CHASING

TRUTH

D0187995

Also by Julie Cross

Whatever Life Throws at You

CHASING

The Eleanor Ames Series

TRUTH

Julie Cross

Entangled Publishing, LLC
2614 South Timberline Road
Suite 109
Fort Collins, CO 80525

Entangled Teen is an imprint of Entangled Publishing, LLC.

Visit our website at www.entangledpublishing.com.

Edited by Liz Pelletier
Cover design by Louisa Maggio and Heather Howland
Interior design by Toni Kerr

ISBN: 9781633755093
Ebook ISBN: 9781633755086

Manufactured in the United States of America

First Edition September 2016

10 9 8 7 6 5 4 3 2 1

To all the Veronicas: A long time ago, we used to be friends.

CHAPTER
1

It's not like I haven't seen a topless girl before. I mean, I am one. Not topless. Not now, anyway. But I *am* a girl.

Seeing a topless girl standing on the neighbor's balcony at six a.m., yelling and tossing clothes from the second floor, is definitely not the norm around here.

From my position on my own apartment balcony, I watch the handful of gray and navy clothing land in the pool, right in front of Mrs. Olsen, mid–side stroke. The old lady stops, looks up, sees the topless blonde. A horrified expression takes over her face. She's out of the pool as fast as a seventy-something-year-old woman can be.

"Got anything else you want me to put on?" topless blonde snaps at whoever is pissing her off next door. New neighbors moved in yesterday while I was having a root canal and sleeping it off with pain meds most of the day. "That's right. Stay in there. Like I care. Have a nice life!"

The girl steps back into the apartment and, seconds later, I hear the front door slam and she's thundering down the steps, a blue sundress now hastily thrown on. I stay hidden until she's peeling out of the parking lot, then I tiptoe through the apartment—careful not to wake my sister and her boyfriend who only get to sleep past six on Saturdays—and head down to the pool. If the topless girl hadn't taken off so quickly, I would have thanked her. I'd been waiting twenty minutes for Mrs. Olsen to get out of the pool. Now it's all mine.

I lean over the side, fishing out the clothes floating near the five-foot end. One gray T-shirt—men's medium. One navy T-shirt—men's medium. Two pairs of navy shorts.

"Uh...sorry about that."

The soggy shorts fall from my fingers and I look up, squinting into the sun at the tall, shadowed figure in front of me. I stare at the tan bare feet then allow my gaze to shift north. His washboard abs distract me for a second, but I reach for the wet shorts again and drop them onto his toes with a plunk before standing up. "Got something against colors?"

Now that I'm standing, I finally get a good look at my new neighbor. I'd expected someone older, but Mr. I-only-wear-gym-shorts-because-I-have-abs-of-steel is definitely more guy than man. Especially with the messy, dark-haired bedhead thing he's got going on.

He frowns at me. "Colors?"

"Yes," I say. "Like red, green, orange. Pink, if you're into that."

"Ah." He shrugs. "Never really thought about it."

The guy swoops down to scoop up the dripping clothes at his feet, and then he flashes me a grin that shows off two perfect dimples. I fold my arms across my chest—I never trust anyone with dimples—and wait for him to offer some kind of explanation. When he doesn't, I prompt him. "Think this will be a regular thing? Should I bring my fishing net tomorrow morning? Or I could ask management to install a pole. If your friend is gonna be here again, in *costume*, she might as well provide some entertainment."

The guy shakes his head and then, to my utter surprise—believe me when I say that I am not easily surprised—he blushes, his gaze bouncing to the parking lot from where Topless Blonde bolted, then back to me. "I'm not— I mean she's not—" He sighs. Defeated.

"What's wrong?" I press. "Not into topless girls?"

"Is it a crime if I'm not?" he says. "Besides, I don't even know her."

"I hear that happens sometimes." I pretend to look deep in thought. "Is it possible that a chemical substance could have been in your bloodstream when you met her? That might explain the memory loss."

Normally I'd roll my eyes and call the guy an asshole inside my head, but there's something almost boyish and innocent about my new neighbor—it wasn't when he first planted his feet beside me, or when he swooped down to pick up his wet clothes, or in his response to my question about his aversion to colorful fashion choices. But when I mentioned Topless Girl—that has me pausing. Curious. It'd been a little bit interesting when the girl was scaring off Mrs. Olsen, but then it was boring. Drunken one-night stand misinterpreted as more.

Now I'm dying to know what their relationships is/was. But as my wise and foolish—yes, you can be both—father taught me long ago, never show your cards. Not in your hand, not on your face. Not even in the way you breathe.

So instead of getting my answer from Hot Neighbor Boy, I toss my cover-up onto a nearby chair and dive into the pool. When I surface, I catch the tiniest glimpse of him still standing there, holding his dripping-wet clothes, his mouth half open. I force myself into a choppy freestyle, kicking and pulling way too hard for this early in the morning. A minute later, my new neighbor is trudging back up the steps.

I stop to rest at the shallow end, laughing to myself. But then I look up at the empty staircase, the completely desolate apartment complex, and I can't help wondering if maybe this is why I haven't made a lot of friends at my new school.

Except Simon.

My only friend at Holden Prep. Maybe my only real friend in my entire life.

"Hey, kiddo."

I pull my head out of my ass and look up at the tall, dark-skinned person standing on the pool deck. "Hey, Ace."

Aidan, my sister's boyfriend, ignores my use of his code name and tosses his towel onto an empty chair, then dives into the deep end. I watch with a hint of envy as he manages to swim the entire length of the pool without a breath and magically appears beside me on the steps. Over the last six or eight months, I've gotten worse and worse at my poker face with Aidan. To prove this, he gives me a look, obviously reading my thoughts, and says, "Ellie, a few months ago, you couldn't even swim."

A few months ago, I fell into this pool and nearly drowned. I shake off the memory and narrow my eyes at him. "I know that."

He flashes me a grin, which is nothing like the fake, dimple-filled grin of New Neighbor Guy. "Have patience, young Grasshopper. We have much to learn." He slaps the water, causing a tidal wave to hit me right in the face. "But you won't get anywhere sitting your lazy ass on those steps. Four laps is not a workout. Don't tell me you've turned all L.A. and taken up sunbathing."

"Virginia is not L.A., last I checked. Plus, I had a freakin' root canal yesterday! And you're taking this spy thing to a whole new level, Ace."

"Secret Service aren't spies," he corrects, though I know

this already. "And yes, I saw your entire workout." He hits more water in my direction, probably trying to get me fired up. "Saw you scaring off our new neighbor, too. Well done. One less boy for me to chase away, Eleanor."

My jaw clenches at the use of my full name. It's payback for my calling him by his Secret Service earpiece name. "Think I should have gone easier on him?"

"Nah." Aidan glances at the balcony beside ours. "Miles can handle it."

"Miles?" I lift an eyebrow. "You've met him already? Does he have a keeper?"

Aidan gives his best "I'm a grown-up and thus privy to more information than you" look. "Don't you think I'd check out anyone new moving in?"

By "check out," he means background check. Criminal record. The irony of this statement is too much to not point out. Though if my sister, Harper, were here, I'd keep it to myself. Aidan is surprisingly tolerant of these mentions. "Clearly you possess the ability to bend the rules if you allow yourself to be associated with Harper and me."

"That's another lesson you haven't learned," Aidan says. "You and I aren't that different, kid. We've both made a living out of noticing things, and we're both experts at keeping secrets."

"Is that why they call it the Secret Service?" I joke, not sure what to do with this idea of Aidan being anything like Harper and me. He's the epitome of good. My family is the opposite of good. "I've always wondered where the name came from."

He rolls his eyes. "We both know you could have charmed Miles Beckett in your sleep. But you didn't. You resisted that instinct."

He says it like it's so easy, pushing away everything I've been taught my whole life and adopting this new mantra.

I mean, I'm glad that I don't have to con people anymore. I'm here because, like my older sister, I don't want that life. But sometimes...every once in a while...like when I'm at Best Buy and the guy "diagnosing" the problem with my laptop has clearly labeled me as a clueless girl he can rip off, I'm so tempted to show him otherwise, to turn on that part of me I've left behind along with my old last name.

Aidan is more military than he's willing to admit, and our chat ends right then because he says I need to get my lazy ass moving. It's September already, and soon the pool will close. So I swim and swim and swim. Until my father's words are nothing but a phantom memory. Like when he told me swim lessons were for kids with social security numbers. For kids who stayed in the same place longer than six months.

I lose count of how many laps I swim—probably more than I've ever done in one session—but when I finally stop, it isn't just Aidan in the pool with me. Miles Beckett has apparently unpacked enough to find his swim trunks and is coming at me with perfect butterfly strokes. He stops at the wall beside me, barely out of breath, and looks at me like I hadn't made him blush less than an hour ago. "Your freestyle needs work."

I snort back a laugh. "Your one-night stand needs work." I miss his reaction because I hear Aidan laugh. I forgot he was out here.

"Come on, Miss Sunshine." Aidan nods toward our apartment. "Your sister's making waffles."

"And you let her?" I push myself out of the pool. "I can't believe they hire you to save lives."

"You're welcome to join us," Aidan says to Miles.

"Don't. Trust me." I wrap my towel around my waist and pat myself on the back. *Daily civic duty? Check.* I give Aidan a nod. "And that's how you save lives."

I'm halfway up the stairs when I hear, "Nice meeting you, Eleanor Ames."

What the— I stop. Turn slowly and look down at my new neighbor. "I don't remember introducing myself."

The grin he gives me is one I'm all too familiar with: guy trying to charm me (aka—guy trying to get in my pants). "Turns out you're infamous around here."

"Is that right?" I laugh to myself. He's being cute. He has no clue how infamous I am. Or my family, at least. "I'm sure everything you heard is completely true."

Aidan catches up to me and tries to hide his amusement. "This should be a blast."

"Whatever. It's not like I see our neighbors all that much, especially since school started up again last week." I shrug. Aidan looks like he wants to say something else but decides against it. "What?"

"He's going to Holden." Aidan turns more serious, his hand now on the doorknob to our apartment. "Miles is a good kid."

"Good? You sure about that?" Clearly he missed Topless Girl. "I think you're losing your touch."

He ignores my jab and says, "Might be nice to have another friend at school."

"Right." I nod. "Because the one friend I had went and offed himself. Good luck, Miles."

Aidan pauses on the stairs and turns to face me. "Ellie, Simon's death had nothing to do with you."

I roll my eyes, but inside I'm shaking. "I know that. God, turn off the therapist voice, will you?" And yeah, I do know all this. It's been three months since Simon—a senator's son and my only friend within the ritzy halls of Holden Prep—well, since he...you know, *went to a better place*. The sting of saying his name out loud is slowly wearing off. But I still have questions. And it's taking every ounce of self-control I have to not seek out those answers.

"Plus, you were the new kid last spring," Aidan reminds me. "You should know better than anyone how hard that can be."

Luckily I don't have to spend too much time feeling sorry for Miles Beckett, new kid at school, because when Aidan opens the door, the smoke alarm is blaring and the entire kitchen is in a fog.

CHAPTER
2

Aidan pushes past me, heading straight through the smoke-filled kitchen. "Harper!"

I'm too busy helping him look for a fire to say, *I told you so*. Both of us are coughing and barely able to see anything through the smoke. But sure enough, I spot flames coming up from what looks like a waffle maker (when did we get a waffle maker?), and while Aidan is looking around for a cup of water and stringing together way too many swear words, I yank the fire extinguisher from beneath the sink. A stream of whitish green foam hits the small flames and suffocates them almost immediately. The beeping of the alarm is too loud to talk over. Aidan grabs a chair to stand on so he can disable it, and I rush to open the balcony door.

Harper's cry of, "Oh no… Oh hell no!" echoes through the apartment and probably floods outside. She's wearing her bathrobe, a towel over her long blond hair. She looks at Aidan and me, pleading with her eyes. "I swear to God it was off before I got in the shower! What the hell happened?"

She rushes over to the kitchen counter. The gust

of smoke that leaves the apartment improves visibility enough for me to notice the small stack of blackened and oddly shaped waffles resting on a plate on the kitchen counter. The counters are littered with eggshells, spilled milk, flour, dirty measuring cups. Harper's expression goes from devastated to pissed off. Just when I'm sure she's about to chuck the waffle maker at the wall, she lets out a yelp.

Fingers are curled around the balcony railing and a second later, Miles Beckett (and his abs) hops the railing and stands on the balcony, barefoot and shirtless, looking into the kitchen like he's poised for a fight. "Everyone okay?"

I roll my eyes. I can't help it. I mean, Jesus, we have stairs for a reason.

Aidan tosses the smoke alarm battery onto the counter and hops down from the chair. "I think we've got it under control."

Miles walks in anyway. He glances at me. I'm still clutching the fire extinguisher, my towel long gone. "That's a good look for you."

I open my mouth to tell him off, but Harper reaches for the waffle maker. "Harper, don't! It was just on fire!"

When my sister gets pissed, she sees only red. Logic is nowhere near her line of sight. It's her greatest flaw—or so my father says. Luckily, Aidan is ready, an oven mitt on one hand. He snatches the appliance before she has a chance, holding it high above her head, the cord dangling behind him.

"God, what is wrong with me?" Harper throws her arms up in the air. "I can't do anything right. Preschoolers can probably make waffles without involving arson."

"It's not your fault." Aidan makes a poor attempt at looking over the waffle maker. "Didn't you get this at a yard sale? It's probably broken. I'm sure the seller just ripped you off."

Harper laughs, but there's not much humor in it. She would never be fooled by a faulty sale. Aidan should know better. *He does know better*, I remind myself. I forget sometimes that people can lie and deceive for good reasons.

I clear my throat and nod toward the balcony intruder just to make sure they both remember that Miles is here. Miles looks at me again and points a finger at the heavy object in my arms. "You might need to get that replaced."

"What are you? The apartment fire marshal?" I demand. What is he still doing here? It's not like we're throwing our problems into the pool. This is private property.

Harper is too pissed to talk about anything rationally and also very aware of this fact. She storms off to her and Aidan's bedroom and slams the door. A second later, she opens it again, poking her head out. "Don't you dare clean up my mess! Either of you."

I exhale and set the fire extinguisher on the table. My heart is finally coming down from the adrenaline rush. I look over at Aidan and see him lower the waffle maker, a smile playing on his lips. He taps the garbage can with one foot and drops the burned appliance inside.

"She's right, you know," Aidan says to me. "A preschooler could probably do this without setting anything on fire."

"Duh." I take in the destroyed kitchen and sigh. "I'll take care of this. Go do whatever it is you do to make her happy again. And refrain from sharing any details."

"Doughnuts on me." Aidan sets a hand on my head, rubbing my wet hair. "Just give me thirty minutes."

He's already nearly to the bedroom door, but I can't resist adding, "Thirty minutes? Is that all it takes these days?"

"Stuff it, Eleanor."

I laugh after he's behind the door. I didn't get to see his face, but it's the kind of comment that would make Aidan blush. Only because it's me saying it. My laughter is cut off quickly, though, when I glance around me. Miles Beckett is still here, and the kitchen is trashed.

"Jesus," I mutter under my breath. I slide the garbage can over to the counter where the waffle maker went up in flames. I'd planned to sweep everything into the bin, but the foam from the extinguisher has hardened and appears to be stuck.

"You'll need to add a lot of water to get rid of that," Miles says. And then he has the nerve to walk farther into my apartment, planting his overconfident feet right beside me. "We should unplug the microwave first."

"We?" I say, lifting an eyebrow. "Your services are no longer needed. Unless"—I clutch the plate of waffles, now half covered in chemical foam, and turn to face him, grinning—"you're hungry?"

"Um...no." He swipes the plate and dumps it into the garbage.

"Thanks. Now you can go." I wave a hand toward the balcony. "Just slide down the fire pole and be on your way."

He laughs. "I bet you're a real blast at parties."

I lean on one elbow and allow my eyes to meet his—just checking to make sure I've still got it. "I bet you're really wondering how much damage you've done this morning. Showing me your dirty laundry. Literally."

He cocks an eyebrow but says nothing. He's cute. I'm not too proud to admit that. And I'm not too proud to admit that his hotness makes this way more enjoyable.

"Good thing for you," I say, keeping my voice soft. "I'm the last person to judge anyone by his dirty laundry."

My mother told me that a lie is so much more effective when it's wrapped in truth. This is the most useful piece of information my parents have provided me.

He gives me a grim smile. "That makes one of us."

I can't hide the shock from my face—not what I expected him to say. But Miles is already on his way to the front door, his back turned to me so he can't see my face.

"See you at school on Monday," he says before walking out the door.

I stand there for a few seconds, trying to figure out what kind of nerve I may have hit, and then eventually I decide it's not worth caring about. I work on the kitchen until Aidan emerges and, as promised because he is a relentless promise-keeper, he leaves for the doughnut shop. I head to the master bedroom and stand in the doorway. Harper is wearing a sundress now, tossed over her swimsuit. She's sitting on the perfectly made bed flipping through a magazine I've seen at the grocery store checkout counters.

I step inside the room and open a dresser drawer, picking out a T-shirt to borrow. Harper and I are exactly the same height—five foot five. But that's where the similarities end. She has our mother's light hair and fair complexion and I have my father's brown hair, brown eyes, and freckles. My sister and I look nothing alike, but luckily we can still share clothes.

"This fucking thing says 'easy thirty-minute meals,'" she tells me. "None of these meals were easy or made in thirty minutes. Can't we sue for false advertising?"

"Let's do it. My physics lab partner has two lawyer parents. We can hire both of them." I flop beside her on the bed.

"Can't believe I paid five bucks for this." Harper sighs and then tosses the magazine onto the floor. "You cleaned up the kitchen, didn't you?"

"Not completely," I say, hiding my guilt. I look her over and finally ask the question. "Why is it so important to you? Being good at cooking? Aidan doesn't care."

"But he will," she says, her gaze fixed on the TV in front of her.

At twenty-four years old, my sister is almost eight years older than me, but when she says things like that, I get a glimpse of this naive side of her. One that keeps her from seeing the truth, even when it's right under her nose. I can't decide if I'm lucky to not have that or unlucky. But then again, I missed a big chunk of Harper's life. Until eight months ago, when she came looking for me, I hadn't seen my sister in years. I thought she'd abandoned me—not just our family but *me*. I thought she didn't care. It turns out that she just couldn't find me.

I scoot close enough to rest my head on her shoulder. "Let's find a class to take. Together. We can tell everyone you've been in a coma for eight years and when you woke up—"

"A handsome man was beside my bed and already in love with me," Harper says, joining my story-time adventure. "A man with a good job and medical benefits."

"Too many holes in this story." I reach across her and open Aidan's bedside drawer where I know he keeps a constant supply of Sour Patch Kids. "Start over."

Harper watches me pop a couple of pieces of candy into my mouth. "You know what we use those for, right?"

My jaw freezes mid-chew, my eyes widening. I can't think of a single thing—which is not a good sign. Harper bursts out laughing, her blue eyes now dancing with amusement. "If I can do that to you, I've definitely still got it."

I don't say anything out loud, but it helps to know that I'm not the only one who feels that need to test out my skills every once in a while. Until recently, being able to con people was all I had. Kinda hard to shake that.

"You know what?" Harp says. "We could just sign up for a cooking class as us."

"True…"

"Good." She's back to her usual assertive self. "I'll take care of that. And you take care of being a better welcome wagon to the poor boy next door." She turns her head, watching me.

I'm not stupid enough to react. I continue eating more of Aidan's candy. On the right side only, to avoid yesterday's root canal. Harper must be too distracted to notice, otherwise she'd swipe the candy from me. "Some angry topless girl was throwing his clothes off the balcony into the pool this morning. I'm not sure he's the kind of friend you want me to make."

"Seriously?" She snatches a few pieces of candy from the box, and I nod. "Jesus. Well, there's got to be a good story behind that."

"Or there isn't."

"You know," Harper says, "it doesn't make you weak or vulnerable, opening up to someone. It can be pretty great."

"Like Simon?" I remind her, knowing the expiration date on that conversation ender is nearing.

Her expression turns grim. "I know I only met him once, but he didn't seem suicidal. I still don't get it."

Neither do I. But like I said, there are still so many questions. It's a rabbit hole I need to not go down. And what if Harper and my gut feeling are right? If Simon didn't kill himself last June, how did he die? More importantly, who killed him?

"I get what you're saying, Harp. It's just that making friends, like at school, and not telling them everything about me…" I glance away from her, a clue to let her know I'm being honest. "It feels like another con, you know?"

"It doesn't have to," she argues. "You don't have to

be defined by our parents and what they've done. You're allowed to be you. Whatever or whoever that is from this point on."

The front door opens and I pull myself off the bed, more than ready for doughnuts and an escape.

"Ellie," Harp says. Waiting.

I sigh before turning to face my sister. "That's the thing…I am defined by them."

More accurately, I'm defined by me. Because it's not just my parents. It's me. I've done things. Very wrong things, and I can't say that I didn't know what I was doing because I did. I still know. Without putting that on the table, I'm not really being me, am I?

CHAPTER

3

"Is the bus always this late?" Miles leans past me, peering around the corner. "My schedule says six fifty-eight."

"I think you've just brought up an important philosophical question." I glance at my cell phone. "Does the term 'late' apply when the time reaches six fifty-nine or when it reaches six fifty-eight and one second? Because by my calculations, it's six fifty-eight and twenty-two seconds... twenty-three..."

"Right. I get it," he grumbles, still looking around the corner for the yellow school bus. "Punctuality equals not cool."

I give him a look. "Even the *word* 'punctuality' equals not cool."

If I thought our last exchange weirded me out, that is no comparison to this conversation. Miles reeked of cool, smooth guy Saturday morning when he was planting his feet beside me, showing off his abs and Spider-Man-climbing my balcony. Now he's too early, too pressed, too tucked in, and way too combed. He's wearing the same white school polo and khakis as I am, but the perfect creases down the legs of his pants, the shiny black dress shoes, make his outfit completely different from mine.

All weekend long, I haven't seen one person besides Miles emerge from the apartment next door. But maybe his mom is in there ironing her life away so he can look like a can of spray starch attacked him on his first day at a new school.

"Right," Miles says again, this time without sarcasm. Like he's taking notes. The bus comes thundering around the corner and screeches to a halt in front of us—at sixty fifty-eight and fifty-seven seconds—and Miles gives me a polite smile. "Thank you for reminding me to trust the system."

"You're kidding, right?" I laugh. "You won't ever get that reminder from me."

I hop on the bus before him and slip into the last seat on the driver side. Miles takes his time walking down the empty aisles—we're the first stop—until he finally decides to sit beside me. I lean back and look at him. "Seriously? Dude, there's, like, every other seat to choose from."

He shoves his backpack—navy blue, of course—between his feet and pulls a folded paper from his pocket. "Yeah, but isn't it bad for my rep to sit alone?"

"No." I keep my voice flat. "It's bad for your rep to have topless girls run out of your apartment."

Where was his ironing mother when *that* was going down? At the store buying spray starch?

"I see." He looks at me, his brown eyes all wide and innocent. "Guess that dirty-laundry thing wasn't so true?"

That's right, I had said yesterday that I wasn't one to judge people by their dirty laundry. Is that his angle this morning? Going from dirty boy to squeaky-clean just in case? Okay, I'm sort of impressed if that's true. Well done, Miles Beckett. I shake my head and hold out a hand. "Let me see your schedule."

He hesitates and then finally hands over the now unfolded sheet of paper on his lap. "You think it's a good idea for me to go out for the football team?"

"When?" I ask, quickly reading over his schedule. AP calc and he's a junior. Impressive. "Next year? Because they started practice in, like, July or something. Where were you last week, anyway?"

Kinda weird to miss the first week of school.

"Uh," he says. "Summer camp?"

Why is he asking me? "What kind of camp?"

He shrugs. "Oh, you know, the regular kind."

"Miles Beckett, calculus extraordinaire. Where are you from?"

"Where am I from?" he repeats. A clear effort to stall. "Well, it's a small town…"

"In Transylvania?" I suggest because seriously? What's the big deal, saying where you're from? That's never the information I'm reluctant to share, and I'm a professional secret keeper.

"California, actually. A small town outside San Jose." He leans closer, pretending to study the schedule, but surely an AP calc student would already have it memorized.

"A West Coast guy," I say as the bus jerks to a stop, sending both of us forward, foreheads slamming the seat back in front of us. "Should be an interesting transition for you. Just don't say anything about Stanford or the cost of living in California. D.C. people are very proud of their outrageously expensive homes."

He nods, and I quickly realize he took all that seriously.

Whatever. I can spot a lie a hundred feet away, and it's clear he's lying. But I'm not sure exactly what part of his story is false—being from California, summer camp, his brand-new starched-up look.

Two sophomore girls get on the bus. I know of them

because they are the notorious, popular volleyball-player type. They both eye Miles, and he surprises me yet again by leaping up from his seat and sticking out a hand to the redhead who stands in front of her friend. "Hi, I'm Miles. Resident new guy."

The girl stares at his hand, and I'm sure she's about to laugh in his face, but then her gaze roams up, taking in all of Miles, and she quirks an eyebrow. Instead of laughing, she looks over her shoulder at her friend and clearly mouths, *Hotty*, then turns to him and shakes hands. "I'm Gabby. And this is Laura."

"What year are you, Miles?" Laura asks.

"Junior," he says right away. "I'm seventeen."

Now that came out much easier than the rest of his story. The girls both look at each other again and giggle. Then Gabby glances my way and says, "Hey, Ellie, how's it going?"

I'm a little taken aback, but then I realize she's done this before. And I've given her a polite nod and nothing more. Maybe Harper is right. Maybe I do need to up my effort with the kids at school. "Hey, Gabby."

The bus is back to full speed, so Miles returns to his seat. He looks at me as if to say, *How am I doing so far?* When I don't honor him with a response, he eventually asks why there aren't many kids on the bus.

"Holden Prep costs thirty thousand dollars a year. How many families, paying that much for school, do you think would put their kids on a yellow bus?"

He angles himself to face me. "Probably only the ones *not* paying thirty thousand a year."

Aidan had to pull a ton of strings to get me financial aid at Holden. He insisted I go to the best school nearby and also that private schools tended to be more lenient on proper documentation. But the waiting list is long and kids start the application process for East Coast prep schools before middle school. Which makes me wonder about my neighbor beside me... Was he on that waiting list?

"Exactly." I nod. "Practically everyone in school has a giant house and a personal driver."

When I started last spring, everyone assumed I had transferred from another fancy prep school. Apparently that can make it easier to get into a school so late in the game. If one top school accepted you then you must be worthy of their school... That's the mindset, anyway.

"Except us, apparently," Miles says.

I'm not sure how much I like being lumped in with him. Not after that comment about my freestyle. "Apparently you weren't studious enough to do your homework on Holden before today. If you had, we wouldn't be having this conversation."

"Believe me, I'm all about homework."

I laugh. "Well, you'll fit right in."

"Right. Because Holden sends fifteen percent of its graduates to Ivy League schools every year," he says.

"Two gold stars for you." I give his shoulder a pat. "You memorized the big flashing words from the front page of the school website."

"I also know the senator from California's son went to Holden," Miles adds, and a chill immediately runs through my body. "The kid who killed himself last June? It was all over the news back home."

It was all over the news here, too. It's not like I hadn't expected him to know about Simon. But the way he says it, like a challenge, like he's asking me personally what *I* know, it hits a nerve. "Yeah, well, everyone around here is a little bored with that story."

I unzip my bag and busy myself with my U.S. history book. But I don't miss Miles stiffen beside me. His expression hard. Almost like it was on Saturday when I made the dirty-laundry comment. Like I've offended him, which doesn't make any sense, considering I'm the one who knew Simon. I'm the one who's been around for three months dealing with all the questions.

I'm the one who saw him last.

Miles Beckett has no right to come in here and bring the Simon Gilbert gossip mill back to life just because he heard about it on the news. Just because he's from California—if that's even true. Simon lived here.

The brakes squeal, and we jerk to a stop. I look out the window and see one of my awesome classmates, Bret Thomas, in a brand-new red Mustang, turning into the parking lot right in front of us. Across the aisle, out the opposite windows, I get a perfect view of a red car taking a sharp turn. I gasp out loud, and several others on the bus do the same. Bret's car stops a few inches from a girl. She spins around, her eyes wide. Bret lays on the horn until the girl, who stood frozen for several seconds, finally shuffles out of the way.

I clutch my chest with one hand at the same time Miles mutters, "Jesus Christ."

The bus finally makes the turn into the parking lot and pulls up front. I stand on shaking legs and make my way off the bus. Parked in front of the school is a black town car. An SUV sits in front of it.

Miles exits the bus and walks up behind me while I'm still staring at the town car. "Who's in the fancy car?"

"You should know him," I say when I see the tall man with stylishly graying hair exit the car and glance around. "That's Senator Gilbert."

Bret Thomas, the guy who nearly committed a hit-and-run in the school parking lot moments ago, walks right up to Senator Gilbert, a grin on his face. They shake hands, and I'm still staring. Awkwardly. I don't know what I'm feeling, but it's a lot. Too much. The senator's head turns, and his gaze freezes on me. For a moment, I'm back at Simon's house the night of the spring formal, shaking hands with his dad, letting Simon put a flower around my wrist.

I can still smell those pink roses like they are under my nose. My breath catches in my throat. Senator Gilbert lifts his sunglasses, looks right at me, and then looks away. Dismissing me. He slings an arm around Bret's shoulders and the two of them, followed by an unusually large security team, head inside. It takes every ounce of my energy not to scowl at Bret. Who does he think he is? He didn't even like Simon.

Gabby walks up to my other side. She's watching this whole ordeal as closely as I am. "I heard they're planting a tree for Simon this morning."

I stare at her. "A tree?"

"Yeah, I know, right?" She shrugs and then walks past me to go in the front doors.

I look to my right, expecting some comment from my new neighbor, especially considering he brought up Simon this morning. But he's gone. I hadn't even heard him walking away.

I guess Miles has bigger things to worry about than a guy he didn't even know. Especially considering it's his first day of school. I, on the other hand, will probably be distracted all day by the idea of a tree with Simon's name on it. I stare down the front entrance of the school, and instantly I'm transported to the first time I walked through these doors, the first time I met Simon.

"So I hear you're my tour guide?" I prompted to the red-haired, freckle-face kid standing outside the office.

"Eleanor?" he asked.

"Ellie." I nodded down the hall. "And you are?"

"Simon." He cleared his throat. "Simon Gilbert. Yes, that Gilbert. But we don't have to talk about our parents' professions. We can go look at the cafeteria and science lab, and I can give you a speech about how Holden is incorporating technology into all its courses."

"I definitely vote for ditching parental talk." I handed him the schedule I'd just been given. "Want to show me where these classes are?"

"We have bio together." He shoved his glasses farther up after they'd slid down his nose a bit. Then he looked at me, serious as hell. And genuine. I could read him like a book. "Feel free to ask me any questions. I promise I'll tell you whatever I know, no judgment; it stays between us. I can think of quite a few things I would have liked to know about this school before I started here."

I stared at him long enough to watch his pupils for dilation. "How about we start with that? What you wished you would have known."

If only Simon were here now, ready to answer all my questions. To tell me what really happened, because he dropped me off after the dance and was dead the next morning. He said good-bye to me, looking happy and normal and just very Simon. And then he killed himself. Before his parents even got home. Before anyone else saw him.

Maybe I can get used to hearing his name again, but how the hell am I supposed to move past those few hours that lapsed between fine and, well, not fine?

CHAPTER
4

Simon's tree-planting was anticlimactic. Only those who had first hour free could attend and, most likely, those kids don't even come to school until second hour. Based on two conversations I overheard between third and fourth period—one near my locker and another in the girls' bathroom—the only people at the planting were a local news crew, several teachers who hadn't had a class first thing this morning, and student government members who were most likely forced to attend. I'm glad I couldn't go, because I can't shake the feeling that Simon would have hated it.

Especially knowing that now, in fourth hour, his tree was already old news.

"We've talked about the nineteen-twenties and the world Fitzgerald creates around this unique time period," Mr. Lance says, pacing the tiny stage in front of my English classroom. "I want to break down the characters now. What makes Gatsby tick? What does he want?" He scans the room, and his gaze lands on the second seat in the far right row—mine. "Ellie? What's Gatsby's motivation?"

I straighten in my chair and repeat the question: What

is Gatsby's motivation?

"Come on, Eleanor, what's his motivation," my dad said in his booming, preacher-like voice. "You can't go into this without knowing what he wants. What does he want?"

I kicked a hunk of perfect country-club grass with the toe of my borrowed golf shoes. "Me."

"What did you say?" Dad asked for dramatic effect.

"Me, Dad." I glared at him. "He wants me. Probably without pants."

He winced but only for a moment. "Good. And are you going to give him what he wants?"

My mouth fell open. "You're kidding, right?"

"The answer is no, Eleanor," Dad snapped. "You will lure and charm. You will not give him anything. Because then it's over. No open door to his rich gullible father, no fifty grand donation to our very worthy cause."

"Which cause is that again? Surely we've saved enough whales for a lifetime."

"Ellie?" Mr. Lance repeats.

I shake my head, refocusing. "I don't know."

"You don't know?" His forehead wrinkles. "Because you didn't have a chance to read the chapters over the weekend?"

"I read them," I say. "I just don't know the answer."

"She means she's conflicted," the guy seated beside me offers. Cody Smith gives a nod in my direction. He's a bit of a stoner who has been in the "I didn't do the homework and I need to BS my way out" position too many times to count.

I glance at Cody, then I turn back to Mr. Lance. "I'm not conflicted. I just don't get it. Gatsby has money. He has power. He has the unofficial attention of Daisy. He knows she wants him. He knows her family isn't going to change. I don't get why he's supposed to be this mysterious character.

There's no puzzle to solve. I know exactly who he is, and I've only read twenty percent of the book."

Mr. Lance tilts his balding, middle-age head to one side and waits a second before saying, "What about Fitzgerald's note about Gatsby in Chapter One?"

"You mean his extraordinary gift for hope?" I ask, and Mr. Lance nods. "I guess he could be a foolish dreamer who believes change is possible."

My teacher grins. "It's possible he is exactly that. And though I admire your cynicism and hatred of predictability, I happen to find Gatsby very interesting, and I've read his story too many times to count."

"What about love," a girl on the other side of the room says. "He wants love. He wants Daisy to belong to him like all his other possessions belong to him."

Mr. Lance looks her way and then back to me. "Is it possible—and stop me if I'm getting too crazy—but maybe Gatsby is chasing the impossible, as Miss Ames so intelligently stated, but he's doing it intentionally."

"You mean like he knows he's going to fail?" someone from the back asks.

"Like, kind of." Mr. Lance paces a few steps and then stops to face us again. "He doesn't *know it* know it, but somewhere he knows. In his subconscious."

"Like self-sabotage?" I ask.

Mr. Lance points a finger at me. "Yes! Exactly. He's chasing this thing called 'happy' and when he gets it, everything will be okay…"

I pick up my pen and write a couple of sentences in my notebook in case I'm forced to relate to Gatsby in a future assignment: *Running after something is easier than standing still. Standing still, you become a target.*

Mr. Lance spins around and draws a big smiley face on the whiteboard, writing the word "HAPPY" above it. "Not just okay, but perfect. Everything will be perfect for Gatsby if he has Daisy. Because it means change is possible. His hope has purpose. Which essentially means that *he* has purpose." He turns to look at the class again. "And who doesn't want purpose for himself, right?"

This always happens to me, despite my immunity to persuasion, when I read something at home that Mr. Lance assigns. I'm so sure of my interpretation. Then I come in here, we start discussing the story, and before I know it, I'm heading down a completely different path. Maybe I'm losing my grasp on my own convictions?

"We have one minute left for me to return your *Color Purple* papers," Mr. Lance says. "Don't forget I'm running college-essay writing workshops every afternoon this week. Room 105. I want to see all of you there. Tonight, let's read the next two chapters and further your understanding of Gatsby's chase for happiness."

I quickly jot down another note: *The green light on the dock = Gatsby's rabbit.*

This immediately reminds me of the dog tracks I've been to in more cities than I can count. The stuffed rabbit the greyhounds all chase. I remember my dad telling me once, when I asked if the dogs liked racing, "Are you kidding? They love it. Chasing that rabbit, the burning desire to get to it first… Who wouldn't love that?"

But they never got it. Ever. And what if they had? Would they chew it to bits in a matter of seconds and then be disappointed with all that buildup? Maybe not, but only because they're dogs. Animals are all instinct. Humans have desire and greed to get in the way of instinct.

I decide to write down that note, knowing we'll eventually have to draw a central theme from the book and turn it into a three- to five-page paper. And Mr. Lance is all about original thought over textbook analysis.

Animal instinct vs. human desire and greed.

Mr. Lance's shuffling feet come to a halt beside my desk. I'm expecting a paper to fall on top of my notebook, but when it doesn't, I glance up. He's reading my notes.

My face heats up. I've only recently stopped "playing" the good student and actually started being the good student, so I have moments of insecurity. Being myself and all. Especially considering the main reason I got into this school was because I nailed the admissions interview— by nailed, I mean created the ultimate sob story about my family and a devastating fire. You know, the kind that destroys birth certificates and social security cards. I also conversed with the dean in three non-English languages, with perfect accents, giving the *impression* of fluency. I'm also gifted at impressions.

He finally drops my essay onto the desk, and then he taps a finger on the notes I just jotted down. "I like where you're going with this."

I work hard not to grin. It's always better to play it cool. I flip the essay over and scan it for the red grade on the front.

98%

Ellie, seriously, remind me again why you aren't in my honors class??

Hmmm... Maybe it's because I came here with no grades, test scores, or transcripts to speak of? Maybe it's because I've never been honors material? Though I played that girl several times, and I have to say, my performance was quite believable.

The bell rings, and there's a mad rush to exit the class. Even Mr. Lance takes off. I read my grade one more time before packing up my stuff. But I stop just outside the classroom door after hearing whispering behind me. Two of Holden Prep's most popular juniors—Bret

Thomas and Dominic DeLuca—are leaning over Cody Smith, who appears to be sound asleep. Bret already got on my bad side twice this morning in a matter of minutes, so I immediately draw the conclusion that he's up to something. Dominic is less suspicious, but he's got that Italian-brooding-lover thing going on—tall, dark-haired, permanent scowl that he somehow manages to make look sexy. Can't trust either of them.

"Come on, he's a stoner, no one will be surprised if he gets caught," Bret says.

I strain to listen—the hallway gets so loud between classes—and catch something that sounds like, "You're sure Benson is doing a search today?"

Benson. The principal.

Footsteps move in my direction. I quickly slide a couple of feet from the door and lean against the wall. My nose is buried in my phone when Bret and Dominic breeze past me.

I have a flashback to those two walking by me in the hall months ago. After a class we all had together, they approached Simon, inviting him to a party at Dominic's that night. Simon's face lit up, but when they walked past me, I heard Dominic say, "Dude, what the hell are you doing inviting that loser?"

"Do you know who his father is?"

I wait until they round the corner, and then I head back inside the classroom. Cody doesn't even stir when I reach in his hoodie pocket. My fingers brush what feels like a plastic bag. I pull it out and look over the colorful pills— definitely not weed—trying to identify them.

Cody lifts his head, drool running across his cheek, and looks around, confused. This is what I meant about standing still and becoming a target. I hastily shove the bag into my pants pocket and put a hand on his back like I'd been shaking him awake. "Hey, time to go."

He swipes his cheek with one sleeve and flashes me a freckle-faced grin. "Oh, shit. I wasn't supposed to fall asleep until sixth period."

"It's fine. You've still got four minutes." I scurry out of the room, my heart beating a little too fast. I'm out of practice.

A shoulder brushes up against mine in the hallway, and then I hear a low, deep voice in my ear. "Did you just lift something off that guy?"

My heart speeds up even more. I keep my breaths even. I glance at Miles only for a second before saying, "What guy?"

"Seriously?" he says. "I saw you lift a bag off him. You're buying drugs."

"Jesus, be quiet." I place my palm on his chest and shove him until we're out of the main hallway, hidden at the end of a row of lockers. "Are you trying to get me expelled?"

He knocks away my hand and narrows his eyes. "Either you stole drugs from a classmate or you bought them. Either way, you're an idiot and you probably should be expelled."

From the corner of my eye, I catch sight of the door to the girls' bathroom. "Excellent point, Miles. Why don't you head over to Dr. Benson's office and let him know all about this. I'll wait here."

He gives me a sarcastic smile. "Right."

Lucky for me, I've been caught and broken free numerous times, so before Miles even lifts a hand, I anticipate his move—the one where my hands end up behind my back, and not in a sexy way—and I sidestep out of his grip. I'm flinging open the bathroom door before he's even pushed away from the wall.

I shove the lock on the stall door and toss the pills—

bag included—into the toilet. The illegal materials are swirling down the pipes by the time Miles pulls himself to his feet after crawling under the stall. His gaze fixes on the toilet bowl. I turn to him and rest a hand on his shoulder. "Thank you so much, Miles. I've seen the light. I don't want to use anymore. I want all my brain cells. I'm going to a meeting right now."

"Y-You…" he stammers, pointing at the toilet bowl. "How could you— Why would you—"

"I've told you kids a thousand times, two feet per stall!"

Miles quickly slides the lock, opening the stall door. One of the P.E. teachers stands in front of us, arms folded across her chest. She glares right at Miles like it's all his fault, since he is, in fact, the boy in the girls' bathroom. "What is going on in here?"

Miles starts to protest, his finger waving in my direction. Thinking quickly, I step forward and raise a hand to stop him. "It's not his fault. I goaded him."

"Goaded him into what?" the teacher asks, her foot tapping, arms still folded.

"Miles has concerns about the number of tampons being flushed rather than discarded into the environmentally friendly wax paper bags." I glance at Miles for a split second, long enough to see his mouth drop open, his forehead wrinkled. "I sort of told him it was impossible to flush tampons, that they clogged the toilets here. And he said it wasn't impossible, which means people are flushing tampons and that's why we need to get signs on all the stall doors. So I told him the girls' bathroom doesn't even have stall doors, and of course he didn't believe me, so he came in to see for himself."

The teacher just stands there like she has no idea what to say. I've learned the hard way the importance of filling a silent moment.

"It was stupid of me. I mean, I care about the environment, too. I really do. And all the statistics Miles quoted about the cost of emptying the septic tank versus taking out the garbage, those are our tax dollars we're talking about! Or maybe not, since this is a private institution, but regardless, it's wasted money all because of a bunch of careless menstruating students." I drop my eyes to my shoes. "It was a really scummy way to win a debate. But I guess I wanted that number-one spot a little too much, you know?"

The P.E. teacher rubs her temples and mutters, "Just get to class. Both of you."

I grab the sleeve of the narc beside me and head for the door. But before we're in the clear, I hear, "And you..." The teacher points at Miles. "Find a new cause. No one wants to hear you tell them how to dispose of feminine products." She shakes her head. "I swear, every year you kids take this college application crap further and further. Someone needs to tell Harvard to shove it."

She pushes past us and walks off, still mumbling under her breath, but she watches to make sure Miles and I both exit the bathroom before heading back to the gym. I'm already late for lunch, so I turn in the direction of the cafeteria. Miles is right on my heels.

"I can't believe you did that," he says. And he really does look shocked. "You'll get in three times as much trouble tampering with evidence as you will getting caught with it."

I turn around and walk backward in front of him. "Or you don't get caught, and..." I spread my arms out wide. "Ta-da! No trouble at all." I tap a finger to my chin. "Yeah, I like that plan best."

I stop at the cafeteria doors. Miles takes a step in my direction, close enough that I smell soap or cologne or aftershave on him, something part mint, part clean. I fight off the urge to lean in even closer. The anger falls from his features, and he's wearing a damn good poker face. "You know what I hate even more than drug dealers who don't get caught?" he says.

I scan him head to toe. "Wrinkles?" I suggest.

"Really good liars," he says, his face still set in neutral.

I laugh and glance over my shoulder into the depths of the loud cafeteria. "Well, Miles Beckett, be prepared to have eight hundred enemies before the end of the school day."

I push open the door and gesture for him to walk through first, you know, 'cause he is the new kid in school and I'm the welcome wagon. He shoots me a glare but eventually walks past.

"Save me a seat right beside you, buddy," I call to his back. Then I lean against the door and release a gallon of tension all in one exhale. I thought Miles would be a pain in my ass, someone who might enjoy hitting one of my nerves every once in a while, but I hadn't anticipated him being someone who might ruin me. And despite my escape just now, I doubt I'm in the clear.

CHAPTER

5

The knife stills in Aidan's hand. "Miles definitely saw you with the drugs?"

"Well, he says he did." I snatch a slice of red pepper from Aidan's cutting board and examine it. "What is this?"

"It's called a vegetable. I read about them in a parenting book." He slides over a few feet to flip a grilled cheese on the stove. "Apparently if you don't eat any, your teeth will fall out."

"Wait, you read a book?" I hop up onto the countertop, sitting beside the cutting board.

Aidan rolls his eyes. "Skimmed it in the bookstore on my lunch break."

He works in several different government buildings in D.C. right now. I can assume if he's in charge of a specific person (I'm not privy to that information), he gets stuck milling around the city with a politician or family member. Which I figured out is Aidan's code for "lunch break."

"Miles was pretty set on turning me in, like it was his civic duty or something." I toss the vegetable and snatch half the sandwich Aidan's just dropped onto the cutting board. The cheese is gooey and hot when it hits my tongue. I chew quickly before speaking. "He even took the time to inform me that tampering with evidence is a greater crime than possession."

Aidan looks over at me, a brow lifted. "He actually said 'tampering with evidence'?"

"I know, right?" I point to the perfectly golden sandwich he's preparing to drop onto the cutting board. "Put that back on and burn it a little."

"Burn it?" Aidan says and then he catches on—he's good like that—and places it back in the pan.

Harper is due home any minute. The last thing she needs right now is to have Aidan serve her a perfectly cooked meal. I grab the remaining half of the first un-burned sandwich. "Don't worry, I'll destroy the evidence."

Aidan rolls his eyes. "You could have just left things alone, you know."

I shrug. I know I could have. Probably should have. But seeing those guys walk past me, like they owned the world, the same way they had after inviting Simon to an exclusive cool kids party… Cody somehow became a less intelligent, stoned reincarnation of Simon.

"I'll go in and talk to Benson tomorrow. Just in case anything drifts his way," Aidan says when I don't respond.

Cheese sticks to the roof of my mouth. "What are you going to tell him?"

"The truth, most likely." He sighs, then gives me his signature smile. "It'll be fine. Don't worry."

I hop off the counter and glance out the sliding door to the balcony. Miles is outside by the pool. "Give me a few minutes to persuade the narc into silence before you go all righteous and visit the principal." I hold a hand to my heart, pleading with him. "My social life is over if the other kids find out you're friends with Benson."

He points his spatula at me. "Don't do anything too crazy, okay?"

"Too crazy?" I scratch my head. "You mean like hypnotizing him?"

When I walk away, toward the bedrooms, Aidan calls, "What are you doing, Ellie?"

"Just putting on that really tiny bikini of Harper's," I yell from my room. I check the battery on my cell: 10 percent. That's enough, I guess. "You know, the one she wears when you guys sneak downstairs for midnight swimming."

I'm out of my room fast enough to see Aidan's mouth close, whatever comment he had been about to utter fading when he sees me still in my school clothes. "Seriously, Ellie, think about letting it go next time. I mean, I get why you wanted to help, but what if they planted drugs on ten different kids? Are you going to flush all the bags?"

The answer to that question is obviously no. How could I possibly know where and when and who?

But while I'm walking down the steps, heading toward the pool, it occurs to me that I could destroy Bret and Dominic if I wanted. They wouldn't even see it coming. All it would take is a little preliminary work—connecting with the source, gaining trust—and then I'd be in. And inside is the best way to know where and when and who. That would be a way better tribute to Simon than planting a tree.

I shove aside the thought. For now. And focus on Miles, who looks up from his book when he spots me. "Hey, Ellie. Just the person I wanted to see."

That's a surprise. I pull up a lawn chair beside his and sit down. "Can we talk about this morning?"

His hair is less tidy now, his shirt untucked and pants pulled up above his ankles. "You mean you want to know if I've talked to anyone about your little drug habit?"

"I told you already, I'm back on the wagon. Even went to a meeting this afternoon. A homeless man held me while I sobbed and confessed everything."

Mile plants his feet onto the concrete pool deck and angles himself to face me. "I hate your type."

I place my feet so they're pointing at his. "What exactly is my type?"

"Blurred lines, too much gray area," he recites. "Someone who thinks she's better than the law—"

"You seriously need to lighten up." I shake my head. What planet is this guy from? "You're gonna end up stuffed in the Dumpster behind the gym. Imagine how wrinkled your pants will get."

"The type who can flip her hair," he continues, ignoring my jab, "walk across the room in a tight dress, ask *really* nicely, and get what she wants."

I should be insulted. I don't need a tight dress to get what I want. I can't even remember the last time I wore a tight dress. I lean in closer, lowering my voice. "Does that mean you *are* going to tell on me?"

"Not this time." He looks me right in the eyes. "But I need a ride somewhere. Think you can help me out?"

"A ride?" I reach into my pocket, pull out a handful of change, and hold it out to him. "The bus stop is two blocks west. That should cover you, round-trip."

Miles rolls his eyes. "I meant in a car."

"Aren't you concerned about getting into a vehicle with someone under the influence?"

He just looks at me.

"I don't have a car," I tell him honestly.

"What about Lawrence—Aidan?" he says. "Will he loan you his?"

So they're already on a buddy-buddy last-name basis? When did that happen? I know he moved in on Friday while I was at the dentist getting that god-awful root canal—thanks, Mom and Dad, for all the dental care you *didn't* provide me in my youth—then I came home, took my prescribed Vicodin, and went to sleep for several hours. All the male bonding must have happened then.

"I don't have a license," I say, going with the truth again over yet another elaborate story. "Too scary. All those other cars plotting my demise."

Okay, so that last part is a lie. I've driven plenty in my lifetime. Just not in the legal sense, and Harper and I are trying to keep it legal now. Mostly. Obtaining a driver's license is a bit difficult for someone without a birth certificate or social security card. But Aidan is working on that. Someday I'll be legal. Not that I wasn't born in America, I was. In Salt Lake City, to be exact. And what's more American than Mormon Country?

Miles looks disappointed by this. I can't tell if my bus money is enough for him to keep his end of the deal. "Never mind, then."

"What about your caretaker? Too busy ironing your pants?" I say, glancing up at his apartment. I haven't seen any adults in there, but he's in high school, so someone must live with him.

His forehead wrinkles. "Ironing my pa— I live with Clyde, and he doesn't iron anything."

"And Clyde is…?" I prompt.

"My uncle." He looks up at the balcony and then back at me. "He travels a lot. For work."

"And he doesn't leave you a car to drive while he's gone?"

His jaw tenses. "Apparently he doesn't trust me enough to drive his car. And have you tried carting groceries on the bus? Not easy."

I stare at him for a beat and then turn around and yell

up at Aidan through the open balcony door. "Hey, Ace! Miles needs a ride to the store!"

Aidan pokes his head out and tells us to give him a couple of minutes.

Then I turn to Miles. "There. Got you a ride."

"I could have done that myself," he says.

"But you didn't," I point out. I watch for signs of annoyance, but I'm impressed again with his poker face. "And did you say you were buying groceries? Is that how you and Uncle Clyde usually operate?"

Miles shrugs. "Don't know. I just moved in with him. And luckily it's only for a semester."

"What happens after the semester?" I slip my shoes back on and then take a moment to admire the hotness in front of me. Maybe I can talk him into shirtless grocery shopping? Or taking a quick dip in the pool beforehand. "You get your own house?"

"I go back home," he says simply, like I should have known. I thought he was home.

"To California? With your—"

"Parents," he says, his voice tense, his gaze drifting away from mine. "They're...not in the country right now."

So his place in my neighborhood is only temporary. Maybe it's for the best. Even though he is nice to look at.

CHAPTER

6

Aidan finished his shopping fifteen minutes ago and took off to run another errand, so now I'm stuck roaming the aisles with my new school buddy. I've never spent lengthy amounts of time in a grocery store, so I really don't know what it is I'm supposed to do. Miles seems to, though. He lifts the largest package of toilet paper off the shelf and drops it into the cart.

"Planning a digestive malfunction?" I ask.

"You know what else I hate?" Miles rolls the cart forward, his attention now on bulk paper-towel packages. "People who comment on other people's groceries."

I flash him a smile. "You really should have kept that to yourself, *buddy*."

He finally chooses his paper towels—twenty rolls— and moves on to the freezer aisles, where he stocks up on frozen peas. It's hard to tell if he's really into reading labels or making a big effort to ignore me. Regardless, I break the silence by questioning each item dropped into his cart.

"Are you sure you wouldn't prefer the store-brand cereal? It's half price today."

He stares at me and moves on, putting three dozen

eggs in the cart. Before I can open my mouth, he says, "They don't really expire in two weeks. You can keep them for months."

"I wasn't going to say that," I tell him. "I'm impressed that you actually know how to cook eggs."

"Eggs and tuna casserole." He grips a gallon of milk in each hand. "That's all I know how to make."

"Tuna casserole…" I have no idea what that is exactly, but there's something about it that sounds homey and warm. Stable. Something a stay-at-home mom would cook. Maybe I do get where Harper is coming from with the cooking stuff.

But I'm too distracted by the voices on the other side of the aisle to bug Miles about tuna casserole. I peer through a space in the tall, long freezers and see Chantel Maloney and Justice Kimura. Two girls who are front and center in Bret and Dominic's circle. Chantel supposedly dated Bret for most of ninth grade, and another one of their friends, Gwen, dated Bret last year.

"Dominic said he's staying on his yacht this weekend while his parents are in China," Chantel says. "Want to blow off SAT prep class?"

"You're the one who's gonna be murdered if you don't get a fourteen hundred. You can't cheat off Fat Matt on the SAT," Justice says. "Plus I have field hockey tryouts."

My back is pressed against the freezer now, and Miles has stopped shopping and is watching me spy on our classmates. One of his eyebrows shoots up. Before he can speak, I grab his arm and yank him close enough to put a hand over his mouth. Then I feel Miles's lips against my palm, and this impulsive move takes on new meaning. My stomach flips over; my heart quickens.

"Ooooh, field hockey. I know who the assistant coach is this year," Chantel teases.

"Shut the fuck up," Justice says, and they both laugh. "I need the ECs for college. It has nothing to do with Bret volunteering to coach."

"Right. We've all had our turn with Bret. Except you." Chantel laughs again, this birdlike chirp that echoes through the store. I imagine her flipping her blond hair over one shoulder. "So, Dominic's yacht? Saturday?"

"I'm in," Justice tells her. "But maybe we should invite Fat Matt. He was totally drooling over your ass in U.S. history today."

"God, gross. Holden really needs higher standards for applicants. The geek population is growing too fast."

Now I see how Justice and Chantel single-handedly sent fourteen freshman girls into the bathroom crying last year.

Miles peels my hand from his mouth and gives me this look like I'd better not do that again. I mean, I wasn't planning on it. I grab his cart and push it quickly down the aisle. He jogs to catch up with me. "What the hell was that?"

"Oh, you know...girl stuff," I say, and then sigh when I see his face. Not buying it. "Fine. If you must know, it's about Bret and Dominic. I'm into them."

His forehead wrinkles. "Both of them?"

Oh, right. Guess I have to pick one. Otherwise that would be weird. "Bret. I meant Bret." I nod in the girls' direction. "Apparently I have competition."

Miles shakes his head. "Maybe you should challenge her to a field hockey duel."

I stop and spin to face him. "That's brilliant! Why didn't I think of that?"

"It was a joke," he says, his jaw tense. "And Bret...he's the douche with the red Mustang who nearly ran a girl over this morning?"

Forgot we witnessed that together from the school

bus window. Bret's handshake with Senator Gilbert and planting drugs on an unknowing Cody Smith had quickly shifted my focus. "He has a really great car. And drugs. You know how I'm into drugs."

"He's not your type," Miles states. Then he takes the cart from me. Control freak.

"He's not, huh? Because you know me so well." I place my hands on his shoulders, stopping him. "Think about it, Miles... You've been on the school bus. You might be out of here after a semester, but I've got nearly two more years of that. I'd be stupid not to put on a tight dress, as you so crudely pointed out, and get myself a rich boyfriend with a car. Not to mention his father being CEO of a *Fortune* 500 company. Hello, letters of recommendation."

The poker face returns, and then Miles pushes past me. "Good luck with that."

I stand there watching the back of his head, and I feel this tiny twinge of something...something new. I don't like that he might have believed me. But wasn't that the point? And now *I'm* jogging to catch up with *him*. I don't like that, either.

"Tell me what you're really thinking," I demand.

Miles looks away from me. "What I really think?"

I cross my arms and nod.

"If you wanted drugs, you wouldn't have flushed a bag full of them. And if you wanted someone like Bret, you'd already have him. You're not the new kid anymore. So why him? And why now?"

"It's that easy?" I scoff. He's smarter than I expected. "Even if I can't afford a boob job like the rest of my competition?"

For the tiniest fraction of a second, Miles's gaze drops to my chest. He shifts his focus up quickly. I point a finger at him. "So you *are* into boobs. I was starting to wonder.

Especially after you left the topless lady hanging the other morning."

"Why do you care what I'm into?" He can't look at me now. Thirty seconds later, he mumbles, "Sorry."

At the check-out counter, Miles pulls an envelope from his wallet. It's labeled: FOOD MONEY. Based on the stack of twenties I spot, he's got at least five hundred bucks in that envelope.

"Guess your uncle is gonna be out of town for a while, huh?"

Miles eyes the envelope as if putting this together for the first time. "Guess so. But I'm not surprised."

After Miles loads up his many bags in the trunk of the car, we're stuck leaning against it, waiting for Aidan. It takes me a few seconds to notice Aidan and his boss, Jack, are standing in the parking lot, just two rows away. Jack, short for his last name, Jakowski, is speaking almost loud enough for me to hear.

I glance at Miles and nod toward Aidan and Jack. "I'm gonna go tell him we're done."

My feet slow while I'm still a good distance from them.

"The parking lot surveillance from June fifteenth shows Ellie getting out of his car," I hear Jack say.

June fifteenth. The night of the spring formal. The night Simon died.

"I can't believe they're going back to Ellie after all this time, after closing the case," Aidan says.

My whole body turns to ice. Months ago, I was told those video files were corrupted. Like several other Holden Prep students, I went through hours of questioning with the FBI.

"No one is accusing Ellie; her alibi checked out fine," Jack assures him, but lines of worry crease his forehead. He rubs the dark scruff on his cheeks.

"What about the Thomas kid? They'll see him on the footage, and that doesn't check out with his story."

Both of them must have felt my presence. They turn suddenly. My heart is off on a sprint, but I keep my face cool and calm.

Aidan forces a tight smile. His buff arms fold over his chest, showing how much bigger he is than his boss. "All done?"

"Yep." I nod toward Miles. "Hope you don't need to buy any toilet paper. They're probably sold out."

They both walk nearer, closing the gap between us, and then Jack offers me a high five. "How's the algebra going? No more tantrums, I hope."

"I did not throw a tantrum."

Aidan laughs, but turns it into a cough when I glare at him. Okay, so maybe throwing a textbook and a graphing calculator at my bedroom wall might constitute a tantrum. But I was frustrated. Enter Jack. Someone who obviously left the shooting range long enough to learn some math.

"Nothing to be ashamed of," Jack says, then he turns to Aidan. "Meet me in my office tonight. I'll get you that stuff you needed."

He heads for his car, and with Jack gone, I'm desperate to ask Aidan what the hell is going on. But I can feel Miles looking at me. I try to ignore him while we walk to Aidan's car and climb inside, but it eventually gets to me and I snap around to face him in the backseat. "What?"

"Nothing. Just excited. That I found your weakness."

"My weakness?" And yeah, I panic a little. Even Aidan seems caught off guard by the comment, because he glances at Miles through the rearview mirror.

"Algebra," he says.

I laugh, trying not to sound surprised. How did he hear that from twenty feet away? "Obviously you haven't seen me play field hockey yet."

"Field hockey?" Aidan turns out of the parking lot and onto the road, then he looks at me to see if I'm serious.

"Ellie's trying to impress a guy with her aerial pass," Miles says, all calm.

"What guy?" Aidan says at the same time I say, "What the hell is an aerial pass?"

I nod toward Miles. "No guy. Don't listen to him."

Yeah, that's my defense tactics. My head is somewhere else. Probably trying to figure out how this video footage suddenly surfaced. Does this mean they'll be investigating me again? Especially since I was the last person to see Simon. Except now there's another Holden Prep student in the mix, if Jack is right about Bret Thomas being in the parking lot that night. At least my story checks out.

I spot a Honda Accord pulled to the side of the road, its owner struggling to change a tire, and take it as a sign. "Look!" I shout as I point out the windshield, causing Aidan to slam on his breaks. Hard.

"Sorry," I say to Aidan when he gives me the death glare. "I just thought he might need some help. Two strong guys ready to help…"

Aidan rolls his eyes but pulls to the side of the road, in front of the Honda. "Miles, coming?"

"Sure," he says, flinging open his door. He's Mr. Polite again.

When they're out of sight, greeting the guy trying to remove a lug nut, I grab Aidan's cell from the console between us and quickly type in his password. He knows I know it and still hasn't changed it. What's wrong with him?

He trusts me. That's what.

Guilt hits me but doesn't stop my fingers from typing. My cousin Denny showed me how to set a phone to forward a copy of new incoming texts and emails to another number. I'm almost done when the car door to the backseat opens. I cancel out the setting and drop the phone back onto the console.

It's just Miles, not Aidan, but still my heart is up in my throat. What the hell am I doing? Aidan trusts me. It can't be *his* privacy I invade. Anyone but Aidan.

I sink back into my seat, relieved that I didn't go through with it and ashamed that the idea had gone all the way to putting my fingers in motion.

When Aidan slides back into the driver's seat, I look him over. He's got a grease stain on his shirt. "Everything okay?" I ask.

"Yep, he's all set." He turns on the radio as he steers the car back onto the road and then immediately flips to my favorite radio station. His least favorite.

God, I'm horrible.

Back at home, after Miles carts his gallons of milk and toilet paper to his apartment, Aidan stops me before we go inside, where my sister is probably waiting for us with a pizza she expertly ordered.

"You heard me and Jack," Aidan states, not a question.

I hesitate but eventually nod. "Is everything okay? Is the case reopening?"

"It's not," Aidan says right away.

To my expert ears, it's clear he's not lying, but the tiniest hint of deception hides beneath the truth. Maybe he's unsure, or maybe he's just worried it might reopen. "And there's video footage of me getting out of Simon's car?"

"It's not completely clear that it's you," Aidan admits. "But there isn't any reason Simon and some other girl would be in our parking lot. It fits the story you told to the police, the one Harper corroborated when she stated what time you arrived home that night."

"And where does Bret Thomas fit into this story?"

Aidan's eyebrows lift, and then a crease forms between his eyes. "I was hoping maybe you could tell me?"

"No idea." But the wheels are already spinning quickly inside my head, recalling everything I do know about Simon's death. "Any chance I can see that video?"

He's conflicted, obviously debating this from every angle. But finally Aidan nods. "Once. And only once. Jack would kill me if he knew I showed you this."

We head over to the table near the pool, and Aidan messes with his phone for a minute and then hands it to me. I watch the dark parking lot pop up on the screen, and eventually Simon's black Audi pulls into the one empty space. It's obvious that the passenger is wearing heels and a dress but not obvious what color dress or hair or anything really.

"Where is Bret?" I ask.

Aidan leans toward me and points to a car only partially visible, hovering far off to the side. "It's just his front plate."

"You can't see Simon." The video ends, and I hand Aidan back his phone. "We don't even know if it's Simon driving Simon's car."

Of course I know because I was there, but from an investigator's perspective, it's not seamless. Especially if the investigator is someone searching for the truth, not just a simple way to fit a bunch of puzzle pieces together.

"Who else would be driving Simon's car?" Aidan presses.

I lift my hands, frustrated. "I don't know, a murderer."

"Ellie," Aidan says so gently I'm sure he's about to dive into another "here is why it has to be suicide" lecture, and I don't want or need to hear it again.

"Okay, I get it."

"Still no idea why the Thomas kid was there?" Aidan prompts. "It's like he's popping up everywhere now, three months in the past."

Everywhere? What else has surfaced and why does it seem like Aidan and Jack are working to cover up some of the evidence? They wouldn't do that, would they?

"Still no idea," I confirm. "But I'm gonna find out."

I abandon Aidan and head for my room. I snatch the first notebook I see piled on my desk.

THINGS I KNOW ABOUT SIMON'S DEATH

1) He dropped me off in the parking lot of our complex at 11:36 p.m. on June fifteenth

2) He went home to an empty house; his parents were at a fund-raiser

3) Around 2 a.m., Senator Gilbert and his wife found Simon dead in their sunroom

4) A gun was involved. More specifically, a gun killed Simon.

And now I can add one more detail.

5) Bret Thomas's car was in the parking lot at the same time Simon dropped me off.

I don't know if Simon left a note, if he went anywhere besides home after dropping me off. I assumed I was the last one to see him, since he went home to an empty house, but what if I wasn't? That would change everything. What if Bret followed him and they pulled over and got into a fight or, I don't know…could be a million scenarios to fill the space between 11:36 p.m. and 2:00 a.m. when his parents found him. That preppy privileged asswipe is clearly hiding something.

A million possibilities, but now one very logical place to start: Bret Thomas.

CHAPTER

7

Growing up, I was taught a strategic, multistep process to approach any long con. My family lives by this process the way other families live by church or religion. And I use the term "family" loosely because we often traveled in large groups. I'm not related to most of those people. So this idea of mine to invade Bret Thomas's privacy—it's not something I'm walking into blind. It requires planning and a bit of prep work—mostly getting to know the source and figuring out how to establish trust.

I haven't actually planned the exact moment of contact with Bret, just that it would be today. Saturday. At field hockey tryouts, if the opportunity presents itself. I want his phone. I want to know what he's been up to, past and present. But first I need him to like me, to trust me. And if things go well, he'll likely offer access to his private space.

"Miss Ames, I see you took my advice?" Coach Haskins (the P.E. teacher who supervises girls' bathrooms for strange activity) says when I walk onto the field. "Ditching debate team for a new extracurricular?"

I decide not to tell her that I've never been on the debate team. "Yep, field hockey. I just know it's my new thing."

"That's the attitude!" She looks over my outfit—P.E. uniform and gym shoes—and then adds, "We'll need to at least find you some shin guards before you can play."

I glance around at the girls entering the field. Everyone has her own stick, plus shin guards, fancy socks over them, and special shoes. Several girls have gloves on, too.

I almost chicken out and take off before this gets any further, but then Bret Thomas walks out of the gym toward the field, and I'm reminded why I'm here in the first place.

"Mr. Thomas," Coach shouts at Bret. "Can you help Miss Ames find some shin guards and a stick in the equipment closet?"

Guess being unprepared has its benefits.

Bret hears Coach and turns and heads back toward the gym. I jog over to him, and he's already holding the door open for me.

We walk across the gym and over to a supply closet. Bret unlocks the closet and points to a bucket of shin guards and a row of field hockey sticks mounted to the wall. "Take your pick."

While I'm sorting through to find a matching pair of shin guards, I can feel his eyes on me. And I know it's my moment. The one where I leave a mark on the target.

He's not into girls who are too forward, too flirtatious. That seems to reek of desperation to Bret, and he's the type to stomp on anyone with that kind of weakness.

And right now, knowing he's definitely checking me out, the door has opened a crack. I spin around to face him, a pair of shin guards now tucked under my arm. "Eyes up, buddy."

His eyes widen, and he lifts his hands in surrender. "Sorry."

"Now I get why you wanted to help coach a girls' team." I snatch a stick from the wall and exit the closet.

Bret locks the door and shuffles up beside me. "Just a reflex. I'm professional ninety-nine percent of the time."

"Okay, I'll forgive you," I say, heading outside again. "But you're gonna have to get me a spot on varsity."

"Oh really?" Bret looks at me, one eyebrow cocked. He's good-looking, in that preppy, blond, rich-boy-with-a-tan way. "Just like that? I haven't even seen you play. And by the looks of it, I'm not sure you *have* played before."

"Then be prepared to have your mind blown." I swing the stick like a baseball bat. "I've watched eight YouTube videos, so I'm pretty much professional level. There is professional field hockey somewhere, right?"

Bret laughs and covers my hands with his, stopping the stick from swinging. "Be careful. You're gonna kill someone."

I catch Justice Kimura, queen bee of Holden's junior class, glance our way, and I immediately step out of Bret's personal space.

Bret shakes his head like he's trying to figure me out. "Just keep that stick down on the ground."

I flash him my best smile. "Thanks, Coach."

He's still watching me when I join the group and listen to Coach Haskins go on and on about teamwork and effort over talent. She explains that we're going to warm up, do some basic drills while Bret takes notes for her, creating a scoring system, then we'll play a scrimmage game. And Monday she'll post the list of who's cut and who's not. Hopefully I won't succeed in making this team.

My goal is just to catch Bret's attention, and I'm well on my way to succeeding.

I watch Justice the whole time Coach is talking. She looks beautiful and exotic thanks to her Japanese heritage. But the more I watch, the more I see her slip back from her usual confident queen-bee self. She ties and reties her dark ponytail way too many times, pretends to examine her well-manicured hands but then proceeds to bite her nails. I don't know her very well, but I do know that Simon had a big crush on Justice. It was what brought him and me together in the first place. The three of us had biology together last spring.

"Do you want her to know you're into her?" I said to Simon after a week of watching him devote most of his attention to the lab table in front of ours instead of to the mutilated fetal pig spread out before us. "Because it kinda seems like you do."

He turned bright pink instantly, his mouth falling open, preparing words of protest. Back then, I'd still been playing the role of regular high school student rather than living it. And for some reason I'd decided that my part would include having a guy BFF.

"And that's totally fine," I'd told him regarding his Justice obsession. "But there is a window on these things." I stabbed a pin into our pig's abdomen, pulling back the skin to reveal the intestines. "After that expires, you slip into the creepy stalker category."

Simon looked up at me, dead serious as he usually was, and said, "How long is this window? Think it's expired already?"

I jotted some notes onto our worksheet. "You blew past it about three days ago."

"Shit," he mumbled under his breath.

And that was the moment I knew I wanted Simon Gilbert as my friend. I'd never met anyone so polar opposite of me. So purely honest and humble. So trusting. And yeah, for one split second, I debated whether he was conning me. Whether I'd become the mark for a change. But my gut told me no. And I'd always had a pretty reliable gut.

Less than an hour later, Bret and Dominic had breezed past me in the hallway, arguing over inviting Simon to that party. But I was too into playing my part, and I didn't think Simon's gal pal would know how to get revenge on those assholes. But I should have done it then. While he was still alive to enjoy it. But then again, that would have meant telling him that they were using him.

The whistle blows, and I shake off the memory of Simon staring at the back of the head I'm now staring at while we jog up and down the field.

After an entire hour of drills and running and chasing around that stupid ball, I'm now aware of the fact that despite my lack of field hockey expertise, Justice Kimura is way worse. I'm not sure it's field hockey specifically; she may just lack athletic ability in general. Still, when I end up a captain for our scrimmage, I pick her first to be on my team. She gives a smug look like she'd expected that, then she takes over choosing the rest of the team, muttering snide remarks about certain girls under her breath.

I really did watch videos on YouTube, and in one of those videos, players were shoving each other with their shoulders in order to get control of the ball. So I figure I'll try out that technique. After Macy Leonard steals the ball from Justice—smirking the whole time, I should add—I chase after her, use my shoulders to knock her flat on her face, then I take off for the goal. I've already swung and sent the ball flying into the net when Coach H. blows her whistle several times in a row.

"Ames, you can't play that way here! Let's keep it clean." She bends over to check on Macy and then gives me a pointed look.

"Sorry!" I yell from across the field. "Should I get ice?"

Justice slides up beside me. "She totally had that coming."

I give her a tiny smile and then return to looking clueless and apologetic. Macy herself is too proud and badass to admit defeat. She stands, her fingers pinching the ends of her nose. "I'm good! No worries."

Guilt washes over me the second I see the blood on her shirt. *Okay, no more cheap shots.* And Jesus, that girl better make the team. Coach Haskins swaps me out for another girl, and I end up on the sidelines beside Bret. He just looks at me, surprise on his face, and shakes his head.

"What?" I say, all innocent.

"Nothing." He marks down a few things on his clipboard, sneaking glances at me every couple of seconds. "Just remind me not to get on your bad side."

You have no idea, buddy.

"It was an accident. I got carried away," I argue. "I'm competitive."

"Me, too." He opens his mouth to say something else, but Justice interrupts us.

"So I'm totally not trying at this," Justice says, brushing off her lackluster performance on the field. "Ellie, right? We had bio together last year."

"Ellie Ames," Bret adds. "Mr. Lance's favorite student."

"I'm so not." I look away from both of them, my gaze fixed on the field. I don't know how this will go down—Bret paying attention to me and Justice crushing on him. Except, oddly, she doesn't seem to be crushing on him despite what Chantel said at the store the other day. I've been watching for signs of this the past couple of days. "I hated on his very favorite book all week. And I argue with him almost every day."

"The guy gets off on that shit," Bret says so matter-of-factly.

"Gross," Justice says, wrinkling her nose. "It should be illegal for any teachers to get off on anything."

Bret studies the score sheet and then looks at both Justice and me. "Hate to say it, but you guys are not making this team."

"Not like I wanted to anyway," Justice mutters.

Sitting in the grass near my left foot is Bret's iPhone. I glance at it for a beat and then look up again. Not yet. Trust first, then invasion of privacy.

"You going to Dominic's party tonight?" Bret asks Justice. After she confirms, he turns to me. "What about you?"

"I was thinking about going to Dominic's thing. He mentioned it in gym the other day." He had mentioned it, just not to me. Definitely not to invite me. But the best way to get an invite to the cool kids' club is to pretend like you already have one. "I've got a ton of homework and college essays to write from Lance's workshop, so we'll see."

"You should come," Bret says.

Justice smiles at me, seeming genuine, which is quite a shocker. "Totally."

Establish human connection: check.

From the field behind us, a guy calls out Bret's name. I squint into the sun and spot Jacob, Chantel's current boyfriend if my school social gossip is up to speed. Bret jogs over to talk to him. I glance at Justice and see her giving Jacob a thumbs-up. She catches me watching and quickly drops her hand.

"So..." I swing my arms and stare out at the scrimmage game. "Should we blow off the rest of this tryout or take our chances?"

Justice glances wistfully in the direction of the girls' locker room. "My parents would kill me if I left early."

"I could give you a bloody nose?" I suggest.

She eyes me, one dark eyebrow cocked. "Somehow I don't doubt that."

Good. You shouldn't.

CHAPTER

8

"A party on a yacht floating around the Potomac River," Harper repeats from her safe spot seated on the pool steps in the shallow end. "Who's driving this yacht?"

I rest against the pool wall, panting from my long swim. "Pretty sure it's anchored."

"Why are you suddenly interested in going to parties?" Harper asks.

I dunk my head underwater, and when I reemerge, I say, "Your lecture about opening up to people got me thinking."

"Uh-huh." She gives me this look like, *Yeah right*, but her focus shifts to Aidan, who's coming down the steps after going up to the apartment to change out of his suit. "And a yacht party will help with this pursuit?"

Pursuit. Interesting word choice.

"It's a start, right?"

Harper narrows her eyes. She knows I'm lying, but she's biding her time, waiting for the right moment to call me on it. Or she wants to figure out on her own what I'm up to.

"A start to what?" Aidan asks.

"A start to launching Ellie's social campaign." Harper flashes me a grin. "She's going to some rich kid's yacht party later."

I stick out my tongue at her when Aidan's not looking.

"Apparently she's decided to make friends at school," Harper adds.

"Hmm..." Aidan stares down at me from the pool deck, his huge biceps folded across his chest, dark skin standing out against his white polo shirt—he looks fierce and intimidating. "And you would repeat this statement while taking a lie-detector test?"

Intimidating assuming I didn't know him so well.

"Sure." I float on my back, staring up at the sun and bright blue sky. "I could pass a polygraph—lying—in my sleep."

"You know this for sure?" Aidan challenges. "I've seen the coolest, calmest agents fail to do that. You must have superpowers."

With my ears in the water, I have to listen over the whoosh of the pool filter to hear him. "Try me."

"My polygraph machine is in the shop, unfortunately. How about a game of memory? Have you looked at the photos since I went upstairs?" Aidan asks.

I put my feet back on the bottom of the pool and head for the steps. "Nope, and you can ask Harper. She's my witness."

Harper hands me a towel and swears to Aidan that I haven't cheated. Over the summer, Harper and I helped Aidan prepare for some tests he had to take with the Secret Service. Tests where they show you photos, allowing you to study them briefly before the pictures are put away. Later, you're asked to recall details from the photos. Turns out, I'm pretty good at this game, and now Aidan likes to use me as his opponent to keep his skills sharp.

With my towel wrapped around me, I take a seat at the umbrella table beside the pool. Aidan is on my right, Harper on my left. Harper leafs through the stack of color images, keeping them concealed from us. "In the image of the downtown-looking area, between the two tallest buildings, what did you see?"

"An alley," I say immediately. Aidan opened his mouth but I beat him to it. I squint at nothing, pulling the image back to my mind. "And a No Loitering sign—"

"A 2005 Ford Fusion," Aidan spouts off. "Dark blu—No, hunter green. And a—"

"Bally's fitness member magnet on the trunk!" I shout before he can. "License plate Land of Linco—"

"Illinois!" Aidan interrupts.

I bang my hand on the glass table as if that will bring me more clarity. "5L62F45."

Aidan stops and turns to face me. "What was that?"

"Plate number. Aren't we supposed to—"

Harper lifts the image closer to her face. "5L62F45. God, I think I need glasses."

"How did you see that? How did you remember it?" Aidan asks, staring at me.

My face heats up, like I've done something wrong. How did I remember that plate number? There was definitely a thought process. I looked at it just so I could beat Aidan, figured he'd do the same. Was that cheating? Those lines have never been very clear to me.

"I-I don't know…" I stutter and then work harder to unravel it because Aidan is still staring at me like I'm a freak. "It was an easy one to remember. Five L…five liters… Sixty two—the age you have to be for senior discounts. F for fuck. And forty-five…because today's my—" I stop, not wanting to finish.

"Mom's birthday." Harp looks up from the picture.

I stare at my fingernails. "Today. She's forty-five today."

Last year, my family celebrated my mother's birthday by conning an eighty-five-year-old woman out of ten thousand dollars. I pulled off an Oscar-worthy performance, selling my dad as a miracle therapist who had taken me from delinquent teen to prim and proper and driven. My mom was the single mother who hadn't known what to do with me. Ten grand and a month in Dr. Ames's reprogramming camp saved my life. And it could save her grandson's, too. Later, while my family dined on steak, lobster, and chocolate lava cake, I sat there thinking about the old woman and the look of hope on her face when she'd watched the reprogramming team show up and pluck her grandson from his downward spiral. But we hadn't been there to save anyone. Quite the opposite. We'd given the kid two hundred bucks, a fake ID, and a bus ticket to Vegas.

I couldn't eat anything that night, and when I glanced across the table at my mother, I noticed her smile hadn't reached her eyes and all she'd done was move food around her plate, hadn't eaten a bite of her birthday dinner. Then there was my dad, on top of the world, no guilt ruining his appetite. And my mom beside him, feeling like shit but pretending she was happy. Forty-four years old and she still did everything for him. Even things I'm sure she didn't want to do. I wonder if she gets to celebrate forty-five years where she's at right now?

My family used that con several times, though fortunately without my parents and me, with a different Dr. Ames each time. But the memory stuck with me. So much that when the FBI suggested Harper and I change our last names, I picked Ames. To remember how I felt after taking that lady's money. Harper was so glad to see me, she didn't care what I picked. Didn't give it a second thought.

Aidan scrubs a hand over his face, giving the mention

of our mother a moment to sit in the air before shifting back to the game. "Seriously, Ellie, swear you didn't cheat?"

"Why would I cheat?" I ask. "Are we playing or not?"

Aidan stares at me for a beat longer and then gives Harper a nod. She shakes her head, refocusing. "Okay, the picture of the warehouse in the desert... Name as many entry points as you can."

"The window," I say, only half as energetic.

"Which window?" Harper presses.

"You can't—" Aidan starts but stops when he sees Harper studying the photo.

Harper mutters something about the manufacturer and the year. "Yeah, she's right. Those locks are pretty basic, wouldn't make a sound to open."

I look between the two adults in front of me and watch what I think Harper has been so afraid of happening. Aidan eyeing her like she's a stranger to him. And I wonder, not for the first time, how they met. Neither will tell me.

Harper drops her gaze back to the photos. "I'm probably wrong about the lock. Why would it be easy to pick?"

"Because it's just a picture, Harper," I say. She doesn't need to be ashamed. She didn't use her skills to take that nice old lady's money. I point a finger at the guy beside me. "Aidan's the one turning it into a bomb factory or something. Regular people use regular unreliable locks."

Silence falls among us. A woman shakes out a doormat over her balcony, and I can practically hear the dust falling to the ground.

"I think that's enough memory for today." Aidan reaches across the table, carefully draws the photos out of Harper's hands, then he says, so quietly I can barely hear him, "I wasn't judging you. I was just floored because everyone in my crew would suggest busting a window to get in. No one would even consider quiet entry. It's smart. Muscles get in the way of brains more often than you'd think."

A lump forms in my throat, and I'm thankful Aidan's staring at my sister and not me. Harper lifts a hand, rubs his head. "We'll have to teach you some tricks."

"I'd like that." He stands, kisses her forehead. "I'll let you ladies talk."

Harper and I both watch him walk away with the photos, and then for some reason we burst out laughing the second he's out of sight.

"He's got such a nice ass," Harper says.

"It's all those squats and lunges." I open her purse and dig until I find a pack of Starbursts, but it's ripped from my hand immediately. "Hey! I'm starving."

"Who was that girl lying on the couch crying," Harper reminds me, still holding the candy hostage, "'My tooth is exploding, I'm dying, Harper, I can't take this any longer, kill me now...'"

I glare at her.

"Is that candy worth a thousand dollars?" she points out. "We're gonna be paying that bill for five years."

"Sorry," I mumble. God, I hate that I cost them that much money. If I could get a job, then I'd be able to help. Or if I pulled a con or two... "I still can't believe we're actually paying a bill."

Harper looks at me for a long moment. "The license plate... You did that thing I taught you?"

I nod. "Five liters for the seniors, and Mom is fucked because she's only forty-five."

Harper laughs. "That doesn't even make sense."

"Well, it worked." I shrug. "Did you remember her birthday? Before I mentioned it?"

"Yeah." She looks up at our apartment. "This morning when I looked at my phone."

I chew on my thumbnail. "Do you think she's okay?"

"I'm sure she's fine." She looks away from me, her face turning to stone.

And with that statement, I know the Mom conversation is done. Harper doesn't care that it's her birthday, and I don't blame her. It's a sore subject for her and now for me, too, since she told me the truth this past summer. My parents had always loved to tell the story of my birthday. Born on the Fourth of July. How American. But Harper was eight when I was born and she remembers details that would disprove this birthdate—cooler weather, the fact that she was in school at the time. Late August is an extreme possibility but September or October are more likely. Today could be my birthday for all I know. Am I even seventeen yet? Or am I still sixteen? Who the hell knows? I guess maybe I'll just have to wait for November to roll around and call it a done deal.

You wouldn't think that would be such a huge thing, and believe me, I've tried to make it not a big thing, but a birthday… It's like the stamp every person gets stating, *I'm here, I exist.*

"Ellie?" Harper says, bringing me back to the here and now. "I found us a cooking class. Or should I say, culinary studies. The guy who cooks for the Feldsteins teaches it."

"Is it expensive? I don't want you to blow an entire paycheck for me to take a class." Harper works part-time as a nanny for a very rich family. Neither of us is legal to work in the U.S., so Harper fakes an accent and the Feldsteins are convinced they've got an authentic, illegal German nanny who will make their children bilingual by age five. It's a lie that Aidan isn't too fond of but goes along with because Harper can, in fact, teach those kids German. It isn't completely fraudulent.

"We are taking the class free of charge." Harper grins. "Thanks to my awesome connections. Sunday night. You and me. Making some kosher meals."

"Why kosher?" I ask but we're interrupted by a red Mustang convertible pulling up in the parking lot beside us. I stare at the car in disbelief.

Miles is hopping out of Bret's red Mustang. And guess who's in the backseat? Dominic DeLuca, Justice, and Jacob, Chantel's boyfriend.

"Thanks for the ride, man," Miles says.

"No problem," Bret responds. "See you later tonight!"

My mouth is still hanging open when Miles breezes past Harper and me on his way to his place.

"Hey!" I yell at him. He stops, turns, pretends to be surprised to see me out here. I jog over to him and keep my voice low. "What are you doing hanging out with them?"

"SAT prep class," he says simply, like I should have thought of that. And damn...I should have thought of that. Would have been a hell of a lot better than field hockey tryouts.

"Yeah, but why were you in Bret's car?" Especially after everything he said about the guy when we were in the store.

"I needed a ride." He spreads his arms out wide. "Beats taking the bus. You said so yourself."

"What are you up to?" I demand.

Miles is Mr. Discipline today, working hard to keep his eyes on my face and not on my bikini top. But I can see the strain, the downward pull of gravity he's fighting. It makes my stomach flutter just thinking about him thinking about checking me out. "What are *you* up to?"

He doesn't wait for me to answer, just takes off. So what now? I have to fight him for Bret's attention? After he closes his apartment door, I turn to Harper. "I need a really tight dress."

She lifts a brow. "Sweet tart?" she says. I shake my head. "Candy apple?"

"No mission," I lie. "Just need to look hot."

CHAPTER

9

"You want a drink?" Bret asks me.

I eye the open glasses of various premade cocktails on the deck bar and shake my head. "I'm good."

Bret flashes me his killer grin that I'm sure gets him whatever he wants and then walks off to greet some of our classmates who just showed. It's getting a little crowded on this deck, and without the khakis and school polos, I hardly recognize anyone. I'm sure it goes both ways, considering I'm wearing a designer dress Mrs. Feldstein gave to Harper because it was "so last season" along with platform sandals that I'm completely in love with but are the most uncomfortable, noisy shoes ever. It's difficult to snoop around in noisy shoes but unfortunately, nothing else went with the dress.

Like Bret, Dominic DeLuca is wearing board shorts and a T-shirt, his feet bare, nose pink, dark hair carelessly messy from swimming, and the scent of sunblock wafting off him. I say hi to Dominic, but he doesn't smile or acknowledge me beyond a quick nod and, "Hey."

He's definitely got the hot-brooding-guy act down.

I do a lap around the deck. Can't believe one family owns a one-hundred-foot yacht complete with built-in speakers—music is playing through them—a bartender, and plenty of standing and sitting places. The sun is setting and the lights on the deck are popping on one at a time, casting a colorful glow all around. The only thing I dislike about this boat are the edges. I've never swum in a river, lake, or ocean, not sure if I even could, and getting anywhere near those railings is not on my to-do list tonight.

Chantel and Justice have just arrived and are now knocking back drinks near the bar. I wait for Justice to spot me and wave before I head over to them. I know better than to assume the camaraderie on the field this morning would continue around her other friends. Her shiny black hair is down, and she's wearing a beautiful dark-blue dress and shoes taller than mine.

"Oh my God, Ellie, you look amazing!" Justice says.

Chantel gives me this fake smile. "You totally do."

"Where did you get that dress?" Justice asks me.

"My sister. The lady she works for—she's a nanny—wears her clothes once and gets rid of them." I smooth a hand over the silky black material. It's made to lie over the skin like butter and appear simple. "It's completely perfect."

"This material is amazing. Durable, too." Justice runs a hand over the shoulder strap. "But the cut is even better."

Maybe the queen bee of Holden Prep has some humanity in her after all.

"She's into designing," Chantel says as if that's the only reason anyone should comment on the durability of clothing. She also wrinkles her nose, indicating it's not a hobby she approves of. She reaches for a glass of something light pink on the bar and holds it up for us to see. "These are amazing. Did you guys try one?"

"Careful with those," Justice warns. She looks at me and

sighs. "God, I miss my nanny."

"Me, too." Chantel downs half the glass in three seconds flat. "Mine did all my homework. It sucks having to do it myself now."

"She did your homework?" Justice says. "You are so fucking lazy, Chantel."

Chantel rolls her eyes. "Whatever."

"So…" I say to Justice. "Are you thinking about design school?"

I never think about college, but everyone else at my school seems to, so it's always a safe topic of conversation.

"I'd kill to go to New York School of Design. But my parents would never let me." Human Justice fades away, and her nose literally lifts up a notch higher. "My dad went to Stanford, and my mom went to Princeton for undergrad and then Stanford for law school."

I open my mouth to ask another question, but Justice decides to shout across the deck to Bret. "Thomas! Did we fucking make the team or what? We know you know."

The grin from earlier slides across Bret's face again. "You both made varsity! Congrats!"

"What?" Justice and I say together.

Bret laughs. "Kidding." He points a finger at Justice. "You sucked ass." Then he swings that finger over to me. "And you were scary as hell."

"Thank God." Justice clutches a hand to her chest. She turns to me and smiles. "He likes you."

"Who?" I reach for a glass and hold it without taking a drink.

"You know who," Justice says. "It was instant love the second you plowed over what's-her-name with the apple ass during the scrimmage."

"I thought *you* were into Bret," Chantel hisses, her voice low like that was only for Justice to hear.

Justice seems to realize she's screwed up something. Her gaze quickly flits across the deck to Chantel's man, Jacob. "I think Jacob's on his fifth vodka tonic... Better go keep him in check."

Chantel huffs and slams down her glass on the bar counter, but she heads over to Jacob. When we're alone, I give Justice a few seconds to 'fess up. She doesn't. "I know you need Chantel to think you have a crush on Bret," I say. Her mouth opens, but I continue before she gets a word in. "The question is why? Either you've got something on the side with Jacob behind your best friend's back, or Jacob's using you to test Chantel. See if she's still into Bret. They dated last year, right?"

Her eyes widen, mouth still hanging open. "How— I mean no way, I'm not hooking up with Jacob!"

"Say that a little louder and Chantel might hear you," I warn. "So Jock-boy Jacob has some insecurity issues, huh?"

The shock slowly dissolves from her face, and she grins. "Why is it we've never hung out until now?"

"Fate," I lie. Fate is bullshit. "Now is our time, I think."

She grabs a glass of pink whatever. "Cheers to that."

"To a new school year, new friends." I raise my glass, clink it against hers. "New crushes."

"And new secrets." She looks me over, silently asking the question.

"I'm not gonna tell Chantel you're part of Jacob's mind game." I set the glass back down, not having taken a sip even though Justice had. "And now it's time for me to stretch my boundaries a little."

Bret is in my line of sight now. I look him over for a moment, trying to decide what tactic to use.

"Get it, girl." Justice smacks me on the ass and gives me a shove. "Make him use a condom."

I cross the deck slowly and feel a small sense of both

satisfaction and relief, knowing my old confidence, my skills, it's all here. Several pairs of eyes turn in my direction. My mother taught me how to do this. How to walk across a room and get people to look my way, any people. As corny as this sounds, it really is about the inside more than the external—*the way you think about yourself affects the way you move yourself*, my mom had said hundreds of times. She'd lifted one of my arms—*if you move this arm, you do it with the attitude, the mind-set that this is my arm. I'm putting it exactly where I want it. This is my foot; it's landing exactly where I want it to. Everything I do is exactly as I want it.*

Sometimes I feel nervous and I can't get into the right headspace, but when I do, I feel it all over. It's powerful. An unforgettable high. That's why I struggle so much with letting go of who I really am and where I came from, because it gives me power. Without it, what the hell do I have? The memory of the Dr. Ames con, that's what.

The yacht railing comes into view, and I almost turn around and head back to the bar, but Bret has already caught on to the fact that I've come over here for him. He lifts an eyebrow—the guy is definitely into bold girls. This makes me hate him 2 percent less, which is useful when I have to pretend not to hate him. I force my vision to blur, not allowing the very near ocean to take over my thoughts, but my heart still picks up, fear slowing down my feet. I turn quickly, my back facing the water.

Bret watches me then slides over, closer to me, stopping when there are only a couple of inches between us. "Hey."

"Hey." I keep my eyes on his—avoiding the water—and pause for a beat before saying, "Justice says you're into physically aggressive girls."

He laughs. "Why? Are you selling your assets?"

"I'm always selling my assets. But I'm extremely picky when it comes to buyers."

"Good to know." His gaze drifts right to my cleavage, but unlike Miles, this guy doesn't blush. "You don't have a drink. Do you want something?"

"You already asked me that," I remind him. "And no. My sister can smell a cocktail on me a mile away. I prefer to limit my substance use to the unscented."

Both eyebrows shoot up. "So that's why you came over here."

I shrug, my stomach bubbling with nerves. Did I jump too soon? I stop breathing, my gaze still locked on Bret's.

He reaches a hand toward the pocket of his shorts and removes a tiny white bottle. I sigh with relief; my timing was perfect. He glances around and then turns back to me. "What's your damage?"

"What are my options?" I keep cool while he dumps a half dozen pills into his palm. Then he slips two pills back into the bottle. "What were those?"

"Nothing I'd give you."

"Why? Are they roofies?" *Jesus Christ, please say no.* Otherwise I'll be forced to twist his balls into a knot, and that really ruins my plan to get on the inside.

Bret shakes his head. "You know people take those as a sleep aid in other countries."

"Which countries?" I press, and then I wave a hand. "Forget it. I don't want to know. What are my options?"

"Molly, acid, PCP, Adderall," he rattles off, his voice low, his palm carefully concealed.

"Adderall? In case I decide to plop down by the bar and study for a test?" I turn my gaze to the crowded deck. "It's more of an ecstasy night for me, I think."

Warm fingers lift my hand, turning it around. Two pills land in my palm, and then the same warm fingers curl my hand into a fist. When I glance back at Bret, the tiny white pill bottle is out of sight. *Smooth.* He'd make an excellent pickpocket.

"How much?" I ask because I'm not sure if he's dealing right now or just being nice.

"It's on me." Bret leans in closer, his breath hitting my ear. I fight hard against the urge to retreat. "But you have to take them in front of me."

My heart pounds, fear sweeping over me. I open my mouth to respond, but Bret laughs and says, "Kidding. Seriously, don't take both of those at once. It'll fuck up your heart, make it feel like it's gonna explode."

I think that's already happening just from holding the pills in my hand. I drop them into my purse in one motion. But I can't get my mind to hold still, my heart to slow.

Relax. Breathe, Ellie. Slow. Easy.

This is my body and I'm putting it exactly where I want it.

My shoulders sink with each lengthened breath I take. *Here and now.* Aidan calls these techniques coping mechanisms. I call them training drills. I may not be playing the games anymore, but I don't plan on getting out of shape anytime soon.

Bret gives me a funny look. "You okay?"

"I have this thing about boats and…" I nod in the direction of the Potomac River behind me. "Railings and large bodies of water."

"Huh." He shrugs but looks less suspicious. "Dominic and I crash here whenever we can. He's been sleeping below deck since Thursday when his parents left for China. It's the best. Party on deck, bedroom below, cleaning crew comes out here daily."

Dominic's been sleeping below deck? Might be a great place to snoop around.

"How long are they in China?" I ask then add, "In case I need to replenish my supply. I'll know where to find you."

"You'll know where to find me," he repeats. "Have you always been this cool? Who usually hooks you up?"

Who usually hooks me up? That's a great question. Let me ask you one first, Bret... What were you doing in our parking lot after the spring formal? Did you follow Simon home? Did he buy drugs from you? Did you give him something that made him want to shoot himself?

"Actually, I haven't been hooked up in a while," I say.

"But who before?" he presses. "Anyone I know?"

I look away from him and chew on my thumbnail. "Just a friend. But I can't— I mean he's not— He's not around."

Beside me, Bret snorts out a laugh. "No way. Simon Gilbert didn't have anything good to share with you. Not in a million years. The guy wouldn't even touch a glass of champagne."

"Neither will I," I point out, hating myself for ruining any image of Simon. "And did I say Simon?"

"Okay, I get it. Not Simon." He lifts his hands. And obviously not a drug deal behind his appearance in our parking lot last June. "But if you do want anything, go to Dominic, if not me. He's the only one at our school I would trust to party with you and not turn you in at the drop of a hat."

"Good to know."

I'm about to make my case for a bathroom escape, but then I catch sight of a guy stepping onto the yacht. My jaw clenches and I suppress a growl.

Miles Beckett.

CHAPTER
10

What's worse than Miles showing up at this cool kids drug party? About four things, all of which I list off to myself the moment he enters the party. First, Bret abandons me to high-five Miles. Second, Dominic rushes over to greet him. Dominic, who wouldn't give me more than a pissed-off nod. Third, Justice grins and whispers furiously to Chantel. And fourth, Miles has ditched the starched-to-all-hell pants in favor of a blue button-down shirt and jeans.

He looks amazing in jeans. He just looks amazing period. His skin is slightly bronzed, probably from all the laps he swam this afternoon when I went inside to get ready. Yes, I looked. Believe me, I'm regretting it now.

I glare at him, refusing to join the parade of Miles Beckett lovers. I mean seriously, how do they even know him? Did he blow all their minds in SAT prep class this afternoon? He bumps fists with Bret despite the fact that he was a hater the other day in the grocery store. And he was about to turn me in for that bag of drugs, and he knows Bret and Dominic were involved. I don't get it. What's he playing at?

He turns toward the bar, and like the cool, smooth guy he's morphed into, he lifts a drink off the counter and "accidentally" brushes Justice's arm. She pretends to have just noticed his appearance here and tugs the sleeve of his shirt. Then she says something that makes him laugh, something I can't hear, and my gut twists.

Am I disappointed that he's made the transition to cool kid before me despite my head start? Or am I disappointed that he noticed Justice before me? But then he glances this way, as if to scan the deck, and his gaze freezes on me.

He blinks. Looks away. And then back at me again. The weight of his gaze, the way his eyes journey from my head to my toes, causes heat to creep up my neck. I shake off the unwanted feelings and move toward the small crowd.

Bret makes a big show of introducing me to Miles, like he's a celebrity or something—what the hell happened in that SAT prep class—and I fake a smile. "We've run into each other a few times."

"They're neighbors," Dominic says, surprising me. But he's still avoiding eye contact, a scowl on his pretty face. He looks at Bret. "Are we swimming or what?"

"Dude, it's been, like, five seconds since you came up with that plan." Bret shakes his head. "If you were ready, you should have told me."

Silent, tense words flow between the two of them.

"You looked busy." His gaze finally falls on me. "Didn't want to interrupt."

Okay, what the hell did I do to Dominic DeLuca?

Miles looks between them, an eyebrow rising as if asking me what I did to cause that bromance tension. I take a couple of steps in Miles's direction, daring him to say something. He looks right at me, eye contact to rival the best.

I return the eye contact long enough to see him tense.

"Do you ever get the feeling you're following someone?"

"I'm not following you if that's what you're implying." A grin spreads across his face. "Can't help it if people invite me to stuff."

"No, you can't, can you?" I shake my head. "Poor helpless, friendless Miles. The tuna casserole not providing enough comfort?"

Before I can ask him what he's really up to, Dominic and Bret pull him away to discuss a night swimming expedition that I want nothing to do with. I find some other classmates to chat up for a while, watch Justice ogle Miles from a distance, and eventually, I make my way downstairs.

Three girls are walking up as I walk down. I press my back to the wall, making room. The lower level of this yacht is nothing like I'd expected. I figured there would be hardwood floors and water and boat thingies. But my platform shoes hit thick, plush carpet at the bottom of the steps and a living room/kitchen combination, complete with a giant flat-screen spread out before me.

Now I get why Bret said they love staying here. It's like having your own apartment. I head over to a chair beside the couch and sift through the purses piled up here. I open the first top one and find a school ID for Justice's friend Briley. I snap pictures of her license, credit card—front and back—and then stop myself. I don't need this information. I find Chantel's purse next. She's got a bottle of penicillin. Yeah, I'd rather not know about that.

Justice's purse is right below hers. Since she's proven to be sneaky, I feel morally obligated to photograph her license. Tucked way in the back of her wallet is her social security card. I snap a picture of it, too, and then I grab her phone. She's one of the few who left a phone down here. And no password protection. A couple more girls head down to the bathroom, and I pretend to be busy texting when they look my way. Justice has definitely been texting with Chantel's boyfriend. I flip through Justice and Jacob's exchange.

JUSTICE: maybe u should just trust her

JACOB: maybe u should just help me.

JACOB: And see? We r on the same page almost. Only 2 words different.

JUSTICE: haha. Fine. Doing it in the name of love. Nothing else.

The phone suddenly feels hot and heavy in my hands, like forbidden fruit. Okay, so maybe she's not the evil sneak I pegged her as. If only guys had purses they abandoned below deck. My work would be so much easier. Then again…

I look around and spot a closed door beside the bathroom. The bedroom Bret mentioned? I turn the knob, but it's locked.

I glance quickly back at the stairs, making sure no one is coming down, and then I pull a pin from my hair and jiggle it inside the lock. The knob gives, and I turn it slowly, carefully, opening the door a crack before sliding inside. The room is dark, but I can make out the shape of a queen-size bed. I close the bedroom door and use my phone for light, shining it on the nightstand. A wallet, keys, and some pocket change are scattered across the surface. I remove the ID and shine the light on a picture of Dominic. He looks sullen as always. Maybe it's just his demeanor. I photograph all his IDs and credit cards even though I'm wishing it were Bret's wallet. Dominic wasn't the one spotted in the parking lot that night in June. I don't need him as much as I need Bret.

At the foot of the bed is a red duffel bag and backpack. I have to hike my dress way up to squat down in front of the bag. With Bret and Dominic both sleeping here, I don't know whose bag this is.

I unzip the duffel first and slide a hand inside, feeling around for something that isn't clothes. Possibly a bag of drugs like the one Dominic and Bret planted on Cody Smith. Or the ones currently sitting in Bret's pocket. I remove one of our school polos and notice the monogram on the tag: Dominic DeLuca. I refrain from laughing at the fact that he's got preschool name tags in his uniforms. So, not Bret's bag. I drop the shirt and reach back in. My fingers brush something plastic. I shift aside the clothes and shine the light, illuminating at least thirty condom packets spread out over the bottom of the duffel. Good boy, Dominic. Way to be safe. And overconfident, apparently. I go through all the side pouches and end pockets but find nothing of worth. Nothing incriminating or even interesting.

I hold still, listening for footsteps before moving on to the backpack. The only sounds are coming from the party above my head. I remove a U.S. history book, then a five-subject notebook—nothing of interest in there. The Spanish book comes out next, and then I know it's Dominic's backpack. Bret's in German III—not Spanish— right before my AP German class. My fingers reach the metal clasps of a manila envelope. I shine the light on it. Luckily it's not sealed. I have to set down the flashlight to remove the contents of the envelope. Several newspaper clippings slide out. I pick up the flashlight again and lean in to see better. The headlines jump out at me.

California Senator's Son Found Dead in his Home: Suicide Suspected...Senator Gilbert and Family Grieve Simon's Death in a Private Burial Today...Simon Gilbert Found Dead...

Dead.

Dead.

Dead.

The words flash before me, and my heart picks up speed. Why is Dominic carrying around these articles? I can hardly bear to read the headlines, let alone see the photo of Simon smiling in the suit he wore to spring formal. A cold sweat breaks out across my forehead and neck, and my chest tightens. The dark room is suddenly too much. Too creepy. I'm used to being on the criminal side of these break-ins, finding people's weaknesses, their vulnerabilities, not letting them find mine.

I tuck the items back into Dominic's backpack. I'm about to bolt, but a pen rolls from the bag. The words "St. Felicity's Shelter" are printed across it. I examine it, yanking off the cap. My breath catches in my throat, refusing to let a gasp escape.

It's a listening device.

Someone bugged Dominic?

The bedroom door swings open before I can make a move to hide.

CHAPTER
11

Miles stands in the doorway, shirtless and dripping wet. Considering he's been witness to my not-so-honest behavior a few times over the last week, I begin to panic before he even opens his mouth.

"What are you doing in here?" he demands, arms folded over his muscled chest. "Dominic told me he keeps this door locked." His gaze drifts from my face lower, to my hands. "What have you got?"

I jump to my feet, smoothing my dress back into place with one hand, the other behind my back, concealing the pen. My pulse is out of control. I need an angle quick before I lose my cool. Considering he's already caught me flushing drugs down the school bathroom toilet to avoid getting caught with them, then lying to a teacher about it, I can't pull a teasing, bad-girl move on Miles again. I need something else, something that appeals to a different sense. Something he won't expect.

"What are you hiding behind your back?" He moves toward me. "Show me."

I put both hands behind me, slide the pen into my purse, and dig for the pills Bret gave me. I attempt to step around Miles, knowing he won't let me. "I don't have anything. I just made a wrong turn on the way to the bathroom."

"Right." He plants his hard, wet body in front of me. If I didn't have other concerns, I would take a moment to enjoy this view. "Then show me your hands, Ellie."

"What are you, the party police?" I snap, then I push myself deeper, further into this role. I take one look at his face, his stance in front of me, and make it clear that I've accepted defeat. "Fine."

I uncurl my fingers, revealing the two blue pills. Miles flips on the light and leans in to get a closer look. "What are these?"

"Aleve," I try.

He rolls his eyes. "Ecstasy, right?"

I channel myself from moments ago, finding those articles, seeing Simon again in the photos, remembering him the night before he was found dead, smiling and strapping a corsage around my wrist. And before I know it, a lump has formed in my throat, tears budding in the corners of my eyes and panic in my voice when I speak. "Please don't tell my sister. Or Aidan. You can keep the pills; I swear I won't take them…"

He lifts a brow. "You want me to lie for you? Again?" He shakes his head. "Yeah, not happening."

I shove past him, suppressing a sob, and head straight for the bathroom, locking the door before he can get in the way. Miles bangs on the door. I check myself out in the mirror and splash some water on my face, smearing my mascara.

"I swear if I hear a toilet flush…" Miles shouts through the door.

"You don't get what it's like," I tell him. *Story, Ellie, come on, you got this.* Teenage drama. It's not rocket science. It all revolves around a handful of subjects—school, friends, boyfriends...parents. *Bingo.* "My dad will kill me. He already sent me away to live with my sister. He hates me. I'm nothing but a screwup to him."

My proclamations must be scaring Miles, because his tone changes. "Ellie, just come out and we can talk about this. Maybe it's not so bad to tell your sister. Doesn't mean she'll tell anyone else. She seems cool. And so does Lawren— Aidan."

There he goes again with the last-name thing.

The doorknob rattles and eventually turns. I place myself on the floor in front of the sink when the door finally opens. Miles steps inside and squats down in front of me. He's got his jeans back on now. Maybe they were in the bedroom with Dominic's stuff? No, they were lying across the back of the couch. Dammit, I could have gotten his wallet. I'm seriously out of practice. I force my thoughts back to the articles in Dominic's bag and the words playing on repeat...*found dead....dead....dead.*

Fresh tears fall from my eyes. My makeup is probably a mess now. I swipe my arm across my face like the mess embarrasses me. Then I open my hand, showing Miles the pills. "I didn't take them. Or flush them."

I expect him to go back to his stiff, I-hate-your-type stance the moment he sees that I'm okay, but Miles surprises me by taking a seat on the bathroom floor right in front of me. "So your dad's an ass?"

"He's..." I sniffle. "He's a preacher. At a church in Utah. I'm an embarrassment to him. He wanted to send me to rehab for smoking pot and doing E a few times. But then my mom and Harper thought maybe I could just..." I sink further into my character and break down in sobs, pressing my face against my knees. "Doesn't matter. They're going to send me there anyway."

Miles's hands land on my bare shoulders. A flutter emerges in my stomach, but I force it away. "Look, Ellie—"

"I wasn't even going to take them." I lift my head, staring into his swirling blue eyes. Despite my suspicions about Miles's sudden appearance with the cool kids, there is something in his face—his eyes especially—that screams honesty. And it's not like he hasn't already made his opinions known, his straightforward, simple thoughts regarding black, white, and gray behaviors. I stand abruptly and wipe my face again with one hand. "Forget it. You're not gonna believe me."

"I might believe you." He stands in front of me again, still shirtless, still blocking the door. He lifts both my hands, takes the pills from one of them, drops them into the pocket of his jeans. Then his right index and middle finger travel to the inside of my wrist. My breath catches; I can't help it. He smells like sun and fresh air and has those eyes that hold layers and layers of thoughts. He steps closer, his face now inches from mine. "Now tell me again… Did you plan on taking the ecstasy you snagged from Dominic's stuff?"

I look right into his eyes. I know exactly what he's doing but I don't know why or how he knows to do this. My pulse picks up, and his face tightens. I release a short, nervous laugh. "Where did you pick up this human-lie-detector skill?"

"A Peter Abrahams novel, I think." His forehead wrinkles. "Maybe it was Stephen King…"

I slide another inch in his direction. I can feel his warm breath hitting my cheek. "And you aren't planning on considering the fact that maybe other influences could cause my pulse to speed up?"

His mouth forms an *O*, but he clamps it shut quickly. Color creeps up his neck. His voice comes out in a whisper, deep and intense. "Answer the question, Ellie."

One slow, quiet inhale, and I've got my heart rate in check. "I wasn't planning on taking ecstasy or any other drugs tonight."

"Good." He continues to search my face. "And several days ago, at school, what were you really doing with those drugs?"

The fingers pressing gently into the inside of my wrist throb as Miles's pulse picks up. Huh. This could be useful. I reach for that emotional duress from moments ago and wait for a few more tears to tumble down my cheeks. "Dominic...he planted drugs on that Cody kid, and it reminded me of..." I swallow the lump in my throat. Truth is so much harder to speak than lies. I can't do it. I can't bring Simon into this tangled mess. "Well, I didn't want anyone else to end up where I'm at. Fighting with myself all the time. Or in trouble for something he didn't do."

"Are you in trouble for something you didn't do?" Miles asks.

His fingers are still on me, his body heat in my space. I lean forward and rest my forehead on Miles's shoulder. He stiffens immediately, so much that I almost back away. But instead, I give him a few seconds. He seems to make a decision about me because his shoulders sink back down, and one hand lands on my back.

"Hey...I'm sorry," he says. "I didn't know what you were doing."

If I wasn't so captivated by the scent and feel of his skin against my face, I would probably be working hard not to laugh. This was almost too easy. Here I thought Miles might provide a real challenge for me, given his no-bullshit approach to every situation. I mean, I'm pretty much 90 percent bullshit.

I turn my head slightly, and my mouth is practically

brushing against his neck. Gravity seems to push me from behind, wanting my lips against Miles's skin. Or maybe it's me who wants that. I've only been with one guy on my own terms. He was part of my "family" (though not a blood relative because ew) and it turned out about as bad as you could imagine considering he's very much like me. For a second, I toy with the idea of being here in this spot and exploring this boy simply out of curiosity. What would that be like? I lay my palm on the side of his neck. Beneath it, his pulse speeds. Uh-oh. Maybe Miles will prove to be a challenge for me after all. Though not the kind I'd originally imagined.

But logic takes over the curiosity. I've done what I needed to do, gained his trust. Now I need to keep it. I slide my arms around his neck and give him a squeeze, one that hopefully feels friendly. "Thanks for talking me down from the ledge. I'm trying not to be messed up but…yeah."

I start to pull away, only Miles is still holding on. He seems to realize this and quickly drops his arms to his sides. The sound of footsteps clambering down the stairs sends both of us glancing out the open bathroom door. I make a move to leave, but Miles touches my arm. "Wait."

He moves closer again, and I suck in a breath, holding it. His hands lift and grip the sides of my face. For a moment, I panic—is he about to kiss me? Then he slides his thumbs underneath my eyes. Black mascara marks his skin. My heart nearly stops. I force the air out of my lungs. He leans back, looks me over, and then nods. "There. Much better."

We step out of the space of the small bathroom before anyone appears. But still, two girls from our class give Miles and me a strange look like they're not sure if we were *in* the bathroom together. They both go in, shutting the door and leaving the area below deck pretty dark.

Miles catches my hand before I can go upstairs.

"Promise me something?"

I spin to face him. "What?"

Lines of worry crease his face. "Let me know if you see Dominic planting drugs on people," he says. "Don't try to handle it alone again, okay?"

I nod. "Okay. But why are you hanging out with them? Why do you even care what I do?"

"I don't know." He swallows. "Sometimes I wish I didn't care. Or want the truth."

And with that, he steps around me and heads back up to the deck of the yacht. I shake off the weird worry that I said the wrong thing. Again. Just when I think I've got Miles figured out, he does something that throws me off my game. And I still don't know what was up with the naked girl last weekend. Did they hook up?

Why do I care? I don't. Definitely not.

And what truth does he want? The truth about the bag of drugs? Or the truth about me? If it's the latter, let's hope he stops searching.

Back on the main deck, the music has grown louder and the voices more animated as everyone gets drunker. Bret spots me and walks over. Like Miles, he's dripping wet, but he's tossed on a T-shirt. "Where have you been? You missed the big race. Beckett cheated, in case you were wondering."

"How do you cheat at a swimming race? Did he drink a Red Bull before? Take some of your Adderall?"

"He said he wasn't that fast," Bret tells me, making an excuse to lean closer. "The guy was like a fucking seal."

"A seal?"

Bret proceeds to give me a play-by-play of the race. I can't focus on what he's saying, though. I'm still all mixed up from the emotional roller coaster I put myself on. My gaze travels across the yacht, down to the end of the pier to the man leaning against a light post.

I touch the front of Bret's shirt. "Hey, I think my ride's here."

"Oh, really?" He sounds disappointed, which is encouraging. He leans down, way too close to my face, and I'm fighting that urge to back away again. "I don't have your number."

I lift an eyebrow, waiting, and then finally I give in. "Are you asking for it?"

He hands me his phone, and I punch in my number. "Eleanor Ames. In my contacts. You look good in there."

"Thanks." I roll my eyes the second I turn my back to him. He's a dumb drunk. I much prefer a wild, table-dancing drunk, but now isn't the time to be picky. I say a quick good-bye to Justice and Chantel. Justice looks ready to drill me with questions about Bret, but then Miles drifts toward her and she's got a new distraction.

When I reach the end of the pier, I stand in front of Jakowski—Jack—with my arms folded across my chest. "And what are you doing here?"

He shrugs. "You know, in the neighborhood."

"Yeah right." I narrow my eyes. "Aidan sent you to babysit me?"

"He may have asked me to swing by and see if you needed a ride." He nods toward the black SUV belonging to the Secret Service. "So…you need a ride or are you planning to join your drunk and disorderly classmates for an all-nighter?"

My eyebrows rise. "Judgmental much?"

"Hey." He holds up his hands in surrender. "Did you see me busting in and hauling your ass out of there?"

"Fine." I sigh and follow him to the car. "I'm still not a fan of Aidan sending babysitters to parties."

Once we're on the road, the pen in my purse is practically burning a hole through the beaded material. I need to disable it. Luckily Jack sticks to my algebra class as a topic for the ride home.

"My teacher wants me to take precalc in the summer," I tell him.

"That's good news. Means you're getting everything down," Jack says. When I don't look excited, he laughs. "Calculus has a rep for being advanced but it's really not. People who hate algebra and geometry end up loving calc."

"Surely someone besides me hates all academic math?" I stare out the window. "Feels like all they talk about at school is SAT and ACT scores and how to get them higher. I barely even think about that stuff."

"Well, why the hell not? I'll make a program for you. When you get past all your 'I'm no good at this bullshit,' you're pretty damn good at it." He looks at me for a second then back at the road. "I think you have a ton of potential; you can't let small things like math keep you out of the game."

The thing is, planning a future, taking tests for college, that's not for people like me. My parents made sure I wouldn't have that life years ago when they decided I didn't need a real identity, when they taught me how to be a criminal. Of course Jack doesn't know any of this. Though sometimes, the things he says…I wonder if he knows something. Maybe not everything, but something.

When I get home, I lock the door to my bedroom and dig for the pen in my purse. I examine it carefully. It's similar to a device I had on me when I walked into that bank expecting my dad to meet me. That one belonged to the FBI. Does that mean the FBI is still investigating Simon's death?

My fingers move quickly over the tiny device and

disable it. Like I would have liked to do nine months ago when my mother took my dad's place during the final stretch of a long con that failed in the worst way possible.

With the device no longer a threat, I sink into the bed and finally allow myself to freak out over everything. Why did Dominic have all those articles about Simon?

Aidan once told me, during a game of memory, one of the biggest mistakes an investigator can make is lumping two separate pieces of evidence together simply because they were found in the same box. Or backpack in this case. But my father always said, someone with diamonds on the ears *and* finger was hiding a pile of cash beneath her mattress.

I flip over the tiny metal bug in my palm. I don't know whose advice is right, but I do know someone is trying to learn something from Dominic DeLuca.

CHAPTER
12

It's dark out by the time Harper and I leave the care of the chef/teacher, after our Sunday night cooking class at the Jewish Community Center. We—by we I mean me—managed to avoid setting anything on fire or explosions in general, which I consider a huge success. Harper is pretty much on top of the world while we walk home, our stomachs full of kosher meat.

"I'm not saying I want to have kids anytime soon. Just someday…" Harper argues.

I've been accusing her of all kinds of things relating to kids and family this evening, trying to get to the bottom of her learning-to-cook obsession. While our food cooked, she had gushed over pictures of the toddler twins she nannies and, after being forced to look at a hundred drool-filled pictures, I'd accused her of wanting babies.

"Think about it," I say, playing devil's advocate. "You bring a kid into this world and he or she will have a mother who uses a fake name, can't legally work—"

"And has a father with a very dangerous job," Harp says. "I know all of this, Ellie. I'm not stupid." She levels me with a look. "I'm also not willing to give up my chance at a real life just because of things our parents did. I'm too young and too optimistic to throw in the towel already."

Yeah, we don't share the optimist gene. I'm about to put up a better, bigger argument, but my senses become alert to something behind me, the hair on the back of my neck standing up. Footsteps. The sound of clothes brushing against skin. It's dark on the street, but the well-manicured lawns around us reduce the possibility of a threat. Or they should, at least.

I glance sideways at Harper. Even in the dark, she catches my eye and moves close. She felt it, too.

"Who?" I whisper. She shakes her head.

"Ellie!" someone shouts from behind.

Harper lets out a short scream. My heart jumps up to my throat.

The shadowed figure shouting my name moves close enough to identify. I clutch my chest with one hand and slap his shoulder with the other. "What the hell, Bret?"

He lifts up his hands in surrender, like he did in the equipment closet the other day. I'm beginning to think it's his signature move. The I-didn't-do-it face is well crafted. "Sorry! I didn't mean to—"

"Well, you did!" Harper snaps. She gives my arm a protective squeeze. "Jesus."

"I went by your place," Bret says. "And the big guy who answered the door told me where you were… I figured I'd catch up to you—" He looks between the two of us, his forehead wrinkled. "Are you two always this jumpy?"

"Do you always creep up behind people in the dark?" I ask.

He laughs. "You guys were seriously freaked out? In this neighborhood? Nothing happens here."

Harper and I take a few seconds to come down from our adrenaline rush, and then we continue to walk home.

Bret decides he's forgiven enough to walk beside us, though Harper continues to glare at him.

"What do you need, Bret?" I finally ask as we're approaching the apartment complex. "And what's wrong with texting? I hear all the kids are doing it these days."

He looks a little embarrassed—very out of character for him—when he turns to me, one hand gripping the back of his neck. "I was hoping maybe you could help me with the English assignment. I'm barely pulling a C and Lance worships you…"

I'm actually impressed that he's got a C in the class. Especially since he's busy helping to coach field hockey and planting drugs on fellow classmates. Hard to keep up with *The Great Gatsby* with all that going on.

But as the saying goes, keep your friends close and make your enemies fall for you.

Harper's looking at me like, *Who the hell is this guy and do you need me to get rid of him?*

"It's fine," I tell her. Then I say to Bret, "I don't do other people's homework."

"I don't want you to," he insists. "Just help me. That's all."

Then tell me what your car was doing in this exact spot last June.

If only it were that easy. The key to undercover operations is to gain trust. Even if doing this makes you want to vomit up kosher meat.

"Okay, I'll help you," I say finally.

We walk between two of the buildings to the courtyard and pool. Even though it's dark out, the lights around the pool and in the water make it easy to see a guy swimming laps. I've become familiar with Miles's butterfly stroke. It's smooth and perfect—the tempo, the ease with which his arms continuously rise out of the water like they'll never tire.

An older man I don't recognize is seated in a lawn chair, a cigar in his mouth, the newspaper spread out in front of him. "Hey, kid, give it a rest," he shouts at Miles.

"Is that Beckett?" Bret says. "Look at him, training for our next race. That shithead. He acts like he's never swam before in his life and then he's kicking everyone's ass."

Smoke from the cigar wafts this way, and my stomach turns. I hate that smell.

"Hey, kid!" the guy shouts louder. "Enough."

Miles stops, and his feet hit the bottom of the pool. He tosses his goggles off to the side and glares at the guy. "If I keep my head underwater, maybe I'll avoid damage from your secondhand smoke."

The man snorts, but he does put out the cigar. Is that Miles's uncle? The one who leaves envelopes full of cash labeled "food money"?

"You're gonna wear yourself down to nothing," the man says to Miles. "You've done at least a hundred laps. What are you training for? Olympics are over."

When Harper heads up the stairs to our apartment, Miles finally looks around and notices Bret and me. He morphs back into the cool kid he was at the yacht party. He hops out of the pool, shakes off the excess water—which is quite a sight—and grins at Bret. "Hey, man, what's up?"

I'm so busy admiring my shirtless neighbor I barely hear Bret when he says, "What do you think, Ellie? Are you up for a threesome?"

I snap around to face him. "What?"

Bret laughs, but Miles stiffens and heads over to grab his towel from a table nearby. "He means to study."

Clearly I missed that part. "You're not in our class."

"But he's reading the same book," Bret says. "And he's in honors."

"That's right, Miles the honors student," I sing.

He turns around to face me, the towel now around his neck. "And Ellie the…" He scratches his head. "What exactly are you, Ellie? Party girl? Field hockey star? Saver of wet clothing?"

We stare at each other, something flowing between us, something that says the trust I built the other night might be gone. But it can't be that. Not completely. He would have told Harper about the drugs.

"Teacher's pet," Bret says. "That's what Ellie is, and I'm using it to my benefit."

I force a smile. "Come on upstairs."

In the apartment, I leave Bret at the kitchen table with Harper, who is all too willing to continue to glare at the guy who freaked us out on our walk home. I find Aidan waiting for me in the doorway to his and Harper's room.

"I know what you're thinking," I say before he gets a word in. I lower my voice to a whisper. "Just let me do this, okay? You want to know what he was doing in the parking lot the night Simon died, and I can find out."

Aidan tenses, cracks his knuckles. "Or I can have a little chat with him one-on-one and find out right now."

"Yeah, and lose your job." I press a hand to Aidan's chest, holding him back. "Plus, he's been questioned by the FBI already, remember?"

"Ellie," Aidan whispers. "As your legal guardian, I can't let you hang out with a kid who carts around bags of drugs."

"They were Dominic's drugs," I lie. "And I'm not doing drugs. I'm not doing anything illegal with him. Right now, we're studying."

"Okay," he concedes. "But I'm keeping a close eye on that kid."

I grab my books from my room and head back to the table to join Bret. Seconds later, someone knocks on the door, and Aidan lets in Miles along with the cigar-smoking guy. Aidan shakes hands with the older man. "How was the traveling, Clyde?"

So it is Uncle Clyde.

"You know, same old."

Aidan offers him a beer, and the two of them head out to the balcony. With Aidan not so secretly watching us, I slide my chair an equal distance between Miles and Bret and open my copy of *Gatsby*.

"So, Mr. Lance assigned us—"

"Dude," Bret says to Miles. "Justice is going nuts 'cause you haven't called her. You going somewhere with that?"

I lift an eyebrow at Miles. He refuses to look me in the eye. "Not sure. Just trying to get by right now, you know? New place, new school…"

"Yeah, I get it. But seriously, she's freaking. And Justice freaking is likely to make you the one to—" Bret's eyes widen. "Okay, I see what you're doing now. Well-played, man."

I lift up the hardcover book and drop it onto the table, allowing the loud *thud* to echo through the room. "Hello? I thought we were studying, not conducting a meeting for Asshole Kings of the Universe."

"Sorry," Bret says, and then he makes an effort to lean over and look at the chapter in the book I've just opened.

Miles, on the other hand, ignores me. "Can you let Dominic know I'm gonna do the boat rental thing sometime this week if he's still up for waterskiing."

Dominic. Miles is hanging out with Dominic. I glance down at the book, thinking of something. "Hey, why don't you ask Dominic to study with us? He's in the class."

"Good idea." Bret picks up his phone and appears to text someone. He turns to Miles again. "Dominic's got a bad rep with the boat rental places. He's banned from all the ones around here. He got wasted, had a bad wreck over the summer. His dad got him off with barely a scratch. He knew a judge," Bret says like this is normal. "He was kind of messed up for a couple of months, but he's cool now. Just don't let him drink and drive."

Both Bret and Miles laugh like we weren't just conversing about breaking some pretty big, important laws. I look at Bret, seeing his presence in my life as an even bigger opportunity. He's a gossip. Or at least he is with Miles.

"Oh, I heard about that," I say as casually as possible.

Bret lifts an eyebrow. "Really? From who?"

Uh… "Justice, I think…or maybe it was Chantel." I shake my head. "I can't remember."

"Justice, probably." Bret rolls his eyes. "She's always hot and cold with Dominic. And when they're cold, she's all about telling his secrets."

Good to know. Maybe there's a way to induce the cold phase so she can fill me in on some of his secrets. Like the envelope of Simon Gilbert articles.

I smile at both guys. "I think this group study thing is gonna work out great."

CHAPTER
13

I t took nearly two hours to get to this tech store in Georgetown, so I had no choice but to skip school this afternoon to arrive before closing. I'll have to make up an excuse for missing class. Aidan and Harper will be on me as soon as I get home because my school sends these automated phone calls whenever anyone misses a class and a parent or guardian doesn't call it in.

I've changed out of my uniform into a yellow cotton sundress by the time I walk into Tech Gear Unlimited. The store is tiny, no customers shopping at the moment, and the girl behind the counter is reading a comic book, her black boots tossed up onto the counter. This is supposed to be the best place for confidential consultations regarding all things tech gear. Hopefully that piece of marketing holds some truth, because I went through a lot of trouble to get here.

"What can I help you with?" the girl asks. She looks about Harp's age, maybe a little older. Her dirty-blond hair is tied in a messy ponytail at the nape of her neck. She's wearing a Star Wars T-shirt, a name tag that reads Connie attached to the front.

I set my purse on the counter and then lean against it, my elbows resting on top. "Promise you won't laugh?"

Connie points to a sign on the wall that says: *Technically challenged? No worries. This is a judgment-free zone.*

"It said on your website that you can identify any electronic or technical gear..." I bite my lip, giving the appearance of nerves, then I slowly remove the St. Felicity's Shelter pen from my purse. "So...my BFFs Sarah H.—that's Sarah with an *H* plus an *H* for her last initial—and Sara C.—"

"*H* or no *H*?" Connie interrupts.

"No *H*," I say. "We were eating lunch on the bleachers because that's the best vitamin D spot and Sarah H. is deficient. I guess it's causing depression, and three pieces of her hair fell out yesterday, so we're trying to help her out. Her cook always makes sushi for us on Wednesdays—not the easiest thing to eat outside, but whatever. I was dipping my spicy tuna when I spotted this pen in the grass. I knew there was something strange about it because none of us had ever even heard of St. Felicity's Shelter and Sarah H. was baptized Catholic so she would totally know."

"Totally," Connie agrees, looking amused. It seems the sign is true. This really is a judgment-free zone, because I would have kicked myself out of this store by now.

"I pulled off the cap..." I uncap the pen and reveal the bug hidden inside. Connie leans closer to get a good look. "And this came out. Obviously it's some kind of computer chip, but why would you hide it in a pen? It has to be top secret. And then Sarah H. and Sara C. got into an argument over whether it belongs to Russian or Chinese spies. Sarah H. says Russians. But Sara C. claims the Chinese are the ones to worry about right now and that Russia is so 1980. I didn't know who was right, so I volunteered to get some help figuring it out." I grin at her. "So here I am."

"Here you are." Connie looks up at me. "It's a listening device."

"Wait..." I fake shock. "So it *is* a spy thing? Spies use these, right?"

"Sure," she says. "Or private investigators, FBI, CIA..."

I clap a hand over my mouth. "Oh my God, the CIA is in our school! I think I know who it is—this one guy in my American lit class is always on the phone speaking Turkish or Lithuanian. Holy cow, I have to tell my parents. They're going to freak. They're so big on privacy."

"The CIA is just one example of who might use a device like this," Connie reassures. "From what I know, clandestine missions in American high schools aren't a primary focus of the CIA. How about we do a little research on the manufacturer?"

I play with my phone and examine my nails while Connie moves a laptop onto the counter and types away, searching for answers. After a few minutes, she says, "This manufacturer definitely has a government contract. It looks like that's their only customer at the moment."

This is exactly what I'd been hoping to learn today. If I can find out who owns this device, I might be able to figure out why that owner wants to spy on Dominic DeLuca.

"Whoa." I lean in closer. "Seriously? This is so *Bourne Identity*. Or maybe *Skyfall*. Have you seen that movie?"

"Sorry, no."

That makes two of us.

"Wow..." Connie says to her laptop. "This is the real deal. Top quality. Probably a few thousand with the receiver."

"Receiver? Oh, like the thingy you use to listen in?"

Connie looks impressed. "Exactly."

"So they just stuck this spy chip in some random pen?"

"No." Connie's face fills with excitement like I've brought her a technical feast. "I think St. Felicity's Shelter might be a code name."

"For what?"

"For a government office or a special division of an existing investigative branch..." she rattles off while scrolling through a web page. "But everything I'm reading is theories other techies like me have posted online. No proof or facts to validate them."

Okay, this shit's gettin' real. Exactly why I need the rich-airhead-girl cover. I don't want her tying me with any government agency in any of her own techie theories. "This is so crazy. I mean, what if we, like, had lunch inside yesterday? This never would have happened."

Connie glances at me again, longing and apprehension on her face. "Any chance you might be willing to leave the pen with me for a while so I can look into it more?"

I shrug. "What good is it to me? I mean, not without the receiver thingy... Now if I had that, I would definitely plant it on Sara C.'s boyfriend. I know he's cheating on her with Gwen Saxton, but she doesn't believe me. She's in denial because she's so in love with him." I stop talking and sigh. "Except my BFFs will kill me if I don't bring it back. They almost didn't want me coming here alone, but Sarah H. had a bio quiz and Sara C. has already skipped P.E. eight days this month for PMS, so she's over the limit."

I can practically see the wheels spinning in Connie's head, while she digs for a way to get me to let her keep this device for a while. I'm hoping for something better in return. God knows I'm too broke to buy any spy gear.

"What if I make you a deal?" she says.

"You mean like money? That's not really going to help."

"I mean I can loan you a similar, though way-less-interesting-to-me device, with a receiver," Connie says.

"Your friends won't know the difference and you can nail Sara C.'s boyfriend—" She closes her eyes briefly and shakes her head. "I'm always doing that. Picking the worst possible wording. I should have said, gain proof or catch him in the act."

"Good, because I would never do that with him. I only date guys who are at least six one and he's five eleven. Plus he's, like, Sara C.'s boyfriend." I'm really beginning to hate my imaginary BFFs. They're assholes.

Connie smiles; she's excited but trying to hide it. She gestures toward a door behind the counter. "Step into my office. That's where I keep all the top-secret gear. I'll show you how to use it and everything."

Connie spends a good forty-five minutes giving me a thorough lesson on how to spy on someone via audio invasion. And despite the fact that I've planted plenty of bugs and searched for them, too, this one is a bit more high-tech than what I'm used to, so I'm glad for the step-by-step instruction.

Before I leave the store, I give Connie my cell number and promise her I'll check back in next week.

The second I walk through the apartment door—my new toy buried in the depths of my backpack—I know I'm in trouble. Aidan and Harper are sitting at the kitchen table, their voices low and serious. Both of them stop talking and look up at me.

"What the hell, Ellie?" Harper says. But I hear relief in her voice more than anger. Which makes me feel like an ass. "Where were you?"

"The automated message said you missed sixth, seventh,

and eighth hour?" Aidan says.

For a second, I let myself enjoy this scene. They're worried about me. For missing a few stupid classes. All the years I didn't even go to school, the times I'd take off with a friend or, well...one particular guy who wasn't a friend... and not come home until the next day—my parents never even batted an eyelash.

I lean against the kitchen counter and smile at them. It's going to piss off Harper, but I can't help it. "You guys are cute."

"Are you high?" Aidan asks at the same time Harper says, "Are you drunk?"

I stifle a laugh. "Um, neither. And even if I were, I wasn't driving or anything like that."

Aidan gives me a pointed look. "Or walking near any pools?"

My stomach sinks. I don't want to think about that night last spring. After I heard about Simon...after Aidan learned that neither Harper nor I could swim. Sometimes I close my eyes to fall asleep, and I'm back in that deep end again, water filling my lungs, my clothes clinging to me, heavy and pulling me toward the bottom.

I look down at my hands. "A bunch of us decided to cut and go to the mall. It was no big deal. I should have told you. I'm sorry."

"Who?" Harper demands. "Which 'us' are you referring to?"

"It wouldn't be very cool of me to rat them out."

My sister glares at me, and I know I need to give her something. I pull out my phone and stare at it for a moment before scrolling to Justice's name. She'd given me her number last weekend, and she knows I know about her and Jacob's little game over Chantel. She owes me. I hit call and luckily, she picks up after a couple of rings.

"Hey Ellie, what's up? How's Bret? I heard you guys were having a study session the other day."

I glance at Harper. "You heard right."

Justice starts to ask for details but I interrupt her. "So my sister knows that we cut class together today. She's not looking to get anyone in trouble, just for proof that I was with you. At the mall."

"Right," Justice says, catching on quick. "The mall. I had that emotional crisis. Needed to get away and buy stuff. Hate when that happens."

I sigh internally with relief. "Mind telling her that for me?"

Justice agrees, and I hand over the phone to Harper. She listens for a minute, looks way less pissed, then hands the phone back to me.

"No more of that, Ellie," Harper warns.

I do the sign of the cross despite our kosher experience the other night, swearing my good behavior is back, and then I walk toward my room with Justice still on the phone.

"Okay, so you have to tell me," she squeals. "Where did you go today? And it better be good. I just told your sister that I lost my virginity to a college guy who has three other girlfriends and now I have chlamydia."

"Jesus Christ, you didn't have to say all that."

"I just got so into it I couldn't stop," she says, sounding like someone with a post-con adrenaline rush. "Now you owe me a favor."

"Funny," I say. "I thought it was the other way around."

"You are something, Ellie. Don't know if anyone would see you coming," Justice says. They usually don't. "Okay then, just help me out, pleeeaase."

"What do you need? Fake ID? Forged absence slips?" I rattle off.

"You can do that?" she says, surprised.

"Um, no," I lie. "It was a joke. Now tell me what you want."

"Miles Beckett."

I glance out the window of my bedroom, checking the pool. He's not there. "Miles Beckett. Any preference how? Scrambled? Fried? Poached? Over-easy?"

"Find out if he's into me," she says. "Carefully, though."

Of course. I roll my eyes, glad she can't see me. "I'll try."

And I will, because she's proving to be quite useful. It's best to maintain the connection. And I'll refuse to notice the twinge in my belly at the thought of Miles hooking up with her, too. *Liar.*

"Text me the second you find out anything."

"You know he's only here for a semester, right?" I tell her. "Then he goes back to California or wherever it is they manufacture spray starch."

"I know," she says. "But maybe we'll sell him on Holden Prep and he'll stay in Virginia? Or maybe I can just have some fun with him and be done with it."

"If you say so."

I hang up with Justice, sling my backpack over my shoulder again, and head for the door. Harper and Aidan both shout at the same time, "Where are you going?"

"A party," I say, but before they can yell again, I add, "To get the homework assignments I missed from Miles."

I think all I had to do was say Miles's name and they would have let me go. Clyde and Aidan really hit it off the other night. Somehow that gave Miles even more credibility.

Me, on the other hand, I don't seem to have much cred with Miles. Which makes our neighborly visits a blast.

CHAPTER

14

Miles's uncle Clyde answers the door. His hair is matted on one side like he'd been napping on the couch. The TV is blasting *Wheel of Fortune*. I try to look past Clyde into the apartment because it seems like many Miles Beckett secrets could be hiding in there. From what I can tell, the living room looks generically furnished like one of those model homes. Brown leather couch, glass coffee table, red-patterned accent chair, curtains to match said accent chair, black TV stand, some colorful decorative items on the coffee table, Linens and Things paintings on the wall—basic pieces to stage a room but nothing personal.

I plaster on a smile. "Is Miles home?"

"Sorry, honey, he went for a run." He scrubs a hand over his face and glances at his watch. "A long time ago. What the hell is wrong with that boy?"

"Oh, well, I'll check back later." I start to turn away, but Clyde stops me.

"Eleanor, is it?" he asks. I nod, though it pains me not to correct him. "Are you interested in having dinner with us later?"

My forehead wrinkles. "Dinner?"

"Yeah, dinner." Clyde nods as if convincing himself. "The kid—Miles—could use a little help making friends."

Oh, I doubt Miles needs my help in that area, but there's no way I'm passing up a chance to get a look inside his place. I smile again. "Sure, that sounds great."

I take my bag and head down to the pool. Hopefully I can catch him when he comes back from this run. I spread out my books on one of the pool tables to start my homework. Before I can do anything, Justice sends me a text.

JUSTICE: Anything????

ME: He's not home. His uncle said he went out for a run

JUSTICE: Hot. Think he runs shirtless? Get a pic for me!

Yeah, this is why I don't do girl talk. There's no way I'm going to tell her that I've seen Miles shirtless pretty much every day since he moved in. She'd probably camp out in the courtyard. And watching Miles move through his butterfly stroke from my bedroom window is *my* guilty pleasure; I have no plans to share it with anyone.

I set down the phone and open my Algebra 2 book. Twenty minutes into my homework problems, and I'm regretting skipping this class. Big time. I'm close to my breaking point when shirtless Miles jogs my way. He's covered in sweat, but his breathing is even.

He's got headphones in and doesn't seem to notice me sitting here. He drops down on the pool deck and begins doing push-up after push-up. I take the opportunity to study him like this. He looks far gone, so deep inside his head I could probably yell his name and he wouldn't notice. And he seems weighted down, too, despite the tireless ease of his push-ups.

I don't want to compare myself to Miles—I mean, I've

never even touched a can of starch—but I get it. I get what he's doing. Because I've done this before. I've thrown myself into something difficult, painful, and challenging just to escape reality for a little while. I think this is why I don't hate all the schoolwork that comes with being at Holden Prep. It fills my head so completely I stop thinking about other things. Like the old woman who's out ten grand and might never see her grandson again.

With a sigh, I leave Miles to his escape and turn back to the integers, equations, and formulas in front of me. I channel Jack and his calm advice and try to break down the problem into simpler terms, to guess the overall purpose and not let the small parts get to me, like he's told me many times before.

"Use the distance formula."

I jump when Miles's finger lands on my notebook and his voice brings my surroundings back into focus. I look up at him, squinting into the sun. "Huh?"

"The distance formula," he repeats. He gently plucks the pencil from my hand and writes out a formula at the top of my paper. Then he solves the problem I'd been stuck on for nearly ten minutes.

I stare at his work. "That's it? It can't be that easy."

He drops the pencil and shrugs. "Obviously not for you."

I wait for him to walk toward the steps before I flip him off behind his back.

"I saw that, Ellie," he says.

The lighter, teasing Miles is back.

But whatever. At least I can do the rest of my homework now. "See you in a little while, for dinner," I call after him.

That gets him to stop and turn around. I grin, feeling a little satisfied. "Your uncle invited me."

"Great," he mutters. "He's decided to be neighborly."

I don't get a chance to answer him because Miles stomps up the steps, probably to have a word with his uncle. I'm even more excited about this meal than I was before.

"What's wrong with eating at your place?" Miles drops a salad bowl onto the table with a loud *thud*. "Your sister starting fires again?"

I shrug. "Probably not. Thursday is PB and J night."

"Sounds great," Miles says. "You shouldn't miss out on that."

Clyde places three glasses onto the table and then smacks Miles on the head. "Don't be an ass."

The way that Miles inhales, his nostrils flaring, his glare trained on Clyde's back, it's obvious they aren't happy roommates. So yeah, this dinner is getting better and better.

Miles points a finger—aggressively, I should note—at a vacant chair, ordering me to sit. Though I think it's more of a "keep your mouth shut and stay out of my way" command. I laugh under my breath. It's nice seeing him flustered for a change.

"What can I get you to drink?" Clyde asks me.

"Water is fine."

He takes a jug of filtered water out of the fridge, fills my glass, and sets the jug in the center of the table. Miles immediately moves the jug six inches to the right. He grabs several bottles of salad dressing from the fridge and sets them in the space where the jug had been. I can't remember the last time I ate salad. Based on their dressing selection, it must be a regular occurrence here.

Clyde releases a frustrated breath, and then somehow

he concedes in this silent argument he's having with his nephew because he takes a seat across from me, leaving Miles to finish up the dinner prep. Miles is fresh from the shower, wearing a T-shirt (unfortunately) and gray sweatpants. Clyde and I watch his nephew move around the kitchen like a pro, pulling a casserole out of the oven, placing it carefully at the center of the table. He fills his own glass with milk, then places the carton nearby like he's planning on having a refill.

Clyde reaches for the spoon resting beside the casserole, but Miles smacks his hand away. "The bread isn't ready yet."

A couple of minutes later, Miles opens the oven again and removes a loaf of French bread. He slices it and then sets it on the table beside a stick of butter. My stomach rumbles at the sight of all the home-cooked food. Finally, Miles sits down with us. He takes my plate, loading it with something white and gooey from the casserole pan. I lean forward to examine it.

"It's tuna casserole," Miles says. "Remember, one of two things I know how to make."

"I remember." I stare warily at the food. "I guess I was hoping for eggs. Or maybe for one of Clyde's specialties."

Clyde laughs. "My specialty is Roni's Pizza Palace. I just figured out how to order on the line."

"Online," Miles corrects, his voice full of annoyance. "Not on the line."

Before I can decide about the tuna casserole, Miles drops a large portion of salad onto my plate. I lean in again to examine the casserole. And yeah, I do have excellent table manners when I need to. But when I don't need them, they seem to go out the window. "What's the crunchy-looking stuff on top? And those are peas, right?"

Miles has this exasperated look on his face that almost

makes me laugh. "Either eat it or don't. Seriously."

He loads up his plate with so much food it's practically hanging off the edges. I sift through the salad dressings looking for a familiar type—Italian. I can do Italian.

We eat in silence for a few minutes, Clyde glancing between Miles and me the whole time. Finally, I turn to Clyde. "So what kind of business do you do?"

Miles chokes on the gulp of milk he's just taken.

Clyde gives him a pointed look. "Mostly check fraud. I work as a consultant for several different companies."

"Check fraud," I repeat. I know a little bit about check fraud. "Sounds interesting."

"Pretty boring, actually," Clyde admits. "Lots of comparing handwriting, reviewing files... If it weren't for coffee, I'd fall asleep on the job all the time."

"Like you don't already," Miles snorts. But when Clyde glares at him, he drops his gaze to the plate in front of him and shovels in food.

Because I can't pass up a learning opportunity, I drill Clyde with questions for several minutes. "Aside from handwriting, how do you identify a serial?"

"Great question." Clyde points his fork at me, obviously impressed with my knowledge. If only he knew the truth. "With the serials, there's always a pattern. Sometimes it's a set of numbers that repeat. One time, I caught this woman who'd stolen more than a quarter million using fraudulent checks, and all her false names had the same middle initial. *V*."

Amateur. "Wow...so she really screwed up, huh?"

Clyde's face is lit with excitement. Doesn't seem like such a boring job. "I think they want to be caught. To be known, at least. These guys—"

"And women," I remind him.

He nods. "And women... They're smart as hell. If I

can follow even ten percent of their thought patterns, I've learned something. It takes intelligence and patience to pull off the big jobs, the quarter-million-and-more jobs."

"They're criminals," Miles says, looking at Clyde like he's dirty laundry. "They're fucking criminals. They steal money. How can you act like they deserve any amount of respect?"

My gut twists and knots. My face warms. The salad on my plate is gone. I have no choice but to fork a bite of casserole and stuff it in my mouth. I wait for my gag reflex to kick in at the mere thought of tuna fish, but I don't taste anything fishy. It's warm and cheesy.

"This is good," I tell Miles, hoping for a change of subject. I shouldn't have taken us down that path.

"I didn't say they were good people," Clyde snaps, both guys ignoring my big taste test. "I just said they were good at what they do. That's a fact. Not my opinion. If they weren't good, I wouldn't have a job."

"Maybe you shouldn't," Miles says.

They stare each other down, tension flowing between them. The table is suddenly small, the room stuffy.

In poetic, sitcom fashion, someone knocks on the door and the ice in the room cracks down the middle. I'm expecting it to be Harper or Aidan checking on me, so I shovel some more casserole in my mouth before I'm asked to leave.

But it's not Harper or Aidan.

It's Dominic DeLuca.

He takes one look at me and tenses. Yeah, this is gettin' weird. But whatever. Maybe an opportunity just fell right into my lap. I stand and cart my plate to the sink while polishing off the rest of the casserole. "I'd better get going. Homework and all that."

Clyde starts to protest, but I head for the door anyway.

I give Miles a pat on the back. And then, despite his entire body turning to stone, I attempt to give Dominic a hug. "Good to see you, Dominic. We should definitely hang out more often."

While he's stiff as a board, I slip the keys from his shorts pocket. I hold them against my stomach and grab the door, flinging it open. "Thanks for dinner!"

Back in my apartment, Harper and Aidan are in their bedroom watching TV, so I'm able to grab the device Connie gave me and sneak in and out unnoticed. I head down to the parking lot and hit the unlock button on the keys, identifying Dominic's SUV. I open the driver door just enough to slip inside, and then I look around for the perfect spot. I glance down at the plastic key chain bought during a tour of the White House from the looks of it.

I split it open and slip the tiny bug Connie from Tech Gear Unlimited loaned me. A perfect fit. I snap the president's house back into place and grin at my work. "Your country needs you, Dominic. Speak all your secrets into this key chain."

My voice emerges loud and clear from the transmitter. It's working. I tuck Dominic's keys into the ignition, making it look like he left them there, and then I take the long way around the complex back to my apartment.

Minutes later, I'm at my desk, homework spread out, headphones on, waiting for Dominic DeLuca to get into his car so I can start listening in.

CHAPTER
15

The screaming punk music turns off and Dominic's voice booms through my headphones. *"I'll have a double bacon burger—"*

"Lettuce, ketchup, and pickles only," I recite out loud from my bedroom. God, this is useless. A week of spying on Dominic DeLuca and all I've learned is his fast food order. In addition, after finding out the transmitter was too small to listen outside a one-mile radius, I had to put on my whining rich girl act for Connie again to get her to loan me a few repeaters to stretch the signal. All for nothing, apparently.

I go back to my homework and try to ignore the blaring punk music, but only minutes later, it shuts off again. I assume he's getting out of his car but then I hear him talking, probably on the phone with someone.

"Dude, we're hanging out at the beach club later. Meet me there…it should be fine. I can sneak away."

I straighten up, my eyes wide.

"Yeah, there… I'll text you… Uh-huh… Behind the—"

"Ellie!" Harper calls, then a knock on my door follows.

I lift the receiver Connie gave me, fighting the urge

to throw it against the wall. Instead, I yank out the headphone plug and tuck the little box under my pillow.

"Harper!" I yell back, my hand on the doorknob. "I hope you know you just ruined a week of—"

It isn't my sister standing in front of me. It's Justice and Chantel. Harper appears behind them, a bit flustered. "Your friends are here."

"Oh…hey." I smooth my expression to a more pleasant one. "Wasn't expecting you guys." Like, ever.

"I know, right?" Justice says. She steps around me and enters my room before I can invite her. Now I know why Harper looked so flustered. I shrug at my sister but wave her away. I can handle these two. But God-freakin'-damn they have the worst timing.

"This place is adorable," Justice says.

Her gaze roams over my room, which is quite bare. When I came to live with my sister, I literally had the clothes I was wearing and nothing else. I've acquired some things since then, but mostly I share a wardrobe, makeup, and hair stuff with my sister. Aside from school uniforms, which I know Aidan went into credit card debt paying for, though he won't admit it.

"Uh…thanks." I close the books open on my bed and pile them neatly. "It's a work in progress."

"I meant the apartment." Justice is still studying my personal space. She practically gasps when she opens the closet and sees that it's nearly empty. "This room, on the other hand…"

My face heats up. "Yeah, well…"

She moves to the window, peeking out the blinds, then raising them. "Oh lord. What a view."

Chantel joins her friend to gawk out the window. "God, that's beautiful."

I roll my eyes and walk over. Sure enough, Miles is in

the pool, performing that flawless butterfly stroke of his. "I'm waiting for winter so I can watch him turn blue out there."

Chantel's boyfriend, Jacob, is standing out by the pool looking incredibly bored. I ask them about it and Chantel shrugs and says he's fine waiting.

Justice slams the blinds shut, spins around, and eyes the books on my bed. "I don't know how you get any studying done with all these distractions."

I attempt to laugh it off like I'm immune to Miles's hotness, but I'm so not. Which is exactly why my blinds were closed before Justice barged in.

"I know a great decorator," Chantel says, her gaze locked on the stack of milk crates I've used to build a nightstand. "Of course he might go into cardiac arrest before he even pulls out the paint swatches…"

"*I'm* a great decorator." Justice holds a hand to her chest. Chantel snorts. Justice stares at her. "What? I am. Remember Catherine's dorm room?" Chantel gives her this blank look and Justice gives up, turning her back to her friend. "Please, Ellie, let me do this project. I promise no cardiac arrest. What's your budget?"

I laugh nervously. I'm being set up for something. "Um, nothing."

"Well, that won't work," Chantel says.

"Bedroom decor for no cost." Justice turns a slow, dramatic circle, a grin sliding over her face. "Challenge accepted."

Chantel snaps her gum. "She just wants to stare out your window."

Probably. I take a seat on my bed and hug my pillow. "So…you guys came over here with Jacob? You could invite him up here, you know?"

"Right!" Justice flips her dark hair over one shoulder.

"You're hanging out with us tonight."

"At the beach club," Chantel finishes, though she doesn't seem too happy about this. "Bret sent us to drag you away from your homework."

He had asked me to come out with him earlier and I told him I had too much homework. It's not easy pretending to be into him, and I have to be in just the right mind-set. But Dominic's phone call earlier has got me suddenly in the mood to hang out at this beach club place. Which is what, exactly? Some kind of nightclub? I haven't owned a fake ID for months now, honest life and all that, so hopefully age won't be an issue at this club.

"It wasn't just Bret who wanted you to come," Justice says, sounding genuine enough. "Chantel's too busy hooking up with Jacob and I need a wing-girl for Miles. That guy is tough to crack."

Tell me about it. "He sounded like he was interested when he and Bret were talking about you. Maybe he's not into short-term relationships? With him leaving in a couple of months…"

"Why is he even here?" Justice states. "I don't get it."

"His parents are on sabbatical or something. They're, like, out of the country, at least that's what Jacob heard from Dominic." Chantel looks at her phone. "We totally need to go. It's a long drive."

Sabbatical? Are they professors?

I change quickly, brush my teeth and hair. I don't look nearly as put together as the two of them, but with Chantel tapping her foot constantly and checking the time on her cell, I'm out of options.

"Did you say it's a long drive?" I ask when we're leaving my bedroom.

"Like, an hour, I think, or maybe—" Justice stops after nearly plowing into Aidan, who's just walked through the front door. She turns and gives me this look, like, *who is this?* "Sorry, that was totally my fault."

"No problem." Aidan flashes both girls a grin, and I can practically hear their internal sighs. He sticks out a hand. "I'm Aidan, Ellie's—"

"Sister's boyfriend," I finish for him. I give Chantel and Justice a nudge toward the door before any hand-shaking can happen. They might not recover from it. "We're in a hurry. Long drive and all."

"Where to?" Aidan asks at the same time as Harper.

I turn to them, shrug, and mouth that I'll text them soon.

Once we're outside, Justice shakes her head. "Like I said, your place is full of distractions."

Jacob latches onto Chantel as soon as he sees us and seems perfectly content to stay that way. In the parking lot of our apartment complex, Bret is leaning against a gray SUV. Dominic climbs out of the driver's seat, a brown fast-food bag in his hand. He sees me, balls up the bag, and aggressively slam-dunks it into a nearby garbage can.

Just the sight of him this close to me, not talking through my headphones, knowing about those newspaper clippings in his bag, I can't fight the chill that runs through my body. He creeps me out. As much as I want to ignore that feeling for the sake of getting on his good side, it's not that easy. Not when it's become so personal.

"Dude, what took you so long?" Dominic says.

Miles appears fresh out of the shower, wearing jeans and a snug-fitting gray T-shirt. "Sorry, I lost track of time." He claps his hands and his eyes land on me for a brief second, though he doesn't seem surprised to see me. "Are we leaving or what?"

This question sends Justice and Chantel into a silent argument over who is riding with whom, I assume. That's when I realize that Bret's red convertible is parked beside Dominic's SUV. Bret catches my eye and nods toward his car. So much for my plan to impress Dominic with my love of screaming punk music. I know all the yells to at least five songs now.

"Ride with me, man," Dominic says to Miles. But when Justice takes a step toward his car, Dominic makes up some lame excuse about his dog getting mud all over the backseat.

When Bret finally backs out of the parking lot—Chantel, Jacob, and Justice reluctantly squeezed into his tiny backseat—I glance longingly at my apartment, cursing myself for not grabbing the receiver and headphones tucked under my pillow.

Bret flashes me a grin and rests a hand on my knee. "You ready for this?"

"Oh yeah, totally." I stare at his fingers curled over my knee. "The beach club. Can't wait."

Bret and I ride in silence for a while, letting the backseat chatter drift our way.

"I just want to get rid of her," Jacob says.

Bret glances into the backseat. "Get rid of who?"

"The adulteress who's screwing his dad," Chantel explains.

"His new personal assistant," Jacob says, his voice full of disgust. "I think she's taking the personal part way too literally."

"What's the big deal?" Bret says. "My dad screws around all the time, and I don't give a shit."

"Must be nice for you," Jacob says. "But my mom's a judge, remember? She catches him and she'll get everything—the house, the cars, my allowance. Knowing her, she'll dump it in some lame-ass charity. My dad knows I know all this and knows I'll keep my fucking mouth shut."

Poor little rich boy. Mom's taking away the trust fund.

"God," Justice mutters. "Why do parents suck so bad at sneaking around? We should give your dad lessons on not getting caught."

"No kidding," Jacob says. "Check this out."

He plays a video from his phone and not five seconds in, Justice and Chantel both squeal.

"Turn it off!" Chantel shouts.

I hold my hand out to Jacob. "Let me see it."

He hands it over without question, and I manage to stomach the home office sex tape better than my peers. Jacob's dad is not what one would refer to as a chick magnet. He's round in the middle, bald on top...geeky software type. And this woman, his new assistant who is concealed beneath the desk for half the video, is definitely in the realm of hot. Blond, long legs, under thirty.

"Has he done something like this before?" I ask. "To your knowledge?"

"No, definitely not. He's... Well, look at him." Jacob lifts a hand to the phone as if his dad's appearance should tell all.

It doesn't tell all. Not necessarily. Where the truth lies is in his history and the fact that he is clearly not in control here.

"She must have filled out some application to work for your dad, right?" I turn around in my seat to face Jacob and hand back the phone. "You know how to do a background check?"

"Probably, but no to the background check. How would I know how to do that? Don't you have to be a cop or something?"

"Get me that application with her Social Security number and your credit card and I'll take care of it." I sink back against the chair. "She'll be gone by the end of the week."

"How?" Chantel says, her snotty voice turned all the way up. "It's illegal to fire someone for having sex with you. That's harassment."

"No one is firing her." I kick my shoes up onto the dash. "She'll leave on her own. And she'll do it quietly without complaint. And then Jacob will owe me five hundred bucks."

Bret glances at me, quirks an eyebrow. "Is that the going rate for a friendly favor?"

"I'm all about the friends, but I've got an empty college fund to fill and a twenty-six-year-old paying my dentist bill. Besides…" I nod to Jacob in the backseat. "He can afford it."

"You get her to leave and go far away from my dad, I'll pay double that," Jacob says.

"Done," I say, and then we fist-bump on it.

"Remind me not to let you negotiate anything for me," Justice tells him. "Like, ever."

I'm high on adrenaline the rest of the drive, going through ideas in my head for helping Jacob with his problem. As soon as I know Miss Mistress USA's weakness via background check, I'll know what to do to get her to quit.

"Badass Ellie," Justice says. "Guess we'd better watch what you do with that knife in your hand."

I flash her my sweetest smile. "What knife?"

"Exactly," Bret says.

Exactly. It's the only way I know how to be.

CHAPTER

16

I t turns out the beach club is at the actual beach. As in sand and seashells and big waves crashing every few seconds against the dock we're all seated on. But this beach is private, part of the exclusive beach club that everyone except Miles and me seems to be members of.

If I had known the location beforehand, I'm not sure I would have left the house. Luckily, I'm too busy keeping an eye on Dominic, waiting for him to text someone about their meet-up location, to be freaked about the ocean. If only I had actually heard where this meeting location is... Behind something. That's all I know.

When we got here, a waiter in dress pants and a bow tie served us fruity martinis and appetizers on the club's dining patio.

I've done the country-club scene many times before but never as myself. Country-club jobs were a favorite of my dad's. The cons didn't involve much creativity, in my opinion. We were usually new in town, having just opened a new branch of our fictional family company, and looking for someone to sponsor our membership to the country club so that Daddy's golf game wouldn't suffer. Of course we always came with the highest recommendations from our previous country club. We made friends; we wined and dined. We came up with a way to get one of those rich, unsuspecting families to hand us a bunch of money. After that, we bolted, taking our fake company and new money with us.

"Is anyone going to fill me in on this tradition of yours?" I hear Miles say from a ways down the dock.

I look over, and he's got a hand on Justice's shoulder, then he leans in to her and whispers something right in her ear. A shiver runs up my spine just imagining being in her place.

God, I'm as bad as her and Chantel.

Speaking of Chantel... The second we drifted from the club's patio to the beach, she and Jacob decided public make-out sessions in the sand were a turn-on, and now we're all forced to keep our eyes away from their spot. Which is why we ended up on the dock—easier to keep our backs to them. I'm hoping they get some sand in hard-to-reach places.

Bret plops down beside me, his pants carefully rolled up. He's got two drinks in his hands. "What do you think?"

"Of what?" I accept the drink from him but set it beside me. I've had enough already. "The rich kids' club? It's tolerable."

"You're funny." He laughs and takes a gulp of his drink. "I mean the plan. Are you game?"

"Game for what?" I glance down at the beginning of the dock, checking to make sure Dominic is still there. When is he meeting this secret person?

Bret puts both hands on my shoulders, turning me out toward the water. He leans close and points a finger out at a lighthouse in the water. "Every year, on the last night of beach season, Justice, Chantel, Dominic, Jacob, and I swim out to that island."

"To the lighthouse?" My stomach knots. "In the dark? The sign says no swimming after six p.m."

"Scared of sharks?" Bret asks, leaning in again.

I am now. Among other things.

Behind me, Justice stands. She makes a big show of helping Miles to his feet. Dominic joins them, and the three of them remove their shoes and outer layers of clothing. Chantel and Jacob abandon their make-out spot and head onto the dock. I glance back at the twinkling lights on the beach club's patio. Surely someone will see us and put a stop to this, right?

I slide back from the edge of the dock. I don't know if I can watch. I turn my back to the water, but the sound of splashing from five people jumping in together is just as bad as seeing it. They're all laughing. Loud as hell. Making no effort to keep this a secret activity. Maybe they're too rich to get in trouble?

"I think I'll stay up here, keep my hair dry," I tell Bret. "Yell if you need anything."

He laughs but doesn't move to strip down like everyone else. Instead he slides closer to me. Like *close* close. "Maybe I'll sit it out this year."

Before I can get myself into the mind-set of a girl who wants Bret Thomas in her personal space, his lips are hovering over mine. I panic. A voice inside my head shouts, *No no no.* My heart thuds against my rib cage. Suddenly the ocean doesn't look so scary.

"On second thought..." I take a step back from him and kick off my shoes. I turn. Run. And then I jump.

Off the end of the dock. Into the ocean.

The water isn't as cold as I expected, but it tastes terrible. My head emerges, and I spit out a mouthful of salty water and tread. See? I can do this. I am doing this. I'm swimming. In the ocean.

Above me, on the dock, Bret is shaking his head like I'm crazy. "You forgot about your clothes!"

Right. That explains the drenched cotton weighing me down. The others are quite a ways ahead. Bret quickly strips down and plunges in.

"Beckett!" he shouts once his head surfaces. "Your ass is dead."

A wave crashes over my face, and I fight to tread properly and keep my head above the water. The dock already seems far away. Shouldn't the waves pull me back toward it?

"Not a chance," Miles yells back. "In fact, I'm gonna float here like a lazy ass and let you catch up."

Another wave, bigger this time, smacks me right in the face. Water shoots up my nose and I inhale, trying to get air, but more water charges into my lungs. I cough and try to turn my back to the waves.

"Ellie, get over here!" Justice says.

I can barely make out her bobbing head.

Relax, Ellie. Don't fight the water. Go with it.

That was the first thing Aidan taught me once he figured out I couldn't swim. *I can't swim. Yes, you can, you idiot.* Even in the dark, the curve of an oncoming wave is distinct, and it's obvious before it hits me that this one is turning rough.

My whole head goes under, my body tumbling. The world tilts itself, blurring the lines between up and down. *Relax. You're okay.*

My lungs scream for a breath. Where is the surface? I try to open my eyes and see my way out, but the water stings so badly and everything is dark.

This is my arm and I'm putting it exactly where I want it. These are my legs and they're kicking me back up above the water.

But none of that is happening, and in the panic, the only thing I can visualize is my body fighting the water last spring, in the apartment pool. And then Aidan's hands grasping my shirt, bringing me up out of the water. But this isn't a pool. It's a giant ocean that goes on for thousands of miles. And I'm drowning in it.

CHAPTER
17

A pair of hands grip my waist. Legs that aren't mine kick up toward the surface.

The cool night air hits my face again. Finally.

I'm boosted up onto the dock ladder by the strong hands that grabbed me beneath the surface. I'm coughing, hot tears rolling down my cheeks, when a body flops beside mine on the wooden dock.

"Ellie?" Miles rolls me onto my side and pats my back. "You okay?"

He's out of breath. And worried. Even in my distress I can hear the panic in his tone. I force myself to nod.

I'm okay. I'm alive. I'm okay.

Water clogs my ears; my head spins. I squeeze my eyes shut and let more hot tears fall.

"Hey, look at me." Miles is leaning over me when I open my eyes again. Creases form over his forehead. "You scared the shit out of me."

I don't even hear the others climbing the ladder to get back onto the dock, but soon Justice and Bret are leaning over me, too.

"We gotta get her out of here," Bret says. "I promised

the club we wouldn't do this drunk. We're gonna be in deep shit."

"Then take her home," Justice snaps at him.

My entire body is shaking, every inch of it.

Bret shakes his head. "I can't drive. Way too many drinks."

"Jacob? Chantel?" Justice prompts. "Can you guys drive?"

"No way," Jacob says. "Not for a couple of hours at least."

The ocean whooshes beside us, and all I want to do is get far, far away from it.

"Give me your keys," Miles says to Bret. "I'm sober."

I sit up slowly, indicating I'm down with this plan. Miles and Bret toss their shirts back on, and Bret scoops up my shoes while I work on standing and try to stop shaking.

Dominic grabs Bret's arm, stopping him from stepping onto the sandy beach. "Don't go, man. You can ride back with me. We'll pick up your car from Beckett's place in the morning."

A silent conversation flows between them, and some realization pops onto Bret's face. He looks at me, slightly guilty. "Is that okay?"

I'm not sure speech is possible for me yet, so I nod and follow Miles to the red convertible. I plop my wet body into Bret's expensive leather seat and watch him and Dominic walk down the beach, away from the others.

I refrain from banging my head against the dashboard. I should have just let him kiss me and skipped the near-drowning. Because I know they're going to do whatever it is Dominic had planned with someone on the phone this afternoon.

I squeeze my eyes shut and shake my head. Miles hits a button, and the top of the convertible rolls over our heads.

He blasts the heat, points three of the vents at me. Even with the warm air blowing on me, I can't stop shaking. Can't stop feeling waves crash over my head. I focus on the road in front of us, hoping it will block out visions of the ocean.

Miles waits at least thirty minutes before saying anything. Before asking me the question I'm sure all of them wanted to ask.

"Why did you jump in if you couldn't swim?" He exhales as if warding off his own traumatic vision of the event. "But you can swim; I've seen you."

"I just learned," I admit, relieved my voice isn't as shaky as the rest of me. "Over the summer."

He glances at me for a moment then turns his gaze back on the road. "Only in the pool?"

I nod. No further explanation is needed at the moment because Miles goes silent again, hyper-focused on driving. He's flying down the interstate, at least ten miles over the speed limit. But it's smooth and easy, like his butterfly stroke. He hasn't even touched the GPS, seems to know exactly where he's going. Which is interesting considering he's supposed to be from California.

I tune out the radio, the click of the turn signal, and allow my mind to drift somewhere else. Somewhere that might remind me how I ended up in the ocean tonight and why I need answers so badly from people who nearly let me drown.

"Our kids are likely to be brown-eyed, brown-haired," Simon said.

"And short," I added, looking over the genetics worksheet. "And right-handed."

Simon nodded his agreement. "Well, that's good. It's easier to be right-handed."

"Why?" I erased a line of our work and began to shift

around some of the variables. "It's not that big a deal."

"It's more the norm," he said. "Easy to blend in."

I set down my pencil and looked at him. "Don't you mean fit in?"

"Right. Fit in." *He laughed, a hint of nerves in it.* "Not that left-handed people shouldn't be accepted in society, they definitely should, but I'm just saying that it's easier to be what most people are. If I had kids, that's what I would want for them. To fit in."

That seemed to be the biggest difference between Simon and me. If I commit to fitting in, I'm in. No problem. The question becomes whether or not I want to fit in. It was obvious Simon wanted to fit in with Bret and Dominic's crowd, obvious he had more on his mind than genetics and dominant hands. But in that classroom, with so many pairs of ears listening in, I couldn't ask him more. And a couple of days later, he was gone.

Had that been some sort of hint or cry for help? Does my intuition work only on people I don't trust? And why do the people I trust keep leaving me? Even Miles is leaving. Not that I trust him. But he did just save my life. Who's gonna pull me out of the ocean next semester? Certainly not Dominic or Bret.

God, I need to stop this. Drowning in my feelings is almost as pathetic as drowning in the Atlantic.

"Maybe you shouldn't go in right away?"

I refocus on my surroundings and realize we're in the parking lot of our apartment complex. Like I blinked and we were home. "Why not?"

Miles scans me from head to toe and then cuts the engine, turning off the headlights. "No offense, but you're a wreck. You're shaking, and you look freaked as hell. Your sister is gonna flip, for one. Maybe if you just come inside with me and get some dry clothes, you'll be more—"

"Yeah, okay," I say firmly, wanting to end Sympathetic Miles's long speech. I'm beginning to return to normal, enough to be embarrassed by what happened at the beach club.

We start to walk across the courtyard, but both of us stop when we hear Aidan's and Jack's voices. They must be hanging out by the pool.

"Is that Miles?" I hear Aidan say.

I dive into a bush. Miles is right, I'm not in a place at the moment to make up a story about my drenched clothes and freaked-out state. Especially knowing that Aidan warned me against hanging out with Bret and Dominic.

Miles walks across the courtyard, exposing himself. "Yep, it's me."

I creep behind all the hedges, making my way around the pool, toward the steps to the second-floor apartments.

"Ellie," Miles says in response to something Aidan must have just asked him. "She's riding home with the others. She'll be back soon. I have a paper to write. Bret let me borrow his car."

My feet are still bare, so they land quietly on each step. I'm nearly to the top when Jack stands and sticks a hand out to Miles. "Agent Jakowski. I went to school with your father. Great guy, top of his class, if I remember correctly."

"Thank you, sir," Miles says, tension biting every word.

"What is he up to now?" Jack asks. "I had him pegged for FBI back in the day—"

"Sorry, I have to take this call. Great meeting you, Agent Jakowski." Miles smoothly puts his cell phone to his ear. "Hey man, everything okay?"

Nice diversion tactics, neighbor.

I roll that around in my head for a second too long because I swear to God, Jack looks up and sees me. But just as quickly, he looks away. I lunge forward, putting

myself out of sight, my back pressed against Miles's
apartment door. A minute later he's in front of me, sticking
his key in the lock.

"I think Jack saw me," I say once we're in the safety of
his apartment.

Miles tenses. "Yeah, me, too."

I open my mouth to ask if he means Jack saw me
or saw him... But they shook hands. Why hadn't that
introduction happened at the store parking lot a couple of
weeks ago? Jack had barely given Miles a second glance.
Maybe he didn't know who he was that day...didn't know
he was the kid of an old classmate. And why is that stirring
Miles up so much? He almost looks spooked. I mean, it is
an odd coincidence. Not as odd as having Jack cover for
me...that one I really can't figure out. He's Aidan's boss.
Seems like he would feel some obligation to tell Aidan if
he caught me in a lie.

"You want some dry clothes?" Miles asks, employing
more diversion tactics.

I follow him down a hallway, an area I hadn't explored
when I came over for tuna casserole night. "No Clyde?" I
ask.

Miles shakes his head. "Business in New York or
Boston. I don't remember."

We pass two closed doors, an open bathroom door, and
a half-open bedroom door. "Didn't realize you had a three-
bedroom."

"Uh...yeah," he says somewhat reluctantly. "Clyde uses
the extra room to store his junk. I've never been in there."

Miles swings the half-open door the rest of the way
open and waits for me to enter the room first. Miles's
bedroom is more bare bones than mine. And disturbingly
neat. The twin-size bed is perfectly made, hospital corners
and all. A pair of shiny dress shoes sits neatly under the

bed. The open closet displays pressed shirts and pants, hung and organized by item. The dresser top and desktop are empty except for a small cup of pencils and pens on the desk—no computer, no books, nothing.

I stand in the center of the room and watch Miles open a drawer. My eyes widen at the sight of the perfectly folded shirts. He plucks out a navy T-shirt, closes the drawer, opens another, and removes a pair of gray sweatpants.

"No ironing board?" I joke when he hands me the clothes.

He's about to spit a clever comeback at me but instead, worry creases his forehead. "You're still shaking."

"Probably the wet clothes." Yeah, that humiliation I've warded off is setting in now. "Turn around so I can change."

He shifts from one foot to the other. "There's a bathroom—"

I roll my eyes. "Just turn around."

Okay, so I like seeing him uncomfortable. It helps with the whole humiliation thing. With a sigh, he complies. I keep my eyes trained on the back of his head while I worm out of my clothes. It's not easy removing soaking-wet clothing. At the sight of my denim shorts and top on the floor, Miles seems to get even more uncomfortable.

I'm feeling like myself again, enjoying this shift in power. Which is why, after I've got on Miles's soft, warm sweatpants, I decide it might be fun to fling my wet panties at the back of his head. "Thanks for rescuing me, by the way."

"No prob—" He snaps around the second the panties hit him.

I'd figured he was way too disciplined to turn around no matter what I tossed at him. Apparently his defensive reflex takes priority.

A squeal escapes my lips but it's cut off the moment

I see Miles's face. He's frozen, staring. At me. Shirtless. I don't move for what feels like ten minutes but is probably only seconds. Heat creeps from my chest to my neck and face. His gaze flicks away from my chest and I jolt to life, reaching for the T-shirt and pulling it over my head.

Miles bends down, scoops the wet clothes off the carpet. "I'm gonna hang these. In the bathroom."

When he disappears, I scrub a hand over my face and exhale. God, what the hell am I doing? What's my angle? If this isn't a con, what is it? Maybe it's me being curious. Or me thinking about Miles laying a hand on Justice's shoulder tonight and hating that image. Or maybe I don't know how to be here, like this, without a game in place.

Miles returns from the bathroom, and I force myself to say something, anything, before it gets more awkward. "So...Jack knows your father? Kinda weird considering you're from California and all?"

He seems startled, either by the question or the shift in topic, I'm not sure. He looks away from me and plays with a pencil on his desk. "I said I grew up in California, not my parents."

"So your parents are—or at least your dad is—from around here?" I watch him closely, studying, looking for any indication of lying.

His gaze stays focused on the pencil. "Something like that."

"And he was destined for the FBI," I press. "What's that about?"

"No idea. Maybe when Agent Jakowski was in school he talked about joining the Secret Service and, you know, those types of jobs came up... Who knows?"

"Come on, Miles, you've got to have a better lie than that," I say. "I've spilled my family drama to you already. You owe me the Dad story."

"I owe you a story, huh?" He looks up from the desk, his expression hard, his entire body seeming to have tensed. "You really want to hear this?"

I plop down on his unwrinkled bed and cross my ankles, hoping this provides enough of an answer.

Miles releases a breath, focuses on his hand tracing lines across the wooden desk. "My parents both..."

"Both what?" Okay, showing my cards a little here, but the anticipation is killing me.

"They work overseas," he says finally. "Government jobs."

"Government jobs, huh?" Yeah, that's about as unspecific as you can get.

"I used to travel with them. But then I started going to boarding schools in the U.S. instead."

I sweep the room again with my eyes. "Would these boarding schools happen to be military?"

He ignores my question and continues. "Last year during break, they were supposed to meet me in Switzerland. We had a whole family thing planned for Christmas."

The eeriness that's taken over his tone is giving me goose bumps. I rub my arms with both hands. "Okay, so what happened in Switzerland?"

Miles abandons his desk, crosses the room, and slides onto the bed beside me. He scoots until his back hits the wall and then leans against it. "I got to the house we rented and...well—"

His voice catches and he drags his fingers over the blanket, maybe waiting to regain control. My heart slams against my chest, my stomach twisting and tumbling. Maybe I don't want to know. Except we've hit the point of no return. I *have* to know. "And what?"

"They were..." He swallows. His eyes lift to meet

mine. They're glossy and haunted. Gravity shoves me from behind, forcing me to move closer. "They were dead. Murdered."

I release the gulp of air I'd held in for several seconds. "How did you—" I clear my throat. "I mean, what did you do?"

"Nothing. I couldn't do anything." Miles rests his head on the wall and turns to face me. Now that he's seated beside me, the warmth of him hits me everywhere. "I was alone in a foreign country with my parents' dead bodies. I wasn't even old enough to buy plane tickets home."

"Jesus Christ," I mutter. "Is that why you're here? With Clyde?"

He nods. "I couldn't afford my boarding school tuition this fall, and I lost my spot. Holden offered me a scholarship for the semester. And my old school—my real school—has a spot open for January and some extra funds, so I'll get to go back soon."

Maybe that explains his relationship with his uncle. He wants his parents, not Clyde. He really wants to be somewhere else, and obviously Clyde can't fix that problem for him. And it could explain his sudden interest in the cool kids. He could be taking my advice and finding connections with money.

My hand decides on its own to find his and lie right on top of it. "I know what that's like, getting stuck by outside forces, being able to solve a problem with money but not having enough."

"Or not being able to solve something with money and having plenty of it." He gently tugs his hand out from under mine, and just when I'm cursing myself for giving in to that impulse to touch him, he reaches out and slides some of the wet hair off my cheek, tucking it behind my ear. "You look better. Less blue. More pink."

The mention of pink causes my face to flush even more. And the fact that he's as close to me now as he was to Justice on the dock tonight.

His thumb roams over my cheek, slowly but deliberately. *What's* your *angle, Miles?* My pulse speeds and my heart thumps loudly in this silent, nearly dark room.

"I'm sorry." My voice sounds thick and unsure. "I shouldn't have pushed you to tell me any of that. It's none of my business."

"It's fine." He lifts his head from the wall. Warm fingers curl over the back of my neck, drawing me closer.

I stare at his lips and try to think of an angle, of something I could gain from getting closer to him. But it's just Miles and me and his hands that saved me from drowning tonight and his mouth, which is dangerously close to mine. And now I want it to be closer. I lean in more, my eyes closing.

"Ellie, wait…" Miles's forehead touches mine, but he stops our lips from colliding. "Maybe we shouldn't—"

But the doubt I'd felt has passed and now I know exactly what I want. And it's this kiss. On me, in me, all around.

My fingers curl around the front of his slightly damp T-shirt, tugging. "No more waiting."

I release his shirt and reach up for his face, bringing our mouths together.

CHAPTER
18

Warmth spreads over my entire body. His lips are soft, and my pulse is pounding. Seconds later, I feel Miles pulling back, resisting. But before I even attempt to form a plan to convince him otherwise, he's diving back in again, hands on my face, in my hair, sliding down my sides...

Why does it seem like I'll combust if I don't get more of him?

Lucky for me, Miles is a mind reader. He slides both hands beneath the T-shirt he loaned me, his fingertips gliding up my back, and then he presses us together. His tongue slips into my mouth, and I'm fumbling around in the dark for the hem of his shirt, for skin I can touch. Miles Beckett skin.

Eventually, after what feels like nothing and forever at the same time, we break apart, both of us breathless, both of us startled by...well, by *that*. All of that.

He adjusts my T-shirt, smoothing it down, and then mumbles, "Sorry."

And it's like that day in the grocery store when he checked out my boobs. An impulse. A completely out-of-control impulse. I work hard not to smile and end up looking down at my thighs so he can't see my face. "That was... It was—"

Miles sits up straight, his body stiff again. "I didn't mean to do it."

"But you did," I point out. *You so did.*

"So did you. And I know why. It's because of what I told you."

"What you told me?" I repeat stupidly. That kiss has definitely filled my head with fog.

"The power of a good story, right?" He lifts an eyebrow and stays like that. Waiting. Waiting more.

Wait...

"A story—" The answer rolls its way toward me, a fuzzy indistinct ball floating above my head.

"How does it feel to fall for someone's fake sob story?" Miles says, his voice flat and lacking the emotion from minutes ago. "Poor Ellie and her overbearing, judgmental preacher father. You sure sold that one to me good."

My jaw drops. "What... Why... H-How?" I sputter.

"Which question would you like me to answer?" He stands, walks over to the desk, and proceeds to empty his pockets like we didn't just cry and make out over his murdered parents.

"Your parents aren't dead?" I watch him move, confident and sure, and I'm still completely floored. I've seen him change colors a few times, but I didn't know he had *that* in him. "You played me."

"I did," he says, unashamed. "But to my credit, you started it. It's your game."

"And what game would that be?" It's a weak attempt at holding on to my lie.

"Fishing," he says simply.

My forehead bunches up. "Fishing?"

"Lure. Hook. Reel." He mimes holding a fishing pole, winding the reel. "Isn't that what you did to me?"

A normal person would be pissed as hell, offended, hurt. But me? I'm impressed. I mean, how can I not be? Because he's right. That is my game. "You murdered your parents just to get back at me?"

I think back on all the cons I've pulled, trying to remember if I've ever killed off my parents... Maybe once. In Birmingham. But that was with total strangers. Not someone who just pulled me from the ocean after nearly drowning.

"Fictional murder," he corrects. "But not to get back at you. To show you what it feels like to have someone take advantage of your kindness. And to show you that just because you *can* lie and get away with it doesn't mean you should. Doesn't mean it's right."

I guess I'm lucky everyone I've conned doesn't use the same tactics as Miles, because I'd be in hell. I jump to my feet. I may have been outsmarted, but I won't sit here gaping like an idiot any longer. "Thanks for that valuable life lesson, Miles. I hope to visit your statue someday after you're dead and voted into sainthood."

He gives a little bow. "You're welcome. Consider it my civic duty."

I set my hands on my hips and narrow my eyes at him. "When exactly did you decide that I fed you a sob story?" He bought it that night on the yacht. I know he did. But the day after, he turned icy toward me.

Miles cracks a smile. "That would be right now."

My mouth falls open again. "Uh-uh. Not true."

"It's partially true," he admits. "I got Harper to lead me halfway there. Asked her a couple innocent questions—"

"Harper would never give you anything to use," I huff.

He does that one-brow-up thing again and I know what

he's thinking. I'm a little bit better at this than Harper, and if he can fool me…

I shake my head and then point a finger at him. "You made out with me! I never manipulated you into kissing me. What kind of lesson is that?"

He lifts his hands. "I already told you I didn't plan that part."

"Well, I didn't hate it," I admit. I look him over carefully. He's different now. More dangerous. More interesting. *God, what is wrong with me?* "Maybe you should not plan more often. Seems to work for you. Definitely worked for me."

I'm not too proud to admit that he isn't a bad kisser. Quite the opposite. Under different circumstances, I could totally do that again.

Miles surprises me with one of his scowls. I had been expecting a Smooth Guy Miles joke. "You don't get it, do you?"

"Get what?"

"It was fake. All of it," he snaps. "It doesn't mean anything to me if it's fake. That's where you and I are different."

Here we go again with my *type*. I let his words sink in and realization hits. A slow grin spreads over my face. "You're forgetting something very important."

"Enlighten me."

I step past him and head for the door. It's time for me to go home. "I believed your story. I bought it. Hard. The only fake person in that kiss was you."

The scowl on his face disappears and is replaced by a blank stare. *Yeah, I know. It sucks, right?* Maybe he outsmarted me this time, but how many tricks like that could he pull? I'm a professional liar. I'll beat him in endurance any day.

I turn my back to him and head out. "Thanks again for saving me."

As I'm taking a step into the hall, two things occur to me: 1) I still don't know why Miles is here at Holden for a semester if his parents aren't dead and that tuition story was bogus, and 2) I may have just admitted that I'm into him. Somehow that doesn't feel like the win I wanted to exit with.

The door at the end of the hallway has me pausing a beat. I glance over my shoulder and catch Miles swinging his bedroom door shut. I hadn't noticed the complicated lock on this third bedroom door earlier. Is it really Clyde's junk hiding in there? Why the extra security? Unfortunately, I can't attempt to pick the lock and peek inside the room with Miles close by, so I head out.

My apartment is dark when I walk inside, but a lamp is on in Aidan and Harper's room. I peek in the open door.

My sister is lying on her back, snoring softly, a cookbook spread open on her chest. I walk over and carefully lift the book, but her eyes open.

She stretches and then smiles when she sees it's me. "Hey, my beautiful sister…how was the beach club?"

"Fine." Except the part where I almost drowned. "Nothing exciting."

"Well, tell me the whole story tomorrow. I'm beat. Those little monsters ran me into the ground today." She pats the empty spot beside her. "Aidan's working night shift."

Harper doesn't like to sleep by herself. She and I shared a bed in our camper for years, and she never had a chance to get used to sleeping alone. But I have. She was gone for years and I was alone in the back of that camper.

I flop onto Aidan's side of the bed, and my eyes close the second Harper shuts off the lamp. I bury myself in the pillows, exhausted. But soon I'm rocking back and forth, the mattress floating in water. Waves crash over my head, smothering me.

I shoot upright, gasping.

Beside me, Harper sits up almost as quickly as I had. "What's wrong?"

"I think…" I clutch a hand to my chest. "Maybe I'll watch TV for a little while."

"'Kay," Harper mumbles. She rolls onto her side and closes her eyes. "'Night, Ellie."

I turn on the living room TV and find the most boring show possible, hoping it will send me off to sleep. But an hour later, I'm still awake and able to receive the text Jacob sends me.

JACOB: Pic of the mistress's application

ME: thx. Has ur dad ever hired a personal assistant before?

JACOB: no

ME: Send me a pic of your credit card, front and back

Of course he does it. Idiot. Not that I'm planning on abusing it, but seriously? All that money and no effort to keep it safe?

JACOB: guess ur ok?

ME: I'm fine. But no more drinking then swimming for me

JACOB: I hear ya. Good thing our boy Miles was there to save the day

Yeah, good thing. But "our boy"? He's all yours, Jacob.

I grab my laptop and get to work.

Turns out Rosa Lipman, age thirty-six (I'd have guessed twenty-five tops from that video), has a squeaky-clean criminal record. Last known address is in Maryland, nothing too weird about that, close enough to have taken a job here. She's been divorced once, went to court over the house, vehicles, and alimony. Still nothing useful there.

But when I run her credit report, I do find something

useful. Eight lines of credit opened this past year but then closed within a month. Her tax returns, even post-divorce, reveal a six-figure income—a bit high for a personal assistant. Surely she hadn't taken a pay cut to come and work for Jacob's dad.

Rosa Lipman appears to be a victim of identity theft.

When my eyes begin to burn, I set aside my laptop and try to focus on the boring TV show, hoping it will lure me to sleep. But dozing off, I bounce from memories of waves knocking me under to Miles's lips on mine, his fingers sliding through my hair. That feeling of him touching me, it's under my skin. It's not going anywhere, but I welcome those thoughts over the ocean waves.

Though neither bring me any sleep.

I open my laptop again and go back to the Rosa stuff. This impersonator obviously has skills, but she's made it too easy to figure her out. Maybe I should have a chat with her, offer some tips in exchange for half of whatever she's stolen from Jacob's family. But that's something the old Eleanor would do.

I'll just have to settle for ruining her con and earning a thousand bucks.

CHAPTER
19

After several days of spying on Rosa Lipman, the distraction of having a new obsession hasn't done anything to help the drowning-in-the-ocean flashbacks. One second I'm following Ms. Swanson's calculations on the Smart Board and then her droning voice grows more distant as if at the end of a tunnel.

I'm standing in the middle of Robertson Bank and Trust in Charleston, waiting for my father. A man in a suit walks past me. His eyes stay on me while he continues to move toward the information desk. I smile at him, wait for the reaction. He bumps into the desk, turns bright red, and looks away from me. I roll my eyes, cool and calm. But under my pressed skirt and top, I'm sweating bullets, my pulse racing. Eyes off the security camera, Ellie. Calm down. Keep your heart rate under control.

And just when I manage to get myself in check, my mother walks through the revolving door of the bank. Her hair is swept up on her head, displaying her long neck and beautiful profile. She's wearing a gray suit, heels, a briefcase in one hand. My newly calm demeanor goes out the window. She can't be here. This can't be happening.

I glance around, looking for someone, anyone. My chest rises and falls too rapidly. And they're watching me. The pen tucked into my skirt pocket brushes my thigh. I look down, expecting it to glow bright, to give me away. I catch my mother's eye. If only I were telepathic. Get out! Abort! *I try, but she looks away, giving the tiniest shake of her head, telling me to calm down, to go with this new plan she and Dad made without me. A plan that ruins everything.*

Mom turns her back to me, revealing something big and metal with brightly colored wires strapped to her. A bomb? What the hell is going on?

She turns to face me, lifts her hand, revealing what looks like a controller of some kind. She lays her thumb over the trigger and before I can stop her, she presses the button in a deliberate motion. I dive for the floor, squeezing my eyes shut, expecting an explosion. Instead, the building rumbles, the floor shaking. People all around scream and run. I glance out the glass windows. A giant wave rushes toward us. I stand staring at it, frozen in fear. The wave hits the glass, shattering it. Water floods in, filling the bank lobby from the floor up. Desks float beside me. I tread and tread, but the moment my head rises above the water, a wave knocks me over again.

"Nice, Kelsey...good use of the distance formula."

I jerk awake, stifling a gasp. I glance around, expecting to see a tidal wave coming from somewhere, ready to knock me over. A few nearby classmates give me that are-you-on-something look.

My hand shoots in the air. "Bathroom break?"

Ms. Swanson gives me a nod, and I grab the wooden calculator prop we use as a hall pass and head out the door. I walk through several hallways, needing to move, needing freedom before confining myself in a bathroom or back in the classroom.

I pass an open classroom door and see my homeroom teacher, Mr. Chin, giving an animated lesson at the front of the room. He's speaking Mandarin, writing Chinese characters on the board. He says something that makes the class laugh, but then he prompts one student to answer a question. Her eyes widen, and she shakes her head. This happens with two more kids. Mr. Chin calls on someone else and I pause in the hallway, scanning the room. Near the back, slumped down in his seat, eyes fluttering shut, is Miles.

Without straightening up in his seat or even looking awake, he answers Mr. Chin, speaking in Chinese. Despite looking a bit like Cody Smith in my lit class, Miles seems to please Mr. Chin, and he even claps for Miles.

At the sudden sound, Miles jolts upright, suddenly looking alert. I scoot quickly down the hall, away from the open door. So Miles Beckett speaks fluent Mandarin. Figures. Harper and I are both whizzes when it comes to foreign languages, especially accents, but neither of us knows a language as complex as Mandarin. That one would take years of learning.

Like Miles, I've become a bit of a teacher's pet in most of my classes—lots of hard work and false enthusiasm—so I decide Ms. Swanson probably won't mind if I take a long time in the bathroom.

I head out the front doors, toward the athletic fields, and take out my phone to dial the school office number.

"This is Judge Cohen… My son, Jacob, left this morning without taking his meds," I say. "You know how he gets without them. I'm two minutes away… Mind sending him out front to meet me? I'm due in court soon."

"Of course," she says. "I'll page him in class."

After hanging up, it only takes about three minutes for Jacob to appear outside. He looks around, probably expecting his mom's car, probably panicking because she's supposed to be out of town. I wave him over, and we duck under an awning, out of range of the school's security cameras trained on both the parking lot and the athletic fields.

"*You* called me?" Jacob asks, startled.

I shrug. "Indirectly."

"What's up?"

I take out my phone again and flip through the photos from the other night. "So, Rosa Lipman?"

"Yeah?" he says eagerly.

"She's a victim of identity theft."

He frowns. "I'm supposed to feel sorry for her now? Not happening."

I lean against the school building, my arms folded across my chest. "Rosa Lipman is a thirty-two-year-old woman who lives in Maryland, works as a CPA, divorced six years ago, and recently had her identity stolen by someone who keeps opening lines of credit in the Fredricksburg, Virginia, and D.C. areas."

Jacob's eyes widen. "So you mean that she—that—"

"That your dad's under-the-desk gal pal is not Rosa Lipman? No, she's not. But she's definitely making Rosa's life hell."

He leans against the wall, still in shock. Then skepticism fills his face. "Are you sure? There has to be more than one Rosa Lipman on the East Coast."

"With the same Social Security number?" I shake my head. "It's not a mistake."

He doesn't argue but also doesn't look completely convinced.

"I can prove it to you, but when I do, she'll be gone," I warn him.

"Gone? Doing what?"

"A phone call," I say. "But maybe it would be better to take this to your dad and let the grown-ups deal with it?"

"That won't work. He's fucking lovesick." Jacob hesitates then says firmly, "Do it."

"Pull up that application on your phone and give me her number." When he does, I dial, put it on speakerphone, and wait for Fake Rosa to answer. It takes three rings.

"Hello, is this Rosa Lipman?"

"Yes, it is," she says all breathy and genuine. She's definitely a professional.

"My name is Betty Summers. I work for the Internal Revenue Service's identity theft department. I have some good news about the claim you filed last month."

"Oh, you do?" Some of the pro in her tone fades and there's a hint of nerves.

"We've traced the perpetrator to an address in Fredericksburg, Virginia." I glance at Jacob and then spit out his address from memory. "Fourteen Germantown Lane... We're sending the local authorities out there now to make the arrest. Our surveillance shows the fake Rosa Lipman on the premises—"

The line goes dead, and Jacob and I stand there for a moment staring at the words CALL ENDED on my screen.

Then Jacob lifts his hands in the air and gives a yell. "Dude, that was awesome!"

I reach up and slap a hand over his mouth, nodding toward the classroom on the other side of the wall. I give him about ten seconds to celebrate because hell, I kind of want to celebrate, too. I haven't done anything like this in forever. Then I turn businesslike. I find a pic I took on the beach the other night, one involving him snorting something from Bret's or Dominic's stash. "I heard you're hoping to go to Columbia, like your mom. Law school, too..."

He looks at the picture and takes a few steps back, away from me. "Damn...that stings."

"Relax." I roll my eyes. "I'm just keeping this in case you talk. Not a word to anyone that I helped you, understood?"

"What about Justice and Chantel a-and Bret..." he sputters. "They were in the car."

"Tell them you did it yourself." When he looks unsure about that, I add, "You can say that I sent you a link to a background check site—any idiot can find what I dug up on your dad's assistant. I'm not worried about that. But if you want to brag about running her off, *you* made the call, *you* posed as the IRS, not me."

"So I'm Betty Summers?"

"Now you're catching on." I pat his shoulder. "Oh, and I'll take my payment in cash."

I head for the school's front doors, leaving Jacob standing there. "Thanks, Ellie! I owe you one."

"No, you owe me one thousand." Realizing my position of power, I spin back around. "One more thing."

He waits while I walk toward him again.

"I need you to answer a question and not mention it to anyone. Ever. Okay?"

He swallows. "Okay."

"You've known Bret for a while, right?"

"Yeah, like, forever. We went to St. Matthews together before Holden."

"Aren't you Jewish?"

He shrugs. "Yeah, but it's a good school. That's all my parents care about."

I lower my voice. "Can you think of any reason Bret would have followed Simon and me from the spring formal to my apartment?"

"You and Simon—" His eyes get huge. "Wait, the spring

formal? That's the night he—"

"Died," I finish for him. The jock brain is getting annoying. "Any ideas?"

Jacob stands there for several seconds looking like the most uncomfortable person in the world. If I wasn't so desperate for this answer, I'd enjoy watching him squirm.

"I don't know, Ellie..." He appears to be thinking. "Simon did hang out with us that one time, and Bret was all buddy-buddy, kissing his ass, probably because of his dad, but he wouldn't— Hell, I don't know."

"Yeah, that makes two of us." I sigh and leave him there while I head inside the school.

When I get back to algebra, Ms. Swanson gives me this look that says twenty-five-minute bathroom trips are outside of the don't-need-to-explain window.

"Sorry I was gone so long," I say. "Mrs. Harris was giving a tour and got interrupted. I offered to show the family around the east wing. I remembered my tour of Holden and how nice it was to have an actual student offer insight."

Her frown turns to a smile. "How nice."

Then she proceeds to tell me everything I missed over the last twenty-five minutes. Unfortunately, not all my teachers are this gullible, even if I am a favorite.

Later, after lunch, I find an envelope full of cash at the bottom of my locker. Jacob is a man of his word. But I still can't believe he's paying me a thousand dollars for that. And he footed the bill for the criminal and credit checks, so I've got no overhead costs.

After school, I'll take this money straight to the dentist office and have them put it toward that bill Harper is struggling to pay. A few more scandals among my classmates, and I might be able to take care of all of it.

CHAPTER 20

"What exactly is she doing?" Harper whispers.

"It's called an accent wall." We're both hovering in the hall outside my bedroom watching Justice slide a paint roller over the back wall of my room. She's got headphones in her ears, iPhone tucked in the pocket of the denim overalls she changed into when we got here right from school. She's dancing and singing along to the music. "I don't get it. Why bother painting? It's a rental."

Harper gives me a weird look. "It might be a rental, but we're not here on vacation."

"I know that," I assure her. But it's easy to forget that this is what regular people do. They live somewhere longer than six months. They paint their walls.

The paint is fuchsia, which is, um, bold. But whatever. She also brought gray paint and, after a quick lesson, she sets me up with a roller on another wall. I take the opportunity to plug in my headphones and check in on my boy Dominic. If only I had more devices. I could keep track of Bret, Jacob, and Miles, too.

But the first voice I hear isn't Dominic's. It's Miles's.

"I don't know, man. You sure about this guy?"

"He's cool. No worries." Dominic laughs. *"Dude, relax. I buy from him all the time."*

The paint roller nearly slips from my hand. Justice glances over, and I quickly re-grip the handle and smile. "This is gonna look great."

She sighs. "My mom would never in a million years let me do this stuff in our house. Not even with a big budget. I had to bribe the gardener to make sure she didn't tell my parents I swiped this paint from the shed."

I'm too caught up in what Miles and Dominic are up to to consider what kind of bribe she may have pulled.

"But you buy weed from the guy, right?" Miles asks. *"Not anything else?"*

"I've bought other stuff from him."

"Like what?" Miles asks.

"Usually whatever illegal Mexican or Russian version of Valium or Xanax Davey can get."

"But you're not doing that stuff anymore?" Miles asks, his voice gentle, concerned.

I almost drop the paint roller again. What the hell is he doing? There is no way to make sense of him meeting up with a drug dealer. Unless he's trying to get someone in trouble? Could he be that crazy? Or that committed to his neurotic drug-free campaign?

"This summer kind of sucked for me," Dominic says, and then adds in a lower voice, *"Here he is."*

Through the headphones, I hear an engine rumble and then shut off.

"Hey, man," Dominic says. *"This is my buddy, M.B."*

M.B.?

"'Sup," a deep voice says. *"Did I hear you right on the phone? You want the new shit?"*

"Only if it's really the new shit." Miles's voice comes through smooth, calm, a tad bit defensive, but with none of

the hesitancy he had minutes ago. He knows how to hold his cards, that's for sure.

Silence falls. Then finally, Davey's deep voice comes through again. *"Not so fast, Slick. I don't deal to new guys. Dominic knows that. We hang first. I get to know you. Starting with where you live. You get me?"*

"Yeah, I get you."

I don't know where they met up, but I know they're headed here. I do the worst job possible spreading paint over the wall while the three guys end up in one vehicle—not sure whose—and make small talk for ten minutes.

The most effective plan of action for a problem like this, when someone defies the laws of predictability, is what my dad calls a "private lesson." Meaning I give myself a private lesson in the science of Miles Beckett by searching his place. This usually requires studying an asset's schedule, patterns. And of course anyone in the household.

Out the window, Miles, Dominic, and a big guy—probably early twenties—are walking through the courtyard. I expect to hear them thunder up the steps, but Miles stops them.

"Let's hang out here. My uncle's upstairs." Miles points out his apartment, lifting a finger to identify it from the ground floor. *"Is that cool?"*

Davey shrugs, and the three of them take a seat at one of the umbrella tables. Dominic and Davey both immediately light up cigarettes.

I know for a fact Clyde is gone all week. He told me himself. Miles won't bring Davey the Drug Dealer up to his place. Which means I may have found the perfect hole in my asset's pattern. Perfect for a private lesson. But only if I act quickly. And get rid of Justice. I glance over at her, checking her progress. She won't be done anytime soon.

"Where'd you hear about...?" Davey asks.

Either he left out the name of whatever they're trying

to buy or he said it so low it didn't come through the device planted in Dominic's key chain.

"You know, around," Dominic says. *"I keep up with your accomplishments."*

Davey laughs.

"You tried it?" Miles asks him. He must have nodded or something because Miles adds, *"What's it like?"*

"It's fucked up. I stayed awake for three days straight. Like wide awake. And I got shit done, you know? And then I just…" He makes a sound like an explosion. *"Not for me. The ups and downs. But if you got something you need it for…could be useful as fuck."*

"How much?" Miles demands.

"I already told you to slow down, Slick," Davey warns. *"And you know it ain't money I want from you. I hear you've got something I need."*

"Maybe."

"You really brought that shit back from Switzerland?" Davey asks, sounding impressed. *"Bet you pissed your pants walking through customs."*

"Only a little," Miles says.

Switzerland. The sight of his parents' fictional murder. Coincidence? Unlikely.

"So it's here?" Davey presses.

"Maybe," Miles repeats.

Okay, it's now or never.

I set down the roller and tell Justice that I need to go to the office and get the mail. I snatch some tools and a flashlight from the kitchen drawer and stuff them in my pocket. I turn the volume way up on the receiver to keep track of my neighbor. Inside the apartment, everything is perfectly in place, quiet, empty. If my time is limited here, I'm gonna start with the most interesting room.

I kneel in front of the mysterious bedroom door—the

one where Clyde supposedly keeps his junk—studying the complicated lock. A lock that definitely didn't come with the apartment. After several failed attempts, I finally get the top lock undone and move on to the doorknob, which is nearly identical to the front door and takes no time at all.

I slip inside the dark room and shut the door behind me. There aren't any windows. It's pitch black until I click on my flashlight, shining it on my bare feet.

"...*Left my bag in your car,*" I hear Miles say through the headphones. "*Let me have your keys.*"

Shit. There goes my security system. I debate bailing and trying again later but then decide I'll still hear him open and close the car door. I stand there frozen for a moment and then, the car gives that clicking sound when it's being unlocked. I release a breath and raise the flashlight. There's a small table and two chairs. I shift the light to the tabletop. My heart stops, the air catching in my lungs.

Spread out across the table is Simon's face. Newspaper articles, at least ten of them. Like the ones I found in Dominic's bag. The shadow of papers hanging from the wall catches my eye. I raise the light and gasp aloud. A large picture hangs above the table. A picture of me. Actually, Simon and me, walking from his house to the car the night of the dance.

Beside it is a photo that looks like it was pulled from the surveillance video Aidan showed of the parking lot. My shoes, my dress, a shadowed figure that looks like me. Another shot of Bret Thomas's license plate in the parking lot that night.

My heart beats at race-car pace, my stomach turning. I spin slowly in a circle, shining the light around the room. Simon is everywhere. Strings are pinned to the wall, connecting photos and scraps of paper with words scrawled on them. I study one scrap of paper and see my own handwriting, my email address. I'd written it down for Simon when he offered to study together after our first week of bio. How the hell did Miles get that? Where would Simon have kept it? In his wallet? His room?

The *thud* coming from my chest echoes in the silence. I've been curious about Miles all along, wanted to figure out what his deal was. But I never thought he was dangerous. Dangerous for my heart maybe, but not like *actually* dangerous.

The flashlight in my hand moves on its own, shining on a note with writing I recognize as Simon's.

I know my timing is really, really bad, but I have to tell you before this is over, before it's too late. I love you. Like love love you. I don't know how you feel and I need to know before it's too late. I know we're friends. Best friends. But maybe...

Sorry I'm too chicken to say all this to your face.
Love,
S

I can't even absorb that note because I'm too distracted by the photo beside it. It's Jacob and me outside the school the other day. How the hell did Miles take that photo? He was half asleep in the back of Mr. Chin's classroom. And how did he know I was out there?

Panic engulfs me. I drop the flashlight and start patting down my clothes. The answer hits me, but just as my gaze drops to the tennis shoes on my feet, something moves across the room in a blur.

Arms grab me from behind. A hand covers my mouth, stifling my scream. A hard, round object presses into my side. *A gun.*

The grip on me loosens and another scream rises in my throat, but light floods the room, freezing me in place.

Miles stands a few feet away, pointing a gun at me.

CHAPTER

21

My hands lift slowly in the air, deliberately. Already I'm replaying all of our conversations... Miles asking me about Simon. Miles digging, watching, always watching. Did he do something to Simon and now he knows I know? If so, I know how this story ends. I swallow and stand perfectly still.

My arms shake, but I keep my hands up where he can see them because there's a gun pointed at me and I'm in new territory. I've been caught before, but not like this. I don't have a trick for this. And he can see me shaking. He can see the fear. See that I'm powerless.

"How did you get in here?" he snaps. Before I can answer, he says, "*You* planted the bug in Dominic's keys, didn't you? You knew I wouldn't be in here when you broke in."

I remain silent, but I do turn my head enough to notice an opening in the wall. A sliding door of some kind. What the hell is this place? Have I been stalked and conned by a con man or a serial killer?

"Was it that night on the yacht? When I caught you digging through Dominic's stuff?" Miles shakes his head, like he's pissed at himself for missing it. "That's why you made up that shit about your parents. To distract me. You're even better than I thought."

"I...I...found a bug in his stuff that night. I wasn't planting anything," I manage to say, my gaze hyper-focused on the gun. "I thought Dominic might be— I just wanted to see if..."

"If Dominic or Bret knew anything," Miles says with a nod. "If they were onto you."

"Onto me?" I drop my arms.

"You can't give it up, can you?" He grits his teeth, jaw tense. There's a fierceness, a deep-rooted anger on his face that steals my breath, and a chill runs through my entire body. I'm not gonna make it out of this room.

Keep him talking. Just keep him talking.

"Give what up?" I force the eye contact, using whatever persuasive power I possess to draw him in.

Please let Justice or Harper come looking for me. Or Aidan. That's who I really need right now. He's the one with the gun and choke hold. Carefully, I pat my pocket. No cell phone. God, I'm an idiot.

"The lie." Miles steps closer, the anger rising in him, filling the small area between us. "You've owned it, haven't you? Simon's dead and you're here playing the good girl, still hurt, still upset over it."

I think I finally understand what it feels like to have a rug pulled from underneath you. "You think *I* killed Simon?"

"You were the last one to see him," Miles argues. He moves another step closer. "I know you've devoted a lot of time to sneaking around, trying to dig up dirt on people in his circle. Making sure they aren't onto you. What I can't figure out is why you'd kill him. But then again, your life before Holden Prep is a mix of many different stories all revolving around a fire I'm not sure ever happened. Convenient how you basically have no identity. You and your sister. Are you working together? Is Lawrence in on it, too? I've heard Secret Service agents sometimes get offers they can't resist to go over to the dark side..."

I back up but soon run into the wall. A photo of Simon holding a corsage slips off it and floats in the air until it lands by my feet. I look up at him, my eyes widening. "I didn't kill Simon."

"Well, I don't think he killed himself," Miles says as if this automatically points a finger in my direction. "In fact, I'm nearly positive he didn't."

He's nearly positive. How?

"What about Bret Thomas?" I point to the photo of his license plate. "He could have been the last one to see Simon. He could have done something to Simon or upset him enough to make him—"

"Or maybe he was waiting for you. To hook up. Or for both of you to hop in his car and go after Simon. The more I think about it, the more that fits. Nice girl comes to Holden, makes friends with Simon. Simon suddenly gets invited to the cool kids' party... Nice girl keeps her distance from Simon's new group in public and no connection is ever made. Parking-lot footage was mysteriously corrupted. Until recently. And it's distorted to not show faces." Miles's hold on the gun becomes less steady, his hands shaking.

A question that should have come to mind at the beginning of this conversation finally hits me. I take a chance and move a step closer, studying his face.

"Don't move," he commands.

I pause. "How do you know Simon?"

"The police report says only Harper was home when you supposedly returned to your apartment, and we both know she'd lie for you. No one else saw you go inside. Not a single witness."

"I didn't kill Simon," I repeat. Is this what murderers do? Turn the tables on their accusers?

"I eliminated you almost immediately. I thought you were just a lonely girl who lied to get her way and push people away. But then..." He releases an angry breath.

"Why would I kill him?" I ask, my voice rising. Having a gun pointed at me is really starting to piss me off. "I was in *his* circle. Not Dominic DeLuca and Bret Fucking Thomas. Neither of those guys knows anything about Simon. I cared about him. He was *my* friend!"

"No, he was *my* friend!" Miles shouts, his eyes glossy.

For a moment, I can't move or speak. I stare at Miles and try to make sense of this. My gaze drifts to the note tacked on the wall, the one from "S" professing love to someone who was just a friend. In the fleeting moment after I had read it, I thought maybe he'd written it for me and that would have been—well, not good because I didn't feel that way about Simon. But the writing sounds too immature for the Simon I knew, too young.

Miles's hand is still shaking, and I'm forced to refocus on the current peril I'm in. "Okay. I get it. He loved you. He was your friend. But he was my friend, too. We have that in common."

As I'd hoped, he loses his focus for just a moment. I hold my breath and then as quickly as possible, I reach out and let my fingers curl over the gun.

"How did you know Simon?" I ask again. I'm close enough to feel the heat of him, feel him shaking everywhere, trying to hold back or pull it together, I'm not sure which. He tenses, showing he might be back on the Shoot Ellie Plan. "Miles, you know I didn't hurt Simon. Deep down, you know it. Because the moment you flipped on those lights, you saw me. You saw that I was scared as hell. Scared of you. Look at this place! It's like a fucking serial-killer cave. And you're out there meeting up with drug dealers, talking about smuggling stuff from Switzerland. What am I supposed to think?"

"You bugged Dominic. You broke into my place."

"Can you blame me? If you heard me conspiring with someone like Davey the Dealer, wouldn't you consider searching my place?" *Based on the photo gallery around us, I'm pretty sure you've been tracking my every move already.*

I keep my fingers wrapped around the gun and rest my other hand on his arm, giving it a gentle squeeze. And then I wait. Let him put it all together. He's smart. Logical. He'll get there.

God, I hope he gets there.

Beneath my hand, his muscles relax just a bit. Enough to give me my answer. He looks at me, and there's pain in his eyes. "I didn't kill Simon, Ellie. I swear to God—"

I gently press down on the top of the gun, forcing his entire arm to lower. I lay both my hands on his arms. "I don't think there are any murderers in this room."

The words fell out on impulse, but I decide they're true. The way he looked at me when he thought I—

I suppress a shudder. That was the look of pure hate. Which brings me back to… "How did you know Simon?"

"Middle school," he says, his voice thick. "We went to—" He stops, frozen as if listening to something. His body stiffens. "Shit."

Suddenly he's Miles again, jumping into action. He lifts the black cloth covering the table and reveals what looks like a radio. He flips a switch, and Davey's voice fills the room.

"*This ain't how I roll,*" Davey says. "*You know that, D. What's the deal with this guy?*"

"He's cool," Dominic says. *"His dad's some fancy diplomat, so it's easy for him to get away with shit."*

"Fuck. He's gonna leave." Miles squats down on the floor, flings open the gun, and grabs a handful of bullets from beneath the table.

My mouth falls open in shock. "It wasn't even loaded?"

"It is now." He clicks it into place and tucks the gun in the back of his pants. He jumps to his feet and pulls something tiny and gold from his pocket and closes it in his fist before I can see it. Except I did see it. And I know what that is. A tracker. He turns to me, a warning on his face. "Stay here. We're not done talking."

Oh believe me, I know. But then I realize what he's about to do. I grab his sleeve before he can take off. "You can't go out there with a gun!"

"Don't worry." He shakes out of my grip. "I know what I'm doing."

"Davey's gonna see right through you. Regular seventeen-year-old kids living around here don't have guns."

Miles seems to consider this, but eventually he steps through the door—still with the gun in his pants. "Stay," he says again, and then he shuts the door behind him.

I kick off my tennis shoes and plop down on the floor, examining them. I pull back the sole of my left shoe and spot the shiny gold circle, barely bigger than my fingernail. I rip it out, holding it up to look closer. Miles Beckett, you sneaky, lying little shit. How long has this been in my shoe? I use the leg of the chair to smash the tracker to bits.

From the radio, Davey's temper rises as he and Dominic argue. *"Dude, what the hell are you trying to pull?"* he says, probably when Miles appears.

"Nothing," Miles says. *"Just got caught up—"*

"We're not doing this," Davey says. *"I told you we*

needed to hang out and you up and vanish. Did you go call someone? You got a friend working with Diplomat Daddy ready to jump me?"

"What?" Miles says, sounding mostly convincing. "No... why would I—"

This is gonna end in gunfire. Which is insane. It would be so easy to turn this around... *Fuck it.* I stuff my shoes back on and push open the door, lock it behind me, and run through the apartment. I don't know why Miles is trying to track this drug dealer; I don't know a lot of things, but the questions will have to wait. Because I do know that he won't quit until he succeeds or gets shot, and I can get that tracker on Davey without anyone blowing a gasket. Or blowing anything.

I slow down when I reach the steps and sigh with relief when I notice Justice's bright yellow car is now gone from the parking lot. I don't know why or when she took off, but this will be way less complicated with her gone.

I tug my ponytail out and shake my hair, hoping it gets that sexy, wild look. Today's a rare uniform skirt day for me. I quickly fold over the waistband, allowing more leg to show, and then release the top two buttons of my polo. I'm still shaking, still mentally in that room freaking the fuck out. But I give myself the usual pep talk.

This is my body and I'm moving it exactly how I want to... And you're gonna look at me. You are definitely gonna look at me.

I stride across the pool deck, my hair bouncing around me, and make my movements loud enough to get the guys to pause and look my way. Even without looking up, I feel Davey's gaze on me. When I do look at him, his gaze roams the length of my legs to the hem of my uniform skirt and then all the way north. I slide right up to Miles, slip my hand into his. Then I whisper loud enough for Davey to hear. "Thanks for…*you know*. I needed that."

The smile on my face is supposed to tell its own story. And when Davey's eyebrows lift, just a smidgen, I know I succeeded. The tiny gold tracker in Miles's palm gets transferred to mine without him being able to protest. I could hang on to it and botch his entire little mission, but for some reason, I decide to go for it. Act now, ask later. And I will be asking. Lots.

I push up onto my toes and plant a kiss on the side of Miles's neck. "Same time tomorrow?"

From the corner of my eye, I see Dominic's mouth fall open. I step away from Miles, closer to Davey. I glance back at Miles, hoping he's as good a salesman as he was the other night when he sold me that bogus story about his parents.

A grin spreads across his face. "Happy to be of service." *Good boy.*

My return smile is real—it's relief. "See ya later, Miles… Dominic." I give Dominic a nod, then my gaze drifts to Davey. Up to Davey because he's big. Freakin' big. "And guy I don't know…"

I stop and look between Dominic and Davey. "Oh shit, were you waiting on Miles?"

Dominic scratches his head, confused as hell. Davey drops the defensive, suspicious look and gives Miles this nod of approval. I refrain from rolling my eyes. Most predictable drug dealer ever.

"Oops, sorry," I say with a shrug.

"Maybe text first next time." Miles gives me that sexy smile he's so gifted at, then he does the eye-roaming thing to me, like Davey had done but better. His look heats my skin. "Or not. I'm good either way."

Davey chokes back a laugh. He looks at Miles and Dominic. "We'll do this again soon."

I sigh internally. Using my fingertips, I work the sticker off the back of the tracking device, planning my move. I twirl the earring in my ear and when I brush past Davey, I pop it right out of my ear. My mother calls this move the Brush and Pop. I've used it to pick pockets, read hidden tattoos, and once to win a bet over whether or not a man had a hair weave.

"Shit..." I drop down onto the pool deck, searching. "My earring just fell out. I think it's..." I nudge Davey's sneaker. He responds immediately, lifting the heel. I roll the earring beneath his shoe at the same time I press the teeny tracker against the heel of his sneaker. "Got it! Thank God it didn't end up in the pool filter."

I spring to my feet and shove the earring post through the hole in my earlobe.

But now Davey's staring at me. My heart picks up again, flying out of control. He leans close, his breath hitting my cheek.

"That's a top-grade diamond," he says. "Have you thought about a screw-on back?"

I don't have to look to know this is making Miles crazy. He told me to stay in the room and I didn't. His feet shift on the pool deck but he stays put.

"They're my mother's earrings. She said they were nice ones but I didn't realize..." I flash him a grin. "Thanks, I'll have to look into getting new backs."

I hold my breath, waiting.

Davey takes a step back and shrugs. He turns around and strides away from us. Miles pretends to study the back of my earring while Davey crosses the parking lot and keeps walking. Wherever they first met up, must not have been far if he's going on foot. Once he's out of sight, Miles exhales and swears under his breath.

"Dude, what the hell is this?" Dominic growls, nodding at me.

I give Miles a light shove and stick my hand out, palm

up. "All right. Pay up. Fifty bucks. Plus five extra for the kiss." I wrinkle my nose in disgust.

Miles gives me a bewildered look, but eventually he removes his wallet and drops a fifty plus a five into my palm. Yeah, I'm so not giving this back. Hold me at gunpoint in your secret room and I will definitely be cleaning out your wallet.

"So, who was the big guy?" I ask. "Are you betting on football games again? Didn't you lose, like, five hundred last time? I heard your uncle yelling at you from all the way next door."

"Betting—" Dominic starts, and then he nods. "Yeah, that's what we were doing. But keep it on the DL, all right? My parents would kill me."

"Duh." I roll my eyes. "It's illegal. Plus, Miles gave me hush money already. So you're covered."

I stuff the money in my pocket and walk away from them, heading back up the steps. When I reach the top, I slide around the corner where I know they can't see me. My whole body sags against the building, and I get light-headed. I close my eyes and take slow, careful breaths.

In. Out. In. Out.

I am safe. I am perfectly safe.

Soon Dominic is gone and Miles is standing in front of me. He tries out a few different words but ends up tongue-tied until he finally manages to say, "Don't ever do that again."

"I saved your ass," I point out. Though I don't know what I saved him from. Davey hurting him? Illegal possession of firearms charges? Him shooting someone?

He leans against the wall like he has to. "Go find out what happened to Justice. She took off like a crazy person while you were picking my locks. Check in with your sister, tell her you're studying at my place. And then meet me back there. Twenty minutes exactly."

Jesus. Bossy much?

But he's gone before I can say anything. Before I can take control of anything. I push away from the wall and head next door to my apartment.

I'm about to call for Harper, but she's waiting for me in the living room, arms folded across her chest. "Did I just witness a Brush and Pop? I was watching out the window, so I could be mistaken...?"

"Maybe." I play it cool, fling open the fridge, grab a bottle of water, and start chugging. I'm dying of thirst. I think it's a sign of shock. Being held at gunpoint will do that to a person. "What happened to Justice?"

"She got a phone call from her parents. Sounded like she was supposed to be somewhere and forgot. She promised to finish painting tomorrow." Harper moves closer, looking me over. "What were you doing out by the pool? With a shorter skirt, two buttons undone, and your hair in post-make-out state."

My head is pounding. I rub my temples and sigh. "Dominic's in some kind of trouble. Gambling, I think. I was just trying to help."

"What about Miles?" she asks. "Is he involved?"

Since I still need so many Miles questions answered, and Harper and Aidan seem to trust him and trust me around him, I decide it's best to leave him out of this lie. For now. "He doesn't know anything. And he's waiting for me to study with him. I don't want him to think something's up. I'll explain the whole story later, okay?"

God, I hate lying to my sister. But I'm deep in the hunt for answers, for truth, and my obsession wins out over keeping Harper in the know.

She slides over, letting me through to get my school bag. And I make a promise to myself that from now on, lying to my sister needs to be reserved for safety-only situations.

CHAPTER

22

When I follow Miles back into the secret room, I'm much more prepared this time. Just because I no longer think he's a murderer or serial killer doesn't mean I trust him. He put a freakin' tracker in my shoe. I leave my hand on the doorknob, gripping it tight. "Put your gun on the table."

He gives me this look like, *seriously?* He sighs but reaches behind him and tugs the gun from his khaki pants before laying it on the table. "What about you? What have you got on you?"

"I did have a tracker in my shoe, but I got rid of that."

Miles nods toward the bits of broken metal on the floor. "I noticed. Thanks for that, by the way. You know how much those things cost?"

I stare at him. "I'm aware."

"You didn't answer my question," he says, taking a step in my direction. "What do you have on you?"

"Nothing." I turn my pockets inside out. "See?"

Miles hooks a finger in my belt loop, yanking me close, and then he reaches right under my shirt, grabbing the cell phone I stowed in my bra. I watch, half in shock, while he takes it apart and lays the pieces on the table.

I stare down at my shirt, trying to figure out how he did that so quickly. But I have bigger concerns. With my grip still on the doorknob, I look right at him and ask, "Where did you get the gun? Are you a cop? How old are you really?"

"Seventeen," he says, like I'm weird for questioning it. "I'm in high school. Like you."

"I'm finding that hard to believe with your secret room and ongoing investigation of murders and drug deals."

I watch him for signs of giving in, of talking to me for real. I need that. Usually I don't fault people for their false identities because I've lived that life for so long, but this is different.

My grip on the door loosens without permission, and I quickly realize how weak my hands are. Then my legs turn to Jell-O. The pounding in my head increases and nausea sweeps over me. Spots flash in front of my eyes. I blink several times to get rid of them. Definitely not at my best right now—due to a lack of sleep and the fact that I barely ate any breakfast and skipped lunch today to get some research done in the library.

Concern fills Miles's face. "What's wrong?"

I shake my head. My hand falls from the door and I reach for the table, gripping it for balance. "Just dizzy. Headache."

The chair is already out, so I fall into it and then lean my head against my hand for support. "I skipped lunch. Didn't sleep much last night."

Miles leaves the room so abruptly that I wish I felt better so I could snoop around under the table. I slide my foot over, trying to feel for something, and end up stubbing my toe on the radio thing.

He's gone less than a minute, returning with a glass

of apple juice and a banana. He slides open another imaginary door, revealing the hallway bathroom. "Advil or Tylenol?"

"Maybe some caffeine," I say, eyeing the juice. "How do I know you didn't put something in this to make me forget the last couple of hours? Or worse."

"Excedrin it is." Miles returns with the bottle and sets it in front of me. "And as for the juice, I guess you'll just have to trust me."

That's not happening. Trusting him in general. But I drink some of the juice anyway, then take two headache pills. The spots in my vision fade shortly after sitting down and getting through half the apple juice. I peel the banana and take a small bite. Miles sits across from me, looking completely together. I'm lost now, not sure where to start.

"Are you really from California?" I ask, making myself believe that I have skills to read him even if he's a gifted storyteller. I hadn't been expecting it before, but I am now.

"No," he says.

Truth.

And now it's clear why he chose that lie. So he could bring up Simon, find out what I knew. Because California is Senator Gilbert's home state.

"What middle school did you and Simon attend together? You told me you went to boarding schools; was that a lie?"

"St. Matthews. It's around here."

Lie.

I lean closer. "Yeah, I heard about that school. From Jacob. Apparently he and Bret went there. I'm sure he'll be able to verify your story."

I reach for the pieces of my phone as if preparing to text Jacob.

Miles sighs. "Fine. It's a military school."

"Good." I nod. "Tell me about this military school."

He leans back in his chair, fingers tapping against the table. "What do you want to know?"

"Where is it, for starters?" I watch him, and when he hesitates for a beat, creating a false answer, no doubt, I add, "I could easily pull Simon's file from Miss Geist's office and find out."

"Then do it," he challenges.

"Sure." I stand and reach for my phone pieces again. "And while I'm in there, I'll make sure to explain to the guidance counselor how I learned that Simon Gilbert had a secret love who likely didn't return the feelings…guess that could have pushed him over the edge." I scratch my head. "Or maybe his feelings pushed you over the edge?"

Miles's calm face morphs into a scowl, but he says nothing.

I shrug. "She's a professional; she'll know how to help me sort out the details. Good thing I snapped some pictures of that letter from Simon."

Warm fingers curl around my wrist, holding me in place. "Sit."

I give him a satisfied smile and plop back down in my chair.

"Baltimore," he says, practically through his teeth. "And yes, boarding school."

Truth.

Baltimore isn't too far from here. It makes sense that Simon might go to school there if his family had already made the move from the West Coast to D.C. "How close were you two?"

The pain returns to his face, and he glances away from me at one of the photos pinned to the wall. "He was my roommate all three years before high school."

Truth.

And okay, maybe he really is seventeen.

"What happened when high school started? You stayed at military school and Simon came back to Virginia?"

"Simon was there because—" He closes his eyes and shakes his head. "We were both there for the same reason. To get into the honors program."

"So you were competing against each other." I take another bite of the banana. "What happened? He didn't get in?"

"No, he didn't," Miles says. "He bombed the entrance exam."

His jaw tenses like he's angry with Simon for flunking a test. The Simon Gilbert I knew never would have flunked a test. Quite the opposite. I mention this to Miles.

"It wasn't that kind of test." He thinks for a minute, deliberating. "It was more...more applied skills than a written exam."

Applied skills? Like climbing a rope or army crawling beneath barbed wire?

"Okay, so you gave up your spot in the honors program to come here so you can dig into what happened to Simon?" The thought of Miles avenging his death, needing to know what really happened in the same way that I need to know, leaves a strange feeling in the pit of my stomach. I'm not ready to be on a team with Miles. Maybe not with anyone.

"Something like that." He won't look at me. He's studying the photos on the wall, and it's obvious he's gone too far with the sharing.

"And tracking the drug dealer—?"

"A hobby," Miles says.

Lie.

This pisses me off. "I can't believe you made me feel like such an asshole for being deceptive, investigating, throwing out drugs. Every word out of your mouth has been a fucking lie. And what the hell are you doing with your free time? Not flushing drugs, oh no. You're fucking buying them from dangerous dealers! Do you have a bloated hero complex? Are you just incredibly stupid? Or are you still lying to me about why you're here?"

His fingers curl around the edge of the table, his jaw tense again. "Maybe I can't tell you why I'm here, Ellie. Did you ever think of that? That maybe, unlike you, I'd be happy to lay out all the facts of my life right here on this table for you to understand, but I can't. So fucking deal with it or go do whatever it is you're threatening to do, because you know what? I'm not as good a liar as you are, and that says something about my character. What does it say about yours?"

"You put a tracking device on me," I accuse. "And you kissed me! For a lie!"

The quick shift in blood sugar appears to be bad for my impulse control.

"And you're sort of dating Bret Thomas even though you've made it clear today that you hate the guy." Miles stands, walks over to the wall with the most photos of me on it, and begins pulling out pins, shifting pictures around.

"So it really was fake?" I sit on that for a minute, a bit stunned he didn't correct me. And disappointed, though I'm working hard to ignore that part.

"You tell me." Miles glances my way, a smile tugging at his mouth. "I've seen you in action. You can turn it on and get every guy to look your way whenever you want. But how do you know the reaction is real? That you've really lured and hooked?"

"Easy," I say. "Change in skin color, pupil dilation, tension in the hands, fidgeting, momentary avoidance of eye contact."

What the hell am I doing? Or does he already know about me? He knows my strict-preacher-dad story is bogus. But then I remember something he said when the gun was pointed at me earlier.

I thought you were just a lonely girl who lied to get her way and push people away.

No, he doesn't know. Sure enough, Miles lifts an eyebrow and says, "Lawrence taught you some tricks."

I shrug. "Aidan says I'm a natural Secret Service agent."

"Lawrence is still pretty green."

My eyebrow lifts up. "You're an expert on the Secret Service now?"

"Wikipedia," he says, tense again. "Heard all the kids are using it."

Lie.

"Another lie," I say, deciding to just call him out on it.

He glares at me. "You're such a hypocrite. You're the one with the skills."

The anger on his face fades, and I sit there staring at him. Suddenly, or maybe finally, we seem to be on the same wavelength. He wants to tell me, but he's not allowed.

If I'm reading correctly between those lines, he wants me to find out for myself.

"Look, I have to go meet someone—"

I sit up, suddenly energetic again. "Are you following the drug dealer? And seriously, what does he think you brought back from Switzerland? And what is this drug that makes you stay awake for three days or whatever?"

Okay, why am I suddenly interested in fighting the war on drugs? Maybe Miles is rubbing off on me. Or it's Aidan's investigation training games.

"I'm not following Davey." He busies himself cleaning up my banana peel.

"Why not?" I demand. "At least turn on the other half

of the tracker so we can see where he goes."

"I don't have it," Miles mutters. Then he walks out with my glass and banana peel, returning them to the kitchen. "Besides, I don't even know what you're talking about. *I* didn't put a tracker on anyone."

"Jesus," I mumble. "Don't get so defensive. You were screwed before I jumped in to save your ass. So you can turn off the courtroom-testimony act. We aren't there yet."

"I really do have to go."

I roll my eyes. We've hit a wall. And I don't have the energy at the moment to fight him through it. "Fine. Go to your secret meeting of the secret people."

He sweeps the parts of my phone into his hand and has it reassembled by the time we're out of the apartment. He drops it into my hand, but his fingers linger over mine. "Go eat something more than a banana, okay? And get some sleep."

I study his face, my gaze drifting to his neck, noting the barely pink coloring creeping upward. He rolls his apartment keys around in one hand, and when I try to check his pupils, he looks away, above my head. Before he can catch me studying him, I walk away, into my apartment.

Now I need to learn a little more about this military school and about Simon's long-lost friend. I head straight for my laptop and get to work, typing: *military school Baltimore* into Google.

CHAPTER
23

It's two in the morning and I'm still awake. I could blame it on the half-painted fuchsia wall in my room, but this is the third or fourth night in a row I've lain awake until unreasonable hours. Every time I close my eyes, the room fills with water, the bed lifting off the floor, rocking back and forth.

I toss back the covers and hop out of bed. I can't lie there any longer. The blue lights in the pool glow bright through my window. I lift the blinds and spot Miles right away. It's too cold for him to swim; he's fully dressed, seated on the edge, his bare feet in the water.

But he must have felt me watching. He tilts his head up toward my window. I debate hiding, but it's too late. He already caught me watching. I don't know what reaction I expected, but I definitely didn't anticipate him standing and then climbing up the balcony. He does it so fast I don't even have time to unlock my window before he's reaching over, knocking on it.

I scramble to pry it open and then back up while Miles basically jumps from the balcony through the window. He lands with barely a sound, crouched down on my carpet.

I stand over him, shaking my head. "I would have let you in the front door."

"Didn't want to wake anyone." He glances around my semi-dark room, taking in the paint job and the furniture moved away from the wall.

"It's a work in progress." I can't remember if I'm wearing the pajama pants with a hole in the crotch. Not to mention my lack of bra. I fold my arms over my chest. "What are you doing by the pool in the middle of the night? Surveillance?"

The second the word exits my mouth, everything I read online hours ago comes back to me. And it isn't easy standing here with this Miles Beckett. The one who is likely good. What had I wanted to find out? That he was a reformed criminal like me? That would make it easier, I think. Easier for me.

He tenses and stares at me, searching my face. Reading me. "Odd word choice."

"Probably not for you...?" I prompt. "Mr. Marshall Academy. How hard is it to get into this McCone honors program? How many experiential learners like you are out there right now playing teenage FBI for the semester?"

Miles smirks at me. "Conspiracy theories? That's your source. I thought you were better than that, Ellie."

"Investigators use conspiracy theories all the time." I walk over to my desk where my list of notes rests beside my laptop. Despite my casual tone, it wasn't exactly easy getting to this conclusion. The Marshall Academy checks out perfectly. Around two hundred years old, founded by a slave-owning dead president wanting to turn boys into men, then came the girls in the seventies...similar story to the nearly two dozen military boarding academies in our country.

"Yeah," Miles agrees. "To find the nut jobs behind them.

Conspiracy theorists are ten times more likely to commit terrorists acts."

"I take it Terrorism 101 is on your honors course list?"

Eventually, while searching online, I started running into chat boards where something called the McCone honors program, where students are handpicked and groomed as future government operatives, military leaders, etc., was discussed at length. This program supposedly includes semester-long undercover field work. Teenage spies in the flesh. It sounded like B.S., like a TV show on ABC Family or the CW.

Since I'm not a genius or a tech expert, I employed the help of my good friend Connie from Tech Gear via anonymous email. My airhead persona she knows me as wouldn't have fit with this question. With her magic tech fingers, she dug up some very interesting details. Turns out Connie is a lover of both conspiracy theories and the truth. Very helpful combination.

"Does the name Kathleen French sound familiar? Apparently you aren't the first honors kid to blow his cover—or hers." I look Miles over, trying to see if I hit his panic nerve yet.

"I haven't blown any cover," he snaps.

And because he did this to me the other night, I can't help but say, "I think you just did."

"Why?" He folds his arms across his chest, not even a little flustered, unfortunately. "Are you planning on turning me in?"

"Haven't decided yet." I glance over my page of notes. "Sounds like someone turned in this Kathleen French girl back in the early nineties. According to a report from the Boston PD, she was arrested for prostitution along with dozens of her fellow sorority sisters at Northeastern University."

"Where did you see that report?" Miles demands.

I ignore his question and continue. "The Feds were able to take down a four-year-long prostitution ring started by a group of MIT guys who saw the future of the internet and decided sex tapes featuring prominent members of society might be worth a lot of money. Unfortunately, those smart MIT guys decided they weren't going down without making a big splash. If they couldn't release the sex tapes they'd collected, they were going to tell the world that Kathleen French was simultaneously enrolled at Northeastern University and Marshall Academy. And somehow had managed to vanish before any of the girls arrested went to trial. Before she could testify against her MIT pimps."

I have to admit, it really is quite a story. If I weren't on the criminal side of society, even I would want to join the FBI after hearing that. Least. Boring. Job. Ever.

Miles has his poker face plastered on, but he says nothing. What could he say?

"You're not undercover as a prostitute, are you?" I ask.

"God, do you take anything seriously, Ellie? Or is it all a game to you?" Miles glares at me. "I'm not some weirdo hiding my dark past." *That makes one of us.* "Unlike you, I have a job to do. And this shit is dangerous. If I'm keeping something from you, it's because I don't want you or anyone else to get hurt. You said Kathleen vanished before the trial. Do you know what happened to her?" I shake my head. "Well, neither does anyone! She either fled the country under an alias or she's fucking dead."

I take a step back, the force of his words coming at me like a physical attack. It's true, I hadn't thought of what happened to her. Figured she went back to her school, her life, but how could she have?

"Whatever means you used to extract that confidential

document from the Boston PD is likely to have left a trail, and if by some miracle Kathleen French is alive somewhere, you've single-handedly exposed her again and put her at risk," Miles says. "There are rules in place for a reason, lines we don't cross because people die if you do."

Goose bumps erupt on my skin. I rub my arms. I stare at him, horrified. "You practically told me to dig up this stuff. Why would you do that? If you had budged an inch from your disciplined self and crossed that tiny line and explained things to me, this wouldn't have happened."

Miles's eyes widen, and then he backs up until he runs into my bed. He sits down and scrubs a hand over his face. "You're right. I'm sorry, Ellie. You're right."

Okay, not what I'd expected him to say.

"I'm sorry," Miles repeats. He drops his hands and looks up at me. "I'm just a little... Well, things have gotten messy, and I don't do messy. Ever."

"Yeah, I kind of guessed that." I move closer, the tension lessening between us.

"I came up here to ask for a truce," he admits. "Can we just be on the same side for a little while? I think there are holes in Simon's investigation and I owe it to him—we owe it to him—to keep looking until we're sure. Don't you think?"

I nod, shocked by these words as well. I release a breath and close the distance between us, taking a seat beside Miles. "I can't believe your school sent you here to investigate your own friend's death."

He looks down at his hands. "They didn't. I'm number three in my class, so I got top pick for the internship. I have other work to do for school."

"Like busting drug dealers," I mutter.

He doesn't confirm or deny this. Doesn't need to. "I'm not doing anything illegal being here, looking into Simon's life since he left Marshall Academy. If we find anything useful, we'll go right to the authorities, and we'll do everything by the book."

By the book. 'Cause I'm a by-the-book girl. "We?" I prompt.

"Yeah." He looks at me again and nods. "We. Both of us have done some digging and on our own we're getting somewhere, but together...we could be highly effective, not to mention efficient, which is good, considering I've got only a couple of months left at Holden."

"Exactly what every girl wants to hear...together, baby, we're just so efficient."

He looks like he wants to give me another "be more serious" lecture but eventually cracks a smile. "I'm good like that. And you were right. I was doing surveillance. Thought maybe you could sleep, and I can keep an eye on things from in here."

"You want to watch me while I sleep?" I snort back a laugh. "Creepy much?"

Miles rolls his eyes. "I'm just trying to help."

Yeah, 'cause I usually like to fall asleep whenever I get a hot guy in my bedroom in the middle of the night.

Miles takes the pillows from my bed and moves them to the other end. "Here's a trick I use sometimes. Switch ends, lay on top of the covers, keep it low commitment."

I'm skeptical of this plan, but I sit on the new end of the bed and lean against the pillows. Miles plops down on the other end, his legs shifting to the opposite side of mine.

I have a vision of Simon and his reddish-blond hair and skinny legs sprawled out on my bed, like Miles is right now, from last June when we were cramming for the biology final.

A lump forms in my throat. I pull my knees to my chest and rest my chin on them. "You sure you want to work with me? What if I'm bad luck? What if somehow I'm the reason Simon's dead?"

Miles looks like he's about to laugh, like I'm joking again, but I'm mostly serious. "I don't know how or why—probably Agent Lawrence's work—but you're good at this. Look at how well you've done wedging yourself into the in-crowd's world. You've got Justice painting your room, Jacob worshipping your genius like a new religion, and Bret Thomas's about to ask you to homecoming. This is exactly what we need. Nothing better than information from the inside."

"I agree with that last part so completely but..." I twist my hands together. "You know that whole near-drowning thing the other day?" He nods. "Well, Bret was about to kiss me, and I just couldn't deal. I couldn't get in the right head space to play along."

"So you jumped in the ocean, at night, even though you knew you couldn't swim well there?" Miles says.

I cover my face with both hands. "Well, I didn't *know* I couldn't swim there. I just knew I'd never tried." I drop my hands and glare at him. "It was stupid, I get it. I would have died if you hadn't pulled me up. And now every time I close my eyes, this bed turns into a boat and waves are crashing over me."

Miles grips my feet and tugs until I'm lying down, then he flops down beside me. "You would have fought your way through the waves. Survival instincts give you superpowers, and so does the will to live. And you *can* swim. I've seen you."

His words drift over me, coating me like a warm blanket. I turn on my side to face him. "So what you're saying is that I'm gonna have to kiss Bret next time."

"You're a gifted liar; tell him you have a cold," Miles says, his voice low and sexy, right near my ear.

"Why didn't you give yourself the same pep talk before you decided to teach me that really important lesson?" I shake my head. "Forget it. I don't want to know."

I liked it too much to have the memory tainted.

"I shouldn't have kissed you," Miles says. "It's less complicated if I don't do that anymore. And I rarely make the same mistake twice."

Disappointment hits me. But technically he hadn't said that he didn't like it.

"If it's so complicated, then why are you all over my bed, putting the moves on me?" I attempt to shove him off, but he stays firmly beside me.

"To talk. To make plans. To help you get some sleep so you don't screw up anything. Sleep deprivation can lead to disasters."

"Oh, I see. So it's all business?"

Miles laughs. "Give me your hand." When I don't move, he reaches for my hand. "When I first started military school, I couldn't sleep, either."

He turns my hand palm-up and I watch, my body sinking farther into the bed, relaxing. "Uh-oh, is this Chinese medicine?" I mumble, feeling sleepy all of a sudden.

"Just a story." Miles moves his thumb in circles over my palm. "I was eleven and nervous about boarding school. So my parents took some leave from work, rented a house in Baltimore for the first month of school. It was less than a mile away. After a rough first couple of nights, I started sneaking out of the dorm and sleeping at my parents' place."

"Did they catch you?" My eyelids weigh a ton. I let them close and relax into the pillow.

"Eventually." Miles continues the circles on my palm.

"Simon didn't turn you in, did he?"

"No," Miles says. "Simon pretended he didn't notice me leaving. Later, he told me that he stuffed pillows under my covers, made up excuses about me being in the shower or bathroom." He slides his fingers down my arm, stroking it lightly. I'm torn between relaxation and stimulation, between falling asleep and rolling on top of him. "I moved around my whole life, lived in dozens of places, so my being homesick didn't make any sense. To my parents or me. Took us by surprise."

I think I can relate to that. Moving everywhere but still wishing for home. I don't want that life anymore, but it is familiar. There's comfort in familiar even if it's wrong.

"The dean caught me walking down the road in the middle of the night about three weeks into sixth grade. They kept a closer eye on me." He slides down farther, his head right beside mine. "When I couldn't sleep, Simon used to tell me stories or read from one of the many books in our combined collection...." His thumb returns to my palm, making more circles. "I think we went through half the Harry Potter series in sixth grade. He'd turn on his flashlight after lights out even though it was against the rules. He'd read just loudly enough for me to hear from the top bunk. That was Simon, for me at least. Just there as my friend. Not judging me, not needing anything in return."

My eyes drift closed again but I'm alert, still listening. And I get what he's saying, at least a little bit, because that's how I felt with Simon stretched out on my bed, chomping his way through a giant bag of Twizzlers. Never once did I feel like he was trying to read me or see inside me when I didn't want him to. My past felt safely locked away when he was around.

"It was complete trust," Miles says. "The truth is, with where I'm headed in my life, trust won't be a part of it. Definitely not safety. If I could go back in time and bring one thing to the future with me, that's what I'd pick. That safe feeling, in that room, with my friend. Back then I didn't get how rare that is—" His voice breaks, and my heart breaks a little for him.

"I can't have it back." He reaches over and brushes the hair off my face. "But knowing that you believe me and that you were already searching like I am... It feels a little like being in that dorm room."

I raise my head and stare at him. God, I could kiss him right now. It would be so easy. And yet, after that move he pulled the other night...instincts kick in and I lean away from him. There is trust and there's *trust*. Usually I don't let myself do either, but with Miles, I'll at least give him my "trust." For Simon. But not with everything. Not my heart.

"You're right about one thing," I say.

"What's that?"

I settle back into my pillow. "Trust isn't a part of the real world. I'm gonna be waiting for you to tell me that story was my next How to Be a Saint lesson."

He exhales, a hint of frustration in his voice. And just like that, our warm little bubble pops. "Like I said, this is complicated."

Like you said, I'm good at pushing people away.

Miles rolls off my bed, returning to his feet. "Good night, Ellie."

I wait to feel a sense of satisfaction, seeing him leave rattled by yours truly, but I'm surprised by how hard that story hit me. How much I'm hurting for him.

Maybe trust isn't a part of my life because I don't want it to be. Because I'm too afraid to be alone in a dorm room with someone, completely open, all the walls down.

CHAPTER
24

MILES: if the housekeeper doesn't let you in, you have to bail. No copying files, no pictures. Just look and report back.

I roll my eyes after reading Miles's text. Like I'm gonna leave Dominic's room without copying everything from his laptop. Miles will thank me later. And I'm breaking the rules, not him.

ME: housekeeper didn't answer. Don't worry, I only broke 2 windows getting in

MILES: what?!

ME: jk

MILES: Rule #228 - no sarcasm

Actually, that's a rule with my family, too. At least not in texting. But Miles has been driving me crazy all week with his rules. As if I'm not the one who bugged Dominic and has been listening in on him for two weeks or who got the tracking device on the drug dealer. I'm just glad to have a break from OCD Miles and his rules, not to mention his sexy voice constantly whispering things in my ear on the bus and slipping notes in my hand in the hallways. If I didn't know better, I'd say he's hooked a fish named Ellie and is slowly reeling her in.

Dominic's house is a mansion, brick with hedges blocking the view from the road. But no security guard, no gated neighborhood. Getting in would be easier than a lot of other break-ins I've done. But no, I'm gonna ring the bell and ask to be allowed in. Thanks for making my job hell—I mean challenging—Miles.

When the housekeeper attempts to understand me, replying in broken English, I switch to Portuguese. I'm pretty good with that language. I explain that Dominic and I were studying in his room last night and I left my notebook. She retrieves a key from a box in the entryway and then leads me to his room and unlocks the door but stands in the doorway watching me like a hawk.

Yeah, great plan, Miles. Look at that, a murder weapon is lying right on Dominic's bed. Right.

Of course, I had to actually leave my notebook here last night—by the book and all—during a *Great Gatsby* study session with about five of us from Lance's fourth period, plus Miles. Too many to fit in Dominic's room. Especially when there are thirty other rooms in this house. Miles left the notebook in Dominic's room before we left the house.

Despite the fancy, immaculate home, Dominic's room is disgusting. I barely manage to find my notebook in the mess, but the housekeeper smiles with relief when she sees my name written in curly cursive on the front. She turns her back to lead me out and old instincts kick in. I flip the lock on one of Dominic's bedroom windows. The kind housekeeper shuts and locks Dominic's bedroom door behind her, making it obvious that this room is off limits even to her skilled cleaning hands.

Minutes later, I'm climbing back inside the window, deviating from the plan. *Miles will thank me later*, I tell myself at least four times. To be safe and because it's disgusting in here, I pop on a pair of latex gloves from my pocket before sifting through items piled on the bed. I snap photos of every paper, receipt, book on the shelf, then I find the laptop buried in the covers. I open it up and type his last name into the password box. It works. *Idiot.* Seconds later I'm inside the computer of Dominic DeLuca. Which might hold zero secrets.

While I'm waiting for his hard drive to copy onto the thumb drive I brought "just in case," I stand in the corner of the room and study Dominic DeLuca's personal space.

His bed is dressed with expensive linens in neutral yet trendy colors. It's also covered with garbage, bags of chips, beef jerky wrappers, soda cans. I walk over to the tall bookshelf at the foot of the bed and scan each shelf individually. The one at eye level is full of books, carelessly stuffed in, some upside down. Papers are strewn in front of the books. I pick up a large envelope and read the front.

University of Pennsylvania Office of Admissions

I slide out the papers and scan them. Dominic's been accepted for early decision. Buried under all the papers is a recent progress report from our school for the first few weeks of the grading period. Dominic's barely pulling Cs in all his classes, has a 2.8 GPA, and is in the bottom half of our class. The shelf below is filled with CDs. I read the first few titles and don't recognize any of the bands, but I do notice that they're loosely alphabetized.

I scan the rest of the room, trying to find connections, any personality leaping out. Even though I've looked through his bag recently, I do it again. The articles about Simon are still there, stowed neatly in the envelope. One thing I can conclude is that Dominic DeLuca takes care of things he cares about and has no problem ruining anything he doesn't.

My phone buzzes in my pocket. I pull it out and read a text from Miles.

MILES: r u still in there? If yes, time to go!

What the hell, Miles? The download is at 90 percent. I shift from one foot to the other, typing a text to Miles.

ME: Stall.

MILES: can't. Just get out!

Come on, come on, come on, I chant silently to the laptop. *96 percent...97 percent...*

The sound of the front door opening is faint but clear enough. My heart slams against my chest. I rest my fingers on the flash drive, preparing to pull it.

98 percent...99 percent...

"Dominic! Where the hell are you?" a deep male voice says. Footsteps follow the voice up the stairs.

Shit. Oh shit.

I squeeze my eyes shut, count to five, and then pull out the drive. I glance at the laptop for a split second, taking in the words "Download complete" on the screen.

Someone fiddles with the lock. The doorknob turns. I dive into the bathroom. Leaving the door open, I slip behind it, suck in a breath, and hold it.

"Dominic, you better be in here!" Black dress shoes stomp past the bathroom door then spin and head right in.

I close my eyes again and wait. The man pauses, glances around the bathroom, makes a noise of disgust, then walks out. Seconds later, he slams the bedroom door. I wait a moment before emerging, then I bury the laptop in the bedcovers again, climb out the window, and make a run for the bus stop a block away.

I take a seat on the bench and try to catch my breath before shooting Miles a text.

ME: Close call but I'm out

MILES: good. You have your cover story but it's easier

this way

ME: yeah, so the story worked. But housekeeper watched me like a hawk. I had to go back in through less legal means

MILES: jesus christ, Ellie

ME: so I should destroy the flash drive full of Dominic DeLuca secrets?

MILES: My place. Thirty minutes.

My text messages vanish seconds later. Miles deleted them. Great. I mentally prepare myself for another St. Miles lecture, complete with guilt trips and reciting laws of search and surveillance. Can't wait for that.

CHAPTER
25

"You can't keep picking my locks," Miles says, striding into the windowless secret room. He's sweaty and chugging a bottle of water. "One of these days, Clyde is gonna catch you."

"Why are you all sweaty?" I bite into a slice of the pizza I ordered while waiting more than an hour for Miles.

"Took Dominic to the gym. He didn't want to go home; his dad was pissed at him."

"Yeah, I noticed," I say, recalling his dad's sharp tone and stomping feet. "And don't worry about Clyde catching me. I'll just tell him we're sleeping together, and you gave me a key."

Miles chokes on his drink. "Do *not* tell Clyde that."

"What's the deal with him anyway?" I offer him the pizza box but he shakes his head. "Is he really your uncle? Or is he like your undercover handler?"

He flinches at the mention of undercover. Still getting used to someone knowing about his secret life. "He's my uncle. Unfortunately."

"Why unfortunately?"

Miles closes the pizza box then wipes crumbs off the

table. "Clyde's a criminal. As skilled in check fraud as the guys he puts away."

Cheese congeals to the roof of my mouth. "Wait... what? So he really doesn't work as a freelancer?"

"The FBI hires him all the time." Miles scoops a fallen thumbtack from the floor and jams it into the wall. "He was never convicted. Got immunity for turning in the big boss running his operation and now everyone thinks he's a reformed bad guy, God's gift to bridging the gap between criminals and the Feds."

I force myself to swallow the bite of pizza lodged in my throat. "And what do you think?"

Miles turns to face me. "I think the larger the body of water between criminals and the people trying to catch them, the better."

I twist my hands together. "But then how do they figure out how to catch the bad guys without informants on the inside?"

"I don't know." Miles shakes his head. "But not like that. Not when I've spent my entire life keeping myself on the right path, all so I can get a job and work beside someone who should be locked up in federal prison?"

"Or live with him." Or live next door to them.

The pizza twists in my stomach, turning sour. I shove the box farther away.

"Exactly," Miles says. "So yeah, I'm not a fan of that plan. But there's nothing I can do about it. My dad trusts his brother, therefore he expects me to."

I was right about Miles all along. He doesn't do gray areas. Doesn't forgive easily. He isn't going to be my ally if he finds out the truth. My secrets are nothing like his. Mine are ugly and kept hidden so I can appear to be a good person. His secrets are important and noble and put lives in danger if they get out.

I dig my fingernail over the surface of the table. "I guess I didn't realize con men could be hired by the FBI."

"Happens more than you'd think," Miles says.

It's true that I didn't know it was a regular thing, and unlike Clyde, I didn't get paid for the job, but I did get freedom. For Harper and me. And my mother, too, though that part hadn't worked out. All in exchange for my father. The boss man. Head of my family's operation. But then my mother walked into that bank and ruined everything.

And speaking of criminal behavior...

"Why haven't you lectured me yet about the wrongs of breaking and entering and illegal search and surveillance?" I ask. "Figured you'd get right to that. Maybe whip out some handcuffs."

He lifts a brow. "Oh, I've got handcuffs."

"Yeah?" I drop my feet to the floor and pretend I'm not curious. "Let's see them."

Miles hesitates, like he's debating that whole this-is-complicated thing. Eventually he sighs and says, "Next time."

I place the flash drive full of Dominic DeLuca secrets on a table between us. "I took this, not you. I crawled through that window, not you. I can look through all of it on my own if you want. But you should know that I am going to look at it no matter what you say in your how-to-be-a-saint lecture."

He stares at the flash drive for what feels like forever, probably reciting laws in his head, then his hand closes over it. He slides it to the center of the table. "Last resort, okay? Let's put together our notes."

A notebook lands in front of me, and he flips it open to a page in the middle. "Here's a list of everything I saw when I planted the notebook in Dominic's room."

The list is long. Really long. Details about which model

of iPad he owns and the brand and color of the pens on his desktop. I read each item carefully until I reach the middle of the page and can't take any more of the dry information.

"There's nothing useful here," I complain. "Nothing to help us get inside Dominic's head, figure out why the fuck he's carting an envelope full of Simon Gilbert articles. He didn't even like Simon. You should have heard him in the hall one day last spring. He was pissed at Bret for inviting Simon to a party. Explain that from your list."

Miles narrows his eyes at me, his arms folded over his chest. "I suppose you did better?"

I wave a hand over the flash drive. I mean, duh.

"Through legal means," he clarifies.

"Well, yeah." I think for a minute, recalling details about Dominic's room. "The guy's a pig. Crumbs all over those fancy sheets. But his music collection is alphabetized."

"ADHD?" Miles suggests.

I shake my head. "Who knows? But obviously he's loyal to some things in his life. When he doesn't care about something he doesn't bother pretending."

Miles sinks back in his chair, thinking. "Those articles were trimmed and cut with precision. Perfectly placed into that envelope."

"You saw them, too?" I ask, and he nods. "Seems like something a psychopath would do."

"What if…" Miles stands, paces the room. "Dominic did have something to do with Simon's death, and what if someone knows about it and is tormenting him with the articles, and planted the bugged pen in his bag…?"

"If that's true, why would Dominic keep the articles there?" I ask.

"You're right. Doesn't make sense." Miles stops pacing and sits back down. "It's more likely the FBI is still keeping an eye on a handful of Holden students."

"Then wouldn't they be keeping an eye on me?" I say. "Also, the device I found in Dominic's bag wasn't FBI issued."

"And you know that how?" Miles drills.

"I have a friend who looked into it for me." Still looking into it, actually. And unfortunately before Miles caught me in his secret room, he found Connie's device on Dominic's keys and promptly destroyed it. Not sure if she'll continue to help me after I tell her this.

"So what you're saying is that we don't know who's spying on Dominic and why he carries around those articles," Miles concludes. "Basically we learned nothing from his room."

"That flash drive's looking pretty good right now, huh?"

Miles eyes it and then picks it up off the table, holding it in one hand. "I think I can get a warrant to view this evidence."

"A warrant? Seriously? On what grounds? You have a hunch that the FBI screwed up a homicide investigation?"

"The grounds for it aren't a problem. Plenty of criminal activity to justify searching that house and online activity."

I perk up. "The house? You mean Dominic's dad? What's he into?" Dominic's family is old money. It's a lot harder to figure out what those families do and what type of trouble they could get into.

Miles gives me a bewildered look. "I'm talking about Dominic. About the crimes I've witnessed." My face must be blank because he adds, "Did you miss the drug dealer he has on speed dial hanging out here last week?"

"Oh, come on," I say. "Dominic's not like a *criminal* criminal. He hasn't established sainthood like you, but still…"

"Ellie, he purchases, uses, and occasionally gives illegal drugs to friends in exchange for cash." Miles pauses, offering me a chance to retract my statement. When I don't, he continues. "Where I come from, that's a crime. And people who commit crimes are called what again?"

I hold my hands up, surrendering. "I guess if you want to get all technical."

"The grounds for search aren't a problem, like I said. It's the deception involved. Making it seem like I'm looking for something related to...to my..."

"Schoolwork?" I prompt, knowing he still won't admit it out loud. Maybe they put a silencing spell on him at that military school.

"But I would be searching for something else. Reporting it like I'm not using the information for my own agenda."

I lean on one elbow, looking him over. "Keeps you up at night, huh?"

God, we are so different. I'd have been halfway through that drive by now.

He flips the plastic thumb drive between his fingers. I'm waiting for a lecture or a textbook answer, but when Miles looks up at me, I'm caught off guard by the intense stare.

"Can I ask you something, Ellie?"

Oh no, not with that look. "What?"

"What are you hoping to find? With all this digging into Simon's death? What's really keeping you from adopting the suicide conclusion that closed the case?"

Right now, I have a gut feeling. Not exactly what Miles wants to hear, I'm sure.

"What's keeping *you* from closing the case?" I ask, turning the table. "Are you really hoping to find proof of an accident or maybe even find a murderer?"

He leans forward, elbows on his knees, his face inches from me. "I'm hoping to find the truth. Something better than evidence strung together to create a believable story."

My heart pounds, realization hitting me. "Because you have a piece that doesn't fit the story."

I think I've known this since the moment he revealed his true self after holding me at gunpoint. I knew there was something real and tangible that brought Miles here.

"So do you," Miles says. "Or we wouldn't have bumped heads investigating the same things."

"Bumped heads, or something else?" Not the time for a make-out joke, but the comment slipped out before I could stop myself. "And if you have something, why not hand it over to the authorities? What's that rule you quoted about destroying evidence again?"

"I haven't destroyed anything. And I need more to work with than what I have. Then I will go through the proper channels."

"So you do bend the rules?" I watch him closely, and after a second, he looks away. My gaze travels to the note Simon wrote him, pinned to the wall. "For Simon, you'll bend the rules," I conclude. "What was it like for you two after he wrote that note?"

"Hard," he admits. "We were both honest and neither of us got what we wanted. He wanted me to feel the same about him, and I wanted my friend back."

Weight presses on my chest. This keeps happening to me. I tease Miles, I get pissed at him for driving me insane, and I daydream about making out with him again, lots of shallow feelings and mostly lust. And then he says something that allows me to see inside him and it becomes this heavy weight on my chest, something more than shallow. Much more. But I can't do the same. Not to someone who hates everything I'm about, all the parts I keep hidden. Not to someone leaving soon. Going back to a squeaky-clean life of civic duty. This is the truth and it hurts already. Imagine how it would feel if I did let him see me?

"Did you keep in touch after he left Marshall Academy?" I ask, getting back to business.

"Yeah, we did. But it wasn't the same. There was always this invisible thing between us, and no matter how hard I tried to get rid of it..." He stops, clears his throat. "All I know is that he would have done anything for me if I'd asked. Despite what happened between us. If I needed him, he would have been there. And I owe it to Simon to do everything I can to find out the truth about his death. Whatever that is."

"So let's find the truth," I say. "No more follow-the-rules B.S. The FBI closed the case. They left us no choice."

"If we're going to work together, we have to really work together," Miles says. "No more deviating from our plans without telling me. No more handing over evidence to secret sources or whatever you did with that bugged pen—"

"That was before our civil union," I argue.

"I know," Miles says. "But from now on, we're a team. And you don't lie or turn on your teammates, got it?"

I swallow, my mouth suddenly dry. "Got it."

But that might be a lie. I'm not sure I know how to be a team player. In my family, we obviously had to work together. The Dr. Ames con would have never worked as a solo job. But honesty with one another was never part of our team rules. If you're good enough to con a con artist, then you should do exactly that. The only person I've ever trusted in my family is Harper. I would add my mother, but if my dad asked her to lie to me, she would, so I never really knew with her.

We sit in silence for a long moment, and I'm half expecting Miles to draw up a contract or make us sign in blood. But he doesn't, and the silence makes me more nervous. "So, does this mean we're looking at the flash drive?"

"Yeah." He tosses it on the table and grabs his laptop. "We are."

"Only took you an hour to get on my train." I pull out my own laptop. "Good thing I already downloaded everything onto my computer because we're gonna have to double time it to make up for the wasted time dealing with your moral compass."

"Jesus, you are impossible," Miles says.

I grin at him. "Impossible or impossibly amazing?"

"You're at least a hundred different impossibles."

"I do like to aim high." I type in my password and open the folder on my desktop labeled "wtf." "Care to be more specific?"

Miles types in his own overly complicated password. "Impossible to get you to turn off your game, impossible if you don't get your way. Impossible to ignore."

Impossible to ignore. Like the view from the window when Miles is in the pool. Unfortunately, they closed the pool for the season last week. My face warms. I try to focus on looking through Dominic's documents, but then I feel eyes on me.

"What?"

"Nothing." He shakes his head, the flash drive poised in one hand ready to be inserted, but he stops and places a hand on my cheek. "Awfully warm."

I shoot a glare at him. "It's hot in here. I'd open a window if you had one."

He's still staring at me thirty seconds later. "Impossible to get inside your head, something I'd love to do right now."

I laugh darkly. "You can try, but you would be going where no man has gone before."

"A challenge," he says. "Be careful with those. I have

trouble resisting."

Resisting a challenge or me? But I don't ask that because Miles is right. It's complicated. I dig my heels into the investigation. "How about you tackle all the folders full of C-level papers and I'll search through the photo and video files."

Miles dives into a piece of brilliant literary analysis by Dominic while I open a picture folder labeled: FAMILY VACATION 2006.

From my experience, studying an asset through computer data, it's always a long, tedious search usually offering tiny morsels of gold buried in thousands of bytes of useless data. So when a very leading photo pops up before my eyes not five minutes in, I nearly fall out of my chair. Instead I lean in closer just to see if my eyes are correct, then I promptly slam the laptop shut. "Oh my God!"

Miles looks up, startled. "What?"

I wave a hand at the laptop. "Uh...think I found something."

"Okay...?" Miles slides the laptop in front of him and opens it. "What— Oh shit."

I shove back my chair and start pacing the room. Several things are beginning to make sense. I conjure up the image of our biology classroom last semester. Simon on my left at our lab table, his gaze constantly fixated on Justice. If I were in Simon's spot, looking the same direction, I'd have a clear shot of Bret and Dominic's—

"How did I not think of this the second I saw that note?" I point to Simon's love letter to Miles on the wall.

Miles expands the photo, zooms in on it. I stop pacing and lean over him to examine the photo. Dominic DeLuca and Simon Gilbert lip-locked. I blink. Check again to make sure it's still there.

"That's the suit he was wearing the night of the dance," I assess.

Miles nods. "It's too close up to tell where they are. Outside somewhere. Do you remember him leaving at all during the dance?"

"He went to the bathroom a couple of times," I say.

Miles flips to the next photo. It's a screenshot of an email sent to Dominic from alleyesonyou@gmail.com. The email is blank, no text, but the subject line reads: PHOTO OF YOU, and a thumbnail-sized version of the scandalous photo is clearly attached at the bottom.

"This is who sent the picture," I say.

Miles nods. "He probably deleted the email to be safe."

We continue to flip the deliberately mislabeled 2006 Family vacay folder and find more screen shots of emails. All blank. All from the same address. Same photo attached. There are dozens of them dated about a week apart, spanning all the way back to the end of last June. Right after Simon died.

I start pacing again, shake out my arms. My head is a mess. Too much, too soon, maybe. "Now we know why he carries those articles."

"And why he hates you," Miles says, jumping up from his own seat.

I turn sharply to face my teammate. "Dominic hates me? I know he glares a lot and barely says anything, but hate...why? Because I went to the dance with Simon?"

"Think about it, Ellie. If this"—he waves at the make-out photo—"happened during the dance, you would be Dominic's top suspect, the most likely to notice Simon vanishing."

My forehead wrinkles. "And then what? Follow him outside, let him make out with another guy, and then kill him?"

"Dominic isn't exactly open about his dating preferences, as far as I can tell. We might be thinking about catching a killer, but he's thinking about keeping his affair a secret."

I stare at him, still not following completely.

"Dominic thinks you're tormenting him," Miles explains. "And he can't say anything because you know something he doesn't want anyone to know."

I sink down into my chair. Dominic thinks I'm blackmailing him. God, that does explain a lot. "But I'm not sending these pictures, and I didn't put the bugged pen in his bag."

"I know." Miles turns to face me. "Someone is out there targeting Dominic. He could be in danger and not even know it."

CHAPTER
26

MILES: Bret's gonna ask you to homecoming

I stare at the text, confused as hell. Especially considering Miles was sitting beside me on the bus less than five minutes ago. Did he exit the bus and head right to a gossip session at his locker?

ME: r u undercover as a 14 year old girl now?

MILES: Rule #228 violated again. And u know I'm not undercover

Right. The experiential learning program. Turning good boys into men who know drug dealers.

MILES: The dance = operation school records. Setting is perfect for this mission

Look who's joined my train for real. Breaking and entering is a big jump for Miles Beckett, Hero Who Barely Bends Rules.

ME: got it. So, to be clear, I should say yes?

MILES: not gonna answer that, Rule #228 again. I'm asking Justice.

I'm nearly done reading Miles's last text when I look up and he's walking past me in the hall. I grab his arm and pull him into a less crowded hallway.

"You do realize that Justice is expecting a grand promposal-type gesture, right?"

Miles leans against the wall looking cool and calm. "I got it covered."

"When did you think up this grand plan? During the ten minutes between the bus and standing here with me?"

"Yes, actually."

I'm not an expert in regular school, either, but I've been around since last spring when actual promposals happened, so I'm schooled in the expectations. "You've got to do better than a pizza with words spelled out in M&M's. Plus Justice is gluten free — doubt she'd eat pizza."

Miles folds his arms across his chest. "Clearly, you have no faith in me."

I roll my eyes. "I have faith in the fact that you haven't devoted your valuable time to studying how to ask a girl to a high school dance."

"Guess you'll have to wait and see."

With that cryptic message, he leaves me alone in the hallway, and I have no choice but to head to homeroom. On the way, Dominic DeLuca walks right past me without so much as a nod. It's weird seeing him now, knowing about his secret affair with Simon. He seems like a different person. Seconds later, Miles appears at his side. Ever since our cryptic conclusion about him being in danger, Miles has kept a close eye on Dominic.

I sit down at my regular desk in the middle of the room and stuff my phone in my backpack.

"Eleanor Ames?" Mr. Chin says, holding a note in one hand.

"Yes?" He strolls over to my desk and drops the note in front of me. It's a request to meet in the guidance counselor's office after homeroom. I don't know what this is about, but it's likely not good. I tap my foot, watching the clock until the bell rings.

The hall floods with students. I'm shoving my way through the elbows and backpacks toward the office when one of several TVs placed throughout the school shifts abruptly from listing tonight's activities to displaying a giant red heart. The letters *J* then *U* pop up inside the heart as if someone is typing it live. I stop in the middle of the hall. All around me, my classmates are doing the same.

```
J-U-S-T-I-C-E
W-I-L-L
Y-O-U
G-O
T-O
H-O-M-E-C-O-M-I-N-G
W-I-T-H
M-E
??
M-I-L-E-S
```

The heart vanishes and question marks flash on the screen. A scream of delight erupts from the end of the hallway. I turn in time to see Justice, several of her friends gathered around her, jumping up and down.

A tiny ball of something unknown sits in my stomach. Am I actually bothered by Miles playing Justice? Or is it the fact that he's not my date?

Miles appears in the hallway near Justice. I can't hear them but I'm sure he's asking her for real. When she obviously says yes, he gives her the sexy grin he's flashed me so many times. And then, before Miles turns around to head back to class, Justice grabs the front of his uniform shirt, yanks him closer, and kisses him. Right here in the hallway, in front of a large audience. Even from my spot far at the other end, I can clearly see Miles's eyes widen. He hadn't expected that. That makes two of us.

I stand there, frozen in place, watching them lip-locked. The ball in the pit of my stomach triples in size.

Jesus Christ, Ellie. Get it together.

The air I'd been holding in whooshes out of my lungs, and I turn back around as the applause erupts in the hall. Several of the office staff came out to watch the show, but they trickle back in when I open the door.

"I have a note to see Ms. Geist." I swallow the lump still in my throat and tell the secretary.

Before she can direct me to the guidance counselor, Ms. Geist opens her office door, revealing Aidan, already seated inside. I refrain from letting my eyes widen, but when Harper appears behind me, out of breath, carting a toddler twin on each hip, I start to panic.

"Come in, all of you," Ms. Geist says, her voice warm and friendly.

My heart picks up. "Okay, what did I do?"

Someone in the corner of the office laughs. Mr. Lance is standing near Aidan's chair. "Right," he says. "Like you could be in trouble."

Aidan chokes back a laugh, and Harper just looks at me, like testing her mind-reading powers.

"Shoes off! Shoes off!" one of the toddler twins shouts at Harper. The other one repeats it in German. You know, 'cause Harper is their native German-speaking nanny.

Ms. Geist ushers us all inside and shuts the door, making her small office very crowded. I catch a whiff of what might be a dirty diaper. I don't know how Harper deals with this all day.

"Thank you both for coming in at such short notice," Ms. Geist says. She eyes the babies and then looks between Harper and Aidan. "Are they yours?"

Considering they're pasty white kids and Aidan is black, I'd say it was a leading question.

Harper shakes her head. "No, I'm just the nanny."

The girl twin, Shayna, yanks off one of her fancy black baby shoes and pelts it at the wall behind the desk and shouts, "Thank you!" in German.

Mr. Lance bursts out laughing and then turns it into a cough. "How nice, they're bilingual."

"I'm so sorry," Harper mutters, her face turning red. She sets both kids down and rushes over to retrieve the shoe.

For a moment, I'm wondering if she brought the wild twins on purpose, as a distraction. Aidan surprises me by scooping up the shoe thrower and holding her firmly on his lap. He whispers something to her and she seems to sit still. She might be the one with the dirty diaper and she's planted it on Aidan's dress pants. Gross.

"As you know," Ms. Geist says, "Mr. Lance is one of Eleanor's teachers, and he's expressed some concerns."

"What kind of concerns?" Harper says. She looks at me, trying to pluck something from my mind, but her guess is as good as mine.

"She's one of my top students," Mr. Lance says. "But Ellie is currently not on the track to position herself for acceptance to top colleges."

"College?" I blurt out. "That's why were here?"

"Junior year is crucial for college planning," Ms. Geist says. "And Eleanor isn't even registered for the SAT or the ACT exam. Most of our juniors are already prepping for their second attempt at both exams. We need to get her into AP courses next fall, college visits, interviews…her ECs are slim to none—"

"What are AP courses?" Harper asks at the same time Aidan says, "Remind me what ECs are?"

Ms. Geist's mouth falls open. She's clearly disturbed by those questions. "It's safe to assume you haven't hired an educational consultant yet?"

"A what?" Harper and I both say.

Mr. Lance interrupts, moving beside her desk. "What Ms. Geist is trying to tell you is that we're here to help Ellie in any way that we can because she is an asset to this school. I, personally, would love to see her in my senior AP English class next fall, and I'm happy to help with her application essays." He opens the folder he'd been holding and hands a paper to Harper and Aidan. "This is the practice SAT exam we gave all the juniors a few weeks ago. As you can see, Ellie scored in the top five percent of the nation. She has the potential to gain admission and scholarship to an Ivy League school. I can speak personally of her literary analysis and writing. According to her admissions file, her foreign language skills are top in our school."

Not anymore. Not with Miles and his Mandarin.

Harper looks at me, and I know what she's thinking. We're good at foreign languages because we were taught practically to imitate accents, to learn enough of a language to give the appearance of fluency. Even our names were given with intent to be a conversation topic. Historically famous women: Harper Lee and Eleanor Roosevelt.

"What steps would you recommend we take first?" Aidan asks.

I tune out the conversation for a minute and chance a look at Mr. Lance. I hate that he thinks I'm good and wants me to be something valuable and important. If only he knew the truth.

"I know it's been months," Harper says. "But we're still having the hardest time getting copies of birth certificates, and without those, the Social Security office won't issue us new cards." She chokes up, popping out a few tears. "We just can't seem to escape the damage that fire did to our family. Look what it's doing to Ellie's future! She can't even apply to college or take Advanced Placement exams without a Social Security number."

Yep, my sister has still got it. An Oscar-worthy performance.

Aidan looks a bit startled but pulls himself together and rubs Harper's back while saying in his stern Secret Service officer voice, "I've had enough of the tail-chasing we've been sent on. I'm going to talk to someone higher up in the system and get this taken care of. It's been long enough."

God, for a second, I wish this were real. These were my real parents and we really had lost everything in a fire and Aidan really could growl at some grumpy Vital Statistics worker and demand copies of birth certificates for two people who never filed for them.

But it isn't real. And despite the fact that I'm here at this school to start over, I'm still playing a role. And it's apparently not going to end anytime soon.

But Geist and Lance buy it with no problem. Harper has to take off quickly, probably to change a diaper, but Aidan lingers in the school hallway to ask how I'm doing.

We lean against a row of lockers, and he pulls a pack of Skittles from his pocket and hands it to me. "Don't tell Harper."

I force a smile. "Thanks."

"The truth," he says, his voice low. "Did you cheat on the practice SAT?"

"I should have." I look down at the candy. "Would have saved you guys the school visit today if I flunked it, right?"

"But you didn't," Aidan points out. "You're competitive. They put a test in front of you and you ace it. They're not wrong, Ellie. You really do have potential."

"I thought I was going to have a clean slate here, you know?" I look up at him and he nods. "But I'm still stuck with all of that crap from the past."

He stares straight ahead. "I'm sorry. It wasn't supposed to be like that."

"Maybe it is," I reason. "I mean, I'm not innocent. Maybe I don't deserve to be completely free. Besides, they wanted my dad, and he's still out there."

"Enough of that," Aidan warns. "You keep winning over teachers, acing tests for real, and I'll handle the rest, okay?"

"You really are going up the chain?" I lift an eyebrow. "Think you can get the boss man to toss in a driver's license?"

He grins. "Don't push your luck."

For his benefit, I force myself to look happy about this. But between the Geist and Lance intervention and Miles's homecoming proposal, I end up in a funk all morning, and I'm in it enough for Justice to notice something is up at lunch.

"You look upset," she says. "Is it Bret? Did he not—"

I shake my head, not wanting that gossip circulating. But damn, Justice really sucks at being a mean girl. Chantel has her beat by a mile. "I had a college intervention this morning. Apparently I'm not doing enough to get on the right track." I look up from my school hamburger, surprised that she's listening so intently. "But I'm not sure all of that is for me, you know?"

"This school has a one-track mind—college prep and more college prep," she says. "I don't agree with it all, not sure I want my parents' life, but I figure what can it hurt to prepare for it at least? Then you have choices. People are always so afraid of choices, but that doesn't make sense. Be afraid when you don't have any choices."

It's smart advice. It really is. But it might be too late for me to have choices. Or maybe I made that choice when I agreed to go into the bank heist under the FBI's direction.

I'm about to thank her but a middle-aged dude in a chef's hat approaches our table holding a dish of something.

"I'm looking for Ellie Ames," he says.

Ruby, one of Justice's friends sitting to my right, says, "Oh my God, Chef Leo! You're, like, on TV."

I sit there like a dumbass until Justice kicks me underneath the table. I clear my throat. "Uh, I'm Ellie."

The guy sets the dish in front of me, and when I ask what it is, he reluctantly says, "Tuna casserole," he says with a wrinkled nose. "Not my recipe."

I snort back a laugh. What the hell is this? He hands me a card and stands there waiting.

"Read the card," Justice hisses at me. She reaches over and pulls it from the envelope, holding it open for me to read.

Ellie,

I heard this was your favorite food, kinda weird but whatever. Go to homecoming with me? Chef Leo promises he'll make this at his restaurant before the dance.

Place your order below.

Thank you,

Bret

Everyone is staring at me so I have no choice but to scribble "yes" at the bottom of the card and hand it back to Chef Leo, who then marches it over to where Bret and Miles are sitting. Bret makes a big show of looking surprised by my answer. We get nearly as much applause as Miles and Justice had this morning.

"What is it?" Justice says, then she peels the foil cover off the dish. "Uh..."

I examine it and smile. There are green peas poking out and crushed potato chips on top. Just like Miles made. Bret slides into the seat beside me, and I immediately dig my fork into the noodles and stuff a giant bite in my mouth to avoid a grand kiss like Miles and Justice had this morning. He settles for planting one on my cheek.

"You like it?" Bret asks.

I swallow the big bite. "Love it. Thanks."

Miles appears beside Justice and digs his fork in, taking an even bigger bite. "That's good stuff. I gotta get the recipe."

I shake my head at him. "I'm sure you can figure it out."

"Okay, guys," Justice says, all businesslike. "We gotta talk details. Limo or no limo…?"

I tune them out and stare at my casserole, pretending it meant I would get to go to the homecoming dance with the person who really created this gift, not just the one who made a call and paid for it. What would that be like to want someone's attention and then earn it? No false pretense, no agenda.

In the midst of the homecoming discussion, Miles sends me a text. I place my phone in my lap to read it privately.

MILES: she kissed me

ME: I know, I saw

MILES: I told her I wanted to go as friends

I look at him, a silent question on my face. He reads my expression perfectly and replies.

MILES: she was cool with it

Justice's voice rises, her feelings against neon-colored limos fueling a passionate response. I study her, replay that kiss in the hallway, and I'm sure she's lying to Miles. She's into him. But in Miles Beckett fashion, he was honest with her. I'm not sure how this will end well.

Before I can fall into another make-out daydream, Jacob taps me on the shoulder. He asks me to give him some chemistry notes but his body language—hand fidgeting, wide eyes—indicates something else. I hurry through my lunch and meet him at his locker, where Chantel is currently extricating her tongue from his mouth.

"Bad time?" I prompt.

I wave a set of chemistry notes in the air and Chantel takes the hint, flashing me her perfect smile before skipping off to class. Jacob opens his locker, keeping his back to the crowded hall. "You know that question you asked me before…"

About Bret and his presence in my parking lot last June.

I glance around, checking for listening ears. "Yes?"

"I was with him that night. We partied together for a little while, and he hadn't said anything about you or… *your date*. I didn't think there was anything to worry about." He pauses, checks around. "But then Chantel was talking about the spring formal this morning and how she drank too much and Bret had to drive her home."

"And…?" I ask, hoping this actually goes somewhere.

"Bret never mentioned that to me, which is a little weird, so I asked her if anything happened, you know, between them. She said no, that she passed out right away and then remembers waking up for a minute and they were parked somewhere, just sitting there." He lowers his voice, leaning in a bit, as if to read my chemistry notes. "Bret saw that she had woken up, and then he turned the car back on and started driving."

"She doesn't remember where they were parked?" I ask. Jacob shakes his head. "Did she say if he got out of the car?"

"He didn't leave the car while she was awake," he says.

"Anything else?"

He starts to shake his head again but stops. "Just that he had a camera in his hand. A nice one."

Yeah, that's an important tidbit. "Did he take any pictures?"

"Not that she saw." He looks worried, really worried. "Do you think he took pictures of Chantel or did something to her? They were dating just a month before—I can't even believe I'm thinking this... God, I'm an ass." He scrubs a hand over his face. "Pretend I didn't say that, okay?"

"It's fine," I assure him. I don't think it was Chantel that Bret wanted pictures of. "It doesn't hurt to ask questions. You're worried. But remember, he was in my parking lot when Simon dropped me off. I think Chantel was there out of necessity, nothing more."

Or an alibi. Nothing better than a drunken girl who can claim you gave her a ride home but can't recall if you drove straight home or not.

"Thanks for telling me," I say to Jacob, and then leave him when I spot Miles exiting the cafeteria. I grab him for the second time today—people are gonna start talking— and drag him away, this time to the back of the library.

"We have to stop meeting like this," Miles says, whispering the words into my ear. No kidding. "Is Jacob trying to get rid of another future stepmom?"

I spin to face him. "No, but I think I know who 'all eyes on you' is."

Miles listens intently, not interrupting me once—he's good like that—and then before I can launch into my plan to get closer to Bret at the dance, he says, "You can't be alone with that guy. We're gonna have to ditch the dance mission. It's too dangerous. Let me—"

"Uh-uh." I shake my head. "You don't have authority to cancel plans. We're a team, remember? Equal partners."

He opens his mouth to protest, those adorable lines of worry creasing his forehead. When he looks at me like that, my stomach gets all fluttery, and I hate myself all over again for being such a liar. I grin at him and start walking backward. "Besides, I've already got the perfect dress for this mission—I mean dance."

"Ellie—" he argues.

I leave before he can finish. Maybe we should have signed our work-together contract in blood. No way am I backing out of this now. If Bret Thomas is secretly harassing Dominic, what else is he capable of?

CHAPTER
27

"Hey, have you seen my date?" Justice asks me above the loud music in the school gym.

I check my cell, hoping for an update from Miles. "Um, last time I saw him he was sucking up to Mr. Chin in Mandarin."

MILES: u got eyes on Geist?

The guidance counselor is near the gym doors, busy checking tickets (aka sobriety checks).

ME: what's taking so long?

MILES: the lock is tricky

I roll my eyes. Amateur.

Bret is across the gym, talking to some guy I don't know. I keep an eye on him while sliding carefully out the back entrance of the gym. I clunk down the hall in my heels, toward the office, and slip through the door.

Miles is kneeling on the floor of Ms. Geist's dark office, a flashlight poised in one hand. "You're supposed to be lookout."

"Fine by me. Assuming you could pick a simple lock."

"What about Geist?"

"She's busy smelling people's breath." I snatch the

flashlight from Miles and examine the lock. I hold my free hand out to him. "Scalpel, please."

He reluctantly hands over the tool he'd been using and even holds the flashlight for me. And when he leans in closer, I hear him inhale. "You smell nice."

My face warms. He smells nice, too. Like soap and cinnamon. I focus on the lock on this ancient file cabinet. I hook the tool inside the slot and wiggle it gently. "Advice for future reference…you can't be too aggressive. And try to put yourself in their shoes."

"Whose shoes?" Miles asks.

"The lock's," I say. "Enter with the least amount of disturbance because deep down, it wants to open for you, wants to let you in. All you have to do is"—carefully, I twist the tool, applying just the right amount of pressure until I feel a pop—"ask nicely."

I hand the tool over to Miles, a big grin on my face. He's staring at me in that way that makes my stomach flip over several times. "What?" I ask.

"You," he says simply, like this should answer everything. "You're kind of amazing."

"Only 'kind of' amazing?" I glance away from him, my face heating. I stuff those feelings way down and turn my gaze back to him, lifting one eyebrow. "What about you? You've morphed into a fully fledged Hermione Granger."

"I'm definitely not Hermione," he says.

"You so are. Mr. By-the-Book, breaking and entering for the greater good. It's hot."

His mouth falls open, words preparing to exit, but he stops and tugs his vibrating cell out of his suit jacket pocket. His eyes widen. "I have to answer this."

I slide the drawer open and head straight for the *T* section to find Bret's folder. I can't believe Geist keeps actual files for students. Paper filing is probably nearly as ancient as this cabinet.

"Hey, Dad." Miles tugs Dominic's folder from the *D* section and lays it open on the floor. He pulls a tiny digital camera from another pocket and begins snapping photos of papers. "Yep, it's going well…I'm learning all kinds of new skills."

I open Bret's folder—not the least bit curious about Miles's conversation. I quickly flip pages, pausing only to snap a picture. We can look through all of this later.

Miles laughs. "I can't learn Turkish by Christmas. Tell Mom to pick a new spot."

I return Bret's folder. My fingers drift slowly through to the *G* section.

"…I'm at the homecoming dance…yes, with someone." Miles glances at me and then turns back to his file. He shifts the phone to the ear closest to me so he can turn a page. I hear a man's voice on the other end say, "Well, make sure you're having some fun."

Miles stands and walks across the room, his back to me. I glance at him and then on impulse, I tug Simon's folder from the cabinet, pulling it halfway out and opening it enough to read some of the papers.

Simon Gilbert is one of the most kind, observant, and self-aware students I have ever had the pleasure of working with. He is an asset to this school, his community and I firmly believe he will be an asset to your university…

A letter of recommendation from one of Simon's teachers last year. I smile at the letter. This is so him. *Was* him. I flip back several pages.

Simon seems to be struggling with sexual identity. We've discussed in great length how he can approach his family and have even practiced conversations. But his wariness seems to increase with each of our interactions. Today he appears especially deflated and negative regarding the topic. I'm worried he's backsliding and have asked him to check in with me again in a few days.

My insides ache, my heart pounding. I check the date at the top of the page: May 19. Last semester. I shove the folder back into place and jump to my feet. I motion to Miles that I'm heading back to the gym. He looks like he's about to say something, but I take off before he can.

Every step on my way back to the gym feels weighted. The dinner we had before the dance is churning in my stomach. I nearly run into Justice near the gym doors and almost forget to plaster on my happy face for her.

"I think Miles is talking to his parents or something," I tell her. "He was on the phone when I went to the bathroom."

"Oh, okay. That's good I guess. He said he doesn't get to talk to them much."

Well, she knows more than I do then. Since he fed me the fictional murdered parents' story, he hasn't told me much truth about them. I do know they work for the government and travel out of the country frequently. Being equal partners and all, I'm afraid to ask him more, afraid he'll do the same with me.

Physically, I'm in the gym, at the dance, but my head is still in Geist's office mulling over Simon's file. I jump when a pair of arms wrap around my waist.

"Easy there," Bret says, his breath hitting my ear. "Thought you might want to dance."

I plaster on another smile and suppress the shiver of warning that races over me. "Love to."

The song is slow, and my false enthusiasm must have been a little too convincing, because soon I'm pressed up against Bret Thomas, the guy many many girls would love to get close to and again, I'm not in the right head space for this. I was earlier. Before the office. I could have nailed this romantic dance moment. Maybe even pulled off a convincing kiss, gotten him to open a bit. But now I'm filled with a thousand doubts.

Across the gym, Miles has ended his phone call in time to slow dance with my interior decorator. And unlike me, he is pulling off a convincing romantic moment. Maybe too convincing.

The air in my lungs feels lodged. My chest tightens. The bodies around me close in and all I can see is Simon, doing his weird jerky-looking dance to an eighties song during the spring formal and me laughing at him, no longer worried about my own dancing. He was here. We were here. And then he was gone. What if I had done something different? Asked him to hang out after, stayed up all night talking. Maybe he would still be here.

I must have tensed, because Bret pulls back and looks at me. "You okay?"

"I'm...I'm just..." Breathe, Ellie. Just breathe. "Excuse me for a minute."

I tug myself out of his hold and disappear in the sea of dresses and suits.

CHAPTER
28

I head out one of the unguarded gym doors, down a dark hall, and into the first classroom I spot. The lights are out, so I sink against the wall across from the door, sliding until I'm seated on the floor. The music from the gym is faint but still floating in the air—a reminder.

Breathe, Ellie. Pull it together. You've got this. Go back out there and turn on the charm.

But the pep talk only seems to make things worse. Because when I came to that dance with Simon, it was under such different pretenses. I wasn't trying to hold on to an asset or steal files from the guidance counselor, or fight off feelings for someone who likely sees me as a resource and nothing more. I was here to have fun. To try to start a new life. With my friend. My friend who is gone. He died along with the hope of me truly escaping my past.

I hear light footsteps near the classroom. I immediately wipe the tears from my cheeks and mentally prepare a cover story to tell Bret, who has likely come in search of me after my dramatic exit. It's too dark in here to see a face, but I don't need to. The moment he sits on the floor beside me, I recognize the soap and cinnamon scent.

"Shouldn't the crying at the dance part happen in the bathroom with a dozen other girls around you?" Miles says.

I use my hands to do a better job wiping my face. I don't think Miles has ever seen me cry for real, and I'd rather he didn't. I'd rather no one saw. "What if we were wrong about Simon? That clue you say you have? Maybe it doesn't mean what you think it means. What if he..." I swallow the giant lump in my throat. "What if he was depressed or whatever?"

"Where is the girl who was so sure of all of this?" Miles says. "What happened to your rock-solid confidence?"

"It was mostly an act," I admit.

He leans his head against the wall beside me. "I take it you read his file?"

Guilt creeps over me. "I know it wasn't part of our plan, but I saw it—"

"He was your friend, too, Ellie," Miles whispers. "Just because I knew him longer doesn't give me the right to take away your grief. You needed him. And he's gone. You deserve answers just as much as I do."

I swipe away a couple of fresh tears and will the rest not to fall. "I can't stand the idea that maybe he was falling apart and I didn't even notice."

"I'm not sure what Simon was doing talking to Geist regularly, but I do know that his family wasn't in the dark about him being gay. Not that they loved it." He laughs, and there's a bitterness to it that sends a chill through me. "But they knew."

"Then what—" I stop myself from asking what his angle was. Simon didn't have angles. That's my world. And it seems to be Miles's world now, too. At least while he's here doing his experiential learning.

"The clue that I have?" Miles says.

I sit up straighter, looking over at him. "Yeah?"

"He made plans to meet up with me." Miles's own voice cracks a bit. "Very simple, clear plans. Days before…"

I can tell there's more. There's something else he's leaving out, but damn does it feel good to hear this. To hear that I'm not crazy thinking Simon seemed so much like himself that night. He made plans to meet up with Miles.

"Thanks," I whisper. "For telling me."

We sit in silence for several seconds, and I try my best to get my head back into the mission but I can't seem to. "God, I should be in there working on Bret. I suck at this homecoming dance stuff."

"Don't be so hard on yourself." Miles stands and holds a hand out to me. "How about we take a short break from our real dates."

"A break?" I ask, but already my hand is landing in his. "What do you have in mind?"

"Dancing," he says simply.

I glance around the dark classroom. "Here?"

The music seems to grow louder. It's another slow song. Miles is more subtle, more gentle than Bret had been when he brings us together. One hand rests on the small of my back, slowly drifting me in his direction; the other hand wraps around one of mine. He brings our fingers to his chest, leaving my face inches from his shoulder.

I attempt to relax, but soon I'm filled with a whole different kind of tension. The kind that feels good. The kind that has the potential to make me forget all my other worries and just be here, wanting more. Wanting skin against my skin and lips on mine.

His hand slides up my back, pausing right between my shoulder blades. He presses gently until my nose brushes his suit jacket and I'm surrounded by the sights and smells of Miles Beckett. I close my eyes and inhale, memorizing this. There is value in this memory, even if it goes no further than right here. It's the first time I've wanted someone, just because, just for me and only me. All my costumes are lying in a heap at my feet.

I rest my cheek against his shoulder. Warm fingers slide my hair to one side, and then Miles's nose drifts over the skin on my neck. I inhale a sharp breath, my body responding a little too openly. My heart speeds, and I'm sure he can feel it.

And for once, I don't care. I've wanted this since that chef delivered a tuna casserole to my lunch table and I imagined Miles as my date tonight.

His heart beats rapidly against mine, his mouth skimming along the side of my neck, melting me into a gooey puddle on the floor. Just when I'm near explosion, his lips touch my ear. "You drive me crazy. You know that, right?"

I work to breathe normally, but my mouth is dangerously close to his cheek, his chin, and lots of other places I'd love to touch. I slide my free hand into the back of his hair and drag my fingers through it. His eyes close and he sighs. "Ellie—"

I can hear his discipline winning, and I can't let that happen.

"Your dad told you to have some fun, didn't he?" I argue. "It shouldn't be all work and no play."

"It shouldn't." His lips press gently against my neck. I suck in a breath; my fingers tighten around his hair. "But how much fun are we allowed? A minute? Five?"

I raise my head, every part of my body aching for more. "Doesn't matter. Just—please—"

His mouth crashes against mine, and both of us groan in response. He releases me just long enough to bring his hands to my face, gripping it tight. He nudges me backward until the wall stops me. Miles's hands roam over my body, over the tight dress, searching for skin. My fingers find their way inside his suit jacket and tug at his shirt until the tails are hanging down. I lean my head against the wall and close my eyes when Miles pulls his mouth from mine and plants kisses up and down the front of my neck.

"One more minute," he whispers against my skin. "Maybe two…"

His mouth finds mine again. He deepens the kiss, our tongues tangling. My fingers dig into his back, bringing him closer. Close enough to feel that he's as turned on as me. I'm not thinking clearly or I'm thinking perfectly clearly, no outside influences getting in the way, when one of my hands slides down to his butt and brings our hips together.

Miles tears his mouth from mine, his lips resting against my cheek when he mumbles, *"Jesus."*

He lifts his head, his eyes meeting mine and staying firmly in place. A hand lands on my thigh, moves north slowly until it's beneath my dress. I swallow a gasp when his fingers pause on the edge of my panties, then his thumb makes small circles just above the waistband.

With his gaze locked on me, he whispers, "Tell me what to do. I'll do anything you want."

I hold his stare, my eyes wide, heart pounding. It feels like this is about more than right now.

"Where do you think they went?"

Justice's voice rings loud and clear from the hallway. Miles and I both freeze. He slides us over until we're tucked away in the darkest corner of the room.

"Hell if I know," Bret says, louder. They're close.

Miles rests his forehead against mine. "We've been gone too long."

I cover his mouth with my index finger. "Shhh."

He smiles, shifts my finger over and leans in until his mouth hovers over mine. "Ten more seconds."

He steals another kiss, this one slower and quiet, more tender. The last thing I want to do is leave this room, but I don't have a choice. We can't stay here forever kissing.

"Don't move," I order before stepping out of his arms. I exit the classroom and wait for Bret and Justice to spot me. One positive from my meltdown earlier is that I'm likely left with red eyes.

"Hey, where you been—" Bret stops when he sees my face. "What's wrong?"

"I'm fine."

Justice isn't wearing the sympathetic expression my date now has on. She's looking me over carefully, eyebrows lifted. She glances over at Bret. "Give us a minute? Girl talk."

He lifts both hands. "Fine. I'll be in the gym with Dominic."

Dominic's here? Miles told me he wasn't coming to the dance. He'll want to keep an eye on him now, and he's stuck in a classroom.

"You haven't seen Miles anywhere, have you?" Justice asks. Before I can answer, she steps into the classroom and flips on the light. Revealing Miles hidden in a corner. When she turns to me again, she looks at me like I'm completely different.

"Wow…" She shakes her head.

"We weren't—" I start at the same time Miles says, "She needed to—"

"Save it." Justice shakes her head and laughs. "I underestimated you, Ellie. I knew you weren't completely harmless but this…this requires top-grade mean-girl skill."

Guilt I hadn't expected to feel hits me hard. "I'm sorry. I really wasn't trying to do anything—"

"I said save it," she snaps. "Can't say I wasn't warned. Miles asked me to homecoming as friends. He was very up-front. But you..." She stops. Exhales. Appears to get her emotions under control. "You should know that Bret is using you."

"What could he possibly use me for?" I ask, completely baffled. Not money—I don't have any and he knows that—or sex—we haven't even gone to first base.

She shrugs. "Guess he thinks you're important."

Justice starts to walk away, and my heart is pounding all over again, for new reasons. I reach out and touch her arm to stop her. "Important how?"

She looks at me, hurt concealed behind her solid composure. "Simon Gilbert told him you were some big legacy at Holden Prep. That your family had power with the school and could make things happen."

Behind me, I can practically hear Miles's thinking. Why would Simon make up that lie about me?

"Is that why you wanted to hang out with me?" I ask her.

Justice tugs her arm back and steps farther from me. "He told me that like ten minutes ago. I was trying to find you to give you a heads-up."

With that, she spins and walks briskly down the hall. It appears that I may have made a real friend without realizing it and in the same moment managed to lose that friend.

Well done, Ellie. All in a day's work.

I'm still processing, so I barely notice Miles step away from me and head down the hall until I see his walk—it's full of purpose and definite action. I'd expected him to go after Justice, to apologize; that's the Miles Beckett way.

I jog as best I can in my heels to catch him. "Where are you going?"

"To have a little chat with Bret."

I grab his jacket, halting him in place. "You are not going near him right now."

He shakes out of my grip, turns to face me, and I immediately panic. He's got that "I'm gonna get what I need from him and I don't care who knows about it" look. I've been in this position before. Listening to someone lie to me, feed me a bunch of BS, and wanting to break character, shake them, and force out the truth. But it's never worth it.

"He was there that night, Ellie," Miles argues. "With a camera. He's harassing Dominic... I need to know—"

"Miles." I wrap my fingers around his biceps, holding him in place. "Let Justice go find him. She'll tell him we hooked up. We need to let that happen. Turn the tables so I can confront him. Me, not you. Not us. As soon as there's an 'us' questioning Bret, we're done."

He knows this. He's told me this a hundred times. But I can tell he's not there yet.

I shove him into a dark girls' bathroom and block the door. "What are you planning on doing? Interrogating him until he talks? Blowing your cover?"

Being the disciplined, compartmentalizing guy he is, it takes only about five seconds for Miles to take a deep breath and look normal again, not like a guy ready to beat the truth out of someone. "You're right. Sorry. I'm—"

"Being an idiot?" I suggest.

"Yes..." His hands land on my face and in the blink of an eye, his mouth is on mine again. He spins me until my back is against the wall. "Last time, I promise."

So Miles is one of those guys who can fuel anger into... well, into this. For several seconds, I turn to Jell-O falling, my body held upright by the wall and Miles's rough hands. Eventually, I grip his face, holding him at a distance, still breathing hard. "What the hell are we doing?"

"Nothing. It's done." He closes his eyes, his forehead resting against mine. "I know you're going to kill me for saying this but I hate the idea of you talking to him alone. I can't—"

"You can be there," I assure him. "He just can't know you're there."

Miles steps away from me, putting some cool air between us. He glances around the girls' bathroom and runs a finger through his hair. "I don't know why I—"

"Can't resist me?" I finish for him.

"I can," he says, like he hadn't been dying for more time in that classroom or glued to me seconds ago. "Or I should. *I will.* We've got too much shit to deal with... Best not to add more."

Right. But would it be so terrible if people thought we were dating? If Miles and I had to "pretend" to be together? I must have done a bad job of hiding my disappointment, because Miles stares at me.

"It was your idea," he says quietly. "Five minutes of fun."

"Yep, my idea. And yep, five minutes of fun. All over now." This time I hit the right inflections in my voice, keeping it light, convincing him. I tug my dress back into place and plaster on the neutral look I've worked so hard to master. I don't know how much more of his intense looks and kissing I can take before my head gets all messed up. "Are you done resisting me so we can make a plan in like the next ten minutes? Clock is ticking..."

I take my cell phone and tuck it down the front of my dress. I look up at Miles. "Now...tell me if you can see anything?"

His gaze locks on my boobs, and then he shakes his head, refocusing. "I...I think that'll work."

CHAPTER

29

Bret leans against the outside gym doors and looks me over. "So, you and Beckett, huh?"

"No, I mean…we're not—"

"Save it," he says, stealing Justice's line. "I've known for a while now. Wanted to play along for Justice's sake."

"It was a onetime thing." Or two. Maybe three-time thing if you count the girls' bathroom separate from the classroom. "Moment of weakness."

"I guessed it during the tuna casserole ordeal," he says smoothly.

Apparently my classmates aren't all complete idiots. Note to self: never underestimate the C student who carelessly hands his drugs to whomever.

I look at him. "You don't seem too upset. Why is that, Bret?"

He laughs. "Justice and her big mouth and self-righteous—"

"What exactly did Simon Gilbert tell you?"

"He told me why he was friends with you," Bret says. When he sees me standing there, arms folded over my chest, waiting to hear the rest, he continues with a sigh.

"Because of your father. And your grandfather."

"Right." I nod. "He said that they're...?"

"Yes, Eleanor, I know your secret." He grins. "The Wilkenson family. As in the two men who gave five million dollars to the school to build that new wing. Harold Wilkenson, who is about to announce his desire to run in the next presidential election."

"And you wanted that connection?"

"That's what people think, isn't it? That I slither around sucking up to important people for dozens of letters of recommendation?"

Isn't that what he had said that day in the hall when I overheard him and Dominic arguing about inviting Simon to a party? "So if you're dating me, then my father and grandfather will help you out with what? Internships? College acceptance?"

"Yeah, no." Bret laughs. "I learned at a very young age that having dirt on someone is much more useful than a friendly relationship."

Bingo. And he led me right there. "Dirt? Like compromising pictures?"

He doesn't admit to anything. Folds his arms over his chest and cocks an eyebrow. I need to get something out of him before Miles turns back into the Hulk and storms out here demanding answers.

"So you have pictures of me," I conclude from his nonanswer. "Doing what exactly?"

"Buying drugs, drinking," he rattles off.

"Drugs that you gave me! For free!" I release a breath and remind myself of the goal and the fact that I don't actually have rich, important family members for him to blackmail. *Joke's on you, Bret; you picked the wrong girl.* "Forget it. Doesn't matter. Because I was using you, too."

"Oh really?" He looks skeptical. "What were you

hoping to gain?"

"Answers," I say, taking a step closer to him, making sure Miles hears every word. "The night my friend Simon died, you were in the parking lot when he dropped me off after the dance, and I want to know why."

He stares me down. "I don't know what you're talking about. Besides, I've already told the police and Feds everything I know. Like you did, like anyone who ever talked to Simon Gilbert has done."

"There's new evidence," I tell him, knowing I'm making it sound like it's a game changer when clearly it hasn't been so far. "Video footage of your car in that parking lot. And I overheard Chantel talking about the spring dance and what happened to her after. Something about your backseat and a long-lens camera…"

Some of the color drains from his face. "And I take it you turned this drunk-girl story over to the police? Should I head home and wait for my arrest?"

"I don't know, should you?" I challenge. "And no, I haven't. Yet."

Bret steps closer. "What do you want, Ellie? Money? That seemed to work with Jacob. What is it you two did together?"

"He paid me a thousand bucks to run a thirty-dollar background check for him. And I already told you what I want. Answers." The cold air hits me and I suppress a shiver, running my hands up my arms. "Let's make a deal, Bret. You have pictures of me, I have incriminating information on you. Now tell me why I shouldn't assume the worst. Why were you following Simon? Did you follow him home?"

Bret's face twists with anger. "I wasn't fucking following Simon! I was tailing Dominic. Check your little video again and I guarantee there's another car there. I thought he was messed up with that wack-job dealer, Davey. I was trying to help him! He's my fucking best friend and he can't fucking tell me he's into dudes? Still hasn't. Like I'm gonna hate him or something?"

"That's why you're tormenting him with pictures," I conclude. "You want him to tell you the truth."

The anger falls from his face. His forehead wrinkles. "What? I don't have pictures of—" He shakes his head. "Okay, I do have pictures but I would never...maybe just for the senator's eyes but I didn't..."

My inner lie detector is sensing he's telling the truth, but it's hard to know for sure with Bret. He's obviously got a conniving side. "So you aren't sending Dominic weekly photos of him and Simon making out the night of the dance under an anonymous email?"

"Why the hell would I do that? You don't know what I've been through with Dominic this summer. The holes I've had to drag him from. It's been fucking hell."

Truth.

"If you feel that way, why do you even have pictures of them together if you weren't collecting items to blackmail him with?"

"The senator, not Dominic. I wouldn't do that to him," Bret insists. "And it's kind of become a habit now. I meet people and immediately look for ways to ruin them."

There's really not much I can say to that. I mean, seriously? Am I supposed to hate him for playing me? I might be a lot of things, but I try to never be a hypocrite. Instead, I move on to a new question.

"So after Simon dropped me off, Dominic followed him and you followed Dominic?" I prompt. "To where?"

"Dominic's house," Bret says. "I saw them together... like *together*, and all my questions about Dominic were answered so I left. Took Chantel home and the rest is secured by the alibi I gave the police."

"Simon went to Dominic's house that night?" I press, my heart pounding, adrenaline rushing. *This* is a game changer. "You're positive?"

"I didn't see them actually go inside. Just outside the house."

"And you didn't tell any of this to the police or FBI? Including the fact that Chantel was passed out drunk in your car?" I don't even need to hear his answer. Obviously he didn't tell anyone.

And this means I wasn't the last person to see Simon that night. I wasn't even the second-to-last person.

CHAPTER
30

I burst into Miles's secret room after a long wait for a bus. I'm near explosion from new information overload right now. And freezing. I should have worn a jacket like Harper suggested, but I didn't have one to go with my dress.

I yank my phone from between my boobs and toss it on the table. Miles looks up from his laptop, and the poker face he's wearing stops me from bursting with words I've held in for over an hour.

"So..." I prompt, waiting for him to tell me I'm awesome and I should win a medal of honor for my interrogation tactics.

"I was sitting right there, Ellie," he says, pushing away from the table and standing. He spins his laptop around so I can see the screen. "You've got balls, doing this right in front of me."

"Sitting where?" I ask, and then, "Doing what in front of you?"

I lean down and barely read the top of the page: MILES HENRY BECKETT, before he hits delete and the picture on the screen vanishes.

Miles's school file. Had I really—

"What did you want to know so badly?" he demands.

"I don't…" My eyes widen, my mind drifting back to hours ago, remembering my fingers grazing the files in Geist's drawer. I went from Thomas to Gilbert, and Gilbert sent my head up my ass and caused me to flee the dance in tears. And then suddenly it comes back to me. Miles stepping away, the phone to his ear. And me moving to the *B* section, tugging his file out and snapping pictures for later. On my phone. How did he even—

He synced my phone to his laptop before I pulled Bret aside to talk. God, I'm an idiot. All the making out must have turned my brain to mush. And man, I'm not much different from Bret Thomas. I couldn't resist the temptation, either. I couldn't leave his file untouched. But it was my subconscious that did the work for me. Old habits and all…

"I didn't read anything," I argue weakly.

"Yet," he says, his voice rising.

"You don't know that."

"Did you see me reading your confidential school records? Do you see me digging into your life?" He snaps his laptop shut, and the sound vibrates through the silent room. "I trusted you. We were supposed to work together, to be a team. You don't even know what that means, do you?"

I shake my head. "Are you hiding something in that file? More secrets?"

Okay, so maybe I'm a hypocrite, although to my credit, there's barely anything in my file. It's what isn't there that I'm hiding.

"Yes! I'm hiding a lot of things in that file." He looks at me like I'm a huge disappointment, and suddenly I feel like one. "My parents' jobs for one. Emergency numbers telling where to reach them if something happens to me. That's confidential information. People could die, Ellie. And you uploaded it through an unsecured network."

"Unsecured by your Fort Knox standards or actually unsecured?" I feel like the world's biggest asshole. Again. But of course I went into defensive mode instead of apologizing. *Like Miles would*, I can't help thinking. He's done that several times. Said or did something to me he regretted, and then he just looked right at me and told me he was sorry. I can't do that. I always have to turn it around, point the blame back at my accuser.

He doesn't respond to my sarcastic remark even though it wasn't sent via texting. He proceeds to pack up his laptop and tuck things away, tidying up the secret room.

"What are you doing?" I ask. "Don't we have work to do?"

Miles finally looks at me and shakes his head. "No. Not together. Not like this."

"Seriously?" My stomach drops, my heart picking up speed. I follow him out of the room. "Were you not listening in on me and Bret? How can you just walk away—"

He spins to face me. "I didn't say I was walking away."

"Oh." I sink back on my heels. *You're just not working with me.* "Guess we're flying solo again."

"Guess so."

While I'm leaving and walking back to my apartment, I call him a dozen different names inside my head, but none of it helps. None of it makes me feel less alone. Or less guilty. I violated his trust. Didn't even think twice about it. Something is wrong with me. Clearly. Or maybe my subconscious has reason to not trust Miles and is seeking out evidence. Hard to tell the difference anymore.

My apartment is dark and quiet but when I crawl into bed, preparing to drift off to sleep—hopefully minus the drowning nightmares—my door opens a crack and Harper creeps in, sliding under my covers.

"So," she whispers. "Just getting in? Thought the dance ended at eleven…"

"And your point is?"

"Nothing," she says. "I just want to gossip. It's two in the morning. What have you been doing all this time? With Bret…"

I snuggle into my pillow and close my eyes. "How about we play that game where you guess?"

"Don't be a brat," Harp says. "Consider yourself lucky. Aidan is convinced you need a sex talk, and I didn't come in here planning on giving you one."

My eyes fly open. "God, seriously? He's not going to attempt that, right?"

"He'd rather die a slow, painful death, his words, not mine," Harper says, laughing. "But really, Ellie, do you want to talk about any of that? Or maybe just tell me you know what you're doing and you're being safe? Not that you even have to take things that far."

I want to tell her right now that I'm not a virgin, but then she's going to ask who and when. And then I'll have to tell her that my story went something like hers. Slightly older hot guy who runs in our family's circle charms innocent girl into sleeping with him, then stomps on her heart. I know it's one of the reasons she left. And it's not that I'm too ashamed to tell her. It's that I know one big reason she came looking for me was to keep something like that from happening. I don't want to take that away from her.

"Not sure I'm quite there yet," I tell Harper, forcing the lie out smoothly. "And not sure about Bret, either."

I'd hoped the last part would provide a distraction, and it does. She breaks into a grin. "Miles. I knew it! Aidan didn't believe me, but I knew it!"

"Shhh…" I clap a hand over her mouth. "We made out. Twice. That's it." I think for a minute, digging for an excuse that doesn't involve the investigation and my broken trust. "He's a bit of a commitment-phobe."

She frowns. "Really? I didn't get that vibe from him. He seems like the disciplined, loyal type."

That he is. Unfortunately. "Well, everyone's got to have their wild side, right?"

"I guess." She climbs out of my bed. "Well, that was pointless and boring. Thanks for nothing, little sis."

"Be glad it's boring."

After she's gone, I try to sleep. Try to forget about all the words Miles tossed at me tonight. Truthful words. But the part of my brain that acts without thinking—the part that copied Miles's file—is on the move again. Soon I'm clutching a notebook to my chest while swinging a leg over the balcony. I pop the lock on the neighbor's bicycle parked on their patio below ours and hop on, and by the time I'm riding off into the dark, I know exactly where I'm headed.

Simon Gilbert's house.

Miles would have never agreed to surveillance of the senator's place.

And thus begins my reentry onto Team Ellie. Flying solo.

CHAPTER
31

CONNIE: how's the new gear working?

I turn up the volume on my receiver and hear Dominic's voice loud and clear.

ME: perfect. And sorry again about smashing the other one

CONNIE: np. Check ur email. Sending you something

I'm eating my lunch outside despite the fact that late October is a little too cold for dining alfresco. But since homecoming, I seem to be lacking people to sit with in the cafeteria. Or people in general. You know, since I'm flying solo again. Which means I get to plant listening devices on him. Fair, right? Connie lent me a new one last week, didn't even get mad that the other one had been destroyed. Would have liked to have planted one inside the Gilberts' mansion, but unfortunately those Secret Service guys look for these types of things. Wonder why?

"How was your date last night?" Miles says to Dominic.

"Fine," Dominic says in a way that is an ending rather than a beginning.

He still hasn't opened up to Miles about being into guys or anything about Simon, though he has opened up a ton about his family drama—Dad's pressure, Mom's drinking and painkiller habit, and his poor little sister who seems caught in the middle all the time.

And apparently I've turned into a narrator for the *All My Children*. I yawn, fight to stay awake. Too many late nights outside the Gilberts' place.

I guess solo investigating meant Miles became Dominic's emotional support. But he has yet to ask Dominic about being the real last person to see Simon Gilbert alive.

I shift my focus to the link Connie emailed me. The link is to a three-hundred-page report written in tiny font, using very technical (aka boring) terms. I skim a page or two, and then go back to the email to read her explanation about the report.

During an investigation of a series of murders taking place in 1968, the U.S. government files a report that linked all victims to a powerful politician. The report focused on this connection, but an interesting note is made regarding items left behind at each murder scene baring an identical logo and name: St. Felicity's Shelter. No shelter, church, or facility of any kind was ever identified on U.S. soil under this name. The investigation ended in 1974 when it was determined that all trails had turned cold.

I agree with Connie that conclusions drawn from the report are interesting, but how many pages of that document did she have to read? And where does uncovering this nonexistent shelter lead me? To some secret religious gathering? And what does any of this have to do with Dominic? Of course Connie doesn't know of that connection. She doesn't know where I go to school. If she did her head would be spinning with conspiracy theories considering Simon's link to a powerful politician and then fact that he's dead, possibly not by his own hands—

Shit. Maybe it is connected. I mean what are the odds? Dominic is the real person who saw him last.

My fingers are flying, texting Connie a million more questions; the sandwich Aidan made for me this morning lies abandoned. I word my questions carefully, keeping personal details and the very public case of Simon Gilbert out of the mix. But I end up forgetting one big detail in this process.

CONNIE: what happened to the ditzy teenage girl who came into my store a few weeks ago?

ME: uh…you know just reading, getting smarter

CONNIE: did u think I'd turn u in to someone just b/c ur curious about a listening device u found?

ME: better safe than sorry. I found it in a classmate's bag. For real

CONNIE: OK then. I'm Connie, it's nice to meet you girl who is much smarter than she looks/acts

I look down at my phone, feeling a physical connection between me and another person for the first time in over a week. Sometimes it's nice to have the freedom to be me.

ME: Eleanor. Call me Ellie.

CONNIE: got it. And I will keep digging through these government reports. Right now, I can only access the released reports, usually 20+ years old

Guess that means she can't hack her way into getting the police report of Simon's death.

"You sure you want to deal with Davey again?" Dominic says. *"I nearly pissed my pants last time with you pulling your disappearing act."*

"So don't go," Miles says. *"I'll meet him alone."*

Oh no. Not this again.

"Dude, you've either got massive balls or a death wish," Dominic says. *"But no, I'm not leaving you on your own. Can't you just buy some weed off the guy? Why this new*

thing? I can get you Adderall if you need it for studying or whatever."

"Just curious. Aren't you?"

"A little, but not enough to get into shit I don't know about," Dominic says. *"You still got what he wants? The Swiss imports?"*

"I got it, don't worry," Miles says. The bell rings, sending a piercing sound through my headphones. *"Later, man."*

Damn. I missed the part where they said when they were meeting up. I storm off to my next class, pissed at myself for missing the most important bit of info, but fifteen minutes in, I get pulled from class. Another note to meet in the office. I debate skipping out—the last thing I need right now is another "let's chat about your future" session in Geist's office—but what if Harper and Aidan are here again waiting for me?

I get halfway to the office when a hand reaches out and pulls me inside the janitor's closet. My heart jumps up to my throat. The door closes, leaving me in the dark.

"If you wanted to listen in on my conversations, you could have just asked nicely," Miles says.

My heart slows a bit, but the scent of him nearby sends my pulse racing again. The apartment pool closed weeks ago; how does he still smell like chlorine?

I'm adjusting to the dark enough to make out the shape of his face, his body. "Didn't think I could. You know, since we're not on the same team anymore."

"I know you've been staking out the Gilberts' house all week," he says. "I just can't figure out why."

God, can I do anything behind his back? Or maybe I'm slipping in covering my tracks. I think I might be obsessed. Not with the Gilberts but with this answer floating right above me. My dad refers to this as Junkie Mode. Anyone in my "family" who fell into Junkie Mode got thrown off the job or pushed into a background part. It was too risky, he'd say. They're not seeing clearly, thinking clearly. Looking back on it now, I'm pretty sure my dad was in full-blown Junkie Mode during that last job I did with them. If he wasn't, he would have figured out that I'd been helping the FBI, figured out that he didn't know the target as well as he'd thought. Maybe my mom pulled him out last minute for that very reason?

"Ellie?" Miles says, snapping me back to the dark closet and him so incredibly close. I can feel him examining me in the dark. "Are you sleeping at all? You look…"

Nice. I miss a little beauty rest and Mr. Always Hot calls me out on it. "What?" I demand.

"Tired," he finishes.

"Thanks, Miles. You look great, too."

He leans in, his breath hitting my neck. "Tired, but still beautiful. And I know you know it. So get over yourself."

We haven't been this close in a while, and now all I can think about is the homecoming dance and Miles pressing me up against the wall, his hand sliding beneath my dress. "Is that why you pulled me into a closest after a week of ignoring me? Didn't you say you had no problem resisting me?"

"The Gilberts' house." He clears his throat, back to disciplined Miles. "Your solo surveillance team. That's why I pulled you in here. What are you up to?"

"You're the one who broke up with me," I remind him, then I jump to clarify. "Broke up our team, I mean."

"Only because you refuse to trust me," he snaps, angry all over again. "Tell me what you're up to."

I shove him aside and put a hand on the door. "Guess you'll just have to catch me there tonight and find out for yourself."

CHAPTER
32

Around ten thirty p.m., when my body is nearly numb from cold and my eyes are drooping, a paper coffee cup appears right in front of my face, blocking the Gilberts' mansion from my line of sight. "Couldn't help spying on me, huh? Now who's having trust issues?"

Miles is dressed in all black. He waits for me to accept the coffee, then folds himself on the ground beside me. "You can see me, right? Not spying."

"Fine then. You're not spying." I rub the warm coffee between my hands and stare straight ahead. I don't know what I'm looking for, maybe because I've gone into Junkie Mode and lost perspective. "And we're definitely not spying together."

"Definitely not," he agrees.

A black town car pulls up in front of the house. The Secret Service agent hops out, glances around, opens the car door, and then Senator Gilbert steps out. I flip my notebook to a blank page and note the time. His arrival home is an hour later than last night and the night before.

Beside me, Miles sits unmoving, watching the house, not writing anything down. He doesn't even have coffee.

I try not to look at him, try to forget he's there, but the more still and quiet he is the more aware I become of his presence. This goes on for two hours except every once in a while, one of us speaks. It goes something like this:

After 30 minutes...

MILES: Five entry points not counting windows.

ME: Yep, cameras only on two of those.

After 45 minutes...

ME: No watchman monitoring the security feed; it's just there for replay.

MILES: Don't you mean watchperson?

After 67 minutes...

MILES: Mind if I look at your notes?

ME: I don't know…that sounds like a teammate thing.

MILES: *Stares* *Stares more*

ME: Fine.

After 72 minutes...

MILES: How did you get the alarm code?

ME: Made a call.

After 114 minutes...

MILES: So either 7:00 p.m. or 1:00 a.m.

I peel my gaze from the house to look at him. "For what?"

"You know what." He turns away before I can read his expression. "It's too risky alone."

"Seriously?" I angle myself to fully face him now. "You—Mr. By the Book or Else—are considering breaking and entering?" Into a U.S. senator's home of all places. But I don't say that out loud. I'm too excited about the prospect of a partner in crime.

"We need to—" He shakes his head. "I need to see his room."

I glance sideways at the house. "It's been months. How do we know it's still intact? That they haven't turned it into a fifth office or ninth guest bedroom?"

This is what's stopped me from breaking in sooner. I need to know for sure it will be worth it. Okay, so maybe I'm not in full-blown Junkie Mode.

"Because I know." Miles stands, dusts the back of his pants off. "Tomorrow. Seven or one?"

"Wait…" I scramble to my feet, scooping the empty coffee cup off the ground. "This will be really really bad if we get caught. Why would you risk that?" I can't believe I'm asking this, or saying what I'm about to suggest. "Or maybe we should just turn in the information we've found. Anonymously or whatever."

"I did," Miles says simply. "Eight days ago."

Eight days ago? Jesus Christ. "Why wouldn't the Feds want to—?"

"Because he's a prominent public figure and people needed an answer quickly," Miles states. "It takes a lot of doubt to reopen a case. More than we have."

"Right now, anyway."

"So tomorrow. Seven is best, I think. Empty house but still dark out." He looks at me for a response, and I nod. Can't argue with that logic. "You need a ride home?"

I open my mouth to say yes, but then decide against it. If he wants to join forces again, then he'll have to make the first move. "Nope, I'm good."

With that, he walks off, calling over his shoulder. "Tomorrow we're driving together."

Whatever. But you are so not in charge. Breaking and entering is a specialty of mine.

CHAPTER
33

can see my breath in front of me. It's cold and dark. Leaves crunch beneath my feet. And Miles refuses to let me hold the flashlight. Mine ran out of batteries twenty minutes ago and we've been walking for at least forty minutes. Mr. Boy Scout USA had the nerve to tell me that I should come better prepared.

"Explain to me again," I say to Miles, "why we had to park so far away and trek through an entire forest?"

"Probably because parking right in front of the Gilbert mansion might make it a little obvious when we break in."

I shove him from behind. The condescending tone is totally not cool. Especially when he's been ignoring me for over a week, then cornering me in janitor's closets, smelling like fresh air and sexiness. "We're not a team anymore. How do I know you're not leading me somewhere that you can murder me, bury my body, and be off the continent long before anyone digs me up?"

"If I wanted to kill you, I could have done it weeks ago."

"Well, that's a reassuring thought." At least we're talking more tonight than last night. Helps with my nerves. Yes, nerves. Despite this being a specialty of mine, even I don't take a job this big lightly. "Or maybe this is how you score chicks. Maybe we'll wander the woods and then I'll wake up topless in your apartment while you throw clothes at me."

Miles turns to face me, the outline of his body illuminated in front of me. "Is that what you want? A wild night in my apartment?"

Maybe. I shove him again, harder this time. He stumbles back. "Hey, you keep bringing it up, like a suggestion."

"Go to hell," I say.

We step out of the woods, and the Gilbert mansion appears before our eyes. It looks different tonight. Bigger. Closer. Both of us stand there for several seconds, shoulder to shoulder, assessing the place.

"Five entry points," I say, even though we went through this last night.

Miles nods. "Six if you want to climb to the third floor."

"Go for it, Spider-Man."

"His room is on the second floor, but I'm not sure which one," Miles says.

I look at him, trying to study his face in the dark. "You've never been here?"

Miles shakes his head. "Simon invited me a few times, but my parents always took me somewhere during breaks or we stayed in Baltimore."

Despite our current business-only relationship, I have to know some things before we go through with this. "What do you think we're going to find? And why aren't you more worried about getting caught?"

"I don't know what we'll find, maybe nothing. But I know his room is exactly as he left it. That's something." Miles looks out into the dark. "And I know someone broke in with no problems."

I spin to face him. "What?"

"Dominic." He says this with no emotion in his voice. I would have never been able to hold on to that detail without looking ready to burst. "I don't think he did it."

Killed Simon. That's what he means. I don't think I could say it out loud at this moment, either. "Don't you think it's suspicious that he felt the need to break into his room?"

"It's not him, Ellie." This time there's emotion in his voice. "I caught him with Simon's school ID, and he confessed to swiping it from his room."

I'm almost too shocked to speak. Almost. "So he admitted to you about his relationship with Simon?" This is huge progress for Dominic, especially considering he still won't admit it to Bret, someone he's known his whole life.

"No," Miles says, sounding defeated. "He lied and said it was a dare that came from the senior Rowman members." The Holden Prep Rowman. I'd heard about the two-hundred-year-old secret society but wasn't sure it was real.

"Dominic said the guys in the secret society would beat his ass if they knew he told anyone," Miles continues.

"Well-played, Dominic," I mutter. "Guy's got some secret-keeping skills, that's for sure. You think he came for a Simon Gilbert memento? Doesn't really seem like a Dominic thing."

"I don't think that's it," Miles says. "I think he's looking, too. Like us."

"Great." I shake my head; "shocker" doesn't do that bit of info justice. "Maybe we should start a school-sponsored club. Think of the college application points we'd all have from this EC. And when we figure out who 'all eyes on you' is, we can invite him or her, too. I'm sure Dominic would love that. One big happy family."

"You done with the sarcasm?"

I give him a pointed look. "I'll be done when I'm done."

"Believe me, I know. That's why I asked."

I roll my eyes but allow him to explain his part of the plan, how he'll shut off the alarm on the far side of the house before we head in. Miles hands me a fancy earpiece and a special phone so we can communicate. He lists each entry and exit point, assigning them a number for quick reference. I repeat the numbers several times in my head, committing them to memory.

"You take two, I'll take five. No surveillance on either, but don't forget to avoid the path of security cameras," he says. "Alarm will be off for thirty seconds, but wait for my signal just in case they've changed the code."

I head for the sunroom door and watch Miles move across the yard, his black clothes blending beautifully into the night until I can't see him anymore. A few seconds later, he whispers that we're good to go. I fish around in my jacket pocket for the right tools to pick the lock and soon, I'm opening the door—slowly and quietly. I listen for voices or movement before slipping inside.

"I'm in," I tell Miles, mumbling the words into the phone strapped to my shoulder. According to the news reports, Simon was found dead in this very room. I glance around. Everything is in perfect order—the furniture, the plants, even the books on the shelf are arranged by height.

"Almost in," Miles says.

I tiptoe around, snapping photos of everything. With my tennis shoe, I kick back the corner of the rug. The polished wood floors shine all around me, even in the dark, but a dull spot beneath the rug stands out.

"I'm in," Miles says. "Walking through the second floor now."

I take a photo of the dull spot on the floor and shoot it to Miles. "Check this out."

There's a short pause, and then he says, "It's been sanded. The only way to remove a deep bloodstain."

I stare at the non-shiny circle on the floor, waiting for it to talk to me, give me answers. "Deep as in it sat there for a while?"

"Ellie." Miles's tone has shifted to something more urgent. "I found his room. Right at the top of the steps, third door on the left. "

"Got it." I'm up the stairs in no time, but a door at the opposite end of the hallway opens. I dive into the laundry room. "Stay put," I whisper. "Someone's here."

"Housekeeper, probably."

Whoever it is heads down the steps seconds later. I sigh with relief, wait for silence before exiting the laundry room. I find Simon's room and open the door only a crack before sliding inside. The room is oddly untouched, as if Simon truly may have been the last person to enter or exit this space. The covers are pulled back on the bed; a glass of water sits on the nightstand. Dust surrounds the glass, and a coat of it rests on the bookshelf beside the window. Something soft squishes beneath my shoe. I look down and stare at the blue suit jacket and slacks.

The suit Simon wore to the spring formal. The suit he wore in the photo of him and Dominic making out.

Miles's gloved hand drifts over a red tie hanging on the back of the desk chair, then he looks over at me. "This is what he was wearing that night. At the dance."

I nod, afraid my voice will shake.

"That means he came up here to change," Miles says, his voice stiff, forced calm. "He put on something more comfortable…"

"Why would it matter what he was wearing if he planned to…" Again I can't finish.

"Yeah, I know," Miles says. "Let's dust the room for

prints. I should be able to run a search of anyone who entered."

I'm sure this task has been done and done again, but maybe those prints will mean something different to us. Miles appears to have come equipped with his own forensics lab in his pockets. I turn off the thoughts in my head and take Miles's directions, shifting into mechanical mode, only following orders.

My plan goes out the window when I spot the calendar pinned above the desk. That Saturday in June, the last day I saw Simon Gilbert, is circled in bold black marker, the words "spring formal with Ellie 8pm" written in the center. Miles's arm brushes mine as he moves to stand beside me, staring at the same words. I glance sideways at him, watch his forehead wrinkle. "What?" I ask.

He steps closer, examines the calendar, and then before I can even blink he tugs it down, revealing a safe built right into the wall.

No wonder he wanted to come in here. No wonder he thought we'd have more luck than the Feds.

My mouth falls open in shock. "How did you—"

"He told me." Miles carefully uses tape to pull any fingerprints from the safe and tucks all the evidence into a small plastic bag. "He built this himself while his parents were in Fiji one summer."

I try and fail to conjure a mental image of middle school Simon building a safe. "Any chance you know the—"

Miles is already twisting the dial with such confidence I'm not at all surprised when the safe door pops open seconds later.

"Guess that's the sort of thing you tell your best friend," I mumble.

Miles shines a light inside the safe, but before we can get a good look, a beeping noise fills the room. It's soft at first, a low buzz, and then it grows louder.

"We must have tripped an alarm," Miles whispers.

I make a move for the bedroom door—we need to get out of here—but already, several pairs of feet are thundering up the steps. Miles heads for the window, popping it open.

"It's probably the cat again," a deep male voice says from outside.

"Never make assumptions," another voice says, one that's familiar. Shit. Oh shit.

Miles swings a leg out the window. "Ellie, come on!"

I glance between him and the door. The footsteps grow louder and closer. If I jump out that window, it'll be the first place they look. We'll never make it to the woods without being spotted. Not both of us, anyway. Since we're not a team anymore…

"Go!" I order him. I give myself two seconds to look over the contents of that safe, close the door and stuff the calendar in place. Miles is still waiting. "Now! Get out of here. I got this."

He's clearly torn, so I take the initiative to peel his fingers from the sill and give him a shove until he's forced out onto the ledge. I have enough time to shut the window, enough time to yank my ponytail out and toss hair over the earpiece, but not enough time to hide.

The bedroom door swings open; a bright light points right at me.

CHAPTER
34

Nearly nine months ago, I was in this exact same position. Caught red-handed in the office of a sleazy banker. Only I hadn't known he was sleazy at the time—as a general rule my family prefers to con innocent, naive people. Turned out the FBI had been investigating the guy for fraud for a long time. Turned out I knew things they didn't about Mr. Sleazy Banker.

Thus began a beautiful relationship with "the good guys" where I was given freedom and a second chance to break in somewhere else, apparently.

But before our fairy-tale ending, I had pulled the performance of a lifetime in that office. It hadn't worked back then because the FBI already knew who I was and more importantly, who my family was. But tonight, it might work.

"Ellie...?" Jack says. "What the—"

A younger guy in a suit interrupts Jack by whipping out his gun. "What are you doing in here?"

I swallow back fear and shake my head. "No...I mean, no one. I'm just—"

Jack lifts a hand, placing it between the younger guy's

gun and me. "Hold up there, Rider."

"I'm sorry...I just...I can't believe he's gone and I don't have anything—" I cover my face with my hands and sink down onto the floor. "He never told me anything was wrong but I should have seen it. He was my friend and I didn't see that he was hurting. If I had just—"

"Should we take her down to the interrogation room for questioning?" Rider asks.

I reach for Simon's suit jacket and pull it to my face. It still smells like him. Like a dozen lab reports, like friendly dances and Twizzlers. I hug it tight.

Above me, Jack sighs and turns to Rider. "I'll take care of this. Go shut off the alarm."

Jack strides across the room, lifts me up by the arm. He plucks the jacket from my hands and tosses it back onto the floor. His grip is tight on my arm until we reach the hallway. And then I'm released.

He brings his phone to his ear, looks right at me and says to whoever is on the other end, "False alarm...I'll check the wiring again...thanks."

He tucks the phone away, gives me this long look silently saying, *this is your one and only chance*. Lucky for me Jack doesn't know about all those other chances I've had.

Rider appears in the hallway. "I wouldn't exactly call it a false alarm," he points out, but it's obvious he's reluctant to call his boss out.

"She came with me," Jack says. "Lawrence's stepdaughter."

That's a bit of a stretch, especially considering Aidan is only twenty-seven. Jack gives me a stern look, but there's no need. He doesn't have to convince me to keep my mouth shut.

"She was supposed to stay in the guest house office to

study, but apparently had other ideas." Jack nods toward the steps. "Let's go, young lady."

I follow him without hesitation, keeping my eyes on my feet. The second his back is to me, I pluck the earpiece out and crush it between my fingers. I shove the bits into my pants pocket and continue moving forward.

Harper jumps up from the love seat and paces the room again. "What the hell were you thinking?"

I glance at Aidan from my spot on the couch, trying to read something from him. He's not moving, not shouting, not giving away one shred of emotion. Unlike my pissed-off, freaked-out sister.

Harper shakes the blond hair off her face. "Do you realize what could have happened to you? Immunity is a one-time deal, Ellie. You do something again and—"

I don't know what to say. How do I begin to tell her that this search for answers about a dead kid I knew for literally three months is more important than all the sacrifices she and Aidan have made for me? I was definitely in Junkie Mode.

"I'm sorry, Harp," I whisper, hoping she believes me. "I screwed up, okay?"

She eyes me suspiciously. "So if you could do it over, you wouldn't break into Senator Gilbert's home?"

No, I just wouldn't get caught. I'm not heartless enough to lie to my sister's face, so I say nothing.

"Yeah, I thought so." She sighs, swears under her breath, and then she's pacing again. "Every month I have to meet with that woman and her fancy FBI badge and—"

"What woman?" I demand.

Harper lifts a hand to her mouth and then closes her eyes for a moment. "Agent Sheldon. She makes me report

all your whereabouts and activities for an entire month.
And she's like a damn lie detector. Jack might have swept
this under the rug with the Secret Service, but I'm gonna
have to sit there and lie to a fucking federal agent. Because
no way in hell can I tell her that you fucking broke into a
United States senator's home and convince her it was an
innocent mistake!"

I shrink back into the couch, pull my knees to my chest.
Okay, I take it back. I wouldn't do it again if I had the
chance. Not after hearing that.

"What do I have to do to get you to understand how
serious this is? How fragile our lives are at the moment?
We are hovering inches from losing everything." The anger
drops from Harper's face. She looks worn, exhausted. "Why,
Ellie? What was so important?"

Again, I don't know what to say. I hadn't ever imagined
how difficult this would be for her, how tense. I never
imagined we would still be answering to the FBI in any
form. I thought we were done with that. But I'm only
seventeen, and apparently the FBI is making Harper
shoulder the responsibility for my actions—past and
present.

"Please, Ellie," Harper whispers. "You have to give me
something. Something so that I know I can trust you."

My stomach knots with guilt and hurt. First Miles, now
my own sister. "Of course you can trust me."

"Swear to God you haven't talked to Dad? You haven't
had contact with any of our family?"

The desperation in her voice, the need for me to prove
myself, is like a punch to the gut. If I don't have Harper's
trust, I'm not sure I have anything.

"I know why she was there tonight," Aidan says,
and both Harp and I stop and look at him, surprised
considering he's been silent this whole time. Aidan stares

right at me, several different emotions crossing his face. "The surveillance video. I should have never showed that to you. That's what started all this, isn't it?"

Harper looks confused, her gaze drifting from me to Aidan for clarification.

"She doesn't think Simon killed himself, and she's trying to prove it."

Harper slowly lowers herself into the empty cushion on the love seat and looks at me. "Is that true?"

There's no way out of this now. "You said the same thing. You don't think he did it, do you?"

Her eyes widen. She shakes her head. "Ellie...I don't know. God, I wish that were the truth, but surely the FBI must have evidence if they stopped their investigation. And they did. They stopped looking for answers. This is a senator's kid. They wouldn't give up early unless they were sure. You have to trust that."

Now my sister is looking at me like I need grief therapy and she missed the warning signs, but both of us are distracted by Aidan, deliberately pulling out his phone and removing the battery. He scrubs a hand over his face.

Harper touches his shoulder. "What, babe?"

"The reason they stopped the investigation," Aidan says, and there's a shake in his voice that sends my heart racing, "is because of me. Because of what I saw."

I sit there frozen, waiting. Harper tosses me a sideways glance.

"I didn't know he was home. I thought you guys were still at the dance." Aidan stands, walks over to the window, looks outside, then shuts the blinds. "The Gilberts had hosted a dinner party the previous night, and I was going through the standard inspections. Simon's room was dark, the door opened a crack, I didn't know he was in there. He was standing in the dark, looking inside a safe. Looking at a gun inside the safe."

He never told me he was assigned to the Gilberts. The idea that Aidan was there that night, that he saw this gun is...well, I'm not sure what it is yet.

"Wait," Harper interrupts. "You confronted him about the gun? How did he end up—"

Aidan shakes his head. "That isn't my job. Not without knowing the history. I was filling in for someone. For all I knew, he owned that gun legally. But when he went in the bathroom, I checked to make sure it was locked up again. I had planned to inform his father as soon as he came home. I stayed parked at the far end of their driveway long after my work hours, making sure Simon didn't leave the house. Making sure no one went in. What happens inside their home...you don't realize how much we have to ignore."

I can't move or speak. Across from me, Harper's eyes are round orbs.

Aidan looks at both of us, desperate for understanding. "I figured he went to the range like his dad, maybe even with his dad. I figured as long as I didn't let him leave—" He stops, chokes up a little. "I never thought he'd use it on himself...never in a million years."

"Oh God," Harper mutters. She drops her hand from his shoulder and slides back a few inches. "Aidan..."

Aidan looks at me. "I'm so sorry, Ellie. I should have told you sooner. Should have seen how much you needed that closure. But now you know why the investigation was closed. There was no one else in that house. And I wish I could change that night. For Simon. For you. Every day I wish that."

"Did you hear it?" The words come out in a croak. I clear my throat and try again. "Did you hear the gun?"

He nods.

"What time did you hear it?"

Aidan shakes his head. "Ellie, just let it go—"

"What time?" I demand.

"Oh one two four."

1:24 a.m.

"If you knew th-this…" I sputter. "If you were so sure, why did you ask me about the video? About Bret Thomas in the parking lot that night?"

"Because I wanted to know if that punk-ass kid did or said something to push Simon over the edge."

Jesus. We were never on the same hunt. Aidan never saw any hope, just a need to right a wrong. "I don't think he did," I manage to say.

Aidan stands, gives me one more long look, then says again, "I'm sorry."

He walks through the kitchen and out the door. I'm still frozen, processing, but I expect Harper to go after him, and when she doesn't, I shift my attention to her.

Harp covers her face with her hands and draws in a deep breath. She lifts her head, eyes on me. "All this time, I thought we were so different—opposites—my life versus Aidan's job, but maybe it's not so different? Maybe we're all lying and keeping secrets."

I want to defend Aidan. I want to tell her that he's still the man she loves, but I'm not there yet.

She gets up, walks toward her bedroom instead of the front door. "It'll be okay, Ellie. We'll be okay."

After she's in her room, I move toward the window, peek out the blinds, and spot Aidan seated in a chair by the pool, his head in his hands. I know he's doing exactly what I've been doing, what Miles has…probably Dominic, too.

We're all trying to rewind time. Earn a second chance at that night. But sometimes there are no second chances.

CHAPTER
35

'd just fallen asleep when I heard the rattling in my room. I peel my eyes open in time to see Miles land softly on my bedroom floor. He tiptoes across the room and locks the door.

"You know, some girls would call this behavior creepy," I mumble, still half asleep.

"Are you okay?" Miles asks. "I heard Jakowski cover for you, but then I lost reception."

I sit up and yawn. "That's because I destroyed the earpiece." Miles winces but doesn't say anything. It's probably school property. "I had to. I couldn't exactly explain the spy gear with the story I came up with."

"The crying thing is becoming your trademark, isn't it?"

"It works. Why wouldn't I use it? Plus, I didn't cry tonight. It was more about the dramatic monologue." I fold my arms over my chest, giving the appearance of being ready for an argument, but really I'm not sure I have it in me. "Are you actually complaining that I kept your ass out of trouble? Again?"

Instead of giving a snide remark he surprises me by saying, "No. Not complaining. What you did—what you did for me…that was pretty incredible."

"We wouldn't have both made it to the woods," I say, trying to brush off the compliment. "Besides, if we were working solo, then I wanted to go down on my own. Get all the credit."

"Maybe we can reconsider that solo thing?"

I look down at my hands, my face heating. "Yeah. Maybe."

Miles sits at the opposite end of my bed, but turns to face me. "I have to tell you something."

"Me, too." I swallow back nerves and all the swirls of confusion. "But you first."

"I ran some of the prints from Simon's room." He exhales, leaving enough time for me to ask how the hell he ran fingerprints? Seriously, does his school have a fingerprint machine it lent him? But I'm too nervous about telling him what Aidan told me to put that question front and center. "The prints we found on the safe…they belong to—"

"Aidan," I say at the same time he says, "Lawrence."

Miles blinks, surprised. "How did you know?"

With a heavy heart, I explain what Aidan told me tonight. Miles just sits there listening, still as a stone. Several seconds of silence follow after I finish talking.

"Did you know Simon had a gun?" I ask.

Miles shakes his head.

"I mean, you have a gun and you're both from the same school so maybe—"

"I've only been training in firearms for two years," Miles says, his voice flat, unreadable. "It's part of the honors program, but the rest of the school doesn't…definitely not the middle school. I wasn't even issued a weapon to use outside a range until right before I came here, and only on probationary terms. Guns are a last resort."

"I would hope so," I say under my breath. I still hate that he has a gun in that secret room, sometimes on him. He probably had it with him tonight. Another reason not to let Miles get caught. Breaking and entering *and* carrying would not fit under any rugs.

"What I mean by that is, we first learn ways to take down an enemy without a weapon. With our bodies, with our hands," he tells me.

I'm taken back to that horrible day in the bank, when I stood there in the midst of a storm, watching FBI agents pop out of every nook and cranny, some pointing weapons, others pouncing on the sleazy banker, on me. I try to put Miles on that team, in that bank preparing to save dozens of American citizens from losing all their money by blackmailing a teenage girl and then assaulting her during the heist you forced her into. I hate the idea of him doing that. Any of it. Hate that he even knows how.

"It doesn't mean anything," Miles says, breaking me out of my own thoughts.

"What doesn't? The gun?"

"That he had the gun," Miles explains. "That it's the one someone used on him. If anything, it makes it even more obvious that someone did this to him."

"But Aidan said no one was in the house. He parked outside and sat there until he heard the gunshot." It occurs to me right then that Aidan probably ran inside at that point. He probably saw Simon—

I shake off the thought because I'm not ready to feel sorry for Aidan. Not yet.

"Did he split himself in two and patrol the woods behind the Gilberts' house?" Miles says. "Think about it, Ellie, we walked that way tonight, went right into the house unnoticed until I messed with the safe. You said he waited for hours, right? Anyone could have gotten in. Plus Jack covered for you tonight. We don't know that he isn't doing that for someone else. Why the hell would Jakowski take that big a risk for a teenage girl he's not even related to? He made up a complete lie to a new trainee."

I guess that's true, but the other scenario makes so much more sense. "But who? Who would want to kill Simon Gilbert that badly that they plotted and planned and walked through the woods in the middle of the night and then took Simon's own gun and shot him with it?"

"I don't know," he whispers. "But we have to find out."

I look at Miles. I need to know what he thinks. I need someone to help me decide what I should think. "Do you think he should have taken the gun from Simon?"

"I don't have the USSS rule book memorized." Miles shakes his head. "But given the circumstances—no one else in the house, he was filling in for someone, didn't know the family details, he made a plan to inform the senator and waited for them—it's likely he followed the protocol."

"But he *could* have taken the gun," I say, emphasizing the word "could." "He had a choice. No, he *made* a choice. He's a human, not a machine. He could have done something."

"You can't make your own rules in the Secret Service. You follow orders, you keep the people you protect alive. It's the only way. I would have done exactly what he did."

I don't know what kind of reaction I'd expected from Miles, but this certainly isn't it. I mean, we're talking about his best friend, we're talking about one broken rule that could have maybe saved his life. "Jack broke the rules tonight. Explain that."

Miles shakes his head. "I can't. I seriously don't get it. But still it's not the same as with Aidan. He's younger, newer. He needed to follow the rules for everyone's safety."

"But he was supposed to protect Simon," I whisper,

barely audible. "And Simon's dead."

"It's not a perfect system." Miles tugs at a thread on my comforter. "It's never going to work all the time, but you still have to trust the system. Otherwise it's just chaos and instinct."

"I would have never left that room until Simon handed over his gun or locked it up, and then I would have locked him up in a separate room."

Miles's jaw tenses. "But you're forgetting something. Simon didn't kill himself. Aidan's actions would have been different if he'd thought someone was trying to hurt Simon."

Right. Except it's hard to know what to believe anymore. Why do I keep doubting Simon's mental state? Why can't I have the rock-solid conviction Miles has and hang on to it? Miles trusts it. Trusts himself. And I'm the opposite. I can't even trust Simon after he's dead.

"Whoever did it got lucky that Simon had a gun, that Aidan had seen it," Miles continues. "But that doesn't mean he or she wouldn't have found another way."

Found another way to murder Simon. I mean who would kill Simon Gilbert, the nicest kid in the whole school. The roommate who helped Miles get through his homesickness.

But what about the Simon Gilbert who made up lies about my past, who secretly hooked up with Dominic and built a safe in his own room to hold his unregistered gun? It's definitely more possible someone might want to kill that guy.

Miles stands up and moves toward the window. "We're gonna figure this out. I swear to God we are. But I need you. I can do it alone, but together...well, we're good together."

I should be rubbing this in his face—he was wrong.

But instead, I stare at my knees, hating the compliments. Hating that he trusts me. That he's putting faith in me. And I'm doubting everything, including whether or not I can pull another stunt like we did tonight. After seeing Harper so upset.

"I need to get Dominic to talk," he says. "It's long overdue, but also touchy. If I go too far, it's over—"

"Miles?" I say, interrupting this new plan.

He was about to swing a leg out the window, but he stops and looks up at me. "Yeah?"

"I'm sorry. About the file in Geist's office. Sorry I didn't apologize right away." The words spill out, relief wrapped around them.

"Okay." He nods and then gives me a little smile. "You know, you're not the villain you keep trying to become. Trust me, I can spot a villain better than anyone."

Not always, Miles.

My heart sinks. Outside of this quest, he and I will never be in the same circle, the same world. Ever. He doesn't know it yet, but he hates everything about me.

After he's gone, I stare at the ceiling, too awake to go back to sleep. I run through every aspect of the last twelve hours in my mind until I pause on something I'd seen but had yet to process. I shoot up in bed, my heart pounding.

Simon's safe.

There was a pen. With the logo of a woman in a long gown, her arms spread out and children seated around her. The words "St. Felicity's Shelter" printed across the pen.

I don't want to fall down Connie's conspiracy theory rabbit hole and I don't want to think about the weird coincidence of that pen popping up in similar places, but I do want to use that information to get her help. It's risky revealing my connection to Holden Prep and Simon, but then again, Connie's the epitome of discretion. No digital footprint will be left when I'm done being her friend. And maybe it will keep Miles from ruining his own future. Which is what would have happened if he'd been caught tonight. I'd like to give him that if I can. For his trust in me.

I take out my phone and send a text.

ME: found something new. About that thing you've been researching

My phone vibrates seconds later. Not sure the woman ever sleeps.

CONNIE: srsly? Come see me!

ME: I need a favor. A big one. I need a police report from a crime scene

CONNIE: how old?

ME: Recent. 6 months.

CONNIE: what state?

ME: Virginia

CONNIE: shouldn't be a problem. Is there a name?

I take a deep breath, knowing I've hit the point of no return. But surely this beats biking between Dominic's house and the Gilbert mansion over and over as if clues will fall into my lap. And it's got to be less risky than breaking and entering.

ME: Simon Gilbert

CONNIE: Ok, now I'm really gonna be up all night

That makes two of us.

CHAPTER

36

Connie lifts an eyebrow when I enter the store not alone.

"You didn't tell me you had a partner," she says, like this changes everything.

Beside me, Miles looks like he's itching to search every inch of this place for bugs, but he manages to hold still except for the hand he extends to Connie. "Miles. Ellie's classmate."

"I got what you asked for."

Both Miles and I stiffen, but after a quick exhale I say, "The thing I wanted to tell you..."

I take a few minutes to explain our adventure the other night at the Gilbert mansion. Miles listens intensely, because I haven't really had a reason or time to explain this whole St. Felicity's Shelter thing in detail.

"How exactly did you see inside this secret safe belonging to the senator's dead son?" Connie asks.

Miles gives me a pointed look. "Great question."

"I was there with a family friend. He works at the Gilberts' home." I flash both of them a smile. "He was helping me with algebra and I took a detour on my bathroom break. Ran right into that safe, crazy, huh?"

"Okay then," Connie says, not as if she believes me, but as if I've left her no room to argue.

"St. Felicity," Miles repeats, his voice eerie and distant. "The patron saint of widows and mothers of dead sons."

"Is that her title?" Connie says at the same time I say, "Wait, what?"

"I think that's right." Miles scratches his head. "Saint Felicitas…Felicity of Rome."

Connie bangs a fist against the counter. "God, I'm an idiot! I didn't even think to look at the religious origin as a metaphor. This changes everything. I need to start back at square one."

"One more thing," I interject before Connie's knee-deep in a whole new research project. I grab a pen and slide her notepad toward me, jotting down: *alleyesonyou@ gmail.com*. "Think you could figure out who this email address belongs to?"

She looks at it and frowns. "Maybe."

I shrug off the disappointment. "Just give it a shot."

"Will do. Now…let me show you what I found." Connie tugs a brown envelope from beneath her laptop and proceeds to open it. "This copy is yours to keep, but I would destroy it after you look everything over." She points to a sign above her head with the words BURN DON'T SHRED and another that says, REAL GEEKS USE FIRE.

The police report emerges from the envelope and Miles says, "How exactly did you manage to get this? If you don't mind me asking…?"

"Friends in high places. Before I opened this store, I was a lawyer," Connie says, rolling her eyes. "I know, right?" When we don't react to whatever inside joke went over our heads, she clears her throat. "Anyway, maybe this isn't what you were hoping to hear, but I'm definitely seeing some holes in this suicide declaration—"

"Like what?" Miles and I both say together.

"Okay, maybe it is what you wanted to hear..." Connie reaches into the envelope and pulls out a small stack of photos. "First off, the angle of the gun technically allows for self-firing, but the window of accuracy is very narrow."

I don't know why we hadn't anticipated this, but it's obvious by the quick intake of air that neither Miles nor I considered the possibility of crime scene photos. As in pictures of Simon. After.

The store around me vanishes, my eyes hyper-focused on the photo in front of us. A large bloodstain sits on the Gilberts' perfect wood floor, right where the rug has since been placed.

"...plus, there's not one mention of that container of ice cream on the table. Why would a suicidal kid go to the kitchen for ice cream at one in the morning? You can see the condensation. I'd estimate it's been out of the freezer about forty-five minutes based on..."

While Connie spouts off mathematical formulas, I shift to the next photo and gasp. Beside me, Miles exhales and his hand shoots out to grip the counter.

It's Simon. Blood spread across the space around his head, so thick and heavy it's nearly impossible to see where the bullet went in. My stomach tosses and turns until I have to look away from the picture. My throat tightens. I hear the jingle of the bell above the shop door before I turn and realize Miles is gone.

With trembling hands, I stuff the photos back into the envelope and then tuck them inside my jacket. "Thanks for this," I manage to say to Connie, who is wide-eyed and worried now.

"God, I'm sorry," she says. "I didn't mean to—"

"It's okay," I assure. "It's just—I mean we were...we

knew Simon..." I point at the door. "I should go check on him."

She nods, not needing any more explanation. I head out the door and pick a direction to head in. I find Miles minutes later, behind a row of stores, pale and leaning over a Dumpster. I touch a hand to his back and he quickly loses balance, swaying. I grip his face with one hand in time to see his eyes roll upward.

I hook an arm around his waist and pull us both down until we're sitting on the ground, leaning against the building. Miles's head falls right into my lap, his eyes closed. My heart picks up, panic engulfing me. He had better fucking wake up, because I sure as hell can't carry him to a hospital.

"Miles..." I give his shoulder a shake, then his cheek a light smack. "Miles!"

He peels his eyes open and rolls onto his back, looking up at me. "I'm sorry," he says.

I sigh with relief. "For what?"

"This." He gestures between his head and my lap. Sweat trickles from his forehead through his dark hair. All the color has drained from his face.

It reminds me of that first day in the secret room when I nearly passed out from not eating enough. "Maybe we should get you something to eat?"

He shakes his head furiously. "Not now."

Okay, I get it. Not after those pictures. He needs a distraction. "So...what else is new?" I ask lamely.

Miles cracks a smile. "My parents will be back in the country in a couple of weeks. They want to meet you."

His parents. As in supersecret agents that we never call supersecret agents out loud. My mouth falls open. They want to meet me? "Why?"

"Relax." Miles slowly sits up; some color has returned

to his face. "It's kind of standard whenever someone becomes aware of their jobs."

"What jobs? I don't know anything about their jobs."

Miles rolls his eyes. "Come on, I know you've guessed enough. And I told them I blew my cover with you."

"Why would you tell them that?" I demand. This is all his fault.

"They're my parents," he says, as if that explains things.

"Does that mean they know why you picked Holden—"

"Some of it," he admits. "They assume I picked Holden to get some closure, learn things I didn't know about Simon, which is basically the truth."

"But not that you wanted to uncover a murderer and avenge Simon's death?"

"Not that," he agrees. "But to my credit, I didn't know that's why I was here, either. Just that I needed to look into it." He shifts topics, probably to avoid another relapse. "So I'll get my parents' schedule and make plans."

I cover my face and groan. "What happens if I say no?"

"It's not a big deal." Miles tugs a hand from my face. "They just need to get to know you better. Since you're in the know about their jobs."

Get to know me better. Comforting thought.

"It will be painless, I promise. Just a little weekend trip. *As friends*. Maybe we'll work in a college visit. Make my parents, Harper, Lawrence, and Ms. Geist happy all at once."

"A whole weekend?" I lean against the brick building and shake my head. "Why not like a dinner meeting. Something simple and in a public place."

"Clearly you have mixed-up information regarding individuals in their profession."

Clearly. Guess I have nothing to worry about. Nothing at all.

Miles pulls himself to his feet, looking much stronger. Then he holds out his hand to help me up. "Coffee on me. Then we've got work to do."

Suspect 1: Justice
    Motive: Taking Simon's spot as #3 in our class
    Suspect 2: Bret
    Motive: Not sure, but sneaky behavior gets him a spot at the top of this list. He's also angry about Dominic keeping secrets from him
    Suspect 3: Dominic
    Motive: Not wanting to be outed, maybe Simon wanted to tell ppl about them and Dominic flipped out? Now known "second-to-last person to see Simon alive"

"If Dominic is a suspect because he was the second-to-last person to see Simon alive, shouldn't we include the last person to see him?"

"You?" Miles says.

I shake my head, guilt already knotting my stomach. "I mean Aidan. If we're making a complete list of any and all suspects, we have to include Aidan."

Miles adds him to the growing list. "Then we need to add any other Secret Service agents on duty or any who have access to the Gilberts' mansion."

"Like that Rider guy," I suggest.

"And Jack," Miles says tentatively, knowing that Jack is the reason we aren't in major trouble right now.

I lift my hands. "So basically everyone is on this list. It

could be anyone. It could be me. Have you listed out my motives yet?"

"Have you listed out mine?" Miles challenges.

No. I haven't. "Well let's see...clearly you were jealous of all his friends at Holden Prep. You were mad that he loved you? I don't know...I got nothing."

In what seems to be an impulsive move, he reaches across the table in the secret room and squeezes my hand. His face flushes, and he tugs his fingers away. "Thank you. I was beginning to question my innocence after all this."

I pick up his pen and write Jack's name down. Under motive, I put: *known liar, good with math/angles.*

"Simon could have known something about Justice. I saw them talking a few times last spring," I add. "And things with her parents are super tense. They seem uptight."

"So yeah, could be freakin' anyone," Miles assesses. "But some definitely stand out more than others, and a few are beginning to connect. We aren't going nowhere anymore."

I draw a line to connect Aidan's and Jack's names, then join Jack's and Ryder's names. Miles connects Jacob to Chantel and Bret since he's the one who told us about Chantel being in Bret's car that night. In fact, Jacob has guided me in a few directions. He could be a mastermind, steering me exactly where he wants me.

I say this to Miles, and he frowns. "Yeah, we better follow that trail a little. I'll work on him."

"And I'll dig into Chantel and Justice some more," I say.

We reach what feels like a good breaking point just in time for Miles to get a text from his dad. He looks up at me, a smile twitching at the corners of his mouth. "Does next weekend work for you?"

"No." I drop my head to the table. "Definitely not."

He laughs in a way that clearly says I'm going to have to make it work. But I think I'd rather face murderers.

CHAPTER
37

Miles's isolated home appears to be out in the middle of nowhere, a little ways outside Baltimore. He's driving Clyde's car, and after three hours on the road, he turns down what looks like a dirt trail. It's a road, I think, but it's hard to tell in the dark. We left right after school today, and now it's nearly eight at night.

There's snow on the ground that fell early last week—the first of the season. I've spent most of my life in the southern part of the country and can't remember the last time I saw snow. We haven't gotten any in Virginia yet, but I've been looking forward to it.

"No wonder you didn't mind tramping through the woods behind the Gilberts' place," I mutter.

Miles laughs but doesn't say anything. The road gets more and more dark until finally I can make out the outline of a small house. It's brick, cottage-like, smoke coming out of the chimney. Windows line the front of the house. The lights are on, and I can see a thin woman with Miles's dark hair moving around the kitchen. My stomach flips with nerves. I wait for him to pull the car in front of the house, and then in a last-minute moment of desperation I shoot Harper a text.

ME: if u don't hear from me in 2 hrs, come find me

HARPER: I said exactly the same thing first time I had to meet Aidan's parents. You'll be fine.

Easy for her to say. Aidan's parents aren't CIA operatives. At least I don't think they are…regardless, if Harper knew that, she wouldn't be laughing at me right now.

ME: Seriously, Harp. 2 hrs

"Ellie?" Miles says.

I stuff my phone away. "Just telling Harper about the snow."

"Ready to go in?"

I look up at him, a grin plastered on my face. "Definitely. Can't wait."

Before we even make it to the front door, it flies open. A tall man with silver-speckled dark hair stands in the doorway, a big grin on his face. "Cari, come and look at this beautiful girl our son has brought home!"

I stop, unable to make myself go any closer. Normally, I'd have the perfect greeting, perfect smile, but I can't do anything but think *CIA agent, CIA agent* over and over inside my head. It shouldn't be this difficult for me, I mean I live with Aidan, but it is different. Aidan knows nearly everything about me and did long before I even met him. I'm gonna have to lie to these people and *CIA agent*…so yeah, it's freaking me out.

The woman from the kitchen window appears beside Mr. Beckett, her smile just as warm as her husband's. "Oh my, look at you…I always knew Miles could snag the prettiest ones."

"Mom," Miles warns. "Ellie is my neighbor or classmate or friend—feel free to use any of those words. But no other nouns, verbs, or adjectives. Remember?"

"Of course," Miles's dad says. "We have excellent memories."

His parents both laugh. Miles just looks at me and rolls his eyes. But seriously? They're Miles but with my sense of humor. Not a good combination.

"It's nice to meet you, Ellie," Mrs. Beckett says, and then she steps outside barefoot and hugs me. I stand there stiff for a second and then work up the nerve to hug her back.

Soon we're ushered into the living room, surrounded by floor-to-ceiling bookshelves and with a blazing fire in the fireplace. The shelves are filled with novels, some very old-looking. But no photos, no personal items at all in the entire living room. Miles shows me to the guest room—a room right off the living room—sets my bag on the queen-size bed, and then opens a door across from the bed.

"Bathroom," he says, leading me inside it. "Towels are in the closet." He opens the closet and then points to another door beside the shower. "That's my room."

I swing my arms, digging for something else to say until we hear Miles's mom shout, "Dinner's ready!"

"The roast is great, Mom," Miles says.

He's already inhaling his dinner before I've even picked up my fork. I study the food on my plate, though much more politely than when I'd assessed Miles's tuna casserole. There's a hunk of beef, some potatoes, and carrots, all covered in a brown gravy. I cut into the meat and it practically falls apart so I'm able to take just a tiny bite.

"I second that," I say. "This is amazing."

Mr. Beckett (Agent Beckett?) returns from the kitchen with an open bottle of wine. He proceeds to pour himself and his wife a glass, then moves on to Miles. Mrs. Beckett stops him from pouring me a glass, and they exchange a look.

"Right," Mr. Beckett says. "We're not related, therefore it would be illegal to provide *you* with alcohol. Which is too bad because this wine complements the roast so well."

I shake my head. "It's fine. I don't need any."

Miles picks up the bottle his dad just set down on the table and fills my glass halfway. "Problem solved."

Worried it's a test, I stare at the glass for several seconds and then back at Miles. He gives a nod, like it's fine. I could definitely use a drink, just to take the edge off my nerves. I lift the glass to my mouth and take a sip. I haven't really had much wine in my life, and what I've had was choked down with great effort. But this one is actually pretty good, less bitter, no aftertaste.

Miles is too busy scarfing down food to talk. His parents take turns sneaking glances at me.

"How long are you home for?" I ask the Becketts.

Mrs. Beckett answers first. "Just until Wednesday, unfortunately. I'm so glad it worked out for you to come this weekend. We may have had to wait months to meet you."

I glance at Miles, but he's staring at his plate. I wish he would have told me this weekend was the only available slot. I figured if I made an excuse, they'd just come after me—I mean invite me—again and again until I went through with it.

"We don't get to do this very often," Mr. Beckett says. "Dinner with friends. As ourselves. Of course, we'd rather keep our circle as small as possible, but if the damage is already done, might as well take advantage of it, right?"

"Usually these dinners are spent discussing our cover jobs," Mrs. Beckett explains. "And of course we don't really do those jobs, so it can feel like we're still on the clock."

I relax a little, take another bite of my dinner. Now I'm jealous that I can't be here as me like they get to do.

"So Miles brings a lot of friends home for you to wine and dine?" I ask.

"Miles hasn't brought anyone here in a very long time," Mr. Beckett says.

A sad look fills his mom's face. "Not since Simon."

I roll a carrot around my plate with the tip of my fork. "We had a class together last semester. Me and Simon. He was really nice."

Mrs. Beckett nods. "That he was."

Silence fills the dining room. Finally, Mr. Beckett raises his glass of wine and says, "To Simon."

Miles raises his glass, so I follow suit. After the toast, I take an extra large gulp of wine—I need it.

"Miles is so shy," his mom says. "He never invited any friends over until middle school. If it weren't for Simon, I don't think he would have made friends at school."

I stifle a laugh. Miles shy? Yeah, right. I'll believe that when…well, pretty much never.

"Mom," Miles warns, shooting her a look from across the table. Then he says something in Chinese that gets her to stop talking.

"Do they teach Mandarin at your school?" I ask Miles.

He nods and swallows the bite he's just taken before talking. "Yeah, but I didn't learn at school."

"He was born in China," his dad explains. "We lived there for six years."

"Did you go to school in China?"

"I didn't go to school until Marshall Academy," Miles says.

Mrs. Beckett adds, "We moved too much—even within the countries we lived in. It was easier to do homeschooling."

"After China, we were in Brazil for two years," his dad recites. "Then down in Texas for a year. Then the Middle East for two years. Miles learned Portuguese, Arabic, Farsi, Urdu, and a little right-wing Texan speak." Mr. Beckett shakes his head. "But we try to forget the Texas part."

"So he was at home with you until nearly twelve years old?" I ask.

"Always," his dad says.

"We never took overnight assignments at the same time," Mrs. Beckett says. "I took leave until Miles was five and then we had—"

"Mr. Lee," Miles says with a grin. "He taught me Chinese, martial arts, and origami."

"We brought him with us everywhere until Miles started at Marshall Academy. He was a fantastic nanny."

Miles looks at me and mouths the word "bodyguard," and now I'm afraid to ask where Mr. Lee is now.

"Enough about us," Mr. Beckett says. "What about you, Ellie? Miles says you live with your sister in Clyde's apartment complex?"

"And Aidan." I swallow another gulp of wine. "Harper's boyfriend."

"The Secret Service agent, right?" Mrs. Beckett asks.

I nod.

"An SS agent saved my life once." Mr. Beckett's forehead wrinkles like he's thinking hard. "Twice actually. Good guys. Department is a little too restrictive for my taste, though."

I look at Miles. "Sounds like the perfect job for you. You like saving people's lives and you love rules."

"That's just the military academy in him," Mr. Beckett assures me. "He'll get more flexible when he leaves."

I wait for Miles to comment, but he doesn't. In fact, he looks like he agrees with them or it's a subject they've discussed in great length.

The topic shifts to school, Holden Prep, and all the college prep they're force-feeding us. Soon I've finished my wine, poured another half glass, and we're feasting on chocolate brownies with ice cream. I even get brave and tell them how I enjoy playing "memory" with Aidan.

"Maybe I can add that to my college applications?" I joke. "Think they'll count it as an EC?"

Mr. Beckett wipes his face with a napkin. "If you ever need a recommendation for any government department or internship, don't hesitate to ask."

"I don't know." My face heats at the mention of me being allowed on the side with the good guys. "Not sure those types of jobs are for me. Plus, I think the guidance counselor has made it her quest to send me to an Ivy League school."

Mrs. Beckett points a finger at Miles. "Let her be a good influence on you."

This time I can't conceal the laughter. I've been nothing but a bad influence on Miles since the moment we met.

"I want Miles to go to Harvard, but he refuses," Mrs. Beckett says. "He's already been admitted, full scholarship."

"Wow." I turn to my friendly neighbor. "Harvard?"

He just shrugs. The way he brushes it off without an explanation, I realize something and look at both his parents. "You don't want him to go into your line of work?"

"We want him to do what he wants to do," Mr. Beckett says. "But no, the CIA wasn't what we hoped for him."

The fact that someone has actually spoken CIA out loud seems to shock only me, but I play it cool.

"You would make a great doctor," Mrs. Beckett says to Miles. "Remember how you performed surgery on your stuffed dinosaur? And you rescued those birds that kept hitting our window in Brazil. Or what about teaching?

Professor Beckett. Nice ring to it."

Miles stands and begins collecting plates. When he takes his mom's dessert plate, he plants a kiss on the top of her head and I swear I hear him say, *I love you.* Really quiet.

My impression of Miles has just been shattered. He's not some machine born and bred to become a government agent. His parents don't even want that for him. He wants it all on his own.

After dinner, Mr. Beckett sends his wife to their bedroom to "take a well-deserved hot bath for all her efforts preparing dinner," and then he pokes at the living room fire and shortly after, asks Miles to get some more wood outside.

I'm already squirming in my armchair, knowing that Mr. Beckett (Agent Beckett?) just orchestrated a private conversation with me. Dinner had been too nice, too relaxed. I should have known things would turn.

He's sitting on the ledge in front of the fireplace staring at the dying flames. But the second the door closes behind Miles, Mr. Beckett turns to me and lowers his voice. "My son tells me you're a smart young lady?"

I think this is the part where the controlling father orders me to stay away from his son, *if I know what's good for me.* I clear my throat. "Why do you ask?"

He pulls a tiny scrap of paper from his shirt pocket along with a pen and jots something down. He gives a quick glance out the window at Miles, tramping through the snow, then turns back to me. "I need you to memorize this number. You can't ever write it down or program it into your phone, understood?"

The urgency in his voice has me shoving away any questions and instead, I watch while he flips the scrap of paper around for me to read. I stare at the number, recite it five times in my head before nodding.

"There's a pass code, too. Miles says your German is good?" he asks, and I nod again. "Die Zukunft gehört denen, die an die Schönheit ihrer Träume glauben."

The future belongs to those who believe in the beauty of their dreams.

"Eleanor Roosevelt said that."

Mr. Beckett nods slowly, assessing me. "Figured it might be easier for you to remember the words of a fellow Eleanor."

This all seems so dark and desperate. I'm not sure what's going on. "Are you anticipating my need for help from the CIA in the near future?"

"I hope not," he says. "Miles didn't want me to do this. Thought it might scare you. But truthfully, we're putting your life at risk by bringing you into our world. The least I can do is offer you some insurance plan. Just in case."

Okay, so he's cautious. That makes sense.

"And let Miles teach you some basic self-defense, okay? It would put some of my and my wife's worries to rest. And it's something everyone should know, in my opinion."

The front door opens and Mr. Beckett smoothly tosses the scrap of paper with the secret emergency number into the fire. It's dissolved into the flames before Miles even reaches the living room. I repeat the number again, testing myself. I glance at Miles, checking to see if he suspects anything, but if he does, he hides it well.

Later, when we bump into each other on the way to the bathroom before bed, I stop Miles from heading back to his room. "I can't believe you have your parents fooled."

His eyes widen. "About what?"

"You being shy." I lean against the doorframe, blocking his exit. "You're the opposite of shy."

He seems to deliberate for a minute, then says, "Now I am."

"And before?"

"I guess it's easier to shed that part of me, starting in a new place where no one knows me, especially with the job I'm doing," he says. "We're all a little more bold in costume."

I look up at him, trying not to seem disappointed. If he's really shy, then that's the Miles I want to know. "So it's all part of being undercover?"

He shuffles closer until only six inches separate us. "That's the thing…I'm not sure it's an act anymore. Maybe I was covered up before and this is the real me, or close to it. Maybe the labels we give ourselves early on hold us back from seeing what's really there."

I'm still standing there, mulling that over, when Miles brushes past me, whispering, "Good night, Ellie."

Just the sound of my name rolling off his tongue gets my heart racing. And he knows it. And he knows that I know he knows. I laugh all the way to the guest room.

Shy my ass.

CHAPTER

38

I wake up to voices outside the door. Light barely peeks in the guest room window. I try to close my eyes and fall back asleep, but the conversation grows louder, more clear.

"If the assignment was for you to help the FBI track the drug dealer, then why do they need you purchasing from this Davey guy?"

Mrs. Beckett.

"The drug sample," Miles says.

The sound of dishes clanking makes it impossible for me to hear his mom's response.

"I'm not sure how many people have bought the drug off him, but probably enough to keep him from pointing a finger at me. Besides, no one is making a move on Davey or his supplier until I'm back at Marshall Academy. I've still got more intel to gather."

"Intel to gather, huh?" Mrs. Beckett says. "I thought this was supposed to be a learning experience for you. Seems like the FBI is getting greedy for progress. Greedy enough to take advantage of children."

Yeah, that's definitely possible.

"Remember, everything goes through my handler,"

Miles says. "No one in the FBI knows which of Davey's seven or eight preferred schools I'm operating from. Or anything about me, for that matter."

"Do they know you're a highly trained student with security clearance? Seems like they're treating you like some disposable informant."

Disposable informant. Like me.

"Relax, Mom. I'm withholding most of my data until the end of the semester. And they're too greedy to settle for simply arresting Davey. They'll want to nail his boss, too, and the entire operation. You know the Feds love their big media shows."

Mrs. Beckett gives a *hmph* of agreement.

"They might want to nail the Holden kids, too. Take down a school drug ring. And I'm the one with names. Without me, they have nothing, and they know it."

The kids from school? Does that mean he's turning in Bret and Dominic to the FBI? For buying weed and ecstasy from Davey? Justice and Jacob both told me they've bought weed and E from Davey before. Will they get turned in to the FBI, too?

God, I can't think about this right now.

I don't want to think about it.

I shove the covers back and leave the room. The second I step into the hall, the conversation in the kitchen ends. I glance at the microwave clock. It's six thirty. Mrs. Beckett is wearing a robe, but Miles is dressed already, with sweat stains on his shirt. He must have gone for a run.

Miles's mom turns to me, a big smile on her face. "Morning, Ellie. How did you sleep?"

"Good, thanks."

Miles grabs an apple from the fruit basket and bites into it. "You mind if I shower first? Or do you need the bathroom?"

"Go ahead," I offer. It all feels so polite and formal. I'm not used to that with Miles.

But when he brushes past me, a wicked grin on his face, he leans close to whisper, "I'll leave the inside door unlocked. In case you need something."

My face heats up, probably turns beet red. I give him a shove, and he retreats to the bathroom. When I look back at Mrs. Beckett, her eyebrows are lifted. She heard that. Of course she did.

"Coffee?" she asks.

I hide my face with my hair. "No, thanks."

"Juice? Water?" she adds, anything to change the subject.

"Sure." I take a seat at the small table in the kitchen. "Juice sounds great."

Soon we're seated together, me with a big glass of orange juice and Mrs. Beckett with a mug of coffee. She watches me for a minute or so and then finally speaks. "Miles and Simon were close. Did he tell you that?"

She emphasizes the word "close." She's feeling out the situation.

"He told me."

"When Simon didn't get into the honors program, Miles was devastated. I don't think it ever occurred to him that one of them might not make it into the program. I thought he'd drop out of Marshall Academy." She looks down at her coffee, hiding a sheepish grin. "Okay, I hoped he would leave school and come to Switzerland with us. But one day, in the middle of the summer, after moping around for weeks, he put on his sneakers, went for a run, and told me he had a lot of work to do before September."

"That sounds like Miles," I say, because it does. His reaction when we looked at those pictures...and then an hour later, he was back to putting clues together, thinking, analyzing.

"And then last June when he heard the news, I thought he'd never try to make friends again. Until he met you. Anyone smart enough to force Miles to blow his cover is a perfect match for my son." She smiles at me. "And now he seems to have some balance in his life. The void that's been around for two years seems to be filled."

I don't know if you could call what Miles and I have been doing anything close to finding balance. Balance between make-out sessions and homicide investigations? Balance between breaking and entering and druggie parties with the rich Holden A-listers? And it's temporary. How is that balance? All I can offer her is a weak smile.

She reaches across the table and pats my hand. "I know, I know. You're just friends. Miles is leaving after the semester ends. It's not meant to be."

Then she rolls her eyes as if to say, *yeah right.* And for a second, I wish with every ounce of me that her perception of us was the reality. It sounds so simple, just the distance and the separate schools being our only obstacle. Not the fact that Miles would hate me if he really knew me. And I don't think he's the type of guy to be with someone and not know them inside and out. It's probably good that he's leaving. That he doesn't want to take anything from Holden with him, physically or emotionally.

"Probably isn't meant to be…" I look down at the table. "I'm pretty good at disappointing Miles. I've done it quite a few times."

"Just because he has high expectations doesn't mean you're not important to him. If you don't believe me, just compare his relationship with you to how it is between him and the other Holden kids," she says. "He's different with you. He's real with you, right?"

I don't know what to say. He *is* different with me. He accepts Dominic's and Bret's screwups because they're part of his job and he has to. But with me, he calls me out on it. That makes me a real friend?

The bathroom door opens, and Mrs. Beckett pushes her chair back and stands. "Time for me to make breakfast."

Miles reappears in the kitchen and leans on the back of my chair. "I wanna show you something outside."

"Out there?" I point at the window. "In the cold? And the snow?"

He laughs. "Don't be a baby."

I look down at my pajama pants and thermal. "I'm not dressed. Or showered."

"You can do that later."

Miles produces a pair of wool socks, some winter boots that are only a little big on me, and a ski jacket. I have no excuse but to follow him outside. Soon we're tramping through the snow, the sun now higher in the sky, brighter.

"Miles Beckett, the wilderness guide," I say as we move through the woods, far from the house. "You look good out here."

He flashes me a grin but doesn't protest or give one of his smooth replies. Instead he picks up his pace, and I have to practically jog to keep up with him.

Just before my fingers and toes are frozen, we reach a creek that flows through the woods. In front of the creek is a wooden fort.

Miles gestures for me to enter first. I duck down and soon I'm free of the cold wind. Miles heads straight for a large wooden box, built into the fort. He punches the code on the outside and flings the top open. I look in and survey the contents—pillows, a propane heater, a camp stove, a container of marshmallows, and several books.

"These are probably stale." Miles lifts the marshmallows from the box. Before I can stop him he rips the lid off the container and shoves one in my mouth. "But you can test them out."

I chew the marshmallow slowly. It's hard to tell if it's stale or just cold. "I've had worse." Miles sets up the heater and soon I'm warming my hands over it. "Did your dad build this for you?"

"I built it," he says. "While my parents were working on the big house, I wanted to make my own. Took me a whole summer."

Not hard to imagine eleven-year-old Miles out here, hammering wood pieces together, mimicking whatever his dad was doing.

"So…" He leans against one of the pillows from the box and looks at me. "What did my dad talk to you about last night?"

Guess I wasn't the only one thinking Mr. Beckett lacked subtlety. Still I feel obligated to keep it a secret. Most of it, anyway. "He wants me to let you teach me some self-defense, and I told him I would."

"Really?" he asks, and I nod. "Good."

"Good," I repeat, staring at his mouth. It's right here. So close. Before we arrived yesterday, I still longed for another time-out from our non-relationship, another moment of enjoyment like we'd had that night at the dance. After getting this window into Miles's life through his family, I want it even more. But at the same time, it feels more dangerous, more risky. More real.

I scoot away from him and head for the wood box. "Let's see these genius books young Miles read."

"Smart move," I tell Mr. Beckett after he lifts his rook, hovering it over a black square.

He looks up at me, narrows his eyes. "You've got quite a game, young lady."

Mrs. Beckett laughs from her spot on the couch. "And not just her chess game."

"Well, she did manage to plant a tracker on a big drug dealer," Mr. Beckett says. "I should have known what I was getting into."

Jesus. He really does tell his parents everything. Weird.

"Wait…" I say. "He actually admitted I did the job for him? Miles…is this true?" I glance over my shoulder at the empty chair where he'd been seated, watching the chess match.

"He went out for more firewood," Mrs. Beckett says. She glances at the clock above the fireplace. "That was seventeen minutes ago."

"Maybe he decided to chop some of the larger pieces," Mr. Beckett says.

"I haven't heard any chopping."

Both parents spring to their feet and head straight for the living room window. Mr. Beckett sighs with relief. "The lights are on in the guesthouse."

"You have a guest house?" I join them at the window.

"We use it mostly as a training room," Mrs. Beckett explains. She looks more closely at the small building behind the house, and her forehead creases. She turns to her husband. "Maybe you should go talk to him."

My stomach twists with knots. It's been such a relaxing day, but I've noticed a cloud beginning to drift over Miles the past few hours. I reach for the borrowed coat on the back of my chair. I might have a better idea what's bothering him.

"Let me go," I offer. I'm sliding on boots before either of them can object.

CHAPTER
39

The "guesthouse" is unlocked. I walk quietly inside, but there's no point in tiptoeing because the sound of Miles, kicking the punching bag hanging from the ceiling, is so loud it echoes off the walls. The only thing homey about this guesthouse is the fireplace. There's a kitchen in one corner and a couch shoved up against a wall, and blue exercise mats cover nearly the entire surface of fluffy white carpet.

The punching bag Miles is currently murdering hangs in the far corner. Miles lays another kick into it. Sweat trickles down his forehead. I jump when he kicks the bag again. It's so loud the house vibrates.

"Dominic won't give me anything. Won't even hint at him and Simon. Keeps making up lies to cover everything." Another kick, this time with the left foot. "Never mentions the psycho that's harassing him, and if I ask him about it, my cover's blown and I risk ruining everything...damn, this fucking sucks—"

He's on the verge of exploding or a breakdown. I grab the swinging bag and wrap my arms around it. "Enough. Before you break a bone."

He lowers his leg to the floor, but tension still ripples over him. "My parents send you out here?"

"I volunteered. But they looked worried." I release the bag and step in front of it. "Why don't you just tell them? Tell them what we're doing. That the FBI doesn't seem concerned with new information. They could probably help."

"I want to." Miles lifts his T-shirt and wipes his forehead with it, giving me a nice view of his abs. "But they seem so happy that I'm doing well. I hate ruining that."

"What about your handler? Can you talk to him or her confidentially?"

"That's who I told." He looks poised to start attacking the bag again, but then seems to notice me. All of me. "No shoes in the guest house. Mr. Lee's rule."

I bend over to pull the boots off my feet. "And where is Mr. Lee?"

"In Miami," Miles says. "Living the retired man's dream. He visits sometimes, though, and checks the mats for shoe prints. This used to be his place."

I unzip my coat and toss it beside the boots. The few seconds of silence is enough to set Miles back on the "beat the hell out of something" plan. I step between him and the punching bag. "You're right. The Dominic situation is infuriating. Knowing he can tell us exactly when Simon left his house, what state of mind he was in, what their parting words were... He's got it on lockdown, so much that he must be willing to risk everything to hold those secrets. Even the truth about Simon. I can't imagine how that's making you feel, but maybe giving your mind a rest, getting away from it all, will give you perspective. You just have to let it go. For now."

"Right." He exhales, looks away from the bag. "Theory of incubation."

"Exactly." I smile, relieved he's always so easy to reason with, even when he reaches such high boiling points. "Your parents are home, and everything we do this weekend is giving that part of your brain a rest and making room for the perfect solution."

"Everything we do," he repeats, giving me a look that warms my insides. "Like your self-defense lessons."

Not exactly where I thought he would head with that. "Why do you want me to learn self-defense? Obviously your dad has his reasons, but you seem to agree…? In case you haven't noticed, I'm pretty good at talking my way out of things. Probably better than I'll be at fighting anyone."

"Davey," Miles says. "That's why. He saw you, knows what you look like, knows where you live. I should have never—"

"You didn't mean for that to happen," I tell him.

"My dad said the same thing." Miles gives me a tiny smile, but it vanishes quickly. "But it did happen. And you—you're so…you're just…I'm…"

"Speechless?" I tease. "What happened to the guy who practically invited me into the shower this morning?"

He breaks out of his funk and rolls his eyes. "Come on, let's get started with your first lesson."

I look down at my sweater and leggings. "I left my ninja girl costume at home. What would Mr. Lee think?"

Miles finds that wicked grin and flashes it at me again. "He'd tell you to ditch the sweater."

"And he's back." I shove him. "Mr. Lee sounds like a dirty old man."

But since I have a tank top on underneath, I follow orders and ditch the sweater.

"Okay," Miles says, standing in front of me. "Show me your best kick."

"You want me to kick you?" This is never a method I'd

use to get my way. "Where? In the balls?"

Miles winces. "Preferably not."

I have no idea what I'm doing, but I lift my leg anyway, thrusting it at him. My foot ends up in his hand. He lifts it just enough to flip me flat on my back. I land with a thud, the wind knocked out of me. "Yeah…no…I don't like this game."

"I'm not going easy on you because you're a girl." He shrugs but at least offers me a hand. "I fight girls at my school all the time."

Unfortunately for me, I have a competitive streak. One that makes me want to beat these girls who get to roll around on the mats with Miles.

Once I'm back on my feet again, Miles says, "Try punching me."

I shake out my arms and wait until he's not expecting it and swing my right fist at him. He catches it easily, just like he'd done with my foot. With a quick turn of my wrist, I'm facing outward, my back pressed to his front.

"I'm beginning to think you're setting me up for something." I attempt to break free, but his hold on me is too tight. "What's the point of this?"

"The point," he says, his mouth right beside my ear, "is that you're overconfident sometimes."

I elbow his side, but his grip doesn't loosen. "And you want to put me in my place. Thanks for that."

"I need you to be afraid," Miles says, so intense his voice sends a chill up my spine. "I saw you that day with Davey, when he got close to you, when he looked at your earring. You were afraid. Right now, I want you to imagine that moment again, but this time imagine you're alone. No Dominic, no me. No Harper keeping an eye on you from the window."

My heart races, my breaths coming quicker.

"Good," Miles says, obviously reading my body language. "Imagine you're walking somewhere, in the dark, and you get that feeling like you're not alone. A guy like Davey...he'd corner you alone, try to talk to you first, and then he'd make a move..."

My body tenses, but I force myself to listen to him, let him keep scaring me. I don't want him to think I can't handle this. But maybe he's right—maybe I can't.

As if reading my mind, Miles says, "You can handle him. I can teach you how. But no playing around, no jokes in the training room, wherever that ends up being. You have to focus. You have to trust me. Can you do that?"

The way he's talking to me, the emotion in his voice... Outside of Harper and Aidan, I don't think anyone has ever cared this much about me. Not even my own parents.

I squeeze my eyes shut and lean into the arms holding me so firmly. It isn't fair that I can't be this person he thinks I am. This person his parents seem to think I am.

"Miles?" My voice shakes, but I still plunge forward. "Why haven't you asked me about my family?"

He's known for a long time that the story about my dad kicking me out wasn't true, so why hasn't he asked about them? Does he suspect something bad and doesn't want to ruin whatever this thing is that we have?

Miles releases me and turns me to face him. He leans against the back of the couch. "Lawrence asked me not to."

I stare at him, bewildered by this. "And you just listened without question?"

"He said it was important. Why wouldn't I take that seriously?"

The weight pressing on my chest grows even heavier. "I don't know, maybe because it's human nature to want to dig for the truth." Isn't that what we were doing with Simon?

"I agree." His fingers land on my hip, and he tugs me closer. "But your parents' truth isn't yours, Ellie."

Then ask me mine. Please just ask and I'll have to tell

you. I can't lie to your face anymore. And then this will all be over. I close my eyes again, shutting down those thoughts. "Miles?"

He pulls me gently until I'm standing between his legs. "Yeah?"

I almost say what's inside my head, but quickly realize that I don't want it to be over. Any of it. I don't want him to hate me.

Instead I say, "Do I still drive you crazy?"

I open my eyes in time to see his reaction, feel his fingers tighten on my waist.

He touches his forehead to mine. "Every. Damn. Second."

My chest rises and falls more rapidly; my hands are shaking from all the emotion, from wanting this so much. I lift both my hands to his face. "I know the feeling."

"What if…" His lips hover over mine. "Another time-out. Just for the weekend? We can turn back into pumpkins when we get back to Virginia."

That's what it's like for me, when we do this thing where we let go and just be…I feel like a statue coming to life. I look at him and draw in a deep breath. He's got those warm, kind eyes trained on me, promising some not-so-good behavior. What is it with the Ames sisters and our habit of falling for these saintlike guys?

I lean in and let my mouth touch his. Warmth spreads over me; my lips linger on his, barely moving, just soaking it up. Miles sighs against my mouth, and then he pulls away too soon. He releases me and strides across the room, turning the dial on the wall to dim the lights. Before I can ask questions, I'm in his arms again, his face buried against my neck.

"Binoculars," he whispers. "My parents have them right by the window. For bird-watching. Figured you might prefer privacy."

He lifts me up off the ground, and suddenly I'm perched

on the back of the couch where he'd been moments ago. His fingers find the hem of my tank top and sink beneath it, pulling the material up.

My stomach flutters with nerves, but I force out a laugh. "So you are trying to get me naked in Mr. Lee's room? I might ask for a refund if this is how you teach self-defense."

I expect him to offer up one of his smooth lines, but instead, his hands come out from under my shirt. He tugs the material back in place. Even in the dark I can make out the creases in his forehead. "Don't do that, Ellie."

"Do what?" I ask, suddenly self-conscious.

He slides closer, pulling my legs around his back. "Don't be that girl. The one who seduced Bret and let Davey stare at her ass. I know that's not really you."

My throat tightens.

"You're allowed to be nervous," Miles says. "I am. And I don't want to pretend I'm not scared of this. Or of you. And me."

Any girl would be an idiot not to fall in love with Miles. He's everything I don't deserve. Fortunately for me, I have a long history of taking things that aren't mine. I tighten my arms around his neck and hide my face.

"I know I seemed experienced around the Holden A-crowd, but I haven't really done much of this," he whispers.

I lift my head and look at him.

"I don't want to pretend to be cool with you, okay? My mom was right, I am shy," he admits. "And I never wanted to—I just—" The smoldering look he gives me sends my heart flying out of my chest. "I never wanted someone so much that I could ditch that part of myself."

Somewhere outside of the puddle I've just melted into, I realize what he's trying to tell me. I bring his mouth to mine. "Okay, I get it. No more artificially cool Ellie. Want to be done talking now?"

"God yes," he says against my lips. He grips my face with one hand and deepens the kiss, his tongue slipping into my mouth. He kisses me for an eternity, finally having time and space to slow down and savor every second.

But eventually I pull away and nudge Miles back a few inches so I can get a good look at him. I push my hands beneath his T-shirt and shove it up and over his head. I've seen him shirtless too many times to count, but I've never really had the chance to touch him like this. My hands roam from his shoulders down his arms. He watches me the whole time, his gaze heavy, intense.

Just to make things even, I finish the job he started a few minutes ago by removing my tank top. Miles immediately steps closer.

"Under the circumstances…" I tell him. "I won't yell at you for checking out my boobs."

In one quick motion, he picks me up and tosses me over his shoulder. "Just for that, we might have to take a walk outside."

But instead of opening the door, he sets me on the floor and then drops down beside me. I'm about to throw some choice words at him for tossing me around like a sack of potatoes, but all those words get stuck the moment his gaze sweeps over me. And for a second, I can see what his mom was talking about when she painted this picture of a shy, slightly sheltered Miles, combined with curiosity that drives an eleven-year-old boy to learn construction by building his own fort in the woods.

Miles is a hands-on learner.

He's still staring at me, maybe searching my face for any hesitation. "Are you cold? I can build a fire…"

I reach up and bring his face closer to mine. "Later."

CHAPTER
40

Miles gives one last poke to the large flames bursting from the fireplace. He tosses a thick blanket over me and sits behind me, pulling me against his bare chest.

I shiver. "Why is it so cold in here?"

"I offered to build a fire an hour ago," Miles says.

"Yeah, well, I was distracted." By sixty minutes of amazingly hot kisses that masked the cold room.

He tucks the blanket tighter around us so no air can sneak in, and then his lips are on my neck, planting kisses in a neat row. I rest my head on Miles's shoulder and close my eyes.

"I could get used to this," I say. "Going home is overrated."

"Me, too." Miles slides my bra strap over and kisses my bare shoulder. "Except I *am* home."

Heat quickly fills the space beneath the blanket, and soon I'm plenty warm. Warm enough to begin thinking about what else Miles and I could do here alone, beyond the marathon shirtless kissing we already engaged in. As if reading my mind, his fingers land lightly on my stomach and begin to drift south. I uncross my legs and then freak out about it. Do I really want his hand there? I think so.

Miles, whose body language interpretation skills are too good for his own good, stops his hand, then moves it again, then stops a second time. I try to play it cool, but I start laughing. And shortly after, Miles joins me.

"I think you just defined mixed signals," he says.

I laugh harder. "To myself as well."

His arm stretches across my midsection until his fingers are wrapped around my side. "Yeah, just gonna leave it here for now."

"You know what would help right now?" I turn my head to look up at him.

"The rest of that bottle of wine from dinner?" he suggests.

"Well, yeah." I brave pulling a hand from beneath the blanket and rest it on his cheek. "But I was gonna say it would help if you let me channel my badass overconfident self. *She'd* tell you exactly where to put your hands."

"You mean she'd know what she wanted me to do," he corrects. "As opposed to you, who aren't sure?" I drop my hand and turn to face the fire again. "I think I'll take my chances with you. Indecisiveness is kinda hot."

"No, it's not." I sigh. Why am I so weird like this? As me. And how is he so good at this? Doing it, talking about it. Maybe I misunderstood him earlier. "Since you said that you haven't done this much, I take it that means—unless you meant that you haven't done that much but you still have done it...at least once? That would make more sense. Or maybe more than once...?"

Miles interrupts my painful stammering by laughing. His chest vibrates against me. "Jesus, Ellie. I'm seventeen, not forty. You make it sound like inexperience at our age is an oddity. I won't quote you statistics, but I'm in the majority."

"Maybe it's just odd to me." I bring my knees to my chest and hug them. "I was fifteen. Guess that puts me in the minority."

He's quiet for a long time, too long. I shouldn't have told him. It had seemed more fact than personal until it sat right between us.

"I was almost sixteen," I add.

"You're right. It's different for everyone. Fifteen isn't that young." Miles turns me around to face him. "But no, I haven't done that before. Or yet. However you want to look at it."

And now I have to assume the topless girl tossing clothes from Miles balcony wasn't what it had looked like.

I scoot forward enough to kiss him. The blanket falls to the floor, and I'm pulled onto Miles's lap, my arms around his neck, his hands in my hair, on my back, pressing us together. He unclasps my bra, slides the straps down my shoulders, and eventually separates us enough to toss the thing aside.

My knees rest on the blue mats on either side of Miles and I'm half tempted to push him until he falls backward and then crawl on top of him. His mouth travels from my cheek to my chest and then back up again until his eyes meet mine.

"I meant what I said that night at the dance," Miles tells me. "Anything you want, Ellie."

I tighten my arms around his neck, let my lips touch below his ear, his collarbone. "I just want this—you close to me—for now."

His arms wrap around me, squeezing me tight. His hand moves through my hair. "I don't think that other Ellie would let me hold her like this."

"No," I agree. "She wouldn't."

...

Sunlight streams into the guesthouse, making it look completely different than it had last night—more training room, less romantic getaway. Except it still feels romantic. Especially with my head resting against Miles's chest, counting his heartbeats while he sleeps. His arm is wrapped around me, a blanket covering us. I'm about to close my eyes and fall back asleep, but something crashes against the window. Miles jolts upright from beneath me, his eyes darting around the room, searching for a threat.

We both spot the wet circle on the clear glass window at the same time. Another white ball hits the window in the same spot. Miles looks at me, a smile playing on his lips. "My parents."

"They're throwing snowballs at the window?" My face warms and I crawl on all fours, scrambling to retrieve articles of clothing and toss them on. I make a grab for my sweater but Miles snatches it and slides it out of my reach. "Hey, I need that!"

"Relax," he says. "They're just messing with me."

I'm about to tackle him for my sweater, but then I glance out the window and see Mr. and Mrs. Beckett walking away from the guesthouse hand in hand, toward the woods. "Where are they going?"

"A walk probably." Miles shrugs. "Or target practice."

I choke down the image of his parents armed. "Romantic."

Miles jumps to his feet and holds out a hand for me. "Come on, we have work to do."

"Work?"

He nods. "For real this time."

"Wait, so last night… That wasn't a self-defense lesson?"

"No." He tries to looks serious but cracks a smile. Then he grips my waist, tugs me closer, and kisses me. But it's over before I even have a chance to really enjoy it. "Enough of that. No more joking. No more kissing."

Normally, I would keep pushing him, but his tone combined with the scary scenario he painted last night stops me. Instead, I give a quick nod and commit myself to doing everything he tells me, minus the snark.

Soon I'm drenched in sweat, bruises forming in various locations on my body. But I get why Miles wants me to do this, why his dad wants me to. There's satisfaction in taking control. That part isn't new for me; only the kicking and punching are new.

CHAPTER

41

I shift in the passenger seat and groan when pain radiates from muscles I've probably never used before. "What did you do to me, Beckett?"

Miles grins, but there's a hint of sympathy on his face, maybe a little guilt. *Good.* "You'll be fine. Tonight's lesson will loosen you up again."

Tonight's lesson? God no. But since I've committed myself to trust Miles, at least in this one area, I bite back my retort. We've just made our way around D.C. and aren't far from home now. "How long before you see your parents again?"

"Christmas, hopefully," he says, his eyes on the road.

"That's right." I recall the phone conversation Miles had with his dad the night of the dance. "In Turkey."

"Only if I learn Turkish, and I doubt I'll have time. Kind of got a lot on my plate at the moment."

"Like gathering names of druggies for the FBI." Yeah, so I haven't committed myself to ending all snark between us.

His hands tighten on the steering wheel. "No more worrying about my schoolwork. I'm number three in my class. I didn't get there by being an idiot."

No, I sigh to myself. *You got there by following the rules—taking names and numbers and handing them over to the proper channels.*

I lean my head back against the seat and stare out the window. I can't shake the image of the FBI hauling Justice and Dominic out of the school in handcuffs. And then there's Bret, who does have a conning secret side, but he probably deserves jail about as much as I do. Or Uncle Clyde, for that matter. So who am I to judge him? Then again, why should it matter to me what happens to any of them? Hadn't I set out to take Bret, Dominic, and his circle down for Simon's sake?

Except every time I try not to care, I replay the conversations I've had with Justice, the ones where she came to life, working so hard to make my room beautiful for no cost. And all the online chats I read between Simon and Dominic, all the dirty looks Dominic's given me since school started back in August—grief masked as hate. I used to think of the kids at Holden as an alien species—a culture I needed to learn and mimic in order to infiltrate. But now I'm not so sure we're that different.

Miles reaches for my hand, lacing his fingers through mine, sending a jolt through my body. How are we supposed to go back to being platonic partners? My face warms and my heart flutters just thinking about last night, about his skin against mine. I suppress a shiver. It wasn't just a hot make-out session this time. He told me things; he looked at me and saw me. It's not easy to go backward after that.

And I feel like I really helped him through things last night. He was overwhelmed, needed someone to vent to, to put things in perspective. It's hard not to obsess over the details of Simon's death. Especially after the photos and Connie's mentions of the angle of the weapon, the ice cream—

"Oh my God!" I shout.

Miles jumps; his foot shifts to slam on the brake. "What?"

"Oh my God," I say again, quieter this time. "The ice cream—"

"Ice cream?"

"Pull over!" Okay, this is the part of the story where we die in a car crash, the important piece of a giant puzzle dying with me. I draw in a breath and speak in the calmest voice possible. "I mean pull over at your convenience. In a safe location. Everything is fine."

Miles nods, his eyes on the road. But tension rolls over him in giant waves. Luckily, there's a rest area three miles down the road and soon we're parked in front of a picnic table.

"The ice cream," I repeat, urgent this time. "In the crime scene photo." God I wish I had the damn thing with me. I was too afraid to bring the stolen police report into the home of CIA operatives. Miles has it locked up in the secret room.

His forehead wrinkles. "What about it?"

"There was a spoon on top of the carton," I recall, pulling the image back to my frontal lobe. "And another one on the table beside the carton." I study Miles, waiting for it to click, but the wrinkles stay on his forehead. "Think about it…we know the DeLucas—Dominic's parents— were home the night Simon died. We know the Gilberts were not home. And we know Bret Thomas followed Simon to Dominic's house, watched them make out and then drove off—"

"Bret never saw them go inside," Miles mutters. "Simon's car was still running…"

"And there were two spoons for that tub of ice cream at the Gilberts' later on that night," I conclude. "Simon probably invited him over since no one was home at his house. Got ice cream for them. Maybe he showed him his gun. Maybe they had a fight and things got out of control."

"Jesus Christ." Miles's eyes are wide now, his knuckles white from gripping the steering wheel. "Dominic broke into their house. His prints were there when we dusted, but not mentioned in the police report."

"And if Simon brought him back to the Gilberts' place that night then that explains why Dominic knew how to get in the house." I add, "He could have watched him punch the alarm code, maybe they dodged the security cameras. Definitely not hard to do, especially for someone who lives there."

"He didn't go back there looking for a killer." Miles's jaw clenches. "He went back to cover his tracks."

Those final words fill the empty space in Uncle Clyde's car. Both of us sit in silence, breathing hard from the adrenaline rush. Finally, Miles strings several swear words together and shakes his head. "I really didn't think it was him. Dammit."

Me freakin' either.

For several seconds, Miles looks lost, unable to move, but then he straightens in his seat and turns to me, speaking firmly, "Seat belt."

The moment my seat belt clicks back into place, he throws the car in reverse, then quickly shifts, speeding forward onto the interstate. I grip the door handle. "I take it you have a plan?"

He nods.

"Does it involve showing up at Dominic's? Because I'm not sure killing him will—"

"We're only about twenty minutes from the FBI field

office," Miles says.

"What?" My stomach flips and flops even more than it had while declaring Dominic DeLuca a murder suspect. "No, we can't—"

I take one look at Miles and stop talking. There's no way I'm reasoning with him on this one. No way he'll change his mind, which means I have twenty minutes to decide if I'm gonna tell him why I'm really not excited about walking into an FBI office. Or jump out of a moving car.

Aidan once told me that the FBI's biggest flaw is its lack of a clear method of sharing intelligence between field offices. And it proved true when I was interviewed after Simon's death. Twice. No one here knew me. Agent Sheldon's office is hours away.

By the time Miles is pulling off the highway and circling the local field office lot for a parking spot, my worries have shifted from concern for the security of my own secrets to Miles's.

Before he hops out of the car, I grab his shirtsleeve and wait for him to turn toward me. "We can't go in there without a plan. A good plan."

"We don't need a plan, we're handing over information. That's all."

I grip his sleeve tighter. "You can't become another Kathleen French. I'm not ready for you to disappear yet."

"Ellie…" Sympathy fills his face. "It'll be okay."

Unfortunately, my trust issues prevent me from accepting that BS. "There has to be a way to tell them our theory about Simon without blowing your cover. Isn't that the number one rule of the McCone honors program? Doing everything in your power to protect the program's mission, which I believe is to remain covert, correct?"

"You're not going in there by yourself," he says firmly.

Damn. There goes plan A. "Okay, we're both going in. Just give me a minute to think."

He looks skeptical, but nods. "One minute."

"Both of you saw these photos?" Agent Riley asks. He's been listening to us talk for at least twenty minutes with barely any interruption.

Miles and I glance at each other, and then Miles clears his throat. "No. I didn't see them."

Good boy.

"I'm new at Holden so I don't really know much about the case," he continues, and I flinch internally at his use of the word "case." Clueless bystanders wouldn't have stated it that way. "Except the research I did for my sociology project. I'm kind of a true-crime nerd." He whips out a tiny spiral notebook from his shirt pocket and flips to a blank page. "Maybe when Ellie's done with her thing, I could ask you a few questions about evidence?"

There you go. Five recovery points for the rookie.

"So just you, Eleanor?" Agent Riley asks, and I nod. "And who showed you the photos?"

The door to the interview room opens and another agent, a woman, takes a seat beside Riley but says nothing.

"Um..." My gaze bounces between the two agents. "I don't know his name. Some freshman...Donnie, maybe?"

"I thought you said Joey?" Miles argues. "I could have sworn—"

"Dark hair, I think?" I say, interrupting Miles.

"The kid you pointed out in the hall was definitely blond," Miles states.

The female agent who just entered the room holds her hands up, stopping both of us. "Okay, so the crime scene photos are floating around Holden Prep and you're not sure who had them first, is that right?"

I give her a satisfied nod. "Exactly."

"And the Thomas kid told you that he saw Simon and Dominic DeLuca"—Agent Riley shifts in his chair—"physically involved the night Simon committed suicide."

"Allegedly," Miles corrects. When Riley lifts an eyebrow he adds, "Allegedly a suicide."

"Yes," I say. "Bret told me that."

"And Dominic DeLuca admitted to being harassed"— Riley glances at his notepad in front of him—"with photos of the incident the Thomas boy witnessed from the all eyes on you email address."

Miles scratches the back of his head. "Yeah, so he was kind of drunk when he told me that. Not me, though, I wasn't drinking. Doubt he'll come clean about it to you guys, but I saw the picture. He got up to pee, and I forwarded one of the emails to myself."

He pulls out his phone, gets Agent Riley's email address, and sends it to him. He must have gotten a hold of Dominic's phone or email password recently. *What else are you holding out on me, Miles?*

Both agents hover over the email for a few moments and then Riley looks up, offering a tight smile. "Thanks for the information." He turns to address me. "We'll be in contact if we have any more questions."

I sigh with relief that Miles has proven useless to them beyond forwarding that email. But then I realize that they don't seem ready to jump on investigating any of our theories. "So...it's possible someone else saw Dominic at Simon's place that night, right? Maybe that's why they're harassing him, to say hey, I know what you did?"

The two agents exchange a look, and then the woman speaks up, "Dominic DeLuca has an airtight alibi at the determined time of Simon's death."

Agent Riley flips open a folder beneath his notepad and glances down at it. "Justice Kimura claimed to be with him that night. They stopped at a convenience store and bought a few items. A clerk identified them and backed up their story."

"Which store?" Miles drills. "Do you have security footage of them?"

Shit. He's losing his grip. It's too personal for him. I turn to face Miles. "Quit turning this into your very own Sherlock Holmes moment. Simon might be a name on paper to you but he was my friend!"

Miles looks startled by my outburst. Or by his, maybe. He swallows, looks away from me. "Sorry."

"Its okay." I shift my gaze to the agents seated across from me. "But seriously? If Simon was suicidal, why would he need ice cream? Or two spoons for that matter? Could the ice cream have belonged to anyone else? Were Simon's fingerprints on the container?"

"It was half eaten," Riley says.

So that's a yes.

The woman clears her throat. "Three sets of prints. Simon's, the housekeeper's, and the checkout clerk at IGA's."

"Then it's possible," I say.

"What's possible?" the woman asks. "That Simon Gilbert would eat ice cream before shooting himself in the head or that Dominic DeLuca was invited into his home, offered ice cream, and managed to shoot Simon at an unbelievably close range leaving no prints or DNA on the weapon, all while upholding an alibi with two witnesses, one with zero personal connection to Dominic or the DeLuca family?"

Well, when you put it like that...

Beside me, Miles shifts in his chair, and I brace myself

for an outburst. He's due for one. Instead he reaches over and takes my hand from the arm of the chair, holding it tightly in his. "Promise you'll at least look into it?"

The stone-faced agents both turn sympathetic and Agent Riley says, "Absolutely. You have my word."

Back in the car, Miles shoves the keys into the ignition and takes off driving but pulls over once we're a few blocks away and cuts the engine.

"Did you know he was with Justice?" Miles asks quietly.

"No." I glance at him. "I take it you didn't know about Dominic's alibi, either?"

He shakes his head. "All we've seen is the police report. Within twenty-four hours, the FBI took over the investigation. There's probably a lot we don't know."

"Yeah." I sink back into the passenger seat, wishing I didn't agree with him.

Warm hands slide up my arms and then rest on my face. Miles leans in and looks me over. "It's still technically the weekend, right?"

Before I can answer, he kisses me. My heart pounds; warmth spreads over me from head to toe. And somewhere, far in the back of my head, a voice is telling me that I'm falling. Way too fast.

Even still, I reach across the center console wanting—needing—to touch more of him. My hands slide inside his jacket. I don't know what I'm doing anymore. I've lost perspective. I've let myself believe I'm worthy of Miles, but deep down, I know the truth is there, ticking like a bomb that will inevitably go off. It's just a matter of time. And I'm too far gone in Junkie Mode to see the explosion at the end of our story.

CHAPTER
42

ME: any luck finding our all eyes friend?

CONNIE: Not even a bread crumb. But I'll keep looking

ME: I noticed something in those pics you gave me.

CONNIE: what?

ME: 2 spoons

CONNIE: Shit. You're right. Why didn't I notice that? This changes things

ME: Glad u think so. The fbi was unimpressed

"No," Miles says for the hundredth time.

He lifts my arm, showing me again how to block his fist from hitting my face. He waits until I look ready before taking another swing at me. I can't turn off the panic, the urge to duck, when his fist comes at me again, and then I take too long to decide what to do and end up half ducking, half blocking. He stops his fist from hitting me, but barely.

"No," he repeats. "Keep your eyes on me. Lift your arm."

It's not just the panic of these fake attacks messing me up, it's all the comments I'm forced to bite back per Miles's self-defense rules. Like why the hell do we have to do this at six in the morning? And what is making the school wrestling mats smell like that? Do I really have to lie on said mats and risk ringworm?

And what if I have the urge to kiss you again? It's Monday. Is that allowed?

Miles drops his arms with a sigh. "When I made you promise to be serious and focus, I didn't mean silent and distracted."

I chew on my thumbnail. "Sorry."

"You need to leave everything outside the door." Miles waves a hand at the doors to the school gym. "Just you and me and this lesson. Think of it as being free of all those burdens…free of competing against yourself for the most witty sarcastic retort."

"Don't forget the sexual innuendos," I add.

He gives me that grin that brings me back to the kissing question, so I do what he's suggesting and shed it. All of it. It's messy and complicated, and this is physical and two-dimensional.

"Ready?"

I nod and wait for Miles to try to punch me again. When he does, I keep my eyes on him, lift my arm to block him.

"Yes. Just like that." He backs away, preparing to repeat the move. "Again."

A little while later, I emerge from the girls' locker room after showering, and Miles is waiting for me in the hall. We've still got nearly thirty minutes before homeroom, but I hadn't expected him to suddenly start hanging out with me at school. "You want to grab a bagel from the snack bar?"

I lift an eyebrow. "This sounds like a breakfast date. Is it?"

Color rises to his cheeks, but he looks me right in the eye. "Maybe."

Okay, this is new. "I guess I could eat."

He leads the way to our school's coffee bar, while I work on braiding my wet hair. He orders a plain bagel with cream cheese and a coffee. Black. Then glances at me before saying, "And a chocolate chip bagel. Peanut butter and jelly on the side. Large coffee with at least six inches of room for cream and sugar."

"Have you been recording my orders?" I tie the end of my braid and lean in closer to Miles to whisper, "You're supposed to order the bagel plain, then come back up later and say that they forgot the peanut butter and jelly. Saves me fifty cents."

The school coffee bar is expensive as hell. I only buy food every once in a while. Miles grins and pulls a twenty from his wallet. "It's all right. I got this."

"You're buying, too?" I fake shock. "This must be a date."

He rolls his eyes. "You really know how to make a guy feel comfortable."

We take our breakfast to a nearby bench. I'm not really hungry, so I watch Miles's precise method of spreading cream cheese on his bagel. I'm surprised he only ordered one. "Did you talk to Dominic last night?"

"Yeah." He sets the plastic knife aside and presses the two bagel halves into a sandwich. "Nothing new. Same as always. You think maybe I should push him more?"

"You want my opinion?" I say, and when he nods I'm even more surprised.

"It's kind of your thing, I think," he says. "Getting people to talk without making it change everything. You did it with Jacob and Bret. With the FBI agents yesterday. They were on information lockdown when I pushed them, but then you got in there and suddenly they were talking about whose prints were on that ice cream."

I take a minute to form my thoughts, wanting to offer Miles my best. "It's one of the things that you can't plan for. Not completely. You have to feel it out, dance around the perimeter, and be able to recognize a cracked door. The way in is different with everyone."

He gives me one of his blazing looks. "How so?"

"Bret respects people who surprise him, who can outsmart him. But Jacob is completely different... I tested him a bit to see if he liked to gossip—not much. And I already knew he had plenty of insecurity. I knew he'd be afraid of me ruining him and that he could keep a secret." It's weird putting this into words. It sounds so calculated, so inhumane. How do normal people manipulate others? "You have to know what or who they love, what's important to them."

He's quiet for a full minute, taking a bite of his bagel and chewing slowly. "You're wrong about Jacob. He's not afraid of you. Or he wouldn't have confided in you about what Chantel told him. He respects you because you're willing to dig for the truth and do what's right."

I choke on my coffee. Me doing what's right? Yeah, no. "See? You've got it figured out. You don't need my help. Besides, Dominic has opened up to you about plenty. He won't speak more than two words to me."

"He could be playing me," Miles says. And I hear what he doesn't say: he could be a murderer. "What about Justice? What's her deal?"

"Justice..." I snatch a napkin from the stack resting between me and Miles. "She tries her best to be a mean girl and appreciates that quality in others, but really, she's not.

Confrontation scares her—"

As the words tumble out, I spot Justice across the hall heading toward her locker and it occurs to me that I know exactly how to get her to talk.

I dump my uneaten bagel and condiments onto the bench and jump to my feet. "Thanks for breakfast," I tell him before slinging my bag over my shoulder and heading after Justice. I'm a terrible breakfast date, but whatever. Junkie Mode and all.

"Justice," I half yell.

She stops in front of her locker but takes her time turning around to face me. "Hey, Ellie."

"Look," I say. "I'm sorry about homecoming. I didn't mean to—"

"It's fine." She shoves her precalc book into her locker, avoiding eye contact. "Miles is hot and all, but it's not like we were in love. And like you said, he'll be gone soon."

God, as if I need a reminder. "Still, I want things to be cool with us, you know? Like before. I could use a friend."

"Not sure I'm the kind of friend you want." She looks away again, finding more to stuff in her locker. "I usually draw the line way before making out with my friend's dates."

"Did you actually see us making out?" I ask.

She laughs. "Um, no, but it was obvious."

"I was upset, you know? The last dance I went to was with Simon and it was also the night he died. And all that caught up to me. Miles was there…" I shake my head. "Not exactly an excuse but, the truth nonetheless."

She lets down her guard just a bit. "Okay, thanks for telling me."

"And as far as Miles goes, I wouldn't fault him too much," I say. "Sometimes we do stuff we probably shouldn't because we feel bad for someone. Like how you told the

FBI that you were with Dominic the night Simon died."

In the length of a heartbeat, she stiffens and drops an invisible wall between us. "What else would I have told them?"

"Maybe that Dominic wasn't really with you," I say, keeping my voice low. "Maybe that he was meeting up with Simon after the dance and you were covering for him."

"It wasn't like that," she hisses at me. Justice reaches for one of her books, and her hand shakes. She quickly pulls the shaking hand behind her back.

"No?" I wait for her to explain, and when she doesn't I add, "I'm not the only one who knows that Simon drove to Dominic's house after dropping me off. Thought you deserved a warning."

I don't think I could have ever orchestrated a better exit than what coincidently follows. Right as I leave Justice, several black SUVs pull up in the bus circle. Half a dozen agents hop out of the three cars. I search the group and spot both Aidan and Jack. They're all stone-faced, intense.

Jacob and Chantel appear beside me, both curious about the arrival of Secret Service. I catch Justice's eye—I'm now several feet away from her—and lift a brow. She swallows, her eyes wide with panic.

Chantel elbows me in the side and nods in Aidan's direction. "Isn't that—"

"My sister's boyfriend? Yep."

"Whoa," Jacob says, "No wonder you know how to—"

I take a note from Chantel and elbow Jacob in the side. "Recite the constitution. But I thought we weren't going to talk about that."

"Seriously?" Chantel laughs. "God, that's weird."

Aidan and his crew breeze past me. He's staring straight ahead, doesn't even see me. The dean comes out of the office and meets them in the hallway. Jack steps forward, does the communicating, while the others hang back, standing like statues.

Homeroom is now minutes away, and the hallways are filling quickly. I start to head away from the entrance doors, but stop when I see the dean pluck Bret Thomas out of the sea of students. I can't hear what they're saying, but Bret's eyes are wide. Panic. He's panicked. One of the agents points down the hall, toward the science wing, and then Bret follows him.

Justice has closed the gap between us and is now clinging for dear life to the sleeve of my uniform sweater.

People are slowing down to take in the scene. The dean plasters on a grin and claps his hands together, telling everyone to get to class. He heads back in his office and the agents immediately split up, half heading inside the office and the other half—including Aidan—going down the hall, toward the science wing.

I turn around and look behind me again, squinting into the sun. Across the street, several news and media vehicles are parked. It's a familiar sight from the last few weeks of sophomore year, but that had ended with the school year. I'm about to text Miles again when two freshman girls breeze past us, their phones out while they whisper loud enough for me to hear.

"If he didn't kill himself, I wonder who murdered him?"

The hair on my arm stands up, goose bumps prickling my skin. Jacob fumbles around with his phone, swears under his breath before flashing the screen toward Chantel, me, and Justice. Right on CNN's website the headline reads: Senator Gilbert's Son Murdered: New Evidence Contradicts Suicide Conclusion. Case Reopens.

I look around for Miles, needing to see his face. Did we do this? Is it really happening? But before I can spot him or even process that this is the Secret Service, not the

FBI, and the FBI is who we talked to yesterday, I'm yanked from the hall into the bathroom by Justice.

She checks under the stalls before saying a word. "What the hell is going on, Ellie?"

"I don't know," I tell her honestly.

"Bret told you about Dominic and Simon, didn't he?" she demands, but doesn't even let me answer. "I knew he knew! God, what a liar."

"I take it you weren't really with Dominic after the dance." I try my best to play it cool. But holy shit. This means—I can't even think it despite the theory we dumped on Agent Riley yesterday.

"Don't look at me like that, Ellie." Her eyes widen even more. "Dominic didn't do anything to Simon and even if he did, I had no idea—I wasn't covering up that." She covers her face with her hands and exhales. When she looks up again, there is desperation in her eyes. "You have to help me. I know you're good at this stuff. You helped Jacob, plus you've got connections with your sister's boyfriend."

"I don't possess skills or connections to help people who lied to the FBI." It isn't easy to stay focused on working this one asset when I'm dying to peel out of here, find Miles, and get the whole story. My phone vibrates right then, Miles's name flashing on the screen. I tilt it out of Justice's view and hit ignore. "And I really can't help you when you're lying to me, too."

"Okay. I'll tell you everything." She nods as if convincing herself. "It started when Dominic asked me if I'd come to his house before the dance. Said his parents would get off his back if he had a date they approved of. So I changed my plans with Austin Mahogany, told him I'd meet him there. Did the pictures thing with Dominic."

"You believed him? That your appearance at his house would make his parents happy?"

"Well, no," she admits. "But that's because I'd caught him texting Simon a week earlier. Looked over his shoulder in Spanish."

I eye her skeptically. I find it hard to believe Dominic DeLuca, who has gone to such great lengths—still—to cover his affair with Simon would be careless enough to put Simon's real name in his phone. I mention this to Justice.

"I didn't see Simon's name when they were texting. Or his photo. But when a new text came in, there was a picture of Simon's cat." She gives me this look like yeah, I know how that sounds. "I take my dog to the same vet the Gilberts use. We ran into each other at the vet's office once last fall."

Growing more anxious with each passing second of Justice's overly long story, I shoot Miles a text.

ME: give me 5 min

"All right, so you already knew about them before the dance. How did you end up covering for Dominic later that night?"

"On the way to the dance, I told him I knew his secret and that he should meet up with Simon later on. He could tell his parents he was going out with me." She pauses for a second. "I went home with him, too, hung out in his room for a little. He wanted me to drive his car to Austin's party after the dance. That way people would spot the car and assume he was there even if they didn't see Dominic. Austin's house is—"

I lift a hand to stop her. I don't need to hear any more. I already know the rest. "Dominic told his parents he was going to Austin's, walked with you outside. Then you drove off in his car and Simon showed up to get Dominic, Bret followed Simon, saw them together, sped off."

"Bret?"

I shake my head, refusing to answer her until I get all of this out. I pace back and forth in the bathroom. "The store clerk didn't actually see Dominic, just Dominic's car," I conclude. "And then I bet Dominic came to you the very next morning, begging you to say that he was with you."

"You didn't see him," she pleads. "He couldn't get out of bed for an entire week. He was wrecked. He knew what it looked like. He knew how bad it was—"

I finally lose my cool. "Because he murdered someone!"

She opens her mouth to protest, but I cut her off. "Did it ever seem strange that Dominic wanted you to drive his car? After you found out what happened to Simon, never once did you consider the fact that he set you up to be his alibi so that he could do something bad?"

Justice looks me dead in the eyes, not a shred of doubt on her face. "No. Never."

I lift my hands in the air. "Seriously? You just sat there thinking, wow…sucks for Dominic that Simon's suicide was so badly timed. At the exact moment they were together!"

Both of us are frozen for a long moment, and then I stand there and watch the truth hit Justice like those waves that had knocked me underwater, toward the bottom of the sea. She flaps her hands around and starts her own pattern of pacing. "Oh my God, oh my God, ohmygod…I fucking lied to the FBI. I'm going to prison. My parents are going to murder me."

Her voice is gaining volume by the syllable. I slide in front of her and grip her arms, holding her in place. "Unless you want the whole school to hear you, I suggest shutting up."

Tears immediately tumble down her face. "What do I do? Turn myself in now? Wait until they come after me? Will that make it worse?"

"It might." I shake my head. "I don't know. We need—"

The bell rings, signaling that Justice and I are now late for homeroom. She looks panicked all over again. "If I cut class, it will definitely look suspicious. And I need to find Dominic—"

What? "No!" I block her way to the door and pull my phone out. "What part of murderer do you not understand?"

I need Miles. He'll know what to do. I shoot him another text.

ME: help! Justice meltdown. In the bathroom where I flushed the you know what

I punch in the phone number for the school office. "What's the name of the Starbucks lady that makes your coffee?"

"Candace," she says immediately. "Wait—what? I'm having a crisis here—"

"Hello, this is Candace over at the Starbucks on Lincoln," I say to the secretary, faking a Southern accent. "There's a Justice Kimura here, and according to her student ID she goes to your school."

"Yes, she does. Is everything okay?"

"Well, she's holed up here in the bathroom and won't come out. It's not a problem with management or anything, we've got two toilets. But I worried about her being tardy. Guess she's taking some kind of test and can't come out until she's got the results. Think maybe y'all should call her folks? Or do you want me to?"

Justice has the most horrified look on her face, but she keeps her mouth shut.

"Um, no, that won't be necessary," the secretary says. "As long as she's okay, we'll just expect her later then. Thanks for calling."

I hang up and tell Justice not to move. I race through the halls to Miles's homeroom and covertly peek inside, preparing to signal him, but he's not there.

Fifteen minutes later, I return to the bathroom where Justice is now on the floor doing what looks like Lamaze breathing. I checked every bathroom, the gym, the locker room, the library—no Miles anywhere.

I start to panic a little myself. I'm half tempted to turn Justice in myself, but something stops me. Something about the way she looked at me saying she never once thought Dominic had done anything to Simon. I don't want something to happen to her just because she put her faith in the wrong person. If Dominic really *is* dangerous, Justice needs to be in a safe place. Safer than this school.

"Here's what you're going to do," I tell her, and she stands immediately. "Go to Starbucks, order a coffee, use the bathroom. Cover our tracks. Then go…" I rack my brain for an idea. "Go to your doctor's office. Tell them you need to see someone right away. Then Google rare diseases, pick one, and start coming down with those symptoms. You'll be there all day."

"What are you going to do?" she asks me.

"I'm going to class." I already hijacked the homeroom attendance sheets and marked myself here, but it wasn't easy to do. "I was never in here with you."

I open the window and tell her to exit that way. To my surprise, she doesn't hesitate, climbs right out. After she's gone, I lean against the wall and take a few deep breaths waiting for the bell to ring.

Miles better appear soon, because I don't know how much longer I can handle all this on my own. Funny how he was the one asking me for advice this morning.

CHAPTER
43

t takes a little over twelve hours for authorities to bring Justice in for questioning. All she said in her nine p.m. text was, "They're here now." And then nothing. For hours. Nothing from Miles since our bagel date this morning. Aidan hasn't come home, so I can't press him for answers either, or a missing persons report for Miles. My sister is being a nanny all night long for the Feldsteins' anniversary. So I literally have no one to gripe to.

Even though I'm the verge of insanity, I accidentally doze off around two thirty in the morning. But I'm woken up only minutes later by a warm body landing on the bed beside me. Before I even open my eyes, lips are on mine. Familiar lips that I haven't kissed in what feels like forever. Miles has his hand in my hair, his chest pressed against mine, heart pounding beneath his shirt. He's so good at this, and it's so completely what I'm desperate for right now that I forget for several minutes that I've been texting him for hours with no reply.

My anger and panic from earlier float their way back to the surface, and I shove Miles out of my personal space. "Where the hell have you been? I've been going crazy!"

"I'm so sorry," he says. "When the media circus showed up, I was pulled out of there by my handler before I could tell anyone."

I let this sink in a moment, unable to say anything.

"I meant to say all of that before kissing you, but it just happened." He eyebrows push together. "Trust me, I've been going crazy, too."

I sit up; the grogginess dissolves among all the urgent matters. "What happened?"

"I don't know." Miles leans against the head of my bed. "Agent Riley wasn't too interested in our help on Sunday, and then it's the Secret Service storming into the school."

"Oh shit," I say, realizing I need to tell him about Justice. "They took Justice in for questioning tonight. Haven't heard from her since, but she admitted—"

"I know," he interrupts. "I heard everything."

My mouth falls open. "You bugged me?"

"Her," he clarifies. "They brought Dominic in, too."

"Both of them?" Shit. This is gettin' real.

"I talked to him before," Miles says, indicating that he likely made his decision about pushing Dominic. "You want to hear it or my summarized version."

He doesn't even need me to answer that. Soon his phone is out, the recording playing. He scrolls through some small talk until I hear Dominic's voice rise, anger laced in every word.

"Believe whatever you want," he snaps. *"I didn't even get in Simon's car that night. He didn't fucking ask me over. And I couldn't go back in after I'd lied to my parents. After Justice drove off in my car. So I let him leave…"*

"Come on," Miles says in a voice that I don't recognize because it's hard and cold. The Miles seated beside me flinches at the sound. *"I know you went over there, Dominic. What really happened? Maybe you're not a murderer…*

maybe Simon thought he'd show off his gun. Maybe he brought it downstairs and you guys were messing around and it accidentally fired. If that's true—"

"Okay!" Dominic shouts. *"You're right, I fucking went over to his house. But not because he invited me. I didn't want to be a chickenshit and not tell him—I walked there. Didn't step foot in his car. And I didn't step foot in that house, either. Didn't need to. I was still half a block away when I figured out why he didn't invite me."*

"Why? Were his parents home?" *Miles presses.*

"Nope. He had another guy over."

"What guy?" I demand to the recording, which is probably at least a couple hours old.

The Miles beside me shakes his head and turns off the recording. "He has no idea. Didn't recognize him. Said it was some young guy, probably Caucasian."

"Probably Caucasian?" I repeat. "Real helpful."

"Oh, and he was wearing really shiny black dress shoes with old beat-up jeans," Miles adds.

I feel like throwing a hard object at the wall. Hearing all these sides, not knowing who's telling the truth...it's the most frustrating thing in the world. "So we have yet another new person we can claim as the last to see Simon."

"Assuming Dominic's not lying," Miles points out. "And what kind of person holds on to that information, lets people believe Simon killed himself, just to keep from being outed?"

I fall forward and press my face into the pillow, releasing a loud groan.

Miles rolls me onto my side and leans in to check on me. "Feel better?"

"A little." I stare up at the ceiling. "What were the Secret Service doing with Bret this morning?"

"I don't know, but I do know that Senator Gilbert was

there, in the science wing. I saw several agents bring him in through the back entrance. I'm not sure why he was there, but maybe he wanted to talk to Bret himself? It's not the norm but then again, he is a lawyer. They could be cutting Bret a deal—he turns in Dominic and they dismiss whatever it is they have on him."

"Maybe they found his stash of blackmail photos." I hug my knees to conceal the fact that my hands are shaking again. "Is it so bad? That the FBI have Justice and Dominic? That they're really looking for a murderer?"

"No," he admits. "It's not a bad thing."

We're both silent for a long time, but eventually I give him a nudge with my foot. "What? You look like you're sitting on a big secret."

"Not a secret." He turns to face me. "But things are changing quickly. With my semester at Holden coinciding with this big case reopening, my school is likely going to pull me from Holden for security reasons. They won't want to draw any attention to Marshall Academy and especially not the honors program."

Oh. That's what he came to tell me. "You're leaving."

Miles nods. "Probably."

My stomach sinks. It's not like this wasn't on the horizon soon anyway, but I thought we still had at least a month. "Right. That makes sense. With the media circus outside the school and your history with Simon…"

"My history with Simon is classified information. The public won't find out about any of that."

"Good." I nod and find myself standing, pacing a straight line in my room. "Now you won't have to deal with Clyde or the druggie kids at school, or me and my—"

"Ellie," Miles says. When I don't stop pacing, he reaches for my hand and brings me closer. "I'm not ready to leave. I just—I'm not ready. But if my supervisor tells me to, I won't have a choice."

We stare at each other in the dark, my chest rising and falling with each breath, stealing the little space between us. I could do it now. Tell him the truth. It would make this a cleaner break. He'd leave and wouldn't look back.

But then Miles pulls me down beside him, lays a hand on my cheek. "I'm not ready to go mostly because of you."

Warmth spreads over my body. It's hard to even get a grasp on everything I'm feeling, but when I kiss Miles, it all pours out, through my lips, onto his. None of my efforts to conceal the tidal wave of emotions hitting me does any good, and I can feel the difference in his reaction; it's heavier, it's more. So much more.

Minutes later we're stretched across my bed, our shirts on the floor. Warm lips trail down my chest and stomach. Already my mind is headed much further than we got in our last make-out session. Miles slowly wiggles off my pajama shorts, glancing up at me every few seconds, giving me a chance to stop him. I don't. His mouth skims along the waistband of my panties and then slides to the inside of my thighs. My heart thunders in my ears, my hands reaching down to touch some part of him. Eventually he makes his way back up, and his mouth finds mine again.

His fingers drag along my side until I can't take it anymore, and a shiver races up my back. His lips touch my neck, move just below my ear, and he whispers, "You smell like sun."

"Like sun," I repeat, half gone. "You smell like a swimming pool."

Just to be sure I'm right, I bury my face in that groove between his neck and shoulder and inhale. While my face is still hidden, I admit that I've watched him in the pool from my bedroom window.

I wait for him to laugh, but when he lifts his head, his

eyes meeting mine, he looks so serious. "I'm sorry, Ellie. For making it seem like I only wanted to work together or hook up."

Miles allows his hand to roam down my stomach and over my panties. I close my eyes and sigh. "I forgive you. You're perfect."

"I'm not." He leans over and kisses my cheek, the corner of my mouth, my nose. "But I accept the ego boost."

He sits up and my eyes fly open, checking to see if he's leaving. His gaze travels from my toes to my light blue panties, to the tiny bow on my bra, and then he stops when he reaches my face. His hand follows the same path his eyes had just gone down. Again, he stops when he reaches my face, resting his fingers at the base of my neck.

I'm warm all over despite the key missing articles of clothing. And when his hand makes the return trip south, this time sliding beneath the waistband of my panties, warm turns to heated. He does everything so slow, deliberate, not the sloppy impulsiveness I experienced in my past life.

Eventually I can't stand the space between us a second longer, and I tug his arms until he's lying beside me. My hand glides over his shoulder, his chest, slowly moving lower. His own hand slides over me again, beneath my underwear, and I have to bite down on my lower lip to keep from making any sounds.

The feelings build the more of me Miles touches, and soon I'm ready to explode. My fingers reach inside his boxers again, gripping him, moving up and down until his breath catches, his body tensing. And then he's kissing me, whispering my name against my lips, and I'm right there with him.

When we both catch our breath and come down from the high, I lay my ear over Miles's heart and listen to the rapid beat slow. His hand is in my hair, moving over it gently, lazily, like we do this all the time. I relax, probably for the first time in twenty-four hours, and my body molds itself to him. I'm about to drift off to sleep but Miles stops breathing, tenses like he's going to say something important. I wait a beat and sure enough, he speaks.

"Ellie?" His thumb traces over my lips. "What if you don't stay at Holden next semester? It's gonna be a mess around here. And you won't be able to—you could go to Marshall Academy."

I lift my head and smile at him. "You want me to go to your military school? Have you seen my dresser? I don't fold. Ever."

"It's not really like that," he says. "The girls don't even have regulation bedding in the dorms or anything like that."

"Why don't they get regular bedding? That doesn't seem fair."

"Regulation," Miles clarifies. "In the boys' dorm we're issued the same bedding and have to make our beds the same way every morning. The girls can use whatever bedding they want.

"I'm serious, Ellie. My dad could get you in. With a scholarship." He tucks my hair behind my ear and kisses me. "You're so smart. It's wasted at Holden. They're a bunch of idiots."

This is like the fairy tale where the handsome prince asks the peasant girl to run away with him. To military school. Yeah, that part needs some work.

I touch his cheek. "I'm not cut out for that place." For one, I'd never pass the background check. "And Harper's here…"

He kisses my palm and says, "I'll wait until Holden turns into a war zone, and then I'll come rescue you."

A little while later, when I open my eyes long enough

to see Miles crawl out of my bedroom window, it hits me that he won't be around to pop in like this anymore.

I nearly call him and tell him, yes. I'll follow you anywhere. Even if it means shining my shoes.

But I'm an impostor. I barely recognize myself anymore. The way I acted when Justice confessed to me, how crazy I thought she was to lie for Dominic. Who am I to judge? My part in the Dr. Ames con is one tiny example of what I've done to hurt innocent people. The list is long. Long and unforgiving.

I reach for my phone and send Miles a text.

ME: so what now?

MILES: sleep? I hear everyone is doing it

ME: rule #228. But I mean now that Justice and Dominic are being questioned

MILES: we let grown-ups handle it from here

I was afraid of that. Afraid of losing our common ground.

CHAPTER
44

"Forget it, I'll buy lunch," I tell Harper. But she won't stop digging through the kitchen, tossing items into a brown paper sack. She throws a bag of croutons in there.

"Aidan manages to pack your lunch every morning, so surely I can figure it out."

"And every morning, I tell him he doesn't have to do this." Aidan made it home an hour ago and passed out cold. He worked nearly twenty-four hours. I glance at my cell again, my hand on the door. "Harp, seriously. The bus is sixty seconds away."

"Fine." She tosses a ten-dollar bill at me.

I snatch the money out of the air and fling the door open. When I spin around, I'm face-to-face with two guys in navy FBI jackets, service weapons strapped to their hips. Behind them is an entire SWAT team, vests and rifles. My heart slams against my chest and I'm frozen.

"Ellie, go!" Harper shouts. "The bus is—"

She's behind me now, I can feel her there, holding her breath, taking it all in.

"We're looking for Agent Lawrence," one man says.

"I'm here. What's going on?" Aidan appears in the kitchen, his sweats hastily pulled on.

Before anyone can get any answers, the SWAT team pushes their way into the apartment and head straight for Aidan.

Aidan lifts his hands, shocked. "Whoa, what—"

He doesn't get to finish his statement because one of the FBI agents begins shouting orders at him. The handcuffs come out next.

"You're under the arrest for the murder of Simon Gilbert—"

My backpack slips off my shoulder and falls to the floor. I stand there unable to move or speak. Shock fills Aidan's face and then, as if processing something, he goes perfectly still, unreadable. Like he'd been the night I was caught breaking into the Gilberts' home.

"You have the right to remain silent…"

"No!" Harper grabs Aidan's arm, refusing to let go.

The cuffs are on him now, his hands behind his back. The SWAT team plus one special agent lead Aidan toward the door, rifles still poised to act as needed. Harper won't let go. She's following them out the door. One agent attempts to pry her hands from him and she elbows him in the side.

"Let go," Aidan tells her so firmly she obeys.

"Do you understand these rights I have just read to you?"

Aidan drops his gaze to the floor and nods. "Yes."

I wait for him to turn back, to look at me, and when he does, I hang on to this tiny thread of hope. *Please tell me you didn't do it. Please, Aidan.* He holds my gaze for several seconds and then is led out.

Harper seems to pull herself together. She turns to the remaining special agent. "You're taking me to the field office. I will not sit around here while you interrogate an innocent man!"

When he agrees to take her with him, I finally grapple for my voice. "Harper…"

She turns to me as if she'd forgotten I was here. "Ellie, God…okay." She exhales. "I'm going to go fix all of this and you're gonna stay right here. Got it?"

She gives me a quick hug, and I almost don't let go. What the hell is happening? The agent leads her out, and I'm left standing in the kitchen, a mess around me — literally. Harper tore the place apart trying to pack my lunch, and then the SWAT team did their own damage.

Some force deep inside me takes over and suddenly I'm in motion, picking up fallen and out-of-place items. My chest grows tighter and tighter. I tug at the collar of my school polo, trying to relieve myself of this pressing weight. Is this my fault somehow? Because I added Aidan to our list of suspects? No, that doesn't even make sense. I focus on the tasks in front of me — put pickle jar back in fridge, pick up cereal box from floor, sweep fallen Cheerios from counter…

"Why aren't you on the bus?"

I jump at the sound of Miles's voice and the appearance of him in the doorway. The open milk carton slips from my hand, hitting the tile floor with a *thud*, and the *glug glug* of milk flowing out follows. My breaths are coming in short spurts, my heart beating rapidly.

"You're not on the bus, either," I say stupidly.

"Yeah, well, I spotted the FBI camped out and figured I should make myself scarce. Looks like we're in the clear, though."

Clyde appears behind Miles. "That was a whole SWAT team on the premises. What'd you do? Make friends with another big-time dealer?"

"Aidan," I manage to say. "They arrested Aidan. For Simon."

I try to draw in a breath, but air won't enter. I shake my arms, the panic increasing. I don't even see Miles's reaction, but soon he's crossing the milk river and right in front of me, his hands on my arms. "Ellie, what's wrong?"

"I…can't…breathe…" I force out; I'm tugging at my shirt, pulling as hard as I can.

Miles undoes the buttons. "Do you have asthma?"

I shake my head.

"Heart condition?"

Spots form in front of my eyes, and I barely notice the larger, heavier steps crossing the kitchen. Then Clyde is beside Miles, the paper bag Harper tried to use to make my lunch in his hands. He forces me to sit down, my back against the wall. He holds the bag over my mouth and nose. "Breathe slowly…relax."

I close my eyes and listen to his voice. Focus. *These are my lungs and they will accept air.* My head pounds from lack of proper oxygen, sweat trickles over me, the bag crinkles open and closed. Even though they're sitting in front of me, I hear Miles and Clyde arguing as if from outside the apartment. Focus. Breathe.

Soon, my lungs relax, accept air. My body turns to Jell-O and I slump over against Miles. For a moment all I feel is relief. Relief from not dying. But I know it's short-lived, and the panic will return soon. I close my eyes and continue to slow my breathing. Clyde pulls the bag away and looks me over. "Good, keep breathing like that. You'll be fine." He turns to Miles. "Let's go back to our place."

For a moment, I'm sure they're going to leave me here, maybe to hide from the FBI, but then Miles places my arms around his neck and scoops me right up off the floor.

"Grab her school bag and phone," he tells Clyde, and I take note of the fact that it's the first time I've heard Miles say anything to his uncle without sarcasm or venom behind the words.

Miles deposits me on their apartment couch, and he and Clyde walk around locking windows and doors, closing the blinds. They move in unison. They're worried about media showing up here. I allow myself a good five minutes to relax into the couch, thank the universe for clean air and lungs and whatever else. And then slowly, with each passing minute, the panic returns. Though this time it's more of an urgent need to do something rather than a pathetic inability to breathe—that's something that happens to amateur con men, not a seasoned veteran like myself.

I snatch my phone from the coffee table and call Harper. It rings and rings and then goes to voice mail. "I need an update!" I say.

I hang up, dial again. No answer. "Dammit, Harper, tell me what's going on!"

Before I call a third time, Clyde plucks the phone from my hand and replaces it with a can of soda. "Drink this. I'll go down to the field office and check in, okay?"

"Try not to end up in a cell," Miles says.

"You'd love that, wouldn't you?" Clyde is already throwing on his coat, unaffected by his nephew's hate.

I catch his arm before he leaves. We aren't related; he doesn't have a blood obligation to help me. "Thanks, Clyde."

He looks embarrassed by the gratitude but gives a nod. "I'll call you in a few."

When the door shuts, I turn to Miles, notice his statue stance, and realize he was dropped nearly as big a bomb as me. I don't know what to say except, "You don't think he did it, do you? I know we said it could be anyone but..."

The silence that sits between my question and his answer becomes an entire continent. I push to my feet and pace the room, despite my shaking legs. "What evidence could they have on him? And what about this other guy Dominic mentioned? Is that not an important lead to pursue?"

Logic might be coming out of my mouth, but in my head, I can't consider Aidan because I can't mentally conjure an image of him, standing before Simon, pointing a weapon at him and pulling the trigger.

Maybe there is logic to that. "He has no motive."

"He was the last one to see Simon, was in the room with Simon and the gun," Miles recites from our notes.

"That's setup," I protest. "A scenario that could be played out, but it's not motive. Other than psychosis or sociopathy making Aidan predisposed to be a killer, tell me one reason why he'd do it."

More silence sits between me and my partner in crime, but eventually he clears his throat and speaks one word. "Money."

I pivot to face him. "Money?"

"He's a trained marksman. Served three years in the military doing that job."

"You think he's been secretly moonlighting as a hit man?" I shake my head.

"He wouldn't need a career at it," Miles says. "One big job could be worth over a million dollars."

"Okay, so where's the money then?" I demand. "Simon's been dead since last June. It's November. Surely he's been paid by now."

Miles winces at my frank statement of Simon's death, and I immediately stop pacing. "I'm sorry. I didn't mean —"

"It's fine," he says.

The walls close in around me; realization hits hard. I look at Miles, desperate for some thread to hold on to. "You're not gonna help me prove he's innocent, are you?"

He locks eyes with me, holding my gaze, and I remember what he said when I discovered his real purpose for transferring schools. *If he didn't fucking kill himself, whoever did this is gonna pay.*

That anger, that hatred, that quest for revenge is in there still, and he's got it aimed at Aidan now. A feeling of hopelessness sweeps over me. Why can't it be Dominic? Or the mystery guy Dominic saw?

"I don't want it to be Aidan," I whisper.

"I know." Sympathy fills Miles's face, and he moves closer.

I brush off his attempt to touch me and pull myself together. "Lead me there, then. We don't agree on the why. So how?"

"The FBI used Aidan's statement to close the case," Miles says, and now *he's* pacing. "The fact that he saw Simon in possession of the weapon that would eventually kill him. Aidan heard the gunshot. He found Simon dead."

"Yeah, but why are they just now arresting him? Two days ago, we were leading them to Dominic," I argue. "And then it turned out Dominic and Justice had a false alibi. And wait...what about the mystery guy at the door? The probably Caucasian guy? Definitely not Agent Lawrence. Where the hell does Aidan fit into this?"

"New evidence surfaced. Could be anything from emails, texts, phone calls to whoever may have hired Lawrence. Pictures of him meeting suspicious persons. Or maybe Dominic's confession led them to this mystery guy, who saw Aidan inside the house."

"But we already know he was in the house! He was supposed to be in the house!" The panic rises in my throat again, and my chest tightens. I shake my arms out and force it away. "But it's Aidan... You don't know what he's done for Harper and for me. You have no idea—"

"Which makes you a great character witness for him," Miles says.

"Me? Yeah, right. Harper, maybe," I say without thinking. I look up and catch something on Miles's face. "What?"

He shakes his head. "Nothing. I'm just saying, you're a good student, no criminal record—"

"What, Miles?" I demand. "What's wrong with my sister as a character witness? She's not capable of seeing the bad? Love is blind and all that?"

CHAPTER
45

My gut is already twisting, knowing this must be something bad. Miles looks absolutely torn, but after he scrubs a hand over his face and looks up at me, I know he's made a decision. He nods for me to follow him into the secret room. He tugs at a corner of the carpet, peeling it back to reveal a small hole in the floor. From it, he removes a package—a large manila envelope, the kind with plastic bubbles on the inside. He hesitates, but eventually he hands it over to me.

"Remember that piece of the puzzle that led me here?" Miles says, giving a nod to the envelope. "There's a reason I kept it vague."

I immediately recognize the handwriting on the front addressing the package to Miles at a PO box. Handwriting familiar to me from dozens of biology lab reports. And in the corner I see his name: *Simon Gilbert.* I almost drop the package. It feels like him, like seeing a ghost, even more so than the crime scene photos. I glance at the postmarked date. It's from June of last year. One week before he died. Miles gives me a tiny nod, and I slide the package contents out. There's a folder with a Post-it attached to the front featuring Simon's neat cursive.

MB.
I need your help. Meet me next week.
You know the place and time. Keep these safe for me until then.
Thanks.
S

Miles wasn't kidding. This doesn't sound like the note of a suicidal person.

I open the folder and glance over a large photo of a woman—a stripper most likely—wrapped around a pole, topless and wearing only a black thong. I give it a closer look.

"Hey, this is the girl..." I glance up at Miles, waiting for confirmation. I've asked about her so many times, and he refused to tell me why she was here in this apartment tossing his clothes into the pool. "But what does this have to do with Harper—"

My stomach sinks, the air stalled in my lungs. Far off to the right, topless and wrapped around her own pole, is my sister. I toss the photo to the floor in order to see the one behind it. This one is a close-up of Harp, upside-down on her pole this time. I toss the second photo to the floor and release a breath when I see the third. Aidan in his Marine Corps uniform, stuffing money in Harper's thong.

So this is how they met. Aidan watched my sister dance topless. And then he paid her for her performance. And this is what Harper left my family to do? I was alone for five years so that my sister could be a stripper?

I shake those thoughts from my head. It's not that simple. Deep down I know that.

"Why would Simon send you these?" I ask Miles.

"I don't know," he says honestly. "I didn't even consider opening the folder until after he was gone. There was no need. He wanted a safe place for the information until we met up, and I could do that. But then after…I thought maybe there was a connection. Maybe it was a clue. So I went to the strip club and found the first girl in the photo, but not the other one. Not Harper. I told the manager I was her brother and she caved, gave me the address. I checked out the apartment and saw Agent Lawrence, the guy stuffing money in—" He shakes his head, lifts his eyes to meet mine. "And then I saw you by the pool. I recognized you from the dance pictures Simon had posted on Facebook. They were the last thing he'd posted. But you hadn't been tagged. I didn't know where to find you other than at Holden."

I stare at him, my mouth hanging open. "So you thought it would be a good idea to move in next door, sign up at Holden."

"That's not a secret, Ellie," Miles says. "You knew that I investigated you first. I told you that."

True. He did. But I guess I always thought our first meeting was the day I fished his clothes out of the pool. That was just the first time I met him.

"Lawrence caught me spying on you guys," Miles admits. "Last June. I was going a little crazy, not being able to cope with Simon… He caught me in the parking lot, found this envelope. I told him Simon was my friend and that I needed to make sense out of the pictures."

"Aidan knows about your history with Simon? Does he know about the honors program?"

"No, I'm sure he doesn't. He was really nice about things when he caught me, considering I had topless photos of Harper…" Miles chews on his thumbnail. "He called my parents, though, took me to a diner while we waited for my dad. He let me keep this package as long as I promised to never show the photos to anyone, especially you."

No wonder he and Aidan seemed to already know each other that first day I met Miles.

"Lawrence told me the pictures weren't what they seemed, and after digging and digging all summer, the only conclusion I could come to was that you or Harper had been in danger and he was protecting you. And Simon figured it out and maybe he was protecting you, too. I felt like I needed to do the same. And to find out the truth."

My stomach twists and turns. "Wait, so you came here for me?"

"A little," he admits. "And for the truth. Simon was gone. I didn't let myself trust anyone until I was sure."

"What about the girl from the photo? Your first night here—"

"I went back to the strip club to investigate again. That woman was about to go home with some sketchy-looking dudes, so I paid her for the night." He scratches his head. "Turns out she's got a bit of an ego, didn't like that I wasn't— that I didn't want to..."

"I get it."

Miles is silent while I study the rest of the contents of this folder.

"Simon didn't take these photos. Aidan had Secret Service training a year ago. He gave up his marine uniform. Simon found them," I conclude.

"Maybe he suspected Aidan of something and was gathering evidence but didn't want it landing in the wrong hands."

I try to imagine Simon snooping around getting dirt on Aidan but I can't. He came over to our apartment; he hung out with Aidan around. There was no weird vibe or tension between them.

"But what would this prove about Aidan?" I protest. "You said yourself that you eliminated him."

"I didn't know about his statement, that he was in the house that night. Even then, it's not enough. The FBI has more on him now. I'm sure it's solid. But I get it, Ellie. I get what it's like to be clouded by your feelings about him. It happened to me, too."

I shake my head. "But why these photos? What is the significance? Nothing illegal is happening in any of these pictures."

"Maybe not illegal, but morally questionable...?" Miles lifts an eyebrow. "And with Harper being his living companion now and his position in the Secret Service..."

"That's why you didn't want to show me," I say more to myself than to Miles. All these feelings, all the anger and betrayal is building, and Miles and his steady moral compass are not as easy to tolerate today. "You knew I wanted to know how they met, but you thought I'd be disturbed by this? Or does your promise to Aidan hold more weight than being honest with me?"

He doesn't say anything.

"I'll admit, I'm shocked because I never imagined Harper doing anything like this, but it proves nothing about Aidan." I stuff the photos into the package. "And it doesn't make Harper less of a character witness than me."

This case from Miles's perspective proves again how different we are, how stuck he is on his convictions and how stuck I am with my past. It was complicated and annoying before. Now it's impossible.

"What Aidan did, it doesn't change how I feel about you, you know that, right?" He's right in front of me now, his hands on my arms. "I already told you that your family's truths aren't yours."

I wipe my face and nod. "But sometimes they are."

"No—"

"My mother is in a federal corrections center right now

awaiting trial for bank and investment fraud."

Miles's entire body tenses.

The last flame of hope dies with his reaction. "My family...that's what we do. Fraud. In nearly every form. We're grifters. We don't have birth certificates or Social Security cards—not real ones, anyway. We live off the grid, move around constantly. All of our money, our resources, we get it by stealing, scamming, or conning. Aidan is the most honest person I've ever known. Harper's second, if that tells you anything about the rest of my family. If it weren't for both of them, I'd still be in that world. Probably still working the Dr. Ames con in a new town, a new desperate victim."

"But I thought... No way." He shakes his head and backs a couple steps away from me.

"You thought what?" I prompt. "Protective custody? Witness protection program?"

"Yes," he says, practically whispering the word. "Wait... Dr. Ames? I've heard of that—that was you?"

"Only the first time. We brought in a new cast for each performance." The look on his face, that mix of hurt, betrayal, confusion, hits me right in the gut. "But it's not like I had other options. It was my life. It was all I knew. And I wanted to tell you a hundred times. But you have this idea of what's right and what's wrong and there's no moving you from your spot, not even if we—" I choke on my words and exhale, getting myself back together. "But you're wrong about Harper. She couldn't stomach my family's life. She took off on her own when I was twelve. She was the brave one. The one who knew who she was. All she wanted was an honest life. A real one. And then she wanted that for me, too. So yeah, she let handsy assholes stuff money in her thong, but she was so sure about doing the right thing. And me, I still can't shake that life, that part of me. If you sift through your memories, if you really think about it, you'll see it. It's all there."

Miles's face hardens, his fist clenched at his sides. "What's her name? Your mother."

"Lenora." I swallow back more tears. "Lenora Hayes."

"Wait…" His eyes widen. "Your mother is married to— You're that Hayes family?"

"Not anymore. The FBI let me change my name. I picked a memorable one." I look Miles over and see the truth. We've gone so far backward, we'll never be able to close this space again. "And how do you know about the Hayes family? Organized Crime 101? Marshall Academy elective?"

"Something like that." His jaw tenses. "You can't be here. I can't be—"

"Associated with a known criminal," I finish for him. I know the top-secret security clearance rules well. Aidan managed to get around that one due to the fact that I'm a minor and Harper has never been formally charged with anything. "Unless, of course, your parents force you to live with one."

"Clyde was never convicted."

"Neither was I. He and I both proved to be fantastic informants. But you know what they say about informants?"

He grips the chair beside him, squeezing until his knuckles turn white. Aidan might not be the only one he'd like to kill. "Don't fall in love with them," he says, forcing the words out.

I nod, wipe my nose on my sleeve. "That's probably good advice."

"You can't be here," he repeats.

"Okay, but…" I stare at the folder on the floor, and then I give Miles one last long look, searching for any hint of conflict, uncertainty, but his look of betrayal, hatred, is rock solid. "I need those pictures."

"No way." He's so fast, the folder is scooped up before I even bend down.

I half turn like I'm about to leave, but instead I lunge forward, slam my elbow hard against his temple—a move he taught me. I gasp when he immediately falls to the ground, out cold.

Tears spill down my face, but I snatch the folder of pictures from his finger. I rip Simon's note from the front, tuck the folder under my shirt. I press the sticky note against the doorframe.

And then I run.

CHAPTER
46

've got Aidan's keys in the ignition when a fist pounds on the window. I'm expecting Miles—I mean, who knew that move would actually work, and his unconscious state is probably short-lived.

Clyde's face presses against the window; he points to the hood of the car, indicating he's going to keep me from driving off. I roll down the window, my hands still shaking.

"You got a valid license, young lady?"

It's obvious he hasn't been in the apartment yet. "Um, no. But I need to see my sister."

He reaches into the window and opens the driver door. "Come on, I'll take you. Another arrest avoided, right?"

Slowly, I get out of the car and follow him to his truck across the parking lot. I try not to glance back at the apartment. The stiff folder pinches the skin at my waist. I can't believe I just did that. But Miles would have handed this over to the FBI, and if Harper couldn't even tell me about this part of her life, I doubt she wants the world to see it. I'm not letting that happen. Maybe that's what Simon was doing? Maybe he protected Harper for me.

Clyde gets us on the road, and I'm wiping my face as

fast as I can but I can't keep up with the tears. If Aidan goes to prison where are we going to go? I pull out my phone and scroll through texts seeing if Harper has contacted me, but I pause on an unread message Justice sent me early this morning.

JUSTICE: home free! Thank God almighty. Dominic, too. Guess there was another guy...idk

There was definitely another guy. Soon she'd know this. Probably think I set her up yesterday or something. Yeah, I don't think I'm going back to Holden anytime soon. I'm surprised, in the midst of so much worse, how this disappoints me. I got in way too deep with this normal-schoolgirl role.

"Did they..." I try. "Is Aidan—"

Clyde shakes his head. "They were processing Agent Lawrence and had your sister in the interview room. I couldn't check in with her." He looks me over and then turns back to the road. "The kid didn't want to go along with your plan to drive illegally to the FBI field office? You two get into an argument?"

I stare straight ahead, holding the folder against my chest. "Something like that."

"Yeah, well, it's not his fault he's that way, you know?" Clyde sighs. "Kid's got a heart of gold, just a bit sheltered, hasn't had to make that big choice yet."

"What big choice?" I ask. "You mean joining a govern-ment agency? Taking an oath?"

"I mean that moment when you choose to believe in someone or something that goes against your beliefs." He drums a finger on the steering wheel, creating a hypnotic rhythm. "Everyone faces it at some time or another."

Realization sinks in deep. I stare at the side of Clyde's face while he drives. "You know who I am, don't you?"

"I didn't at first," he admits. "I work on the FBI task

force at headquarters in D.C. quite a bit. Mostly white-collar crimes, financial fraud. Worked on your mom's case from a distance. Took me a while to put two and two together."

I stare down at my hands. "And you didn't tell Miles."

"Didn't think it'd go over so well."

It hadn't.

We're silent the rest of the drive. My heart is still drumming, my stomach sick imagining Miles on the floor, out cold. But when Clyde pulls into an empty space outside the FBI field office, my thoughts return to protecting my sister. "Do you think you could destroy some evidence for me?"

Clyde's mouth falls open, preparing to protest. I remove the folder from under my shirt and pull out a picture of Harper. He glances at it, looks away, and then takes the folder from me without any further questions. He nods toward the doors to the building, letting me know I can go in.

I open the car door but glance back at him. "You should go right back home. Check on Miles. Tell him I'm sorry." My voice cracks. I clear my throat. "I'm really sorry."

And then I leave him there and join my sister inside and face my worse nightmare—being stuck with nothing to do, no way to help or move forward.

I stare down the doors of the interrogation room where Aidan is and will them to open, will them to let me look at his face one more time. But I'm not sure it would be enough. I want to trust blindly, but I'm not sure I can. I need proof. I need to know he didn't do it.

I need to be inside that room right now, hearing all the evidence, all the accusations.

Harper watches me stand, and I stop her from following. "I'll be right back."

I walk out the doors of the building and stand in the middle of the parking lot where the cars on the busy road can conceal my conversation. Then I dial Connie's number.

I quickly explain to her what's happened, who Aidan is, and the briefest summary of my family history that I can give.

"Can you find some way to sync phones with the agents in the interrogation room?" I ask. "Or maybe you can tap into the camera feed?"

Connie is silent for several seconds, and I immediately regret calling her.

"I'm sorry," I say in a rush. "Forget I called. Please. Just forget it."

"Give me forty-five minutes," she says finally. "Don't go anywhere."

CHAPTER
47

Justice calls for the third time, and I hit ignore again but she texts right after.

JUSTICE: R u ok? Wtf is going on????? Call me ASAP!!

My finger hovers over the keys, attempting to form a reply to combat more phone calls, but a familiar voice has me looking up. Forty-five minutes on the dot.

"I'm legal counsel representing Agent Lawrence."

Connie is wearing a tailored suit, her hair in a neat bun on top of her head and designer glasses perched at the end of her nose. If I didn't recognize her voice, she may have slipped right past me.

"Are you with the DA's office?" the desk worker asks.

Connie shakes her head. "Agent's Lawrence's fiancée asked me to be here."

Fiancée?

Connie glances at me and Harper and smiles. "There she is..." She walks right over to Harper and hugs her. "I came as soon as I could."

Harper turns to me, her eyes narrowed, but she plays along. "Thank you, I really appreciate it." She nods in my direction. "This is my sister, Ellie."

Connie shakes my hand and in the same motion, passes me two small objects. I wait for the desk worker to lead her back to the room Aidan's in, and then I look down at my palm. Earpieces.

I hand one to Harper and quickly slip the other into my ear.

"Is she really a lawyer?" Harper whispers.

I start to say no but then remember something Connie said the last time I visited the store. "Actually, I think she is. Or was."

It takes nearly ten minutes but eventually, the voices inside that room are broadcast loud and clear through the fancy earpieces. Harper's spine straightens, and then she realizes her reaction and slumps down again in her seat.

"If you could please restate the charges against my client so I can advise him properly," Connie says.

The agent in the room sighs. "What your client needs to do is give us the name of the person who hired him as a hit man, and then we can talk deals."

Beside me, Harper swallows a gasp. I nudge her in the side, reminding her to be quiet.

"My client has already assured me that he isn't nor has he ever been a hit man, so I believe we're at a standstill."

Papers shuffle, and then several seconds of silence.

"A series of international investment accounts opened under various forms of your name between last July and earlier this month," the agent says. "The funds total over a million dollars."

My stomach sinks. Money. Just like Miles said.

"And then one of my agents captured this photo of you in the middle of a business transaction… Do you know who this man is?"

"No, I don't," Connie says.

"We've been trying to catch him for nearly two years. He works for the DMV, and on the side, he makes authentic false identification. What did the two of you discuss? Maybe a passport or two... Or possibly three?"

I suck in a breath, holding it in. This can't be right. Aidan would do anything for Harper, anything to give her the life she truly wants, but not this. Not Simon. I squeeze my phone tightly in my hand, wishing I could call Miles, wishing he could hear all of this and help me dissect it.

"One job, one pile of cash, and your girlfriend, the little sister... They get a new life. For real this time. Isn't that what you promised them?" the agent says, his voice escalating with each word. "You're a good man, Agent Lawrence. Loyal to those you love. It must have been a painful decision, taking that job. But Harper and Eleanor, Lord knows the Charleston field office has kept a close eye on them. That can't be easy to deal with. They were always going to be stuck with their past, defined by it. And you weren't willing to let that happen, were you?"

"Tell us who hired you." The booming voice of another agent emerges. The Bad Cop, it seems. "Tell us who you used as bait that night. The kid who opened the door, who'd been luring Simon into an online relationship for months. Or maybe you didn't handle that part, Agent Lawrence. Perhaps your organization requires a multitude of talents, much like the FBI. You'd need some brains between the accounts and covering your tracks. You'd need a pretty face to hook the Gilbert boy, and a marksman, like yourself. Because we both know you're just the muscle, Agent Lawrence. Help us bring your team in and we'll take that into consideration when it comes time for sentencing."

"That's enough," Connie says, her voice now low, barely above a whisper. "I'd like a moment with my client."

The second the room is cleared, Aidan speaks for the

first time since we started listening in. "Who the hell are you?"

"A concerned third party," she says smoothly. "I'm going to need passwords for your email, bank accounts, cell phone…"

Harper pulls the earpiece out, stands abruptly, and walks over to the desk. "Do you have a number for a taxi service?"

The guy looks up from his computer. "I'd be happy to call a cab for you."

"Thanks."

"Harper—" I start.

She waves a hand to stop me. "Let's get out of here."

I don't know what she's thinking, where her head is at; has she lost faith in Aidan's innocence? I barely hear Aidan, reciting the information Connie's requesting, but he does comply with her request, despite knowing nothing about her.

Connie exits shortly after, offering us a brief good-bye.

Our cab arrives quickly, and after we hop in and are down the road, I explain who Connie is and how I know her. Harper stares out the window, listening but saying nothing.

When Connie finally calls me, hours after leaving the FBI office, I jump to answer. "Hey, what's up?"

"The mystery email address," Connie says. "It belongs to a Bret Thomas. I believe he—"

"Goes to my school." My stomach drops. I knew it. I knew that guy was bad news. He lied right to my face and I didn't catch it. "Oh shit, this could mean…well, it could mean that Bret is capable of…" Murder? God, I can't even.

"Ellie, listen to me," Connie says firmly. "You and your boyfriend have to stop this Nancy Drew stuff. You heard the agents in the interrogation room earlier. They don't believe this was a solo job, and since Agent Lawrence was the only taken in, someone else could be watching you two—"

"Wait," I interrupt. "My boyfriend? You mean Miles? He's not my—"

"Whatever he is, he asked me to help him get access to the FBI database."

"Did you?"

"No," Connie says. "And I'm not going to. Let me snoop around for now. If Agent Lawrence is innocent, that means someone went through a lot of trouble to frame him. Whoever killed the senator's son is likely to go after anyone caught digging for answers."

My heart bangs inside my chest. Miles seemed so sure that it was Aidan this morning. Why would he dig around more?

After hanging up with Connie, I hunt around the apartment for my shoes while texting Dominic.

ME: this is Ellie. Have u seen Miles today?

DOMINIC: how did u get my number?

ME: from Miles. Have u seen him???

DOMINIC: Party at my house right now. He's supposed to come over any minute

ME: Great!! Don't let him out of your sight! And stay away from Bret!

I pause in the middle of the apartment, trying to figure out what I should do first. Connie told me to leave things alone, but this Bret info…it has to mean something. He lied to my face. He had me fooled. Bret has to be a part of this. Is that why Aidan was so concerned with the surveillance footage of the parking lot? Did he and Bret work together? I swallow back that thought. I don't even know what to believe anymore.

I need Miles. Now.

Dominic said Miles was coming over soon. But maybe he hasn't left yet.

My phone rings for the millionth time today. Jack.

"How are you two holding up?" he asks.

"Bad, I think." I glance into Harper and Aidan's room where my sister has left behind a tornado of papers and folders. "Harper tore up the entire apartment, wouldn't tell me what she was looking for, and then took off for the Feldsteins' to get her paycheck."

"She thinking about leaving town?" Jack asks.

"I don't know," I say honestly. "If she is, she hasn't told me yet."

"Well, that's good, then. She won't go anywhere without you," Jack assesses. "Give her space. Let her process. Try not to worry. I've got my eye on you two."

He's got his eye on us.

All eyes on you.

Alleyesonyou.

I was about to walk out the apartment door but suddenly I'm frozen in place, ice running through my veins. I manage to stutter out a reply, "Uh…okay. Thanks, Jack. Talk to you later."

I stuff my phone into my pocket and race to Harper and Aidan's room. It's in post-tornado state, but Aidan's phone still sits on the nightstand in plain sight. With shaking hands, I grab it, punch in the password, and scroll back through his texts with Jack. Way back. To June 15. My heart nearly stops when I see what Aidan sent to Jack at 9:32 p.m. on the night Simon died.

AIDAN: want anything from WaWa?

JACK: sure. My usual hoagie
AIDAN: meet u around back in twenty

Aidan never mentioned Jack when he brought up that story. They worked together that night. At the Gilberts'. Either they're still working together or Jack set him up.

I drop Aidan's phone onto the bed and run out the apartment door toward Miles's place.

I bang on the door. No response. I bang again but no luck. I'm about to pick the lock and break in, but the knob turns. It's unlocked.

Two steps into the living room, and I let out a scream.

Clyde is lying in a heap in the middle of the carpet.

CHAPTER
48

Ohmygod, ohmygod, ohmygod.

I drop to the floor beside Clyde and lay my ear against his chest and listen. I try to hold perfectly still, but I'm shaking all over.

His lungs expand; a rise and fall of his chest follows quickly after. I release a breath of relief and shake his shoulders. "Clyde! Clyde, wake up!"

He stirs but doesn't seem to regain consciousness. Is this what Miles looked like when Clyde found him? I look over the rest of the apartment. Chaos swarms around me. Every drawer, cabinet, and container has been opened and taken apart. The door to the secret room has been drilled and removed from the hinges.

Oh God, this is bad.

"Clyde! Please wake up!" Nothing seems to work, and I begin to panic about shaking or touching him; what if he has a neck injury?

I take in a slow, deep breath and force myself to prioritize, mentally form a list of tasks in order of importance. I shoot Dominic and Justice the same text. Then just to be extra safe, I add Chantel and Jacob.

ME: Do NOT let Miles out of ur sight .

I remove Clyde's phone and dial 911.

"My neighbor is unconscious but breathing," I say in a rush. "I think he hit his head or something." I give her the address and then hang up.

By the time I'm backing Aidan's car out of the parking lot, sirens are already blaring in the distance. It's dark now, too, and what had been drizzling rain turns into a downpour with pellets of ice hitting the windshield. I try not to speed on the way to Dominic's house, but my adrenaline levels are too high. When I pull up to the DeLucas' house and hastily park the car among the sea of my classmate's vehicles, I send Harper a text.

ME: don't go back to the apartment. Not safe. Get a cab to FBI office and STAY there . Stay away from Jack!!!

I don't know if she'll do what I'm asking, but I can only hope. I shut the engine off and and hop out of Aidan's car. Dominic's house is packed with kids from school, and it's loud as hell. I shove people aside, searching the entryway.

What if Bret is here? What do I do? Is it Jack and Bret and some mystery guy and they framed Aidan? Or Aidan and Jack and they framed Bret? Or all three of them?

I spot Justice hanging with Chantel. Both of them are decked out in full party wear, drinks in hand. I'm still in my school uniform, my legs now wet and muddy from running through Dominic's yard in the rain.

"Oh wow, you've had a rough day," Justice says, assessing me. "Let's get you a drink."

I swat away the cup she thrusts in my face. "Where's Miles?"

"I think he's in the kitchen—"

I'm already pushing my way through to the kitchen. I glance around, scanning the room. No Miles. I hear Dominic's voice and head straight for him. I yank him from a deep discussion on the best nineties punk bands and spin him to face me. "Where is Miles?"

"Jesus Christ. Who invited you?" He tugs out of my grip and gives me his signature glare. Then he stands there like an ass for a good ten seconds, takes a hit off someone's joint before finally answering me. "And Miles was here, but his dad came to get him."

"What do you mean his dad came?" I demand. "What did he look like?"

"He had some like you know hair and eyes, kind of big eyes." Dominic holds up a hand several inches above my head. "And he was sort of tall."

"Oh my God, you suck," I groan. "Who else saw this guy?"

I grip Dominic's arms and shake him. "Focus! Tell me what the guy looked like. Was he thin? Did he have any gray hair?"

Dominic's eyes widen like maybe I'm scaring him. Good. "Uh... Normal, not thin. His hair was kinda like mine. Definitely not gray."

"Definitely not Miles's dad."

"Relax," Dominic says. "Let me call our man Miles Beckett."

Seconds later, I hear the buzz. I drop down on the floor and look beneath the center island. A black cell phone vibrates against the ceramic floor.

Panic hits me from every side. I pull the phone out and look it over.

"Well, there you go. That's why he's not answering."

Miles would never leave his phone lying around on purpose. I stuff it in my coat pocket and stand. "Call me the second you see or hear from him."

I don't wait for Dominic's response.

I head straight out the back door and run around the

house, looking for signs of something, but what, I'm not sure. I fight the urge to shout Miles's name at the top of my lungs. Cold rain hits me in the face. Mud and water splash up my legs. I make a full circle around the house but nothing. No Miles. No anyone.

A classmate nearly plows me over, trying to avoid a puddle in his dress shoes. I zoom in on his feet, staring at them for several seconds. Shiny shoes. No, super-shiny shoes. Like Aidan wears. Like the Secret Service all wear. And old jeans. Someone who'd been on duty and changed into something more comfortable. Didn't bring a second pair of shoes to work.

There must be an agent that fits the profile Dominic described, someone like that guy at the Gilberts' —

Shit. Oh shit. What was his name? Rider, I think. But he couldn't have posed as Miles's dad. Neither could Aidan for a number of reasons, one being that he's locked up at the moment.

Jack.

Jesus Christ, it is Jack. And he has Miles. But why? Why —

Come on, Ellie, think. You need a plan.

I'll just have to get to the FBI office and tell them everything. But that could take too long. It might be too late by that point.

I pull out my phone in the dark, rain landing on the screen, and with shaking hands, I dial the number Mr. Beckett scrawled on a slip of paper and then tossed into the fire.

"Please state your pass code now."

My voice is shaking, but I force it steady when I recite the German words Mr. Beckett had quoted me. I wait two seconds, and then the automated voice speaks again. "Pass code verified. Thank you for calling voice mail box six-three-four-seven-two. Expect a return call from your party in twenty-four to forty-eight hours."

The line goes dead, and I stand there shivering in the rain, staring at my phone, stunned and utterly let down. Why had Miles's dad made it sound like an emergency number if it was nothing more than a super-secure answering service?

I hop in the car and peel out of Dominic's neighborhood and head for the FBI office. I take a back road, not wanting to get stopped. It's dark, and the rain pounds hard against the windshield. I can barely see where I'm going. I feel around on the left side of the steering wheel, searching for the brights. My elbow makes contact with something. I glance down and gasp.

Fingers. A hand.

Two faces appear in the rearview mirror, and a finger presses down the lock button. I don't even have to look. I already know who it is.

CHAPTER
49

The car swerves toward a ditch. My heart jumps up to my throat. Then what feels like a gun presses into my right side. I stifle a scream.

"Easy there, Ellie. Keep that car on the road, understood?"

Jack is in the backseat of Aidan's car.

I chance another glance in the mirror and spot the young agent who caught me in the Gilberts' house. Rider. I was right. I'm shaking, but I manage to regain control of the car.

"Good girl," Jack says. "Just keep on driving straight, hands right on the wheel, ten and two, where we can see them."

"I told you she'd be a problem." Rider digs his gun harder into my side. "She even got a license?"

"Enough," Jack snaps. "Two more miles and then make a left, okay?"

"What are we—" I push the words out despite the fear. "Where are we going? And where is Miles?"

Rider pats down my coat pockets with his hands and snatches both my phone and Miles's. The sound of the screens cracking follows seconds later. "We're going to a better place," Rider says, laughing.

"Enough," Jack repeats. "Here, Ellie. Left turn."

The left turn takes us on an even darker, more desolate road. This is not looking good. Not at all. "If Rider is the bait, then are you the brains or the marksman, Jack? And which one of you is 'all eyes on you'?"

Jack doesn't respond for several seconds. I can see him shaking his head through the mirror. "You just can't stay out of shit, can you, kid? It wasn't supposed to be like this... *dammit.*"

Fear tumbles through my stomach; my hands grip the steering wheel tighter.

"You were in Dominic's house," I whisper. "You did something to Miles."

I choke back a sob. I might be too late to save Miles.

"Kid had it coming," Rider says. "Running around like he's in the fucking teenage FBI? If he wants to play cops and robbers, we're gonna show him how it's done."

"Shut the hell up," Jack snaps again at Rider. "You have no idea what you're talking about. No idea who that kid is. We're gonna have to..."

I tune him out and focus on a sound barely audible. A soft, repeated *thud*. Jack and Rider couldn't have been at Dominic's much earlier than me; they couldn't have taken Miles far. In fact he could be very close by.

The rain pounds against the windshield. I lean forward, grip the steering wheel tighter, and wait for the right moment. A tree appears in the distance. I tug my seat belt, checking it twice. And then I do probably the stupidest, most dangerous thing possible. I turn the wheel sharply to the left. The back end of the car swings counterclockwise. Both Jack and Rider shout and slide across the backseat. Rider's door hits the tree, throwing them toward the other door. The impact is harder than I expected. My head bangs against the driver's side window. Spots form in front of my eyes, but I manage to fumble around for the button near my knee and pop the trunk. I fling the door open and race around the car.

Before I can even glance inside, a leg swings over the edge and Miles is standing in front of me. There's a cloth tight around his mouth and his hands are cuffed in front. My fingers tremble when I tug the cloth off his face.

"Hurry! Get these off me." Miles lifts the cuffs and glances over his shoulder, checking for movement from inside the car. "My pockets."

Water drips from my nose and chin, but I dig in his pockets until my fingers land on his pocket knife. I find the corkscrew on the knife and squat down in front of the cuffs. "Where's the lock? I can't see!"

"Come on, Ellie," he says. "You know how to do this."

Hearing my name rolling off Miles's tongue in that familiar way urges me forward.

He looks over his shoulder at the back window and presses to the balls of his feet. They're moving around in there. Jack and Rider. I shake the water from the cuffs and locate the lock. I've got the corkscrew working inside it when the rear car door opens and Jack tumbles out. He reaches in and pulls Rider to his feet.

Shit. Oh shit.

The lock pops, freeing Miles's hands just as Rider lunges at me. Miles kicks him square in the chest, sending him flying backward. In a flash, he's got Rider's gun. He aims it at Jack while Rider gets to his feet again. Miles grabs the back of my coat and pulls me behind him.

"Run!" he orders.

A shot fires, ringing loud in my ears. I turn to run, but duck behind the hood of the car. Miles joins me, taking cover. He fires two shots into the dark.

"Go!" He points toward the woods.

I take off running, my heart pounds, mud sloshes up my legs. Miles catches up to me, his steps splashing mine, his breathing just as rapid as mine. We run in the dark, dodging trees, not slowing down even to glance over our shoulders. I can't see anything ahead. Can't make out a road or opening other than the one behind us. And we definitely aren't going back the way we came.

Miles is moving slower than I expected. When I look over at him, he's got one arm draped carefully across his stomach.

Oh my God, did he get shot? I open my mouth to ask him, but Jack's and Rider's voices grow louder. Or wait... are they ahead of us now? Miles hooks an arm around my waist and pulls me against a tree.

"What happened—?"

He lifts a finger to his lips. "Shhhh."

I clamp my mouth shut and hold perfectly still. He presses himself against me, concealing both of us behind this tree. We're making great effort not to gasp for air, silent except the rise and fall of our chests. But when Miles rests his forehead against mine, I notice his breathing is more labored. I keep my eyes on his, internally panicking. I slide my hands beneath his shirt, feeling for any sign of a gunshot wound. As if I even know what that might feel like. Stickiness from blood? A giant hole blasted through him?

"It's my shoulder," he whispers. "I think it's dislocated."

I locate his right shoulder in the dark and gently slide my hand over it. My stomach rolls conjuring a mental image of what this probably looks like. I set my arm beneath his, trying to support it, take the pressure off his shoulder. I follow the path of his left arm all the way to the gun in his hand. He's right-handed. Can he even shoot with his left hand? I shake that thought. It's not the time to ask.

"Come on out. We're gonna find you two eventually, might as well cooperate," Rider's voice echoes through the woods. He's pretty far away. At least it sounds like he is.

My heart pounds. Miles's thuds just as fast against mine. We both hold perfectly still.

"They're not over here!" someone shouts. A new voice. One that doesn't belong to Jack or Rider. "You sure they're armed?"

"Considering Teen Rambo took my fucking gun…"

I'm soaked through my clothes, and it's only forty degrees out, so my teeth begin to chatter. Miles presses his cheek into mine, attempting to stop the chattering and giving me a good view of his temple. The one I elbowed this morning. A wave of regret hits me. I lift my hand, brushing my fingers over the bump.

"I'm sorry," I whisper, "I didn't mean to—"

"Shhh," he says again, his lips right beside my ear.

We both listen for a moment, judging the distance of the footsteps, guessing how many there are. Miles shuffles closer, his feet tucking right beside mine, framing them between his.

"Surround the place," another new voice says. "Let them freeze to death, and we'll collect the bodies in daylight."

Miles stiffens but then sags against me shortly after. They've moved farther away. For now. I try not to shake, to not be the girl who gets cold easily, but it's freezing and I've been soaking wet for at least thirty minutes.

"Pretty sure we broke Beckett's arm getting him in that trunk," Jack says.

Miles raises his head, speaking in a low whisper. "What do you see behind me?"

At first I'm surprised by the question. It sounds like we're in the school, Miles prompting me with questions as part of his self-defense lessons. Some good those do when you're trying to operate a moving vehicle. But then I realize that he can't look over his shoulder, not with it dislocated.

"Nothing." I shake my head. "Trees. More trees."

"There must be something out here," he whispers. "Jack was leading you this way and at least one other person is out here—" He stops, listening to the footsteps carefully. "Two other people."

I stare and stare at the shadows of trees in front of me and finally, I spot a slight opening. "I think maybe there's a cabin or some sort of building. I can make out an opening in the trees."

Miles nods. He lifts the stolen gun, raising it to both our faces, and opens the barrel. "How many bullets?"

I look and feel, giving my best assessment. "Four, I think."

"Okay, that sucks." He snaps it closed again and holds it at the ready. "You don't have a cell phone on you, I assume?"

I shake my head. "Rider smashed mine and yours."

His forehead wrinkles at the mention of his phone.

"I found it at the party," I explain.

Miles rests his cheek against mine again. "You came looking for me?"

"A few minutes too late."

"Ellie?" Miles whispers, and my heart takes off again. Is this the part where he reminds me that he hates me? Or where he admits that he doesn't? "I need you to help me pop my shoulder back in place."

Or there's that.

"How?" I say.

He starts to explain and then stops; his whole body turns to stone against me. The slosh of footsteps nearby is barely audible. I open my mouth to warn Miles, but he's already raising his gun.

I squeeze my eyes shut when he pulls the trigger. He only fires one shot. A cry of pain follows.

Miles pushes away from me. "Go!"

He points in the direction of the cabin or building or whatever I had guessed was out here, but I can't move. I'm in shock. He just shot someone.

"Jesus Christ!" a voice yells.

"Rider's down," someone says.

"Ellie, go!" Miles says again.

I come to life finally and we run, our cover blown from Miles's gunfire. I keep moving forward, but he turns around twice to shoot at someone. His back is to me when a large bright light shines right in my eyes from a distance. I stop, and Miles bumps into me from behind.

"What—" he starts, but spins to face the light. He aims at the source holding the flashlight and pulls the trigger. It clicks but no shot fires. Our eyes meet and I can see him panicking. He's out of bullets. Two more flashlights appear on either sides of us.

We're surrounded.

"I've been counting your bullets," Jack says, revealing himself as the one with the flashlight. "Knew you didn't have enough for all of us. Though I must say, you're quite the marksman, son."

A man I don't recognize appears beside us. He's got a rifle, a bulletproof vest and head cover—government issued. "Move! Both of you."

I can see Miles debating in his head, calculating any possible ways to get out of this.

"Go on," the guy repeats. "Let's get this over with."

"How about I follow you," Miles says. "And you leave Ellie here in the woods. She's not gonna tell anyone about this. She's a gifted secret keeper."

That feels like a dig, like he may still sort of hate me. "Or..." I interrupt. "You can leave the valuable asset here in the woods and take the girl with virtually no identity."

"The girl with no identity," Jack repeats. "You know I was counting on that. Counting on you. But it looks like I was wrong."

"Enough talking!" The tip of the rifle wavers, but the guy holds it steady again and then pokes it right into Miles's dislocated shoulder.

He's brushed against me, so I feel him wince but he makes no sound of pain.

"Move!"

Miles concedes, walking forward. I move beside him, fighting the urge to reach for his hand.

"I'm sorry, Ellie," Jack says when we reach him. "I didn't want it to be this way. You have so much potential." He looks at Miles and shakes his head. "St. Felicity's had your name on their list, right beside your buddy Simon, but I told them you'd never go for it. Your father wouldn't even give them the time of day."

With all of that creepy shit, it takes me a moment to realize he's about to shoot us, or rifle guy is, but the *whoosh* of a helicopter flying above sends them all in a panic.

"What the hell?"

Rifle guy pokes Miles with his weapon again. "Did you call someone?"

"Get them inside, now!" Jack shouts.

CHAPTER
50

A helicopter flies over us yet again. I feel around on the walls looking for any possible exit.

"If there's a window in this room, it's way above my reach," I say through chattering teeth. It's freezing in here. Nearly as cold as outside.

"I'd estimate eight feet by eight feet," Miles says.

"Why are they freaking out about the helicopter?"

"I don't know." But his tone indicates he might know something.

I jump up and down in the dark, hitting the walls in various places, feeling for a window. "Where are we?"

"South of Fredericksburg," he says immediately. "Maybe eight or twelve miles."

"I know that," I snap. "But what is this place? What is this thing that I have so much potential for? And why are you on the St. Felicity's list with Simon? Does that mean they're going to kill you?"

"Assassins. Honorable ones who devote their lives to a mission to serve without personal gain," Miles says. "I think that's what St. Felicity's is. I've heard rumors of a group but I never knew…"

"Okay, but why would Jack think I have potential in this league of assassins?" I demand. "I would suck at assassinating."

"I think Jack is doing his own thing on the side," he says. "Some kind of splinter organization."

"Something for money," I assess, the truth hitting me square in the chest. "Something an invisible, experienced con artist could help with."

Miles is quiet, but it sounds like he's sitting down. I roam in the dark until I bump into him. I feel around for his face and end up poking him in the ear.

"Are you okay?" I ask. "Of course you're not, your shoulder's fucked up."

Outside the door, the voices grow louder. They're arguing.

"Get into the damn dispatch system and find out where the chopper is coming from!" someone shouts.

"I'm a little busy keeping Rider from bleeding to death!"

"How bad does it hurt?" I drill Miles. "Scale of one to ten?" The nurse asked me that after my root canal. I figure it might be a good question.

"I don't know," Miles says, his voice strained. "Six... maybe eight."

My gut twists, but I rest a hand on his good shoulder and say, "Okay, if you want me to help you, I will. Just tell me what to do."

He pulls himself up straighter. I wish I could see his face, see if he's as scared as I am. I listen carefully to his directions and then place my hands exactly where he tells me to. But before I do anything, he stops me. "You can't go halfway. Might make it worse."

"Got it." I shake my hands out and take a breath. But then I lay my hands on the dislocated right shoulder and freak out all over all again. "Tell me everything one more time."

Miles rests his left hand on my cheek and draws me closer until our foreheads touch. "I wouldn't ask you if I didn't think you could do it. I trust you."

I exhale. My eyes burn with tears. "You shouldn't trust me."

His thumb brushes over my cheek. "But I do."

"Okay..." I place my hands on him again but hesitate. "Okay."

"Do it fast," he instructs.

I try my best to do as Miles says, visualize the shoulder as a ball that needs to slide back over into the right hole. Adrenaline is pumping through me, giving me strength. What I'm not ready for is Miles's shout of pain and the crunching sound that follows. But even in the dark, I felt it. Felt the bone return to its place.

"Are you okay? Please tell me you're okay?"

He slumps back against the wall, his breathing ragged, but I hear him nod.

I'm shaking all over, my heart pounding, but I fold Miles's arm carefully against his stomach. I tug my jacket off and use it to make a sling. I'm knotting it at his neck when the lights come on and the door flies open.

I slide over, sitting against the wall beside Miles. His left hand crawls toward mine and squeezes it.

The rifle guy has ditched his helmet, but not the gun or vest. "What was that noise?"

He points his weapon right at us and I hold my breath.

"Lock that damn door and get over here!" Jack shouts.

The door slams shut again, and I release all the air in my lungs in one long exhale. Clicking and banging follows the door slam. I listen closely, trying to identify the locks. "God, what is this place? A dungeon?"

I turn to look at him and realize that the lights are still on. And he's pale. So pale.

Miles's eyes are half closed, but when my teeth chatter too loudly for him to ignore, he looks over at me.

"Come here," he says. I scoot over until my arm touches his good shoulder. "Closer…"

He swings a leg around me and pulls me in until I'm seated between his legs, avoiding the sling. My cheek is against his chest, my leg over his, helping to prop up the sling.

"What's your pain level now?" I ask.

"Six…maybe five." He touches a hand to my cheek, and then tightens his whole arm around me. "God, you're cold."

"Do you believe there are honorable assassins??"

"That's a tough question," he says. "Apparently my dad turned it down, so that makes me wonder. Then again, if someone had killed Hitler before World War II, how many lives would that have saved?"

"That's what St. Felicity's does? They take out the next Hitler?" I ask, shocked.

"If the rumors are right, yeah," Miles says, his voice weak. "But then does that mean someone paid Jack to kill Simon?"

"No," I say after a long pause. It's all making much more sense now—Simon having the photos of Harper, trying to get information out of Rider, letting him play the bait. Simon knew what was going on. He was protecting me. "He killed Simon because Simon was onto him."

Miles nods, appearing to put everything together himself. "All this time I thought I owned my secrets, but Jack knew. Simon probably knew. No wonder Jack covered for me when we broke into the Gilberts'. He was waiting to proposition me to join his million-dollar-a-head long con. Maybe he doesn't know my feelings on firearms? Or my lack of self-defense skills?"

Miles doesn't say anything, but I feel him tense, maybe

at bringing up my dark side, the part of me he likely hates.

"If we'd just stayed out of it, none of this would have happened to you." I press my face against his shirt. "I'm sorry, Miles. For this morning. I didn't want to—"

"Shhh." He leans his head back on the wall again and closes his eyes. "Let's not do this now. You're here. You didn't have to be. You didn't have to look for me at that party or crash the car for me."

"But—" I start.

"No buts." Miles's warm lips touch my forehead. "These guys killed Simon, Ellie. We have no phones, no weapons, no way out. The odds of survival are not in our favor. And the thirty percent of me that is furious at you, the part of me that doesn't even know who you are—he's not in this room right now. I ditched him back at that party."

Despite my freezing cold exterior, his words warm me from the inside. But it's bittersweet, because the reality scares the hell out of me. "How are you always so sure?"

"Because I've never really had to make a difficult choice." He smiles at me. "Until you, anyway."

Outside this tiny room, Jack's voice rises above the others. "See? It's a medical chopper trying to land in Richmond. The weather's bad. They're circling."

Miles tenses, and then he tilts my head up and his lips touch mine, gentle at first and then more urgent, more desperate. And sure enough, the door opens and Jack and the rifle guy stand in front of us.

Miles releases me and pulls himself to his feet. He looks right at Jack. "Where's your weapon?"

Jack nods at the rifle guy beside him. "Right here."

"Come on," Miles says. "We know you killed Simon. He turned around to face you, then you shot him dead with his own gun."

Jack flinches.

"I deserve that same respect." Miles's voice rises. "If you're going to kill me, Jakowski, be a fucking man. Grab a weapon and look me in the eye."

My legs are shaking so bad I'm afraid they'll crumble beneath me, but I get to my feet anyway and stand beside Miles.

With a bite to his movement, Jack snatches the rifle from the other guy and clicks it into place. "Happy?"

I glance around the room, still searching for a way out. I'm not as good at this martyr thing as Miles. "What I want to know is how you pulled this off, Jack. We wrapped the Dominic-the-murderer theory into a perfect package for the FBI. How did you make everything fit so perfectly to frame Aidan?"

The end of the rifle bobs up and down. "Dominic DeLuca never fit the profile, wouldn't have held up through conviction. Unfortunately, he got a peek at Rider, so we had to shut him up, and that got a little messy. Framing Lawrence was plan B. If you two had kept your damn noses out of things, that case would have stayed close."

Jack positions the weapon and turns it first on me. "All right, you have one tiny chance at survival."

"Let me guess," Miles says. "You want me and Ellie to join your club of dishonorable assassins?"

"I've always wanted Eleanor on my team. From the moment I dug into Lawrence's new girlfriends' family. I reunited them, got Ellie into Holden, set her up to make friends in high places," Jack says to Miles like I'm not even here. "You haven't seen her in action. She has a gift that can't be taught. With the right resources we could bank millions, maybe even without picking up a weapon."

Okay, so he hadn't wanted me to kill people, just lie and steal. And make friends in high places. Basically my old life.

"But yes," Jack continues, looking at Miles. "You could also prove to be useful."

A groan of pain erupts from outside the room, and the rifle guy shakes his head. "We're gonna need to replace Rider. That your first human target?"

Miles stands there, his good fist clenched. "Yeah."

"Femoral artery on the first try. Impressive. Bet you're top of your class at Marshall Academy. Who's recruiting you for internships?" Jack asks. "FBI? CIA? NSA?"

Miles glances sideways at me for a split second and it's enough for me to guess, to feel his next move. "Harvard," he tells Jack, and then he dives forward, shoving me out of the way with his good arm. The gun fires at the ceiling, and I immediately cover my head. I hear the rifle hit the hard floor and land near me. I fling myself toward it, pulling it under me before the guy who owns it has a chance.

Jack manages to get Miles to the ground, his hands around his throat. I panic, fumbling to get to my feet and aim this rifle at him. Miles's eyes widen, watching me try to figure out the weapon. I've never even so much as held a firearm before. But even as the other guy races toward me, I've got the rifle backward. A smirk begins to spread across his face, and my blood instantly boils. Since I can't figure out how to shoot him, I jam the weapon right into his temple like I'd done to Miles this morning. He stumbles a little, begins to fall, and I swing the rifle like a bat, smashing it against the back of his head.

I finally get it turned around and aimed at Jack. "Let him go," I demand.

But there's no need for my orders. Miles does some kung fu fighter move and sends Jack flying several feet away. He hits the wall and comes down with a *thud*, but he's on his feet immediately.

Miles carefully extracts the weapon from me and

points it at Jack. And it's like that day in the secret room, all that hatred, that desire for revenge, it's back on Miles's face. It fills the room from floor to ceiling.

"Ellie, leave."

I move closer to him. "We're both leaving."

Jack watches this exchange; his gaze falls on me. He glances for a second at his fallen teammate. "Listen to him, Ellie. Get out of here."

"I'll be right behind you," Miles says.

I'm literally torn in half, one foot planted and the other looking for the exit. But before I get a chance to decide, a bloody leg crosses into the doorway and then Rider is there, a pistol in his hand.

"I believe this game is called chicken," Rider says. "You shoot him, and I shoot her."

An elbow swings out to hit Rider, then a fist to his nose; he falls down on all fours, hollering in pain.

"Never had the patience for chicken."

I stand there in shock while Miles's uncle Clyde hovers over Rider, pointing his own gun at him.

CHAPTER
51

Rider looks up at Clyde, eyes wide.

"That's right," Clyde says. "I'm the old man you knocked out earlier. Thought I'd forget your face?"

Rider reaches for his weapon, and Clyde doesn't even hesitate, shoots him in the other leg. And Clyde isn't alone. Dominic and Brett hover behind him. Bret swoops down and swipes Rider's gun. He turns it expertly on him.

"Damn," Bret mutters. "I made that look good."

What the hell is Bret doing here?

Okay, what the hell is Dominic doing here? His gaze sweeps the room and then lands on Rider. His eyes widen, jaw tenses. He recognizes him. From the Gilberts' house. The night Simon was murdered.

"So all of you…" Bret swings his free hand around the room. "Are responsible for taking our boy Simon out?"

Jack shoots a glare at Bret. "We had a deal."

"No more." Bret shakes his head. "This is not what I signed up for. You fucking used me so you could harass Dominic into silence and frame Agent Lawrence."

"Seriously?" Dominic asks.

Miles is working hard to conceal his shock at their

arrival, but he answers Dominic with a nod.

Clyde reaches out a hand for me. "Come on, honey, let's get you out of here."

I scoot right around Miles and Rider, who's still lying on the ground. Clyde pulls an arm out of his coat and then looks at Bret. "Fire at will if he moves."

Clyde sets the gun in Dominic's hand long enough to drape his coat over me and then he's back in position. "All right kid, time to go."

Miles shakes his head and grits his teeth. "Go ahead. I'll meet you back at the road."

"Goddammit, Miles," Clyde snaps. "Put that fucking rifle down or so help me God I will wring your neck…"

"He killed my friend," Miles says. "He stuffed me in a trunk, brought Ellie and me out here to die. This is my fight to finish."

"Thomas." Dominic holds a hand out to Bret. "Let me see that gun?"

"No, you don't," Clyde says, not even looking at Bret. He's still focused on Miles. "For once in your goddamned life you're gonna listen to me. I don't care how angry you are or how much you need to make things right, you're still a boy. You aren't ready to kill someone."

Miles's hand shakes. He's so angry, but Clyde is right— he's not ready for this. "Miles…don't," I plead. "Please. Let's go home."

His eyes gloss over. He swallows and glances sideways at me for a fraction of a second.

"Come on, son," Clyde says, quieter. "Put the gun down and get out of here."

Miles tightens his grip on the gun. I squeeze my eyes shut, hold my breath.

But seconds later, the rifle hits the ground with a loud *clank*. I grab his shirt and tug him out of that dungeon.

Dominic follows us and then Bret behind him, making a big show of pointing his gun at every corner. We step back outside in the rain, trudge about thirty feet through the mud, and then a gunshot rings out loud and clear from the cabin. We all freeze, turn to face the door. A few seconds later, Clyde steps out, tosses the rifle onto the muddy ground.

Miles walks toward him and sputters, "What…why—?"

"I said *you* weren't ready," Clyde tells Miles. "Not that he didn't deserve to be shot. I'm not gonna let someone walk free who tried to murder my nephew."

Miles stares at Clyde, and I'm waiting for him to get angry, but he instead gives Clyde a one-armed hug and I hear him say, "Thank you."

Clyde grabs Bret's stolen gun and tucks it into the back of his pants. "That the deal you made with the devil, boy? You take some pictures for him and he gets you a legal registered weapon? I'm not even gonna ask what you wanted to do with that gun."

Guilt fills Bret's face. He looks away from Clyde. "I didn't know he was in the assassin business. Didn't know he killed Simon. Just thought he was a dirty agent looking for more money."

"Well, turns out you were right. That's exactly what he is." Clyde releases a groan of frustration. "Now let's get the hell out of here."

We move quickly through the woods, but soon it's too much for both me and Miles. I think crashing Aidan's car is coming back to bite me in the ass now. I press my palm against a nearby tree to steady myself, and Miles ends up leaning beside me. He's out of breath and dangerously pale.

"His shoulder," I explain to Clyde. "It's messed up."

Clyde frowns. "Think you can make it to the car?"

Miles and I both nod, neither of us wanting to admit

defeat. We struggle our way out of the woods, back to the road where Dominic's gray SUV is parked. Dominic opens the car door for me and then I hear him say, in the lowest voice possible, "I'm sorry. For earlier. I should have helped you."

"Forget about it," I offer, taking a note from Miles. "How did you end up here, anyway? How did you find us?"

"It's a long damn story," Clyde snaps. "Get in the damn car."

Dominic starts to go back to the driver's seat, but Clyde plucks him right out. "Oh no you don't. You drunk idiot."

After I climb in the back with Miles, Bret slides in beside us, Dominic in the front, and Clyde takes off down the road.

"Still want to know how you found us," I say to Dominic. He glances into the backseat. "Bret showed up a little while after you left, asked about Miles, I told him what had happened...some chick at the party said she saw a dude stuff Miles into a trunk..."

"I had a feeling Jakowski was involved in this," Bret says. "Dominic and I went to Beckett's place to look for him. Señor Grouchy Ass told us we needed to quit tripping on acid, but eventually he believed us."

"Three minutes," Clyde corrects from the front seat. "I couldn't understand a damn thing they were saying. I have a head injury, just chased away the paramedics, and these fools come knocking."

"But how did you find us in the middle of nowhere?" Miles asks.

"I saw Lawrence's car was missing, ran the plates. Got it located via GPS. Then we got here and saw the wreck, followed the muddy footprints to the cabin in the woods."

I notice Dominic sitting still and quiet in the front seat.

I tap his shoulder and wait for him to turn around. "You okay?"

He shrugs. "I don't know. I mean, Jesus...I was right there at his house. Maybe if I had fucking gone inside—"

"Jack would have killed you, too," Miles says.

"Well, there's a happy thought," Bret says. "At least I don't have to wonder if Dominic's a killer any more."

Bret stares at Dominic, serious all of a sudden. "You could have told me, man. Why didn't you? After last summer, after I dragged you from that hole you dropped yourself down, you couldn't just tell me what I already knew? Fuck, Justice knew. And Beckett. You'd only just met the guy and you told him."

"I didn't tell Miles about Simon," Dominic says, then he turns to Miles. "He was your friend?"

Miles nods.

"When did you start working with Agent Jakowski?" I ask Bret. "Before or after he killed Simon?"

Bret stiffens, turns to face forward, and says nothing. Before.

Dominic looks at him like he's a stranger. Tension fills the car, but it's obvious we're all setting Bret's involvement in Simon's death aside for now.

I lean my head against the seat and allow the day's drama to roll over me. To replay itself. Miles said he could see me as me in that room. But now that we're out, who am I to him?

Miles watches me, a sad smile on his face. "Don't look at me like that."

"Like what?"

He reaches his good hand over and lays it on my cheek. "The answer to all your questions right now is, I don't know."

"Don't know about me?" I prompt and lower my voice to a whisper. "Or about the guys who rescued us tonight and your plan to put them on your FBI watch list?"

"Both. All of that." He groans and rests his head beside mine. "What are you doing to me, Ellie?"

"Nothing bad, I hope," I tell him honestly.

He plants a kiss on my lips. It's soft and warm and so inviting. "Things used to be so much easier."

"And now?" I prompt.

"Now?" His mouth slides over, and he kisses my cheek lightly, then my temple. "Now I'm afraid you might be worth the complication."

Might be?

Whatever. I'll take it for now.

The dark street is illuminated in front of us by the dozens of red and blue police lights. Clyde slams on the brakes, and the vehicle is quickly surrounded by various law enforcement agencies.

Clyde rolls down the window to talk to the officer shining the light at him. "Got an FBI agent in that mess?"

"We'll need to search your vehicle," the officer says. "Amber Alert. The victim was reported within a three kilometer range. Miles Beckett, age seventeen, dark hair, medium build, five nine…"

Miles pulls himself up, his eyes wide.

"No searching without a warrant," Bret shouts from his seat.

"Shut it," Clyde tells him. "What are you planning to do with this Miles person if you do find him?"

I grip Miles's arm, squeezing it tight. What if Jack's group is bigger? There could be some in the police force blocking this road.

"We have orders to escort him to an address in D.C."

"CIA headquarters," Miles whispers for only me to hear, then he shouts up at Clyde. "Did you call my parents' emergency phone?"

I shrink down in my seat. "Uh-oh."

"The boy's in the back, but he's not going anywhere without me," Clyde tells the officer. "If it's okay with you, I'm gonna reach into my pocket, offer you my identification, and you'll see that I'm authorized to transport Miles Beckett." He yells over his shoulder at Miles. "I take it you're gonna want to stop at the hospital before heading to D.C.?"

Miles gives a weak nod. "If you don't mind."

"Feel free to follow us to the local hospital and then you can get all the statements you need," Clyde says to the officer. "God knows I won't turn down a little sober backup tonight."

Clyde offers his ID, and the officer takes it and returns a couple minutes later saying that Clyde has been given permission to take Miles to the hospital. "So I assume we can call off the chopper search?"

The Becketts sent a helicopter searching for Miles. Okay, so maybe that phone number isn't just a glorified answering service.

"Sorry," I say, my face warming when everyone turns around to look at me. "But we did almost die."

CHAPTER
52

The late-afternoon light streams through Harper and Aidan's bedroom. I turn on my side, and Harp is awake, watching me.

"Need more ice?" she asks. "Pain meds?"

I shake my head. "They make me too loopy. And please no more shining flashlights in my eyes every hour."

"You have a concussion," she argues.

A mild concussion among other scrapes and bruises. I sit upright and lean against the headboard but keep the blankets around me. I might never leave these blankets. "What's happening with Aidan?"

Lines of worry crease her forehead. "I don't know. I was told to sit tight, so I am."

"Harper?" I swallow. "What were you doing yesterday? Leaving the FBI office like that, digging through the whole apartment... You were planning to take off, weren't you?"

"Yes." She stares at her mug of coffee. "With you."

"You thought he did it," I whisper. When she doesn't respond, I add, "I did, too, at least for a little while. I mean, it was hard not to after hearing the evidence."

She looks at me and smiles. "I knew he didn't do it. But

I had information you didn't have."

"What's that?"

"That night when Aidan told us about seeing Simon's gun?" she prompts, and I nod. "He didn't exactly ignore the evidence like he'd said. He passed it along to the agent who clocked in after him. That person promised to put the information in the log and to handle it. Aidan covered for him."

"Jack," I say. "He worked that night. I dug through Aidan's phone yesterday and saw them texting about grabbing coffee and hoagies."

"Jack," Harper repeats, her face tense.

"That's why Aidan never mentioned seeing Rider at the door or Dominic down the block," I say, clicking those final pieces into place. What a mess.

"Aidan trusted Jack unconditionally. I did, too. God, I can't even..."

"And he knew about me." I look down at my hands, hating the involvement my past had in all of this. "He knew about us, our family. He wanted me to help him with his for-profit assassin organization. All this time when he was around, invested in my life, helping me with school..."

"I would seriously murder him right now if I could." Harper shakes her head. "And Simon...all because he knew too much about Jack's side business. I can't believe Jack killed someone—how is Aidan supposed to go back to his job and trust any of these guys if they form secret assassin societies?"

We sit in silence for a minute, and then I revert back to the earlier question. "If you knew Aidan was innocent, why were you planning to leave?"

Harper looks at me. "I love Aidan. I'd do anything for him, but you are my priority. I decided if things got bad, if the odds were truly stacked against him, then we would need to leave. In fact, Aidan and I had prepared an escape, just in case."

She removes a large envelope from the bedside drawer and dumps the contents out on the bed between us. A stack of bound hundred-dollar bills sits between two passports. I open the first and flip through it until I land on the picture in the center. A picture of me.

"Josie Whitcolm," I read aloud. "Has a nice ring to it."

"I thought so, too."

I look Harper's false passport over. "Suzanna?"

"My stripper name," Harp says. "Had a soft spot with Aidan."

Last night, while Harper sat with me at the hospital to get my head X-rayed, I told her that I knew about her old job and that Clyde had destroyed the photos Simon and Miles had, but it was a brief conversation with very little info on her end. I'm about to ask more details regarding this first meeting, but the apartment door opens. Harper and I glance at each other, and then we're tossing back the covers and racing into the living room.

Clyde holds the door open. "Look who we sprang from the joint. Right before they handed him an orange jumpsuit."

Aidan walks in, followed by Mr. Beckett.

My sister runs right into Aidan's arms. She's already crying. I want to join her, but I'm not sure I deserve to. Harper never doubted Aidan, but I had. Even if for a short while, I had.

Mr. Beckett rests a hand on my shoulder and gives it a squeeze. "You were the only one who called me. My brother and my son seem to think they can take on an army alone. You were the smart one."

Clyde clears his throat. "Who busted up the little meeting of assassins and got your kid out of there alive?

Not that chopper you ordered. Not the law enforcement blocking the road."

"Who did I thank first?" Mr. Beckett says to Clyde.

"I can't believe my call did all that. Glad it actually was an emergency." Or I would have been really embarrassed.

Mr. Beckett nods as if I've brought up an intelligent question. "It wouldn't have turned into the massive manhunt if you had answered the return call that followed four minutes later. But when we discovered the phone you used to call from was destroyed it became necessary to take every precaution."

Yeah, that's all pretty creepy, but whatever. Can't say I didn't ask for it.

"How's Miles?"

"His mother's bringing him here soon. Doctor just released him."

Mr. Beckett and Clyde excuse themselves to go and wait for Miles at Clyde's place. Harper finally gives Aidan a second to breathe, and he looks around the apartment, his gaze finally landing on me. "You can't stay out of trouble, can you?"

Last night, I wanted to fall apart so many times but I hadn't, and now it's impossible to stop the tears from flooding out. I wipe my face with my shirt, but more tears follow right behind. "I'm sorry."

Aidan crosses the room and pulls me into a hug. "What are you sorry for, Ellie?"

I turn my head, hiding my face in his shirt. "For doubting you. It won't happen again."

He's quiet for a moment, as if absorbing this, then he says, "Okay."

"Also…" I step back and force the words out. "I'm sorry for wrecking your car."

His eyes widen, but he shakes his head. "You know

what? I don't need to know everything right this second. Let's ease into it."

He makes his way over to sit on the couch, and Harper heads into the kitchen to get us all coffee. I sit beside Aidan and keep my voice low. "The guy the FBI photographed you with? You were working on getting Social Security cards, weren't you? It was right after the meeting with the school counselors."

Aidan looks at me, guilt on his face. "I shouldn't have done that. But I wanted—"

"I get it," I say. "You want me to go to college."

He nods. "Absolutely."

I glance in the kitchen making sure Harper is out of earshot, then I turn to Aidan again. "And you want to marry my sister."

He stares at me for a long moment. Finally he nods. "Yes. I do."

"And you've already learned your lines. Got a ring yet?" I press.

He grins and then glances into the kitchen, checking to make sure Harper isn't listening. "Maybe."

"Hopefully you didn't hide it anywhere in this apartment because after yesterday, it's likely she either found it or lost it. Or both."

"I'm not an idiot." Aidan roughs up my hair as Harper appears with two mugs of coffee, and the conversation is over.

More than anything, I would love to ask Aidan if he's part of this St. Felicity's Shelter. I've been going back and forth on this all night. On one hand, Aidan is the noble do-gooder type who will break the law for the greater good. But on the other hand, it sounds like members of St. Felicity's pledge their duty to the group over anything else. Aidan will always put Harper first.

I don't ask Aidan any of this, because Miles has taught me that some things really are on a need-to-know basis and people's lives are at stake.

I curl up in the corner of the couch, enjoying my warm sweats and the blanket Harper offers me. I just sit there and listen to Aidan and my sister talk, watch her curl up with him and finally close her eyes.

My family might be small now, but there's enough love and loyalty right here to fill the entire world.

When Harper dozes off, Aidan elbows me and says, "I still can't believe Miles broke into the Gilberts' place with you. Can't believe you two have been running around playing teenage detective duo right under my nose. I thought you hated him?"

"How could you not notice them?" Harper mutters, her eyes still closed. "I lost count of the number of tracking devices that boy planted on people."

"What?" Aidan and I say together. Aidan adds, "Why didn't you say anything?"

Harper tightens her arm around Aidan, giving him a squeeze. "I thought you knew, thought he was just going through a phase. Isn't that what boys do?"

"Um, no," Aidan says, laughing. "You know what? I've caught nearly all the Becketts doing some strange things, but they're good people. Let's just leave them to do their thing and not ask questions." He looks at me. "I take it you don't hate Miles anymore?"

"Hate?" Harp says. "She's totally in love with him."

"Am not," I say automatically, but Harper hears the lie. I look down at my hands. "But no, I don't hate him. The real question is, does he hate me?"

My sister pries her eyes open long enough to give me a sympathetic look. "He knows?"

I nod. "I told him right after Aidan was dragged out of

here. He didn't take it well."

"But then he saved your life," Harper points out.

"Yeah…true." I leave the topic alone, not wanting to ruin the celebration. I wait for Harper to fall asleep again, and I elbow Aidan in the side. "Your babies are going to be beautiful."

His forehead wrinkles, but he laughs. "Thanks?"

"Just wait until I'm long gone."

Aidan pats my knee. "Done."

A knock coming from somewhere in my room pulls me from sleep. I sit up, my heart racing, my eyes scanning every dark corner of the bedroom. Then I spot the shadow at the window. I rush over and open it. Miles lifts his sling a few inches. "Can't make the jump like this. But I figured the sentiment was still there."

I smile at him, my insides warming. I give him a hand getting inside. "You're using the door to get out. No breaking any more bones."

The joke was me testing the waters. Seeing if I need to deal with us being friendly and nothing more. But one look at Miles's face and it's clear he's here to discuss serious matters.

"What?" I press. "Any word on Jack? Is Bret in trouble for the pictures and working with Jack? What about Rider and that other rifle guy?"

Miles shakes his head, his face tense. "Bret went in to the field office for questioning. But they found nothing at the cabin where we were held. No trace of Jack or Rider."

My stomach turns. I never asked Clyde where he shot Jack. I assumed he killed him, but maybe not.

"I talked to my dad about it," Miles says. "He said an organization like St. Felicity's doesn't take any chances. They cover their tracks, even when it's members who betrayed them. It's likely they took care of the three who held us themselves and cleaned up the mess."

So Jack is likely dead. I swallow back that thought and turn to Miles again. It's obvious he hadn't come for that. Or at least not only that.

"I need you to tell me something, Ellie."

I stand awkwardly in the middle of my bedroom. "I'll try."

"Do you still want to do it?" he asks. "Steal from people. Cheat. Do you stop yourself only out of fear of getting caught? I need to know who you really are under all the costumes and the glimpses of real feelings I've seen."

So he doesn't doubt my feelings for him, only my morality in general. I'm not sure which is worse.

I shake my head. "That's impossible to answer—"

"No, it's not," he argues. "You are either someone who can take things that don't belong to you for personal gain. Or you aren't."

"That question isn't fitting for someone who knows how to con. I can take things that don't belong to me. What you really want to know is if am I compelled to." I wait a few seconds, and then he nods. "The other problem with that question is that personal gain is relative. Am I greedy? Do I want to be as rich as most of the kids at Holden Prep? No. Does that mean I won't ever cheat someone out of money or something of value again? No."

His face falls. That was the wrong answer.

"Here's an example… Let's say Harper got sick," I tell him. "She has cancer and we don't have insurance. I've got enough experience in insurance fraud to know how to work the system. I could get her fully covered for free. And yes, I would do it if there were no other options. In a heartbeat. And I wouldn't feel an ounce of guilt."

That isn't completely true. I would probably feel a little guilt, because Harper would tell me not to do it and I'd do it anyway.

He's silent, thinking.

"Maybe that was a bad example. Or just an extreme example. My sister isn't sick and we do have insurance. Maybe we should just cross those moral bridges when we get to them," I suggest, not expecting him to buy into that plan.

"Mr. Lee always told me that I have a gift for seeing into people's souls. Seeing if it's pure or not. I guess it's ancient Chinese belief or maybe a fairy tale, I don't know." Miles sets a hand on my waist and slides it up my back. "Until you told me about your past, all I could see in you was good. And honestly, it's still all I see."

I lean into him, my eyes burning. I bury my face in his neck. "Was that a conclusion on your end, or are you just trying to figure out if your soul-seeing superpower deactivated?"

He laughs. "I'm not sure."

"I guess I can't really answer your question. I'm not a hundred percent sure what my soul is made of yet." I lift my head, look at him. "But if we can't— If you're not part of my life…" I sniff and force back the tears, trying to cover it up with a laugh. "We're so different, but you're also my equal in a lot of ways. It's challenging and exhilarating and—"

Miles's mouth crashes against mine. His hand is in my hair, on my face. I'm drowning in him. Finally, he pulls away, both of us breathless. His forehead rests against mine. "Don't let me down, Ellie."

Nerves flutter in my stomach, but I nod. I need this. Not

just Miles, but something real and valuable to drive me in the right direction. A moral compass.

"You're still leaving, aren't you?" My heart sinks at the thought of the apartment next door empty again.

He nods and heads for the window despite my orders for him to use the door. He swings a leg outside and turns to me, giving me his most real smile. "Don't worry. I'll be around. Someone needs to continue your self-defense education."

I shake off the thought of me and Miles rolling on the wrestling mats. His shoulder will need to heal first. "Funny how you were all worried about Davey and it ended up—"

His face tightens. "Not a mistake I'll make again. Ever."

I lean down and kiss him until both of us are out of air. "Go, before your parents send out another Amber Alert."

He nods but gives me one more kiss. "Stay out of trouble, okay?"

"Definitely." I use my shirt to dry the tears from my face. "Mostly. Probably…"

"Promise you'll call me the second you need something?" Miles says, and then he waits for me to nod.

After he's out the window and gone, I close it slowly, feeling the weight of his absence. Again. But there's hope now. Because I'm not hiding anything from him anymore. And it's one of the best feelings ever. Maybe it will be too hard, but maybe it will be amazing.

A few seconds later, my phone buzzes.

MILES: check ur pockets

I reach into the pocket of my pajama shorts and remove what feels like a paper card. I flip the lamp on so I can see and then gasp at the sight of the blue card with "Eleanor Virginia Ames" written across the front. And a nine-digit number above the name.

A Social Security card.

ME: how?

MILES: I know a guy…

ME: Miles!!

MILES: kidding. Totally legal. Just had to press the right buttons

ME: u r kind of amazing

MILES: this girl on the card? I looked her up. She's got a perfect record.

I smile down at the card. I wonder when he slipped this in my pocket? Before or after he decided to believe in me? But I have a feeling Miles wouldn't have crawled in my window tonight if he hadn't already put his faith in me.

Now it's up to me to be this girl on the card. To believe in myself.

ACKNOWLEDGMENTS

First off, I'd like to thank my editor Liz Pelletier, who introduced me to *Veronica Mars*, helped create the concept for this series, and gave me the freedom to make it my own. My agent, Nicole Resciniti, for always having a new plan in the works for me. Roni Loren, my best writer friend, thank you for the much-needed brainstorm sessions. Thanks to some amazing Entangled team members: Stacy Abrams, Heather Riccio, Christine Chhun, and Melissa Montovani to name a few.

Thanks to my family for their constant support, especially my husband, Nick, and my kids, Charles, Ella, and Maddie, because it can't be easy living with a writer. And lastly, thanks to my readers, new and those of you who have followed me to every pocket of YA/NA literature.

GRAB THE ENTANGLED TEEN RELEASES READERS ARE TALKING ABOUT!

LOVE ME NEVER
BY SARA WOLF

Seventeen-year-old Isis Blake has just moved to the glamorous town of Buttcrack-of-Nowhere, Ohio. And she's hoping like hell that no one learns that a) she used to be fat; and b) she used to have a heart. Naturally, she opts for social suicide instead...by punching the cold and untouchably handsome "Ice Prince"—a.k.a. Jack Hunter—right in the face. Now the school hallways are an epic battleground as Isis and the Ice Prince engage in a vicious game of social warfare. But sometimes to know your enemy is to love him...

THE SOCIETY
BY JODIE ANDREFSKI

Not everyone has what it takes to be part of The Society, Trinity Academy's secret, gold-plated clique. Once upon a time, Sam Evans would have been one of them. Now her dad's in prison and her former ex-bestie Jessica is queen of the school. And after years of Jessica treating her like a second-class citizen, Sam's out for blood. But vengeance never turns out the way it's supposed to...and when her scheming blows up all around her, Sam has to decide if revenge is worth it, no matter what the cost.

OLIVIA DECODED
By Vivi Barnes

This isn't my Jack, who once looked at me like I was his world. The guy who's occupied the better part of my mind for eight months.

This is Z, criminal hacker with a twisted agenda and an arsenal full of anger.

I've spent the past year trying to get my life on track. New school. New friends. New attitude. But old flames die hard, and one look at Jack—the hacker who enlisted me into his life and his hacking ring, stole my heart, and then left me—and every memory, every moment, every feeling comes rushing back. But Jack's not the only one who's resurfaced in my life. And if I can't break through Z's defenses and reach the old Jack, someone will get hurt...or worse.

THE REPLACEMENT CRUSH
By Lisa Brown Roberts

After book blogger Vivian Galdi's longtime crush pretends their secret summer kissing sessions never happened, Vivian creates a list of safe crushes, determined to protect her heart.

But nerd-hit Dallas, the sweet new guy in town, sends the missions-An Vivian's zing meter-into chaos. While designing software for the bookstore where she works, Dallas wages a counter-mission.

Operation Replacement Crush is in full effect. And Dallas is determined to take her heart off the shelf.

WAKE THE HOLLOW
BY GABY TRIANA

Forget the ghosts, Mica. It's real, live people you should fear.

Tragedy has brought Micaela Burgos back to her hometown of Sleepy Hollow. It's been six years since she chose to live with her father in Miami instead of her eccentric mother. And now her mother is dead.

This town will suck you in and not let go.

Sleepy Hollow may be famous for its fabled headless horseman, but the town is real. So are its prejudices and hatred, targeting Mica's family as outsiders. But ghostly voices carry on the wind, whispering that her mother's death was based on hate...not an accident at all. With the help of two very different guys—who pull at her heart in very different ways—Micaela must awaken the hidden secret of Sleepy Hollow...before she meets her mother's fate.

Find the answers.

Unless, of course, the answers find you first.